# The Evening Hero

Marie Myung-Ok Lee

**SIMON & SCHUSTER**
New York  London  Toronto  Sydney  New Delhi

Simon & Schuster
1230 Avenue of the Americas
New York, NY 10020

First Simon & Schuster hardcover edition May 2022

SIMON & SCHUSTER and colophon are
registered trademarks of Simon & Schuster, Inc.

For information about special discounts for bulk purchases,
please contact Simon & Schuster Special Sales at 1-866-506-1949
or business@simonandschuster.com.

The Simon & Schuster Speakers Bureau can bring authors to
your live event. For more information or to book an event,
contact the Simon & Schuster Speakers Bureau at 1-866-248-3049
or visit our website at www.simonspeakers.com.

Interior design by Kyle Kabel

Manufactured in the United States of America

1   3   5   7   9   10   8   6   4   2

Library of Congress Cataloging-in-Publication Data has been applied for.

ISBN 978-1-4767-3507-8
ISBN 978-1-4767-3509-2 (ebook)

To my parents,
William Chae-sik Lee (b. Pyongyang)
and
Grace Koom-soon Lee (b. Bukcheong)
and my unni,
Katherine Min (b. Champaign)

Division along the parallel made no sense economically or geographically as far as Korea itself was concerned.

—Dean Rusk

There is nothing in history to justify the use of the caduceus as the emblem of the physician.

—Maurice Boigey,
*Presse Médicale*

A wrong decision can cause a lifetime of pain.

—Korean proverb

# Prologue

His name was Yungman.

The components of his name were, as custom dictated, selected by his paternal grandfather, just as his father's had been selected by his grandfather, and so forth back to the origin of the clan. The grounding character "Yung" — "Hero" — cemented him to all his cousins (Yung-jo, Yung-ho, Yung-chun, Yungbok) in this twelfth generation of Kwaks, whether he knew them or not; "Man" meant "Evening." "Evening Hero" would thus be carved into all the family trees on male Kwak headstones henceforth, chipped into his jade name-stick — his legal signature. Yungman's place as first son was evident by contrast to his younger brother Yung-sik, "Vegetable Hero."

To his patients, he was no Evening Hero but Dr. Kwak. A little Asian man (certainly short of stature, at 5'4"), the hospital's obstetrician. He was distinctive to the white townspeople not just by being Asian but by being the first doctor from somewhere, anywhere, else. First North Korea, then South Korea. In America, a year first in Birmingham, Alabama, repeating his internship, as all foreign-trained physicians had to do.

And though he was a graduate of the "Harvard of Korea," no hospital even bothered to reply to the American job search of this man from Asia, a region of the world America had decided it didn't want and made laws to ban and expel. Yungman would end up so desperate for employment that he would drive straight north with his wife and infant child to this Arctic Circle of the US—the Iron Range of Minnesota—where winters were almost lightless, where schools closed for blizzards only when temperatures fell below minus fifty degrees.

Horse's Breath, so named because the only way the early settlers (49ers who got lost on the way to California) could discern whether their horses were still alive that first winter was by checking for their breath, or alternatively, the name was a white man's mangling of the Anishinaabe word *ozhaawashkwaabika*: the purplish undertone on the area's rocks—signifying iron—which gave these speculators a reason to stay.

Towns in this area were spaced apart, individual stars in a constellation. A person from the next town over, Apple's Gate, whose main characteristic to the Horse's Breather was the unholy smell of rotten eggs from the paper plant, was a stranger. Movement between towns was rare.

Into Horse's Breath's mix of the descendants of the immigrants brought to work in the iron ore mines (Swedes, Norwegians, Finns, in that order; a Dane, three Icelanders, Slovakians, Slovenians, Serbians, Germans, Croatians, Poles, an Italian, and an Irish or two, and admixtures thereof) came Dr. Kwak, William (Will, I am) on his official documents; his Korean wife, Young-ae; and his Korean-ish son, Einstein.

# BOOK I

# William Y. Kwak, MD

HORSE'S BREATH
20XX

Yungman's office was strategically placed between the surgical suites and the labor and delivery rooms. You walked by the imaging room, whose door had a sign that said

> Please do not SMOKE during your ultrasound

then through a door with a sign that said

> MATERNITY WARD

and

> Push Push! PUSH!!!

above its automatic opener.

This heavy door kept the noise of the ambulances out. But Yungman was always imagining he heard sirens.

Yungman waved to his secretary, Rose, whose half-size office was umbilically connected to his. She had left his white coat on its hanger behind the door, pressed and cleaned and sheathed in protective plastic. He had to deal with his shoes first. The unseasonable winter rain had left the physicians' parking lot flooded, and he had picked his way across archipelagoes of dryish asphalt, stepped lightly into what he thought was a one-inch-deep puddle, and been so shocked when his foot disappeared up to the ankle that he put his other foot down into a different mini-lake. From his desk, he took out his package of emergency socks, crisp in their cellophane and with the Stuffer's Drug price tag still on it from 1989. Both shoes were damp, so while he hid them under his desk to dry, he transferred his feet into his squishy white surgical clogs even though it wasn't a surgery day.

Then he remembered the letter. He patted his jacket pocket— *whew; still dry*. He opened the slim middle drawer of his desk and placed it in the back, even beyond his RX pad and stash of Tic Tacs.

He checked the ER whiteboard. His longtime patient Mrs. Maki had called him at home this morning complaining of indigestion. She wasn't due for two more weeks, but she tended to deliver fast; three children, each labor faster than the previous, so he told her to come in. Better safe in the hospital than sorry, especially since recent cuts meant fewer ambulances were available. Of course, this would add to his workload; normally, Maude, his nurse-midwife, could do the workup and monitoring, but there'd been sporadic layoffs for months. It had seemed there was no more flesh to cut, but she had been a casualty of last week's "Friday-night massacre" along with Kate Javorina, the hospital's social worker.

In this vacuum, the hospital hadn't come up with a better system than having all OB-GYN cases come through the ER and wait for him in bed #5, the last one. Yungman didn't feel comfortable mixing emergency and nonemergency. It was also a systems problem—deciding for, say, a vehicular accident with a pregnant victim whether the person needed Dr. Rasmussen the ER doc or him. "If I'm busy with another patient, without Maude there to assess it could be dangerous," he'd challenged Odin Tinklenberg, the young hospital president with the curiously old Norsk name.

"We all have to do more with less, Dr. Kwak," he'd said, "if we're going to keep Horse's Breath General viable in this market."

*Market!* Yungman scoffed to himself. They were talking human beings, not rubber balls or boxes of cereal.

Tinklenberg's predecessor, who'd been with the hospital more than twenty years, had been an MD with a master's in public health. Odin was an MBA, brought in two years ago by the private management company Synergistic Action Network–US Health Systems, which had made the tantalizing promise to the board of trustees that Horse's Breath General would be debt-free in a mere two to five years; the precipitously aging and dwindling population of the town meant a shakier financial footing. The hospital could regain its former stability *if* they gave Tinklenberg free rein to do his magic. But all they'd seen so far was fewer staff, fewer supplies—even basics like IV saline and Tylenol were troublingly often in short supply. Telephone problems, which used to get fixed right away, languished for days. Also, their ER had been downgraded one trauma level, then another. The new sign at the entrance read

MINOR INJURY ONLY /
NOT 24 HOUR
FOR EMERGENCY PLEASE DIAL 911

The remaining doctors, nurses, and staff were busier than ever. The ER whiteboard was filled already.

| PATIENT | DOCTOR | NOTES |
|---|---|---|
| Aas, S | Rasmussen | fell off ladder |
| Maki, M | Hokkanen | Well child |
| Maki, A | Hokkanen | Otitis med |
| Maki, L | Kwak | P4G3 (Fedex) |
| Zimmerman, R | Rasmussen | abdominal pain |

The Finnish name Maki was by far the most common surname in the town. Whether on the ER whiteboard, in the high school honor roll in the paper, or in the phonebook, Yungman was continually squinting into a thicket of Makis.

There she was: Lorraine Maki, the one who had called this morning.

"Hello, Mrs. Maki!" He was pleased to see her already hooked up to the fetal heart monitor, the two sensors correctly placed.

"Guess it wasn't just the hotdish, huh?" She burped delicately. He watched the monitor. She was in labor all right. The baby's heartbeat flattened and then bounced back nicely after each contraction, no decels. An uneventful, advancing delivery. He often became crampy himself when it was time to push. He felt faint twinges in his pelvic area now; this baby would be out by early afternoon.

Yungman made sure she had plenty of ice chips to chew on and told her to call a nurse if she was uncomfortable. Lorraine Maki smiled at him. "I don't even need Stadol. I'm fine."

"You're a tough cookie." *These descendants of the pioneers*, Yungman thought admiringly. He went to the supply closet and made sure the instruments and vacuum suction were there if he needed them; things had a way of disappearing from the closet these days.

"Dr. Kwak," said Patsy the ER nurse, from behind him. "Mrs. Maki said her water never broke. I have the amnio hook if you need it."

"Hello, Patsy. Did you learn all that from Maude?" Yungman said. "Were you the one who hooked her up to the monitor?"

She nodded vigorously. "You can't work in the ED for coming up on thirty years and not pick up some stuff. Mr. Tinklenberg keeps saying we have to remember that ER and OB are the 'brand introduction' to the hospital." She rolled her eyes. Probably no one in the hospital was a fan of Tinklenberg's officiousness, or that he didn't seem to care that he remained an outsider in Horse's Breath even though he'd been here for two years now, a single man for whom the hospital bought one of the biggest houses in town, when the 2008 mortgage crisis had caused so many townspeople to lose theirs.

"I heard she delivers fast, so that's why I wrote 'Fedex' on the board—get it?"

"I do get it," said Yungman. He was not always happy about the lingo the ER staff used among themselves. So many staff were talking about racoons recently he thought there was some kind of infestation before figuring out "racoons" was what they called opiate overdoses, for the dark shadows and hollows users had around their eyes. But each department had its way, and he needed to operate within the ER's parameters, to coexist with his medical brethren. Patsy at least was willing to extend herself; the temp ER nurses Tinklenberg had brought in after firing the regulars would openly reject his polite request that they get a patient a birthing ball: "Not my job!"

"So—you need this to pop that sac?"

Back when the Ladies Auxiliary existed, they used to gather in the upstairs conference room to drink coffee all day and crochet tiny hats for the newborns. Yungman had once noticed how metal crochet hooks looked exactly like the Briggs perforator. Ha—maybe with Tinklenberg's new austerity they'd have to start using knitting supplies. They probably cost a dollar at Hobby Hub versus fifty bucks for a Briggs. Do more with less!

"You can put it back," he said to Patsy now. "That might speed up the labor, and that's something we don't need."

"I can monitor the dilation for you," Patsy offered. She held up three fingers in the Boy Scout salute. "These are 4.78 centimeters across."

Yungman smiled, remembering the first time he put his own fingers crosswise on a ruler so he could use them, like a human ring sizer, to measure how wide a cervix had dilated.

Of course, it wasn't 100 percent kosher to have her do this. But she offered. And he had to do more with less. Also, to be honest, his entire Birmingham hospital internship—thirty-six- and forty-eight-hour shifts routinely—would be illegal today.

"If Mrs. Maki consents, why don't you do an exam right now, and I can see if our measurements match up?"

"Awesome," she said. And: "Sure hope that blasted rain stops soon. It's like a swamp out there." No Horse's Breath conversation was complete without a little dig at the weather.

Yungman heard the door to the ambulance bay whoosh open; he reflexively stutter-stepped back to dodge an orderly careening down the hall with a gurney.

Ken Hokkanen, the hospital's internist, also narrowly avoided being sideswiped as he entered through the door. The ER bay was their de facto employee entrance, if only because it was closest to the physicians' parking lot. Drops of rain glistened atop his thick white hair.

"You've still got the moves, Dr. Kwak!" he said, waving to his friend, performing a quick cha-cha-cha. He, smartly, had waterproof chukka boots on.

"Morning, Dr. Hokkanen!" cried one of the lab techs, passing by with a tray of blood.

"You're looking lovely today, Kathy," he said, and she blushed. Ken's boots clonked on the floor as he walked down the corridor toward his office in the clinic wing. He would change his boots for clogs (Swedish wooden platforms, not surgical), clip a koala bear toy to his stethoscope (he was double-certified med-peds), and start his rounds, visiting his patients with their tonsillectomies, appendectomies, pneumonias, and bariatric surgeries.

Ken glanced at the ER board as he passed it. "Mrs. Maki is a Fedex?"

"Same-day delivery!" called Patsy.

In utero, the baby was Yungman's responsibility; ex utero, Ken's. The two men had a well-oiled handoff routine; it helped that the two doctors not only respected each other but were also best friends.

"I'd plan on as early as midafternoon," Yungman said, returning to his office.

Rose had slipped a schedule on Yungman's desk. Today was clinic day. Every slot was taken. He'd have to finish his morning inpatient rounds promptly, then get started on the lineup of women who needed birth control, STD checks, annual exams. He liked to complain about how busy he was, especially lately, but the truth was, he loved his work. Even in a small way, he mattered.

Yungman returned to his desk midafternoon. Today's lunch from the physicians' dining room was grilled cheese and tomato soup. His favorite.

"Dr. Kwak, just to let you know, you've got an incoming, a Carol Maki," said Patsy, materializing in his office doorway, leaning on the jamb, one sneakered foot held up like a stork, her trick for staying on her feet all day. "But—"

Rose appeared behind Patsy. Patsy had been on the high school basketball team in the '90s, and Rose was so short that she was able to peep out through the space beneath Patsy's arm.

"President Tinklenberg called. You're wanted upstairs, stat." Stat? Rose never used the word "stat." Stat was not part of her work life.

"But I have an emergency case coming in." He looked at Patsy. He willed himself not to look at the two slabs of char-flecked toast, the cheese oozing on the plate (just the way he liked it), the soup still hot enough it hadn't developed a skin atop it yet.

"I'll take care of her," Patsy said. "She's a frequent flier."

"Frequent flier?"

"People who just come in repeatedly for free stuff like a turkey sandwich. Or they're looking for a lazy way to get their primary care, whatever. Then they get their FF wings on the whiteboard. This one's also an FF-NAD, according to the EMT."

NAD = No Apparent Distress. She'd pronounced it like the "nad" in "gonad."

"But she came in by ambulance? What's she presenting with?"

"Besides presenting with free ambulance abuse, her complaints are mild vaginal bleeding. And it's not new—she's had it on and off but said she decided to come in today. Ohya, I'm betting perimenopause. Those people have some nerve, using the ambulances like taxis when they know they're broke and can't pay it back, and then *we're* going to be broke."

"That's fine, Patsy," Yungman said. "I need to make that assessment."

"She'll be fine to wait a few," Patsy said. "I won't let her die. *Promise.*"

He looked over at Patsy. This patient probably could wait. Her name, Carol Maki, didn't ring a bell. In a crunch, he prioritized his own patients because you had to reward people for their loyalty, their history with him. "Okay, Patsy, why don't you monitor. I wouldn't delegate this unless I felt sure you were capable of assessing and handling it. I need to do more with less, and I'm sorry, this is really more Maude's job."

"I got you," she said. "I'll have you paged if anything looks concerning."

Yungman shut his door for a second. He had been looking forward to some quiet time—just him and his soup and sandwich. He allowed himself three long slurps. Just having that much warm soup in his belly was helpful. Tinklenberg's "stat" at least couldn't mean a patient's life was at stake.

He opened the middle drawer of his desk and dug around to find the tiny hand mirror and some Tic Tacs. Quick check of his face; no debris. He popped in a minty-fresh Tic Tac and tossed the box back into the drawer, where it landed atop something that made a crisp noise, like an autumn leaf being stepped on. Ah, the aerogram. Drat that. After he grabbed it from the mailbox this morning, it had been too late to go back in the house and hide it. He supposed that here, in his desk, it was just as secret, if not more so, than being stuck between the pages of a book at home.

But he couldn't help pausing. The return address—Sajik-ro, Scoul-si—stared back at him.

Yungman had always been careful to leave no return address when he sent the annual money. But a few years ago, the letters started coming. Of course he didn't reply. Every time he thought and hoped his brother had given up, another surprise reply popped up, like another bright dandelion after he'd saturated the lawn with Weed B-Gon. At least one or two a year. Checking the mail was his domestic task. Young-ae had once even mused, "You just checked the mail this morning—are you going senile?" He didn't say anything. Better to let her think he had Alzheimer's than for her to discover the real reason he was so hypervigilant.

On the third floor, the business floor where he rarely went, he saw this wasn't a private meeting. It was being held in their conference room, the same one where they had their monthly morbidity and mortality conferences, and it was packed with doctors. There was just one chair open, and Ken had his arm resting on the back of it. "Dr. Kwak!" he said, pointing. In any other man this might seem like jerk behavior, but not Ken. Everyone knew he had his own unerring sense of balance and decency, and everyone—even Mitzner the surgeon, who *was* a genuine jerk—respected it. Which was probably why Ken had been drafted into the position ("a pain in the keister!") of medical officer, the liaison between the doctors and management. Tinklenberg had chosen Ken because "it's hard to find a person everyone in the hospital likes," but he soon regretted it—"You're supposed to be a liaison for the doctors, not an activist."

"I don't know when we've all been back here like this," mused Dr. Rasmussen. He must have been referring to when they would meet to use this room for job interviews, talking to the prospects, trying to figure out if they would be good colleagues. The hospital hadn't had a new hire, Yungman was realizing, since Clausen the "young doctor" anesthesiologist, who had been in his thirties then but now was fifty—no spring chicken. Tinklenberg certainly hadn't hired anyone; he only fired. No wonder they had all grown so old on the vine.

The door opened. Mitzner strode in. A tall man with a stoop from both age and decades of leaning over an OR table, he'd once looked like Charles Lindbergh, but now his shiny bald pate was strategically covered by a Minnesota Twins surgical cap. He was trailed, as always, by Clausen, who also had a stoop because he unconsciously copied everything his idol, Mitzner, did. Seeing no chairs left, Clausen immediately pivoted and left the room.

Mitzner stood behind Yungman and crossed his hairy forearms. Yungman turned partway around. "Hello, Dr. Mitzner," he said. It was a civic duty, he felt, to be pleasant to everyone in the workplace, no matter how he was feeling, or felt about the person.

"Ahoy to ol' Dr. Quack," he replied. Ugh. Mitzner hadn't deployed "Dr. Quack" in ages. Yungman had even dared hope that odious nickname had gone on to the graveyard of unfunny jokes. He recalled with some shame that when he first started at Horse's Breath General, he didn't even know Mitzner was making fun of him. Yungman had still been getting used to the heavily Scandinavian-Canadian inflection of Horse's Breathers' speech ("Jeet?" Rose would say, for "Did you eat?") and had just chalked "Quack" up to regional dialect. Indeed, some Horse's Breathers cleaved Kwak into two syllables: Ka-walk. But Yungman vividly remembered Mitzner hello-ing him and shaking his hand, saying, "So nice to meet you, Dr. Quack, is it?" He had stagily winked at some passing nurses in the way GIs had, during the war, when trying to get the attention of a Korean woman.

Later, Young-ae, whose English was more sophisticated than his, explained that "quack" was like being called a tol-pari surgeon, a pseudo-doctor. What an insult!

Mitzner looked down at him and winked again.

Yungman kept his face pleasant. He was highly allergic to conflict. But: "Speaking of 'old,'" he said, extra pleasantly, "isn't your birthday coming up, Dr. Mitzner?" Mitzner was going to be *eighty*, the oldest grape on the vine. Yungman was also nobody's chump. He turned back in his seat.

Tinklenberg strode in on his Abraham Lincoln–esque legs. He wore a navy-blue suit, expensive pen in the breast pocket. In one hand he held a travel mug from St. Thomas' Business School. In the other was a sheaf of papers with extremely fine print on them, which he now looked at without glasses. It must be nice to have young eyes.

"Gentlemen," he said, ignoring Sue Sorensen the osteopath. "I have some good news and bad news—"

"Good news first," demanded Mitzner. Chest hair poked out of the top of his scrubs. Yungman almost never left the surgical suite in scrubs or took equipment out of the suites. Mitzner acted as if he were operating twenty-four hours a day, but he only did general surgery—how many inguinal hernias could there be? His surgical magnifying eyeglasses hung around his neck on a neoprene band that said BEECHCRAFT. He fiddled with the glasses and, to Yungman's disgust and astonishment, put the tip of the left earpiece into his mouth. Yungman made a note that if he ever needed surgery, he should go to UMD hospital.

"The bad news is"—Tinklenberg was the one person in the hospital unbossed by Mitzner—"I regret to inform you that the hospital is closing."

A dozen mouths fell open.

"For a hiatus?" asked Ken. "Are we being furloughed?"

"I mentioned six months ago that the hospital was having financial problems."

Dr. Rasmussen raised his hand, as if they were in class. "*You* said the balance sheet would be saved if we okayed that last round of cuts, like sacking longtime employees like Kate Javorina, the social worker, and making the rest of the staff forgo raises. You also didn't let me replenish my lifesaving clot-busting drugs."

"Yes, but we have the classic situation of too many people using medical services without being able to pay, plus the hospital not having any real revenue-generating arms like a cancer center. The debt is so overwhelming that the cuts aren't enough."

"Not enough for what?" said Rasmussen. Mining was dangerous work, so the mining company in 1925 had established a fund for the hospital, precisely so they wouldn't have to worry about balance-sheet issues from day to day—the company had *promised* there would always be a hospital here.

"For corporate headquarters."

"'Corporate'?" said Mitzner. "We're an independent nonprofit community hospital."

"Nonprofit, yes. But independent? Oh, gentlemen, not for a long while. That's the whole reason I and Synergistic Action Network–US Health Systems were brought in—to fix decades of no one minding the store. Horse's Breath General had been part of Synergistic Action Network–US Health Systems for an entire year before I even set foot in this place. You must have seen the new logo."

There had been a series of new logos and mottos in the front hall. This month's:

SANUS: A Passion for Care

Yungman had thought SANUS was some early medical philospher like Hippocrates.

Also, what did "a passion for care" even mean?

"Okay, then hit us with the good news. Maybe we could finally consider converting to employee ownership, like I've been saying we should all these years." Mitzner's grandfather had come to town with a brace of Kentucky mules and started the mercantile. He was supposedly there when the mining company made the promise to the town to electrify the streetlights downtown and that "the hospital will always be open, doctors' salaries paid, no matter what. Miners and their families need their care, and this is the way to make physician life up here attractive to this generation and the next." Indeed, the doctors' salaries were more comparable to those at Duluth or the Twin Cities than to those in other rural towns in Minnesota. (Even still, Yungman noted, no one wanted to be the always-on-call OB here before him.)

"The good news is that anyone over fifty-five will get their full defined benefits pension."

"Of course we will," said Ken. "That's our money."

"Well," said Tinklenberg, "you're the lucky ones. For people not fully vested, the pension becomes liquid assets for creditors. But as I was saying, the hospital will officially close on Friday."

"What?"

"Impossible!"

"But what's going to happen to our patients?"

The door opened: Clausen, dragging in a chair for Mitzner. It screeched on the floor. "What'd I miss?"

"You aren't getting your pension," said Mitzner.

"Is that a joke? I've been paying into it for twenty years."

Tinklenberg tapped the edge of the papers on the table to straighten them. "This is all coming from corporate; I'm just the messenger. I wouldn't mind a word of appreciation for saving your pensions—in the M&A transaction, Synergistic Action Network–US Health Systems, SANUS, and its consultants inherited all assets of this hospital. I was able to do a clawback for a small portion."

"How can they just close a hospital?" asked Yungman. "Our hospital."

"Without a plan for our patients," added Sue Sorensen.

A glum silence followed.

One by one, they all got up. No matter what happened, they still had patients to attend to.


Bed #5: "Hello, Mrs. Maki, sorry to keep you waiting—it's been a very busy day." Yungman's second Maki of the day. She had blond hair, darkening at the roots, and ear piercings that went all the way up her ear. Around her neck was a delicate gold chain with a cross. Not a regular patient of his. He looked at her chart: age forty-four.

Patsy, passing, hooked her thumbs together and made her hands flap. *Frequent flier.*

"So, what brings you in today, Mrs. Maki?"

"Bleeding," she said. "Pain."

"Did it come on suddenly?"

"No, it's been going on for months. So I finally thought I should come in."

"Any history of endometriosis? Of fibroids?"

"No. I mean, I have moved around a lot these last couple years and haven't been to a doctor for a while, so if I do have any of that, I wouldn't know."

Forty-four was a little early for menopause, but not out of range, especially for these heavyset white women. Young-ae had had a gentle, late menopause. There wasn't even, Yungman realized, a Korean word for "hot flash."

"Are you still menstruating? This isn't your period?"

"I'm totally regular—like, you could set a train schedule to my periods."

Yungman glanced again at her file. There was nothing in it except her name, address, birthday, and OCCUPATION: UNEMPLOYED.

"A change in flow or frequency can happen with perimenopause."

"I honestly don't think this is my period. I also have pain in my abdomen and lower back. Sometimes it goes down the back of my legs. Worse when I lie down."

Yungman inwardly sighed. Diffuse pain was the hardest to pinpoint for a cause. It could be anything, including nerves (sciatica) or nerves (anxiety), a bad hot dog, a strained muscle, constipation, menses. Or a more serious orthopedic issue whose origin might not even be at the site of the pain. Cancer was also possible, but, although most patients immediately thought that, it rarely ever was. Dr. Rasmussen had let Yungman in on his ER "trick" for abdominal-pain patients. He started them first on a "special medicine"—a double dose of Maalox.

"Nine times out of ten we treat 'em and street 'em within the hour." They also, lately, had to be careful of people who came in seeking drugs and knew to say "back pain" because they couldn't test for it, like they could for a heart attack.

Solely because of vaginal bleeding, Mrs. Maki had been assigned to him. Yungman conducted the Alvarado test and ruled out appendicitis, which still left him with dozens of other things. He thought about Tinklenberg's entreaties for them to do less testing, but since the hospital was closing anyway, Yungman filled the lab slip like a bingo card: pregnancy test, STDs, iron and vitamin D levels, thyroid for general health, cholesterol.

"Have you had a Pap smear recently?"

"Where they stick that thing up your vagina?"

"Yes. Because you're bleeding right now, I can't do it."

"I did do it, the other time I was in the ER."

"But there's no record of your visit."

"Oh, it was the ER in Apple's Gate, I think." That hospital had closed within the last few years as well. And even if it hadn't, they didn't share records. American health care was pretty strange.

He diagnosed perimenopause, possibly compounded by orthopedic problems. Maybe he could get her in for an MRI to see what else might be going on. However, the radiology department had been largely outsourced to India (another Tinklenberg "innovation"), and, he confirmed, they couldn't get it read by Friday.

"If the pain and bleeding persist, I would recommend getting an MRI—unfortunately we can't do one for you, uh, into the near future," he said. "It would also be a good idea to start getting wellness exams more regularly," he added gently.

"God is my ultimate doctor." She shrugged.

"Of course," Yungman said. "But you still could do well to have a regular checkup. A Pap test should be done every year."

"Can I get another Kotex?"

"Of course," he repeated. He had plenty of those, and thus got her two.

Yungman's phone rang. "Dr. Kwak—incoming!" It was Patsy. Her normally ruddy face had paled, making her freckles stand out. "This one looks bad—pregnant lady bleeding out."

At the same time, Rose stuck her head into Yungman's office. "Asia Maki, your patient, seems to be having a placental abruption—she's coming into the ER via ambulance."

Yungman was already halfway down the hall. "Patsy, call the blood bank and get all the O-neg they have." He continued his sprint to the ambulance bay; he could see the flashing lights just ahead.


Before he went home for the day, Yungman checked the ER board and was pleased by the soothing blocks of blankness. He had managed to see his appointments in clinic, deliver Mrs. Maki the "Fedex," do an emergency surgery (his third Maki of the day), *and* clear the ER board. There was still a ghostly residue—MEDEVAC TO UMD NICU—for the Maki baby. Asia Maki was one of his younger, healthier patients (an athlete in high school, she was always in the paper), but for whatever reason, for this her first pregnancy, her placenta had started to separate from the uterine wall and firehosed blood everywhere, including in the ambulance. Yungman had sectioned the baby out. Even though a bit premature, she was fine; so was the mother. He'd used up the hospital's entire supply of O-neg but had needed more. Luckily, one of the last equipment upgrades the previous president had invested in was an auto-infuser for blood emergencies.

Yungman made sure to stop by the nurse's station. "Thank you, Patsy, for your help today," he said, genuinely grateful. "You went above and beyond."

"I heard you were super fast removing that uterus," she said. Yung-man nodded. How he wished he could have saved it, but with placental abruption, there weren't many options.

Asia Maki (birth name: Cathy) had been a patient ever since she'd been having painful periods as a teen. He knew she wanted to have many children, so he had even put aside his pride and asked Mitzner to take a look, just in case he'd missed a way to save her uterus. Mitzner peered into the rising lake of blood in Yungman's midline incision, and muttered "Tsch! Dr. Quack, how many arteries does a uterus have?" Surely all physicians must know there were four (umbilical, vesical, uterine, vaginal); Mitzner's comment had seemed oracular but his tone suggested he was wasting precious seconds of Yungman's time to make some kind of point. Yungman had also been annoyed that Clausen had raised the table for Mitzner but hadn't immediately moved the table back down until Yungman had pointedly asked him to. Who was the primary surgeon here? Two intervals of wasted time; he had to move extra swiftly after that.

"Hey, I brought in a pineapple upside-down cake. Let me wrap some for you—I bet you barely got anything to eat today."

Yungman's stomach rumbled. She was right. Three sips of soup and a Tic Tac was it.

Blondish cake, glistening maraschino cherries in the center of each pineapple ring. Between Patsy and Rose, both fans of cooking shows on TV, Yungman never lacked for sugar.

Yungman walked out through the ER bay juggling his briefcase and an entire half cake in its tippy foil tray. Young-ae had her Bible study today. She wouldn't be home until after midnight. He would, then, dig into this cake at home like it was a personal pan pizza, indulging his sweet tooth (pulling out the cherries, first), and go straight to bed, because tomorrow was surgery day and he had to be at the hospital by six. He paused to balance the cake better and stuck his hand out to see if it was still raining. It wasn't.

He noticed the bench out front, because for the first time ever there was a person sitting on it. The single wrought iron bench had always seemed just for show, like TV stage scenery.

"Hello!" he said, picking his way across the lawn, spongy from the rain. It was Carol Maki, the "frequent flier." "Are you waiting for someone?"

"No," she said, with seemingly genuine misery. "I'm trying to figure out a way to get home."

He supposed an ambulance couldn't make the reverse trip.

"I'm on my way home," he said. "No trouble to drop you off."

"I live outside of town, past the drive-in."

"No trouble." Yungman motioned toward the parking lot. He put the cake in the back seat of his car. He had to yank open the passenger door with some force, because it could get stuck, as it was now. He wondered if that's why it had been retired as a police car. You could still see the ghostly imprint of the HORSE'S BREATH POLICE medallion under the mint-green paint.

"Wait, is this an old police car?" Carol Maki noted the dashboard button for SIREN. He nodded. The Kwak family cars had always been a series of decomissioned police cars bought at the sheriff's monthly auction, where one could get a reliable car for dirt cheap, the paint job thrown in for free, except you couldn't pick the color. Yungman had thought Einstein would think a police car was "cool," but as he got older he would only groan, "Can't you get something normal? Even a minivan!" By then Yungman was financially stable enough to afford a "normal" car, but the inexpensiveness and practicality of purchasing a lightly used government vehicle had thoroughly won him over.

"My father had an old Ma Bell utility truck. Got it at the sheriff's auction."

"Ah, I as well. Thank goodness for it, too: when we first moved up here, I needed a winterized vehicle in a hurry," said Yungman.

He thought of Mrs. Elmer Severson. One of his first patients. He'd been so young then, hardly able to believe he was a doctor telling other people what to do. "One of my patients—well, her husband, Elmer Severson—told me about the auction," he said. He'd had so many things to learn to get up to speed about living in Horse's Breath. How was he supposed to know his Birmingham-purchased car would die in the cold? That Horse's Breathers kept little houses for their cars, and their cars had special cords hanging off the grille that you had to plug in at night? A kind of heart-lung machine to keep the vehicle alive in the below-zero cold. "Until then I had to have my neighbor give me a jump—every morning." Dear old Clyde Lungquist, so uncomplaining, getting up at 5 a.m. on Yungman's surgery days. He had been dead now for more than a decade.

"That's my dad!" she exclaimed. "I mean, my late dad."

"Clyde Lungquist?" Yungman was puzzled. He and Duckie had never had children, at least as far as he knew.

"No, Elmer Severson."

Elmer . . . oh! Carol Severson! Of course! Forty-four years ago! Maki must be her married name.

"Ah!" he said. Recent studies showed that one's memories were most vivid when things were new. He'd just started his job in Horse's Breath, when he'd met Elmer Severson and could picture Carol's father perfectly. His stubble, his big ears, how he slumped in that rickety second-class chair reserved for husbands. He was such a Silent Sam and then there'd been the time Mrs. Severson had during her appointment suddenly decided she needed to use the lavatory, leaving the two of them together.

Fine; frequent urination is the purview of the heavily pregnant, but couldn't she have been just a *tiny* bit more considerate and gone *before* the appointment? He was on a schedule! At that time in his life, he'd been fretting about everything, every second. Maybe people didn't know it then (or even now), but his employment at Horse's Breath General was, like an astronaut's tether to his spacecraft, the single thing keeping him from floating off into space. His student visa had run out, and this job was the only thing keeping him from immediate deportation. That this job existed at all was a miracle. Horse's Breath General Hospital had to be the only place in the world so desperate to attract an OB that it could cheerfully ignore his lack of a green card.

Elmer had been so laconic, Yungman had worried he had some kind of selective mutism. Into this conversational void, he didn't say anything, only unlaced his steel-toed workboot. Right in the office! He then peeled off his red-topped thermal sock.

Yungman disliked feet. Koreans were a clean, polite people who almost never showed their feet to one another. As he tried to think of a diplomatic way to point out the illogic of having the town OB-GYN look at a man's foot, the foot was there in his face. A prominent big toe. Stubby, bulbous smaller toes, the last two missing. Diabetic necrosis? Frostbite while sitting for too long in a duck blind? Snowmobiling? It smelled like an old closet.

"Fought at the Chosin Reservoir," he said. "Middle of winter. They called our battalion the Chosen Frozen."

"I see," said Yungman.

"Our rubber-bottomed shoepacs were so cheap our feet would sweat when we marched and freeze when we stopped. They were slipperier than hell on those slopes. Guys would take 'em off, feet would swell, and they'd be walking around on bleeding stumps later in the day."

Yungman was frantically telepathically summoning Mrs. Maki back from the lavatory. In his year in America, it had seemed to him Americans expected Koreans to be abjectly grateful for America's part in their war. Elmer must have been a lad of eighteen or nineteen when he was shipped from his home in this tiny mining town to fight a war he probably didn't care about, or understand.

Yungman would have liked to say something about America's occupation of his country, right after they'd been freed from the Japanese in World War II. How, in the heady days following Japan's surrender, Koreans poured into the streets. How good it was to see the Korean flag waving again, taking down the hated Rising Sun.

But Korea's history was too predictable.

*The flower that blooms in the morning is dead by noon.*

*When the whales fight, the shrimp get hurt.*

America worried over the prospect of Communism spreading throughout Asia. Since the US military had carried out the abhorrent bombings of Hiroshima and Nagasaki, which "won" the war (and killed twenty-five thousand Korean forced laborers, a dozen American POWs), America therefore claimed Japan's colony Korea was up for grabs. It was the Americans who lacerated and split their peninsula at the 38th parallel. America gave the portion above that line to the Russians, who'd entered the war late but on the Allied side, to reward and contain them, thus inscribing the burgeoning global Cold War on Korea's land and people, not unlike how the Japanese soldiers had entertained themselves with teen Korean sex slaves—"comfort women"—by carving the Rising Sun with their military bayonets on the bellies of the screaming girls.

Not five years later, what Americans called the Korean War and what Koreans just called "war" began.

"Boy, I hated that place. Those two toes hung on for a while but then fell off like little Sun-Maid raisins. At least then I got sent home. But every winter they ache and ache like it's happening again. I hate that place.

"The men were all thieves; the women stank of garlic and walked around with their tits hanging out. You know, those gooks, they don't even have proper sewers! A beautiful mountainous country, and they cover it in human crap." There was a new hint of uncovered menace. Yungman realized he preferred the selective mutism. "Yah, *I* wouldn't have minded if Truman nuked the entire thing."

Mrs. Severson, finally returning, looked at her husband putting his sock back on. She sat down with a sigh. "You found a new audience," she said. "Outside of your VFW drinking buddies." Yungman had, earlier, smelled alcohol, and was sure it wasn't from her.

"You're Japanese, right, Dr. Kwak?" Elmer Severson was suddenly concerned. "I'm talking about the Korean gooks, real gooks, not Orientals in general. Kwak is a Japanese name, right?"

Mrs. Severson looked on in alarm. "What are you going on about now, Elmer? And Kwak's not Japanese, it's Chinese."

"Kwak is a Chinese name, yes," Yungman said evenly. His professional method was to find some way to agree even when the other person was wrong. His life here depended on his being agreeable, never making anyone mad. Yungman had already overheard, in the aisles of the grocery store, men vowing they'd never let a "slant-eye" touch their wives. It was lucky no "round-eye" ever wanted his job. It had been Yungman or No Man.

And, as unlikely as it sounded, Mrs. Severson had been right to a degree: there had been another Kwak in Horse's Breath.

"That little Charlie Kwak," Mrs. Severson reminisced.

In his year in America, Yungman had noticed that even the smallest, most rural towns, whether in Alabama or whichever state they'd driven through on the way to Horse's Breath, always had a Chinese restaurant. That meant that each town, unbelievably, had at least one Chinese person.

Horse's Breath had had the Golden Dragon. A youngish man, Charlie Yuchen Kwak, had apparently debarked from the Greyhound bus, single-handedly revived the dead Ember's Restaurant on Highway 20, and announced it as a Chinese restaurant with a plywood pagoda on the roof and a fire-breathing dragon in the window. The Golden Dragon became an attractive alternative to Horse's Breath's other restaurant, the Iron Grill (Dr. Rasmussen called it the "Iron Stomach Grill" for its periodic outbreaks of salmonella), for birthday celebrations and graduations, or when people just wanted a taste of the exotic.

Yungman presumed their surnames shared the Chinese character 郭, the same way Bruce Lee and the Korean name Lee, 李, shared the character for plum tree. A few months before the Yungman Kwaks arrived, a Horse's Breather *swore* she saw Charlie on Highway 20, dragging a raccoon carcass off the road and putting it in his car.

"Blew in and blew out like a tumbleweed, that little Charlie Kwak." Mrs. Severson shrugged. "No wife, no family. I always wondered if he was queer."

"They had good flaming pu-pu platters," Elmer conceded, now turning back to Yungman. "Doctor, tell us how Carl is doing."

Elmer Severson, after a parade of daughters, was set on a son named Carl. Yungman, again trying to be agreeable, did not remind him that probability made the sex determination 50/50, no matter that he already had a passel of daughters.

Two months later, Elmer Severson paced the smoke-clogged maternity waiting room, a box of cigars under his arm, holding a balloon that said *It's a Boy!* He looked astonished when Yungman handed him a female baby. He was still in shock when the social worker arrived a few hours later to fill in the birth record. The couple just stared. It was Yungman's suggestion to insert an "o" to make "Carol" out of "Carl."

"I'm so sorry for your loss." Yungman had seen Elmer's obituary in the paper some years ago and sent the family a card, as was his wont. Rose helped him keep track.

"His liver," she said. "Cirrhosis. He drank too much."

"He was a very nice man."

The giant screen of the drive-in poked up from the dead grass, ripped panes of fabric flapping in the wind. The sign still said FOR LEASE and EDWARD SCISSORHANDS AUGUST 20. This was the unofficial mark of the town's line.

"I told you I live far out." Carol directed him to turn down an unpaved road. The mailboxes read *RR* for Rural Route. Another mile down the road, behind a copse of planted trees, was the Lincoln Courts, a trailer park.

There was a range of age and upkeep: some looked like real homes, with wooden porches and concrete foundations. Others were dilapidated, sagging containers. They all had to be brought in here by semitruck; none were particularly "mobile." A number of them had sun-bleached American flags on giant poles or spread over windows like drapes. From inside the park, a dog started to bark, a dull clank as he ran up to the end of his chain.

Her yard had a medium-size flagpole that flew an American flag. At its base, one of those signs he had seen proliferating around town. This was the first election he could remember where people erected signs *after* their candidate had won. He had also, frankly, been shocked to learn so many of the townspeople had voted for the man.

Carol's plastic sign said

*152 SPECIES OF ANIMALS GO EXTINCT EVERY DAY*
*LET'S MAKE NORTH KOREANS NEXT!!*

As well as one that said

*OUR GUY WON*
*GET OVER IT*

"You know, you're right—" she said, looking back at him. "I do need to start seeing a doctor. Are you taking new patients?"

Yungman had no idea how to explain the closure.

"Unfortunately, I and many of my colleagues are going to be retiring soon." His reflex was always to help: "Please, take the cake." He'd noted her eyeing it as he'd carried it to the car. Not the best for long-term health, but temporary sustenance.

"Oh, I couldn't take your cake."

"Please. I actually shouldn't eat it. I'm prediabetic." How easily he could lie if he thought it was for a good deed. She didn't have to be asked twice. She went to the back seat and gathered the tray, the napkins, and every one of the half dozen forks Patsy had thoughtfully included, then walked into her mobile home past the sign calling for a genocide against Yungman's people—the president-elect had spent a good part of his campaign saber-rattling, especially against North Korea, and he not only didn't seem to be slowing, he was already calling Supreme Leader Kim names and bragging about the US' nuclear arsenal. Yungman supposed each president needed his war. He could see the bold red of the maraschino cherries winking in the fading light as she walked into her trailer. Right by the door there was a tipped-over Tonka truck (plastic, not metal like when Einstein was a boy) and a baby doll, its face streaked with dirt. She shut the door without looking back.

The next day, Yungman broke the news to Rose, who cried.

He spent the morning discharging his inpatients.

Mrs. Lorraine Maki had had a fast delivery (he refrained from saying "Fedex") yesterday. She was cleared to go home with her healthy baby. These kinds of safe and happy births, he was aware, made very little money for the hospital. Horse's Breath had been lucky in some ways. In Apple's Gate, the maternity ward and ER were the first departments to close. Tinklenberg made notes and suggested Yungman do more C-sections for "iffy" cases; basically, anything that came into the ER. Surgeries brought in more money and a much longer hospital stay—and more pain and recovery time for the mother. Yungman ignored him.

Mrs. Maki #2, Asia Suhonen Maki, was recovering from the trauma of her emergency C-section. She'd lost a good portion of her blood volume; he'd had to cut directly through muscle and fascia instead of taking his time, pushing it aside. It would be quite a while before she could stand and go to the bathroom by herself, much less hold and nurse the baby, Beyoncé, who was currently seventy miles away in the University of Minnesota Duluth's hospital's neonatal unit, as Horse's Breath didn't have a NICU (and it was a good thing Mr. Maki was a teacher and they had good insurance). It was obvious Mrs. Maki should be admitted there as well so she could provide breast milk and be close to her baby.

The UMD hospital intake, to his surprise, refused: "She's not a patient here."

"Then assign her to someone. She's not well enough to be discharged, and she's upset about being away from her baby."

"She began her treatment at another hospital; we can't take her here."

"There won't *be* a hospital here in two days," he said, his anxiety rising. The baby had been admitted through a long-standing agreement between the two hospitals when a NICU was needed.

"Also, will Horse's Breath pay for the transport? Insurance is unlikely to pay for an ambulance just to transfer a patient to a different hospital."

Yungman resisted the urge to clutch his head. Would the local ambulance service go out of business at the same time as the hospital?

He had the wild idea to drive her there himself, but that would be stupid. What if she started hemorrhaging in the car? "I don't know."

"I'm sorry about your patient, but it sounds like we really can't help you."

"I need to talk to Dr. Rock Nelson," he said. The equivalent of calling her manager. Yungman wasn't normally the type to be pushy. But what was the downside of cashing this chip he'd been carrying for decades?

Use it or lose it, was what Ken would say.

The intake secretary passed him to another secretary.

"You can't just 'talk' to President Nelson." This secretary audibly sniffed. "Does he know you?"

"Actually, he doesn't," Yungman said. "But I knew his colleague, the late Dr. Jarvis, whom I met during the Korean War."

"So are you saying you want to make an appointment to speak to him? Are you press? He's booked until after Thanksgiving."

"I need to talk to him about Professor Jarvis—the Dr. Jarvis of the Jarvis Medal for Research Excellence—immediately."

Mention of the Jarvis Medal got her attention. He was put on hold. He counted to three. He was patched through.

"This is Rock, how can I help you?" The man was very self-assured, faux-humbly using his first name with a stranger.

"Hello. My name is Dr. William Kwak, from Horse's Breath General Hospital. I knew Dr. Jarvis from the Korean War. In fact, he was the one who arranged for me to get a student visa to come to the US."

"Very nice. I would appreciate you getting to the point. I'm a busy man."

Jarvis may have wanted to wash his hands of Yungman, but the blood of history is not washable. Yungman's eyes had popped at the notice in the *Journal of the American Medical Association* that a memorial research award had been established in Jarvis's name, even more so that the honor was being bestowed for his "groundbreaking research into the effects of frostbite on mobilized troops during the Korean War." Yungman had laughed through his nose. And cried.

When Yungman had first met Jarvis, Lieutenant Jarvis, he was twelve and working as a houseboy on the American Air Force base, Chilpal, which was near his village. Jarvis appeared on the base one day. His Scandinavian eyebrows were so pale they made his face look science fictional. The houseboys had been told he was a very important doctor in Miguk and to do whatever he asked them to. Oddly, he gave them packets of balloons and told them to befriend the harlots who lived in the ramshackle shacks a few yards from the rear gate of the base. Yungman had been trying to soak up any English at the time and noted these balloons were called "lovers."

The harlots laughed later when they saw the boys kept a few for themselves and blew them up into funny cucumber shapes.

Then Jarvis wanted them to spy on the women to see if any were itching in the poji and to make note of their name, their hovel number, or even better get the number of their ID card. Subsequently, uniformed American police would visit these hovels, sometimes Jarvis himself. The women never looked happy being led away to that dark concrete structure everyone on the base called The Monkey House.

Decades later, now a doctor himself, Yungman came across the study "Prophylactic distribution and the mitigation of STD spread among wartime troops," his mentor's name hidden by initials in a thicket of coauthors as Jarvis was by then well-known and lauded as a frostbite researcher; however, Jarvis's methods of getting the data for his STD study had been flagged for being problematic in terms of consent and transparency, but after all these years, there was no one but Yungman to put these two facts about one man together.

Yungman explained Mrs. Maki's situation.

"Dr. Kwak, I don't know why you're taking up my time here, but I don't exactly do admittance for the hospital. I'm its CEO."

"Yes," said Yungman. "You see, Horse's Breath General is going out of business as of Friday."

"I'm truly sorry to hear that, but the mother is your patient. I hope another hospital will take her. Good day."

"Wait—you don't want to have *sexually transmitted diseases* attached to the Jarvis Award, do you?"

"Excuse me?"

Yungman pressed on. He quickly summarized Jarvis's harlot project. Yungman had learned later that the harlots with the itching pojis were taken to The Monkey House, and at the behest of the US military, who wanted to make sure the soldiers had only "clean" women, were pumped so full of powerful antibiotics and other drugs that the side effects made their shoulders sag, their arms and wrists dangle near their knees, like monkeys, and they walked that way even after they got better. Some of the harlots—Yungman knew them all by sight—never came back. Yungman had overheard the GIs talking about how a nearby squash patch had to be repurposed as an unmarked graveyard for the dead harlots, some of whom had originally been kidnapped as sex slaves for the Japanese. Some were not much older than Yungman. Yungman's benefactor Jarvis really should have been punished for this somehow. But so many terrible things done to Koreans by their "Allies" seemed to just be chalked up to the "cost of war."

"What do you want?" Rock Nelson barked, but with a hysterical edge that suggested to Yungman that he knew things. Maybe he knew that Jarvis, like so many others, had also taken up with a harlot when he was there. The youngest, prettiest one who had ended up at the camp because her entire extended family had been killed in an American bombing and she had nowhere else to go. That was so long ago, and now Jarvis was gone as well. But his legacy was still at stake.

"Just for your hospital to take this patient."

"Give me her name," Nelson said. "Will ground transport be sufficient?"

On Yungman's list of patients, he checked off that last, most difficult Maki: *Asia Suhonen Maki*. His inpatients were all finally taken care of.

The last day.

Much of the equipment had already been vacated, presumably for sale. About all that was left were the framed pictures of the gala celebration for the hospital's opening in 1903 that decorated the reeption area: black-and-white photos of Samuel Van Sant, the governor of Minnesota, unveiling the newfangled operating room with real ether. A phalanx of blond nurses fresh off the boat from Sweden. A bunch of company men standing on the lip of the Vermilion mine.

Tinklenberg was not there, and no one missed him. The motley crew of doctors, nurses, techs, Helen from records, and one last ER patient all ate supermarket sheet cake doled out in pink emesis basins, with tongue depressors for spoons.

Outside, it had started to snow, heavy and wet.

Instead of leaving as usual through the ER bay, the doctors filed out the front, past the black-and-white pictures of champagne bottles popping and miners' families celebrating. Outside the bevel-paned double doors, they gathered by the ionic columns of their hospital, gazing at the buff-colored building, made of a local sandstone.

"This building could have easily lasted another hundred years," Ken remarked.

The janitor was shutting off the lights. Even the never-off EMERGENCY sign that had always been a beacon to Yungman, no matter the hour. As the inside went dark, the solar-powered light that shone on the cornerstone grew brighter.

Vermilion Mining Company, Pittsburgh, Pennsylvania, 1903
To the people of Horse's Breath. Heal the sick, take care of the injured.
That we may leave to our children a heritage worthwhile.

Yungman remembered the letter was still in his desk drawer. Well, he'd been too preoccupied these last days with getting his patients squared away. That should count for something, right? Sitting there unopened, sitting unopened in the house—what was the difference?

Midway into his first week of "freedom," the Evening Hero found himself at midday, lunch finished, dishes rinsed, dried, and placed back in the cabinet (he never understood wasting soap for light soil), and was contemplating his new chair, the insultingly named La-Z-Boy.

Upon waking, he'd jumped up in a panic at his lateness, but slightly less panicky than the previous day, and less panicky than the day before that—slowly acclimating to a life of indolence. Young-ae was already gone. She'd left a note, at least.

> *Gone to Mrs. Kimm's*
> *Don't know if I will be back for dinner Probably not*

It was Tuesday. Or was it Wednesday? With no appointments, his grasp on the numerical calendar had started to slip frighteningly away.

*Ring! Ring!*

He had never not answered the phone, in case it was the hospital or a patient. He'd suffered through robocalls, police benevolent drives, lonely elderly patients, persistent telemarketers insisting doctors needed to invest in diamonds.

*Ring! Ring!*

This felt like an experiment: Would the phone explode if he didn't answer it?

*This is Dr. Kwak. Hello. I am currently unable to come to the phone. Please leave your name and number and we will get back to you. Have a nice day!*

*BEEEEEEEEP!*

A shuffling noise, a whispered, "I guess he's not home!" and then the warbling of his son, daughter-in-law, and grandson, to the tune of "Happy Birthday": ". . . Happy retirement, dear Gran-n-n-n-n-ndpa, happy retirement to youuuuuuuuuuuuuu . . ."

". . . and many mooooore . . ."

"Reggie, no, not that part!"—his daughter-in-law.

"Hi, Sir! I hope your first week of retirement is going great and that your chair arrived okay!" said Einstein, Yungman's son. "Sorry I couldn't deliver it personally, but things have been crazy at work. Can't wait to tell you and Mom about it. It was absolutely the right decision to move back to Minnesota. SANUS is going to change the world."

Wait, was that the same company that had taken over Horse's Breath General? Tinklenberg had pronounced it *SAHN-USSS*, almost like "sauna," while in Yungman's head, he'd pronounced it *SAN-U.S.* like it was spelled. Einstein was pronouncing it *SANE-us*, to rhyme with, well, "anus."

Einstein's wife, Marni, chimed in: "Excited to see you guys tomorrow, show you the castle, eat a lot of turkey." She was like those ladies on the morning TV shows—bright, if a bit two-dimensional. "Um! Okay! See you tomorrow!"

"Bye, Grandpa!"

"Bye, Sir! Drive safely!"

Einstein's voice became muffled, underwater. ". . . Maybe this is a good sign. Mom said for the last two days he's just sat in his chair and moped. Like the whole day. He was there when she came home from her Korean church meeting. I'm worried about situational depression, which could trigger any latent tendencies toward dementia."

"Why does your mom drive all the way to Minneapolis to go to church?"

"That's new. When I was growing up we went to First Presbyterian, right in town. Haha, but now that I'm thinking about it, she often didn't go—*she* slept in. I wish I could have."

"I suppose you wouldn't have a Korean church in Horse's Breath."

"Are you kidding? I didn't even see another Asian until I went to Harvard."

"I'm aware of where you went to school, Einstein," said Marni. "So, your dad. Does Bill have hobbies? How's he going to fill up his day? Don't doctors play golf?"

(Bill! How could he ever have envisioned "Bill" would emerge, like an insect from a hidden pod, as a diminutive of "William"?)

"Nah; even as a kid, I never saw him doing physical activity other than mowing the lawn. Horse's Breath Hospital did have a country club so the doctors could play golf, but that closed ages ago. Anyway, he didn't really have hobbies; he was always at the hospital."

"Apple did not fall far from the tree."

Clinking of dishes in the background. Was it wrong to be listening to this? But Yungman hadn't set out to eavesdrop. He'd read somewhere that if Amazon accidentally sent you something, it was lawfully yours to keep, as the mistake wasn't yours but theirs.

". . . No, what I'm doing now is the opposite. I hustle like a boss, cash out while I'm still young enough to enjoy it. Believe me, I don't want to be him."

"I don't want you to be him either . . ."

". . . Retailicine is what's going to make it happen. Seriously, it's going to be the future of medicine, babe."

". . . Yeah, like I'd get my kidney dialysis at the Mall of America. No thank you." A delicate, feminine snort.

"Remember, everyone thought that Steve Jobs was crazy to insist that one day we'd be able to hold a computer in our hands."

". . . Da-ad, you didn't press End Call—*again.*"

"No wonder our family minutes keep getting eaten up so fast, *Einstein*—"

"Ah, oops! Hello? Anybody there? Hello?"

The elderly answering machine beeped, the MISSED CALLS counter turning from 0 to 1.

He stood up. From his vantage point on the chair, he'd inadvertently memorized the order of the books on the living room bookshelf, yearly Christmas presents from their neighbors, Duckie and Clyde: *The Da Vinci Code, Shōgun, The Apple Cider Vinegar Cure, Tuesdays with Morrie, Awakenings, The Andromeda Strain, Fatherhood,* and one children's book, *The Five Chinese Brothers.* A set of Encyclopædia Britannica from 1974.

Next to the encylopedia was Einstein's baby picture from the Sears store, his comically large head propped on pudgy arms, a simultaneously pop-eyed, surprised and anxious look on his face that he often still had. Next to that sat his framed Harvard admission letter.

*Ring! Ring!*

*This is Dr. Kwak. Hello. I am currently unable to come to the phone. Please leave your name and number and we will get back to you. Have a nice day!*

". . . I'm so sorry to call you at home, Dr. Kwak, but this is Christabelle Haugen. I'm feeling a little weird. It sounds dumb, but something's off. I'm light-headed—"

Yungman picked up. Christabelle Haugen's case was still fresh in his mind. With advanced maternal age, she was having a bit of trouble with this pregnancy. Without his files, however, he couldn't exactly remember how far along she was.

"Is this something to worry about, Doctor?"

"If you feel worried enough to have called me, you should probably seek medical attention."

"But I feel like . . . like I can't drive. It's like my head is filled with air." Her voice indeed sounded slurred, loopy. Would a doctor meeting her for the first time think she was high? Drug seeking? He knew she wasn't.

"I'm truly sorry," he said. "I can't give you medical advice."

"I'm not trying to get something for free; I'm worried!"

"No, I mean as I'm not an employee of the hospital anymore, I can't lawfully treat you. Is there someone I can call for you? A taxi service—" He couldn't remember her insurance status, but he did know that an ambulance ride without insurance cost $800 at minimum.

He kept talking into the silence; she'd hung up.

Yungman felt awful as he reclined into his recliner. He could be *doing* something, but instead he was lying down in the middle of the day.

*Ding-dong!*

It was harder to extricate one's self from a La-Z-Boy than one would think. *Ding-dong!*

"I'm *coming!*"

It was Ken. Rain beaded on his white hair, because it was raining out—again.

"Please come in!" Yungman said to his friend. "Did we, er, have plans?"

"Well, I was calling to ask you if you wanted to do something—your phone was busy."

"Yes," he said. "Talking to my son. How are you?"

"I was thinking about crossing another item off the list."

"The list?"

"My bucket list."

Yungman wasn't sure he knew what that was. Had Ken mentioned it before? Seeing each other every day in the hospital, they discussed anything and everything. Now Yungman worried he hadn't been listening attentively enough. One of the things he liked least about Mitzner (among an abundant list) was the way you could talk to him but were never sure he was listening. It made you feel unimportant. He wouldn't want Ken to feel that way.

"So, should we go?"

Fake it 'til you make it. It would make sense that bucket lists weren't affected by water. "Of course!" Yungman said, as if there were nothing more logical, or important.

"I'll drive," said Ken. "Iron Tower's about an hour away."

*Iron Tower? The town?* Horse's Breath was just one of a constellation of small towns: Iron Tower, Marble, Iron, Mountain Iron, Biwabik ("place of iron ore," in Anishinaabc), Aurora, Thief Rapids, Hibbing, Virginia. Virginia had the Walmart and a bookstore, Hibbing had the regional airport, but besides that, there was little reason to travel to another town.

"Wasn't Iron Tower where you took Shaggy for his obedience lessons?"

"Oh my stars, how Scotty had begged for that mutt." Ken groaned. "You remember Shaggy's habit of biting the mailman? That time he flew through a plate-glass window to get his bite in? He was as undisciplined as his owner. That was Mountain Iron, different town. Every Thursday night for three months I drove them over. He won Most Improved—the dog, not my son—and bit poor Nelson the very next day." Still, Ken's voice was colored with a soft nostalgia for the time when the kids were at home. Scotty had proved to be an itchy-footed wanderer, taking off the minute he graduated from high school; Yungman couldn't recall the last time he'd been back to Horse's Breath.

They walked the two doors down to fetch Ken's car. By happenstance or design, all the doctors lived on this fake hill made of ore tailings. It had originally been a ski jump built for the entertainment of all the Scandinavian miners. To the post office, it was Mineview Lane, but everyone in town slightly pejoratively called it Pill Hill.

"The Underground Mine Museum, 'highly recommended—TripAdvisor,'" said Yungman, reading the sign. They'd just driven through the town of Iron Tower, which looked even more economically devastated than Horse's Breath. Maybe one retail establishment was open at two in the afternoon—a bar called The Viking Lounge. Also: What did any of this have to do with buckets?

A man in red flannel and faded overalls came out to greet them. He wore a miner's hard hat with a light clipped to it.

"Welcome to the Iron Tower Underground Mine, the *only* underground mine in the Iron Range." Yungman was vaguely aware that upper Minnesota, the "Iron Range," was famous for "open pit" mining, where they just blew up the earth with explosives and gathered the rubble with giant steam shovels, leaving what looked like the Grand Canyon behind. "I'm Pellet Pete. And if you're claustrophobic, let me remind you this elevator goes down half a mile, and some parts of the tour get verrrrry narrow." Pellet Pete raised his voice as if he were in a Broadway play, projecting, even though it was just the two of them in the "audience." Yungman wondered if he'd ever had childhood dreams of being an actor, maybe even at the Chanhassen Dinner Theatre.

The rain slowed to a drizzle. When their children were small, there was always a good, firm carpeting of white by Thanksgiving, a white that smoothed out all the edges and made everything look clean. By Christmas the drifts could be seven feet tall. Snow, snow, snow, and cold so unending that it could fuzz your brain like static (indeed, also called "snow") on your TV. They, like the Eskimos, had a hundred words for snow: snow, more snow, damned snow, darn snow, dang snow. Soon, Yungman supposed, the expression would be "What snow?"

Above them, a buzzing noise.

"Yah!" Yungman yelled, and hit the sodden ground. Ugh, what a mess. Ken helped him up. "Yungman, are you okay?"

"Um, yes." Yungman did his best to brush off the reddish muck sticking to his elbows and knees. He had jumped like this when first hearing the dynamite of mining blasts; he'd once even upset a crash cart at the hospital. The nurses had laughed in wonderment—they didn't even seem to hear the *booms* at all.

"I just startle easily," he said. Above their heads, a small plane buzzed. It circled, then headed the other way.

"Stan," said Ken. Mitzner couldn't have normal hobbies. He had to be Charles Lindbergh with his *plane*.

"So where are you all from?" asked the guide, resting his eyes an extra second on Yungman.

"Horse's Breath," Ken said, for both of them.

"All right, then. Why don't we get started? Shut your eyes and picture warplanes and battleships coming off the assembly lines during World War II." Yungman felt silly, but he did it.

"Iron Range ore is in every bit of it. Every piece of US steel made between 1890 and 1940 had our ore in it. The country could not have been built if not for our people here, our ore."

"Our ore, say that three times fast," said Ken.

"This mine's ore has an unusually high oxygen content, prized for high-quality steel. Many, if not most, US warships in World War II had steel made from iron from this very mine."

The elevator clanked up to ground level, pulled by a giant winch. Yungman eyed the single rusty cable that would lower them into the shaft. They boarded the cage, and the winch reversed with a jerk and a shriek. Yungman tried to imagine eight men crammed in there, ready for the day of chipping at these rocks, pasties prepared by their wives stuck in their pants pockets for their lunches. The shaft was just a hole drilled right into the ground. Bands of quartzite went by, the slight pinkish blush making them look like chunks of ham, Spam. The sole source of light was the guide's headlamp, which briefly illuminated the next bands of rock: granite, schist, the dull-gray taconite.

"Ken," he said, "you didn't get enough of mines in Horse's Breath?" The Horse's Breath summer festival was "Mines & Pines." Every year of elementary school, students were sent on at least one field trip to the mines; science classes were devoted to the formation of iron ore, while career fairs in the high school were mostly about the mines. Yungman had no idea there were so many jobs that needed to be done:

> shovel runner
> electrician
> welder
> production truck driver
> millwright
> janitor
> schedule clerk
> groundskeeper
> accountant
> secretary
> track gang
> laborer
> Caterpillar operator
> carpenter
> painter
> service truck driver

foreman
track boss
superintendent
train operator
mechanic
steam jenny operator
kiln operator
quality control sampler
bin operator
drill operator
labor boss
engineer
geologist
machinist
oiler
salvage yard worker
shovel teeth changer
high rail

Clyde Lungquist, their neighbor, had been a service truck driver; Duckie had worked on the track gang until she was laid off in the big wave of the '80s. For an elementary school project of Einstein's on "What do people do all day?" mercifully, Clyde offered to bring him to work for a day. Given Einstein's reaction (and his A paper), he had had an enjoyable day with Clyde, especially cataloging all the different kinds of people who were needed to mine the ore, while Yungman pictured it like the Iron Man statue on Main Street, just a guy with a pick over his shoulder.

When the two families would grill together, after a few drinks, Clyde would often talk about how he used to carry binoculars to "zoom in on the fanny of the pretty lady on the track gang," who turned out to be Duckie. In their house they had a picture of Clyde beaming next to his massive dust-covered dump truck, which looked to be taller than a three-story building.

"Yungman—" Ken was the only person who had ever inquired if William was his birth name and, finding it wasn't, used his real name and actually pronounced it correctly: *Yeong Mahn*, not "Young Man"—"I'm only the first Hokkanen in three generations who didn't trundle off to the mines. Some of my bucket list is seeing what, by the grace of God and medical school, I missed."

"I didn't know that."

"What's on your bucket list, Yungman?"

"Mine? Well, probably number one, to purchase a bucket to put it in."

"You know there's no actual bucket in 'bucket list,' right?"

Yungman hated being confounded by idiomatic English. He thought by now he would know everything. "I have to admit I don't one hundred percent understand the concept."

"It's a *kick*-the-bucket list—a list of things you want to do before you kick it."

"Oh," said Yungman.

The elevator's descent abruptly halted as it bumped into something. Metal screeched and groaned.

"Uh-oh," the two men heard the guide say. As if on cue, everything went black. Yungman couldn't see the hand he waved in front of his face. Was this what it was like being *dead*?

"Sorry," the guide said as the light came back on, blinding them for a second. He let them out onto the floor of the underground mine. "Switch got flipped when I scratched my nose. The complete darkness part was supposed to come later in the tour. But see, this is what the miners felt, should the candle stub tucked in the band of their hard hat fall out, or in a cave-in."

46

Yungman was still thinking about the World War II warships. Many had been refitted for the Korean War, including Elmer Severson's marines evacuating at the port of Hungnam. The navy captain used guns to make sure only military personnel boarded. But a Korean interpreter pleaded for the lives of the 100,000 stranded North Korean refugees who faced certain death. He convinced the US to dump the tanks, the jeeps, the big guns—to evacuate the Korean civilians. Yungman tried to picture the massive ship-to-land carriers, their frightened human cargo (including Elmer Severson and his frostbitten toes), the steel of those ships containing some of the earth on which Yungman was standing right now.

It was evening in Horse's Breath (4:00 p.m.) when Ken dropped Yungman off. The drizzle had turned back into a steady, pattering rain. Ken would return to his dark, empty house. Yungman felt a terrible sort of survivor's guilt but didn't know what to do about it, so instead he just said "Thank you" when Ken winked and handed him a paper bag from the back seat that he said was Yungman's retirement present.

At home, Yungman opened the bag. A card with a picture of a recliner.

### GOODBYE TENSION HELLO PENSION
Happy retirement, Ken

A bottle of Johnnie Walker Black Special Minnesota Twins Edition. Such a Ken gift. He must have noticed over the years that Yungman eschewed foamy beers in the hottest summers, glögg, Christmas Tom & Jerrys because he was always thinking, what if he was called to the hospital? He averaged thirteen emergencies a month, which meant no matter what he was doing—sleeping, eating, watching TV—there was about a fifty-fifty chance of him being called in. Not worth the risk of drinking, even a sip. Obviously, his friend had noticed.

It occurred to Yungman that perhaps he should have invited his friend to Thanksgiving. But then again, he would be inviting Ken to his son's place. Not that his son would mind, but Marni tended to be fretful.

*Goodbye tension, hello pension.*

He plonked himself into the recliner, which caught him like a baseball in a mitt. It sighed as the Naugahyde compressed. He'd been working his whole life to reach a place where there *would* be no tension (immigration problems, work problems, child problems). He just never realized that work had served as a fan belt that kept his days moving. A sudden loss of tension just meant spinning at loose ends. At work, the surgeries needed to be done; the babies came and he had to help them get them out, no hemming and hawing allowed. Now he couldn't even decide how best to please both his friend and his son (and his son's wife). He also did not want Einstein to feel pressured. He closed his eyes.

He was still in this position when his wife came home. She didn't disguise the disgust in her eyes.

"Yah! Some Evening Hero," she said. He was about to explain that he had actually been out doing things, but she was already heading upstairs to wash. He'd wait a few minutes so he wasn't following her like a pet. They'd go to bed, more or less synchronously, but sleep on opposite sides, as they'd been doing for years.

The next morning, despite his intention to rise early, Yungman woke to the sounds of Young-ae puttering about downstairs.

He ran the Norelco over his stubble and patted some Aqua Velva on his cheeks. His father used to do military-style calisthenics every morning, so he did, too. Marching in place: one . . . two . . . three . . . hup! Touching toes, rotating the trunk. His joints made noises like chicken bones cracking.

From his closet, he shook out his silver sharkskin suit, the one he preserved for the most special occasions: weddings, funerals, the time he spoke at the Rotary Club, Einstein's PTA meetings. The padded shoulders gave him a bit of gangster flair.

He paused, considered the probability of food mishaps (no one can remain dignified with a gravy splotch on their lapel), then switched to his daily olive-drab suit, whose variegated colors—algaeal green to mushroom brown—should accommodate any number of situations.

From a plastic box he extracted his special-occasion clip-on bow tie with the Harvard seal.

Then, to show that he could be professional enough to keep an article of clothing pure and unsullied, he chose his white patent loafers. He took a moment to remove the dust with a shoe cloth. He felt more purposeful than he had in weeks.

He started to smile when his wife entered the room, but then saw the expression on her face, a kettle just off the boil.

She had a pale-blue envelope in her hand. An aerogram.

*That letter. What the heck?*

Sajik-ro 302
199-2 Sinchon 2-Dong
Seodaemoon Gu
Seoul-si 346
SEOUL, SOUTH KOREA

TO: Dr. WILLIAM Y. KWAK
207 MINEVIEW LN
HORSE'S BREATH, MINNESOTA 55736 USA

"I was going to bring this up last night, but I knew it would ruin my whole night's sleep."

She shook the letter in front of his face. It was open—not slit open, but it looked like it had fallen open, the tabs jostled during the transpacific journey. The English letters were painfully copied one by one, each a slightly different size, giving the letter the look of a ransom note.

"You know, it's a federal crime to look at other people's mail."

"Who is this, this Bo-hae?"

"Bo-hae?" he echoed.

She fluttered the missive under his nose. Inside one of the flaps was written, in graceful hangul Korean letters, certainly *not* his brother's:

*I don't really know how to address you. We are family after all, aren't we? This is to say thank you for the money, all these years.*
   *Sincerely,*

                                                   *(Cho) Bo-hae*

" 'Sincerely'?—That's a good one!" Young-ae tutted.

"I'm still not comfortable with you going through my mail," Yung-man said with a convincing harumph. The address on the letter was definitely written by Yung-sik. Why would the inside be different?

Young-ae returned the aerogram to him by crushing it into his chest. He instinctively smoothed it out.

"I didn't go through your mail. Marge Rasmussen stopped by. It was in your desk." Her still-black eyebrows dove into a frown. "I didn't read it; I just saw that much of it. Just as it's not eavesdropping when someone blabs a secret in front of you, like all those white people in Horse's Breath who thought I didn't speak English!"

"This was also in your desk." With an underhand throw, she tossed him his box of Tic Tacs.

"I have never met this Bo-hae Cho," he said, rattling the box like maracas for emphasis. But Young-ae was already gone from the room.

\*　　\*　　\*

Yungman popped a Tic Tac, enjoying the jolt of mint. He couldn't help feeling that there was something mystical in the way the letter had returned to him instead of going to whatever auction or trash heap the rest of his office furniture was going to. It would be too much to read it right now, and so he slipped the letter inside *Shōgun*, which was, unbeknownst to Young-ae (who was not a big reader), full of earlier unopened missives.

Yungman brought the white Samsonite out of the closet and filled it with his Dopp kit, clean underwear, his spare white shirt. He did not own leisure clothes. Cuffs could be rolled up, hems could be pushed up to make shorts when he mowed the lawn. The trusty undershirt absorbed the sweat and dirt of any kind of activity.

For a moment, he worried that Young-ae wouldn't go to Thanksgiving dinner with him. She often did that—went on a personal strike, stayed in bed. Most mothers, especially Korean mothers, wouldn't be able to wait to see their son. Their last visit to see Einstein, he was realizing, had been back in Connecticut, maybe more than a year ago. However, Young-ae was not most Koreans, or most mothers—or wives.

"Do you want me to pack anything for you?" he called. No answer.

He was relieved when she came downstairs with her own small bag that said KNITWIT, which Marge Rasmussen had gotten for all the ladies of the Hospital Auxiliary back in 1972 to hold their hat-knitting materials. There was a pair of slippers sticking out the top.

The extra space in the suitcase was filled with emergency winter items: flares, Fix-a-Flat, jumper cables, foil blanket, granola bars— one never knew. Einstein said once they hit the Twin Cities, the new expressway would bypass the downtown and take them to directly the verdant greens of Custom History Valley.

"You won't be able to miss it—the exit right after the Mall of America." Just to be safe, he was having them sleep over; he didn't want his parents driving home in the dark, when the night was full of urban hooligans.

On the way out of town, the dead grass of the prairie gave one little to see except the continuous low wire fence along 35W. Yungman shook his head to stave off sleepiness. He was grateful when his wife spoke.

"What is Ken doing today for the holiday?"

Not *that* question. "What's he doing *today*?" he repeated, to stall.

"Yes. Today. Thanksgiving. When family and friends gather, once a year."

"He, ah, has plans." When did it get so easy for him to lie? "I just saw him yesterday," he added, for detail.

Young-ae wasn't ready to let it go. "Are his children in town? Scotty seems to be always off somewhere, Polly so busy with her own kids. I don't recall Mrs. Mulvanen saying anything." Mrs. Mulvanen and her husband owned the Go Away Travel Agency. She knew exactly who was going out of or coming into town, and freely gossiped about it.

"Well, he didn't say he needed a place to go. And don't you think it would be *awkward* to invite him like that, like he's pitiful?"

"So in order to not underscore that he's been abandoned by his kids, you abandon him?" She made as if to rap his head. "What, is there just rock inside? You have no nunchi!" Ah, nunchi.

Koreans are famous for their nunchi—an extrasensitive psychological antenna, emotional mind reading. It's a necessary skill, because Korean verbal conventions, both decorous and ornate, tell you nothing. For example:

*"Oh, I must get going."*

*"Oh no, Mr. Park, you must stay and have some dinner with us."*

*"Oh no, I really must get going."*

*"I wouldn't think of it. Sit down, I'll get you some more tea."*

*"Really, I don't want to intrude on your family dinner."*

*"It would be an honor to have you! And no trouble at all. In fact, I insist!"*

*"Well, if you insist."*

*"But of course! I made too much food anyway; you must help us eat it."*

Then, later, *"Why didn't Mr. Park go home so we could have our dinner? He has no nunchi!"*

"You think he's sitting there alone appreciating your thoughtfulness? Do you think it just takes one year to get over your wife's death, and then you're fine?"

Yungman wavered. Should he turn around and fetch Ken? But then they'd be late—Marni would probably be upset, the food would get cold. Also, they were staying overnight. That would probably be more togetherness than Ken would want.

On the other hand, how could he abandon his friend? What if he *was* just sitting miserably at home right now?

The moment when Yungman could have, should have, turned around passed. They were more than halfway to Einstein's now.

"So anyway," Yungman said, to try to provoke a change in subject. "Ken has this thing he called a bucket list. Like 'drink wine on the Rhine.' 'Go see the glaciers in Alaska before they melt.' What would yours be?"

"Hmm; I'd need a moment to think. What's *yours*?" She punted it back immediately.

Yungman had to admit he was a bit spooked to realize that he didn't have anything in particular that he was driven to do, besides work. Travel held no appeal: any interesting sight they saw would actually be a local person's mundane view, so what was the point? He didn't really have hobbies (he had to confess that he envied Mitzner's having a hobby, his plane obsession; Ken diligently followed sports on TV, as well as the high school football team). What spooked him more was thinking about a talk that the hospital's social worker, Kate Javorina, back when she was still employed, gave to the doctors; she'd been talking about end-of-life directives, like DNRs, and then veered to what she called "the unlived life."

"That happens to a lot of people at this transition," she said. "They look back and realize they've crammed their life full of work, chasing after success, taking care of their kids. These things are all fine, but not if you use them to numb yourself so you miss out on your own life as it's actually happening." Her talk had been about easing the pain of people who were afraid of dying. "You need to hold space for them." It had haunted Yungman, especially when she said, "Believe me, at the end of life, *no one* wishes they'd worked more."

But work was basically all he had. Wasn't that why he had gone into such a noble profession?

When he concentrated, he did come up with one thing he would like to do, irrespective of money: humanitarian work.

Work again. However, he'd always admired Doctors Without Borders. They provided for patients who truly needed them, and without thoughts of compensation. That was work but not *work*. In fact, in a bit of a Walter Mitty moment, when he wrote them a donation check most recently, he slipped in a CV and a cover letter stating that he was now available, if they needed volunteers. He wasn't going to mention it to Young-ae, because *that* had been her entire dream, humanitarian work. That is, until she accidentally became pregnant.

"We haven't been on a road trip like this for a while," he said instead.

"Hardly a road trip," Young-ae said. "This is more like a very long drive for an errand."

Technically true. If they'd gone north rather than south, for the same amount of driving time, they could be at the picturesque shores of Lake Superior. Instead, the scenery of the boring blacktop and soggy dead prairie grass wouldn't change until they neared the Twin Cities.

Yungman politely inquired how things were going at her Korean church, which she had found via Kim's Oriental market in St. Paul. They'd been in the Cities last July for one of Yungman's regional American College of Obstetricians and Gynecologists meetings. Yungman, in his search for dried squid, had entirely missed the flyer for the Good News Korean Church & Institute of Edina. Edina was one of the most expensive suburbs in Minneapolis. Horse's Breathers joked that Edina stood for

Every

Day

I

Need

Attention

It was most famous for the Galleria, a fancy one-story mall that sat primly across the street from Southdale, a several-storied monstrosity that was the US's first indoor mall. Yungman could not imagine that Young-ae, who hated to drive, would drive for almost two hours to go to church, of all places; this the person who refused to attend church in Horse's Breath. But through the dogged heat of August she went, and had started attending various social functions.

"Well, the Kimms—" said Young-ae.

"Ah, the Kimms," Yungman said, with studied neutrality. Young-ae had a kind of crush on these people, the homecoming king and queen of the church. The Kimms this, the Kimms that. The Kimms-with-two-Ms. Dr. Kimm. Yungman felt oddly resentful of people he'd never met.

Young-ae had mentioned more than once that "Dr. Kimm" also referred to Mrs. Kimm. She was apparently some kind of superwoman who had worked even when the children were young—can you imagine? What neglect.

When Einstein entered junior high, Yungman's darling Young-ae had suggested she go out and get a job.

"Why?" Yungman had been incredulous. Hadn't he spent his whole life expending effort so he could provide for his family, for her comfort?

"Maybe I would like to work and earn my own money."

Yungman had always provided a nice allowance. In the book where he kept the budget, he always made sure there was a column for her; he labeled it saengwhal pi—life expenses. "What would you *do*?"

"I don't know. Maybe medical coding."

"That's ridiculous," he said. "Who will be here when Einstein gets home from school?"

Young-ae hadn't brought it up again. Yungman suspected she'd saved up decades of her saengwhal pi and used it to buy the light-blue Hyundai Bongo (new, not used) that she used to drive away from him three, four times a week now.

They entered Custom History Valley, where every "estate" had its own name. Einstein's was KING ARTHUR'S COURT, but they must have somehow missed it. Yungman made a U-turn at GONE WITH THE WIND, drove through the onion-shaped shadow of the half-constructed TAJ MAHAL, and then found the winding driveway to KING ARTHUR'S COURT; the fancy script on the sign had made it somehow invisible to his eyes. The drive led to a drawbridge that took them over an actual moat, which used a motorized pump to circulate the water, so it flowed like a river.

Marni, Einstein's blond wife, opened the door to their castle. She was smiling, and not angry at their being late, it seemed.

"Welcome, welcome to our new home, Kwaks!" she cried. Then she took a moment to take in the battered white Samsonite suitcase Yungman was pulling behind him by its cracked plastic leash.

"Are you moving in?" Her smile turned more tentative. "You know, if Einstein told you we have an in-laws' apartment, that's just what it's called in real estate terms."

Yungman smiled back.

"Oh, this?" he said, motioning to the Samsonite. "See, Einstein was worried that after dinner we'd be too tired from all the tryptophan — that's an amino acid in turkey — to drive home. He did tell you we're staying overnight in your lovely house? Not forever, just overnight."

Big smile, lips lifted over gums. She was wearing a high ponytail like a bobby-soxer; it twitched like a horse's tail. Einstein must not have informed her. Yungman silently congratulated himself for not also having an extra guest in tow. His daughter-in-law was easily rattled.

He politely shucked off his shoes. Einstein wore his dirty shoes in the house, copying Marni, but Yungman just couldn't. Even during the war when they lived in the shantytown in Pusan, where smoke from the smokestack blackened their skin, his mother had meticulously cleaned the pallet that made their "floor" several times a day. Young-ae reached into her bag and brought out her slippers to keep her feet warm, and also to protect herself from the dirt and dog poop Einstein's family inevitably tracked into the house.

Twelve-year-old Reggie slid down the bannister to greet them. Because the foyer was so grand, he gained quite a bit of momentum by the time he got to the bottom and almost knocked his grandparents over like tenpins. "Grandmaaaaa! Grandpaaaaaa!" Yungman was pleased; they saw the boy so rarely that, each time they met, he feared he might have forgotten them.

"Reggie!" said Einstein, hurrying into the foyer. "Careful!"

"We're sturdier than you think," Young-ae said. She had briefly caught Reggie on the rebound, held him aloft like they were pairs figure skaters, then set him down with exquisite care on the marble floor, richly veined in blue.

"This is a lovely house," Yungman said. "Your home literally is your castle."

"Thank you," Marni said. "But if you really want grand, you should see what's going up next door: the Taj Mahal."

"We saw. The greatest love story ever told," Yungman said. "A monument to grief."

"Maybe, but it's blocking our early morning sun. And it's tough to feel good about finally having your castle when the freaking Taj Mahal appears next door."

It was a very American thing, the house tour. If you were rich enough, your Korean house would have an anbang, a receiving room, and the rest would be hidden. Here, Marni took them through every nook and cranny, even to the bedroom, proudly showing off her walk-in closet, her lingerie hanging on padded hangers. Yungman had to pretend he was interested instead in the dozen wedding pictures clustered on the bureau. Marni and Einstein. Einstein and Marni. Marni and Einstein getting engaged on the beach, hips touching frontally (he averted his eyes). Marni getting ready with her butterfly-colored attendants. Marni looking demure. Marni throwing her bouquet. Marni leaning against a tree. Marni and Einstein with their band. Marni and Einstein in full matrimonial regalia in front of the Harvard Club in New York.

They had had two photographers and a professional videographer. Less than fifty people in attendance. Yungman suspected the wedding would have been much larger except that neither of them had many close friends; Marni's cleaning lady was her maid of honor. If she had siblings, Yungman had never met them. Her parents had also not shown up. If she had aunts and uncles, they didn't show up, either. She had a few friends from various jobs (stewardess, bank teller), and

Einstein's roommates from Harvard had been there also, as it had taken place at the Harvard Club in New York.

He thought of his own wedding, held between shifts at the hospital in Birmingham, Young-ae wearing a stiff yellow dress, snug at the abdomen, that had been handed down from the Thai intern's wife and would be passed on to the next woman who needed it. It happened in the living room of some professor whose name now escaped him. Tea and small cakes had been served. The sole documentation was from Mohan, his best intern friend, who had taken a picture of them reciting their vows. The camera, as cameras did at the time, had a bare bulb as a flash. They both looked shocked and spectral, like ghosts, so they never displayed the photo. It was hard to imagine the reckless abandon they'd once shared. They were so stiffly formal with each other, Mohan had asked Yungman if their marriage had been arranged.

In Einstein's cluster of wedding photos, there was only a single one of Young-ae and him. At the end of the ceremony, the guests marched out via a narrow aisle between two banks of folding chairs, the taxidermied animal heads on the wall observing all the guests as they marched. The photographer was stationed at the end to take a picture of each participant as they passed.

Young-ae and he were the first to march out after the bride and groom. With everyone's eyes on them, Yungman found himself unexpectedly overcome with sentiment. He'd reached for Young-ae's hand. And she rejected him at the moment he most wanted to hold a piece of her—any piece. He ended up grasping her wrist. It looked like he was grabbing a runaway toddler. He was smiling; she was not. Her gaze was aimed toward the lower corner of the picture, expressionless, reminiscent of those pictures of Patty Hearst in court.

"Grandpa, let me show you our media center!" said Reggie, tugging at his sleeve. Yungman peered: Was that a mustache hair poking out of his upper lip like an errant cactus thorn? If so, the Caucasian genes were certainly dominating. Yungman didn't have to shave until he was almost twenty, and then just a few hairs, the beginnings of a yangban beard.

He was at an age of abrupt endings: his ability to sleep through the night, his job, his ability to urinate without thinking about it, and now his one and only grandchild was growing a beard. He tried not to sigh audibly.

Reggie led his grandparents to what Yungman would ordinarily call the garage. Two vehicles occupied half of it. The other half had two rows of actual movie-theater seats, various beanbag chairs, and a full-body office chair, all facing a huge screen. On the wall were movie posters that, when he looked more closely, Yungman saw were all of Reggie as various action heroes. On the shelves, dozens of cardboard boxes: MARNI'S CRAFT SUPPLIES, M'S NOVEL NOTES, WINTER SPORTS STUFF, R-LACROSSE, HOCKEY, KARATE, ROLLER BLADES, XMAS. The whole place was toasty warm; there was even radiant heating in the floor.

"The media room," Reggie said happily. "Here's where I do most of my gaming, although I also have an Xbox in my bedroom."

"Gaming?"

"Video games."

"So where do you study?" Yungman inquired.

His grandson laughed, though Yungman couldn't figure out why. "Grandpa, we don't start getting grades until, like, high school."

"But you need to start—"

"So, Sir!" Einstein, accompanied by Marni, strode into the space. He walked over to the cars. "Say hello to my new favorite child: the Stryker."

"Da-aad!"

"Kidding, son! Kidding!"

The Stryker was a military-esque vehicle, much larger than the open-topped military jeeps that Yungman had ridden in as a houseboy. Samurai armor–plated, with a tiny windshield, a gun turret on top, gigantic knobby tires, a pointed-tooth grille.

"It's a MURV—Military Utility Recreational Vehicle," Einstein explained. "Largest vehicle that you can drive without getting a special license."

"That gun turret on top doesn't actually work," Reggie pointed out with disappointment.

"My signing bonus," said Einstein, so proudly he almost sang.

The pointed-tooth grille was certainly intimidating. So were the armor plates and the gun, even if it was fake. Yungman tried to fix his mouth into a smile, to not let his face show his inner thoughts regarding the ridiculousness of his son basically driving a Chaffee tank. Some disapproval must have become external because Young-ae elbowed him. "Kwak-ssi"—Mr. Kwak—she said warningly. "Let's have a nice time." At least, from upstairs, the good smells of Thanksgiving were warming the house.

The Thanksgiving table was already set. A white cloth covered the long wooden table, and orange and yellow leaves were scattered across the tabletop as if a door had opened and they had blown in. Real leaves no longer made a "fall" anymore. The days were shortening, but spikes of eighty-degree weather confused them; they withered on their branches or rotted in clumps, like wet green wads of tissue. From the air, some of the forests looked like fields of black mold with speckles of red and yellow in between—and those colors were from some fungal disease that was affecting evergreens.

Ah, the familiar green Jell-O topped with pink whipped cream: Minnesota "salad." When it was passed, Marni put a generous dollop on Yungman's plate, along with green beans, mashed potatoes, and baby onions in white sauce. During the war, this amount of food would have fed half the village. Yungman felt wickedly indulgent pushing away the onions just because he didn't like them.

The turkey didn't seem to be forthcoming. Yungman thought it impolite to ask, as Marni was a big "wellness" adherent and could possibly be trying a vegan diet or something. He took a bite of the Jell-O, which had bits of red candy suspended in it. He made sure to get a good swath of the whipped cream. He expected something sweet, but got something fishy. Ugh, the deceptive red pieces: pimiento.

"Ah," he said, tasting again. This strange stuff *was* fish. Salmon gelée with clam meringue, Marni would explain later. "It's molecular gastronomy."

"In this family," Marni said, reprimanding him casually, "we say grace before we eat."

"We say grace, too," Young-ae said, just as lightly. "Einstein, don't you remember the grace we used to say? The one Duckie taught you: 'Thank you for the world so sweet . . . thank you for the food we eat . . .'"

"You used to say *that* as grace?" Reggie hooted.

"What's so funny about that, buddy?" said Einstein.

"It just sounds so stupid."

Yungman agreed it sounded stupid—grace in general. The concept had been forced on them via the Western Christian missionaries who passed through the village, trying to get people to convert. Every few months there would be a different group. None could speak more than a garbled word or two of Korean, but they did know how to tempt them: with food. The Seventh-Day Adventists had the best: actual rice, mountain vegetables, as much soy curd as you wanted. In the years after their father went missing, Yungman and Yung-sik would fill their bellies to the maximum whenever they were offered a meal, a few minutes of mystical mumbo-jumbo being well worth making things easier for their mother, who was now the family's sole support.

In Birmingham and then in Horse's Breath, it solidified to Yungman that respectable people said grace and went to church. Nonrespectable people did not. Yungman and Young-ae made saying grace a habit so that, if they were dining with other people, they wouldn't forget. In upper Minnesota, almost everyone had a print of the famous picture *Grace*.

As soon as Einstein left for college, Yungman and Young-ae stopped saying grace, the way one day in late spring you stop wearing socks. Also, the photographer who had taken the *Grace* picture had died, and the local paper revealed the devout old man in the picture was just a drunk stumbling by the photo studio, enticed off the street with the promise of more booze; the photographer had been inspired by his raw, rough-hewn face, added the Bible and other props, gave the gent a fresh drink to stop his DTs, then a ride to the train station. Did this hobo ever find out how his visage had inspired so many—including Koreans—to adopt Christian ways?

Yungman decided he would get Einstein and Marni one as a housewarming present. "I'm hungry!" Reggie whined. "My gravy is getting cold."

Einstein stood up. He cleared his throat and started in on his own extemporaneous grace full of baroque "thees" and "thous."

Yungman was taken aback. When Einstein was in sixth grade, for reasons still obscure to him, elementary school kids had been shipped via their usual schoolbuses to their respective churches for two hours of mandatory Christian instructions on Wednesday afternoons. Einstein, citing the separation of church and state and in solidarity with Connie and Bonnie Mitzner, who had nowhere to go on Wednesdays because they were Jewish, refused to board the schoolbus to First Presbyterian. Yungman had secretly applauded this protest, but because Einstein had been officially marked "absent" from a school class, he had also been obliged to spank him.

His sudden bout of religious fervor was puzzling.

". . . And I am so thankful to be here, now, thanks to our heavenly Father, together with my whole beloved family." His voice even shook a bit with emotion.

"Ahem," Marni whisper-shouted. "What about my side? Aren't they your family, too?"

"You hate your family," he whisper-replied. ". . . And for all this we pray, Father God, in Jesus's precious, precious name, amen."

Einstein disappeared into the kitchen and returned to the dining room in an apron.

"Husband," said Marni, "what is that? You look like the guy from *Halloween*." The corded implement Einstein was holding looked disturbingly like a bone saw.

"Hammacher Schlemmer," Einstein said proudly. "An ultrasonic turkey carver. More precise than any knife. I can ultrasonically slice and dice leftovers into deli-style slices for sandwiches. You should have seen the guy doing the demo at the mall—he removed the fuzz from a peach."

"Bea!" called Marni, looking to the kitchen. "We're ready!"

There was someone else here?

A beautiful young African woman in a hijab that hid everything but her face and hands entered the living room holding a twenty-five-pound turkey in front of her. She set it in front of Einstein, who plugged in the knife.

"Folks, this is Bea, our kitchen helper."

She acknowledged the introduction with a little tic of her head and glided away.

"Bea?" said Yungman.

"Her name's not really Bea," Einstein said. "She's Somali—or maybe Nigerian? She has an incredibly long name that's hard to remember."

"It's Jawaahir. Mommy came up with Bea," said Reggie. "Now, *that's* funny."

"This knife vibrates at a hundred pulses a second," said Einstein, pausing to look up and smile as Bea depressed the shutter on a camera set up on a tripod in the far corner of the room.

*Nnnrgh!* Shards of meat, skin, cartilage, and bone flew around the room like shrapnel. "The silk wallpaper!" Marni shrieked, knocking over her glass of red wine.

"Oops—sorry, honey!" Einstein said as he hastily returned the turkey to the kitchen, one leg hanging precariously off the tray. They could hear a faint whine emanating from the other room, then cursing, then the clatter of a knife drawer being opened.

Bea sponged the pinkening tablecloth with club soda.

Twenty minutes later, Einstein returned, the acromegalic bird triumphantly deconstructed on the tray. He forked a massive drumstick onto a plate, which Bea ferried, as if it were a royal crown on a pillow, to Reggie, who eyed it suspiciously.

"Don't worry, Champ," said Einstein. "I literally carved your name on the other one."

"*Two* turkey drumsticks?" Yungman said. One was enough to feed a whole family—in fact, one had often fed the entire Kwak family. They'd pretended the single drumstick was a whole turkey. Yungman had carved it with exquisite surgeon's care, making beautiful, almost translucent slices that floated atop piles of buttered peas the way fancy waiters showered truffles. He turned to his grandson. "You know, the spirit of Thanksgiving is about sharing, like the Indians and the Pilgrims. Maybe someone else might like one?"

Reggie looked at him as if he were daft.

"Sir," said Einstein, "he waits all year for these."

"And one thing we're thankful for this Thanksgiving is that he has all his teeth," Marni said. "After one was removed *a bit prematurely.*"

Ugh, the tooth. That Thanksgiving five years ago, Yungman and Young-ae had dutifully flown out in a similar manner to see and admire Einstein's "new" house in Greenwich, Connecticut. Einstein explained that on the East Coast, "old" was better; their house had been built in 1929. Einstein had had trouble affording a house there in the first place, so the house's amenities were limited to new copper gutters, which they duly admired, and a small pool, which seemed to collect a lot of scum. He said he'd wanted slate shingles, but they would have to make do with the asphalt ones for now. The house was at the end of what could only be called a dead-end road. Across the street was the local driving school, Ahmed's Driver's Education, where Ahmed's family apparently also lived. The other doctors in Einstein's practice mostly lived in a town called Stamford, which was much cheaper, but Marni said she didn't want her son attending an "urban" school. Yungman knew nothing about the geography of the East Coast, but Einstein assured him that the George Bush family was from Greenwich and seemed to assume that explained everything.

All weekend Reggie had been showing off his loose tooth, wiggling it with his tongue, yammering about how he couldn't wait for it to fall out so he could get five dollars from the Tooth Fairy. Of course, the Kwaks had never promulgated such nonsense with Einstein; who makes money from a natural bodily process? With his grandson, however, Yungman found himself softening about, say, 10 percent on all things—and why not? It wasn't his child. He had no other job than to love and entertain him. He would contribute a dollar to the fund. And:

"I know a way to make it fall out faster," Yungman said.

"Okay!"

"Let me see you wiggle it again."

When Reggie opened his mouth, Yungman plucked the tooth from the gum. Reggie didn't even know it was out. There was, however, a pomegranate seed's worth of blood trapped in the socket. Reggie opened his mouth in front of the mirror, saw the blood, and began to cry. Marni, seeing the tooth in Yungman's fingers, had become a bit unhinged herself.

She had yelled, "Einstein, come help your son!" and spirited a wailing Reggie away in her arms, running up the stairs to the second floor as if they were being pursued by baying hounds. "Reggie, I promise that man will *never* hurt you again!" Her voice floated down to them like dust as Yungman argued, quite ineffectually, that he would never hurt his own flesh and blood. And who was "that man"?

Einstein had gone halfway up the stairs when Young-ae yelled for him to stop. "Are you going to do that, make your son think his grandfather is a bad person?"

Yungman's heart had fluttered at such a spirited defense.

"Ein-*STEIN*!" yelled Marni. "Don't you care about your son?" Einstein then continued up the stairs, not looking back.

Things had artificially calmed down a few minutes later with the arrival of the dessert crew: various neighbors, middle-aged white people who sagged slightly in their preppy, nautical-themed clothes. But the next morning, Marni's sulky silence, the force with which she hurled Yungman's bowl of oatmeal at him, was so punishing that Yungman and Young-ae had left early. Normally the two-hundred-dollar change fee per person would have been unthinkable, but once on the plane, Yungman and Young-ae looked at each other and sighed with utter relief.

"It was a baby tooth," Young-ae pointed out now. "Reggie *wanted* it out."

"That's a mute point, Young-ae," Marni said. "Irregardless. For all intensive purposes, Bill—" How he hated that odd diminuitive that didn't even make sense, Bill from *William*. "—did *not* ask my son for consent."

"Aiguuu—"

Yungman swiveled his head to make sure that sound was coming from his wife. This Koreanism intruded on their gathering like a pile of kimchi dumped on the mashed potatoes. Young-ae, hewing to Yungman's insistence they keep a scrupulously English-only household (so that Einstein wouldn't absorb an accent), usually used "Oh my goodness" or the classic Horse's Breath "Oh, for Pete's sake." In this instance, she might have even deployed the ultimate phrase of Minnesotan disapproval: "Well, that's *different*."

But "aigu"? The cry of annoyance, of despair, of surprise, of being old and tired, of feeling someone else's stubbed toe as your own pain, of sadness at missing a lover, a parent, of a monsoon season gone on too long, too hot, too wet—all these feelings, all the way to the keening cry for the freshly dead. Aigu, aigoh, ay-gooooooo, whose tones depended on severity and dialect but was always recognizable as the lament of the Korean people, shot through with years of sadness over its history, pessimism for its future.

He pondered.

His son, whose dream it was to be a doctor and "help people," was now a grace-saying businessman working at the Mall of America; Yungman's wife was becoming a Korean nationalist. Why was everyone insisting on mystifying him at this late age? Not understanding his white daughter-in-law was one thing, but his family?

"Did you know that the Korean word for 'turkey' is 'chilmyunjo'?" said Young-ae. "Seven-faceted-head bird. I learned that from one of the church ladies. We googled pictures of turkeys after and still can't figure out why 'seven.'"

"Hmm," said Yungman. "On the base we just called it 'tuh-ki,' same as what the GIs called it."

"Young-ae, Bill," said Marni, fully flustered now, "would you please not speak a foreign language in the house? We don't want Reggie to get confused."

68

Young-ae smiled benignly. "During the Japanese colonization of Korea, we were all forced to learn a foreign language," she said. "Imagine if someone today told you you would have to stop speaking English forever and speak, I don't know, Esperanto instead."

"What foreign language did you have to learn? Like, if it was French, it might be okay."

"Never mind."

Yungman quietly rejoiced to see the gravy boat arrive. Gravy was his solace. He could happily drink the stuff from a mug. He made sure to compliment Marni: "Beautiful gravy!" Last time it had been full of lumps.

"Bea made it."

"Well," Yungman said, pivoting to turn a failed compliment into new compliment, "you were the one who arranged it and made it possible, Marni."

"Thank you," she said. "And Bill, it's *Marni*."

"That's what I said: Marni."

"No, you did it again. You said 'Manny.' I'm not a man, I'm Marni. Mar-KNEE."

Yungman looked to his son, who had suddenly decided to decamp to the kitchen.

Had Einstein done that on purpose—married a woman whose name contained the maximum number of fricatives and diphthongs that were most difficult for the Korean mouth to pronounce? Most tragically, in Korean, when *R* and *N* were together, they produced a melodious sound, *rrrnnRRrnnNrrrn*. But in English, *R* and *N* stayed hard, as separate as enemy countries—and he never remembered which sound to make first, so was forced to guess. On the base, Lieutenant Jarvis, being so Christian, had suggested Yungman become Matthew, Mark, Luke, or John.

Maddyew, Marlurku, Rlnuku, Cho-nru.

Yungman had rejected them all; why have a name he couldn't even pronounce?

Mal-uh-rnee?

Marulnnrrrnnn-ee.

MalrnR-rhee.

Manny!

Yungman decided to talk to Reggie instead.

"So, Mr. Reggie! How's your new school been? Have a lot of chums?"

Reggie poked sulkily at his mashed potatoes. The first drumstick had a few bites taken out of it. The second sat capsized in a gravy lake. Yungman never let a piece of protein go until every scrap—muscle fiber, fascia, cartilage—had been consumed, the bone licked clean, split, and hoovered of its marrow. When he'd first had KFC with Ken, Ken had marveled, "Yungman, where did the chicken *go*?" Yungman had eaten most of the bones; they were that soft after being fried.

"Ah, so you have no time for friends, because you're so studious?" Yungman was undeterred. "Your father was the same way."

Reggie looked at him, his mouth hanging open, exposing masticated stuffing in the back. "Wha?"

" 'Studious' means someone who likes to study."

"Oh."

"Where do you think you might like to go to college?"

"Um, Sir," Einstein interjected, "how about some more green beans almandine? Stuffing?"

"How about Harvard, like your father?" said Yungman. "Or even Yale?"

"Ein-*stein*," said Marni. "Reggie, honey, it doesn't matter where—or *if*—you go to college. You know that, right?"

Yungman was aware that Marni (Manny!)'s goal in life for her son was only that he grow up without "pressure." She (scandalously) had not gone to college herself. See, valuing education was called "pressure" in America! Einstein used to complain about schoolboy bullies calling him a nerd, even stuffing him in a locker, kicking his books down the hall. But where were those bullies now? Did any of them go to Harvard?

Reggie shrugged off the adult malaise—he might not even know what "malaise" meant. He likely did not receive 1001 *SAT Words* as his sole Christmas present. In fact, books seemed to have gone out of style as presents in general. He played video games in lieu of reading books. His confidence and self-possession, even while knowing full well he wasn't very smart, irked Yungman but also intrigued him. Where did that come from? What was it based on? Did it have to be based on anything? How malleable Einstein had been; obedient and studious, especially compared to Ken's kids, who were wild from day one. However, while Scotty was an itinerant almost-hobo, Polly was a researcher at the Jonas Salk Institute. What was Einstein besides bland, like the floury white sauce swaddling the baby onions? Maybe it would have been nice if Einstein had shown a bit of fire once in a while (which Yungman would have been obliged to beat down, but still).

"How old are you, again, Reggie?"

"Twelve."

"That's definitely not too early to be thinking about college. You know, I sent away for a Harvard catalog when your father was only six months old! And in his room, he made a little sign that said 'Think Harvard, 199—'"

"Second call for beans almandine, Sir? Sir?"

"In fact, your father was reading college-level biology books when he was in junior high. He spent his school breaks coming with me to the hospital. He even learned how to take blood."

"He won the science fair in sixth grade by doing a quite sophisticated project on macrophages," Young-ae added.

"Uh, Sir? Mom?"

"—and he was younger than you when he did all that because he skipped a grade!" Yungman couldn't help adding.

"I can't imagine my dad being younger than me."

"Than I," said Yungman.

"Than *you*?"

"No, you should say 'my dad being younger than *I*,' as it's the nominative case. Likewise, you say between you and *me* when it's the object of a preposition." He hoped Marni was listening, as she always said "between you and I" because it sounded sophisticated, but it was wrong.

"Uh-huh," said Reggie. "Right."

"You need to do well in school so you can have a successful life."

"Nah," he said with a sudden winsome grin. "I got it covered."

"Then what do you plan to do?"

"I'll just inherit. This house is worth a million dollars!"

"A million dollars!" Yungman whistled. He turned to his son. "How big a mortgage did you have to take out?"

"I sold off some of my 401K."

"You sold some of your retirement funds? What about the penalties?"

"Dad's counting on his company blowing up on the stock market, like Facebook," said Reggie. "But it could always crash and burn like MySpace."

"This is not great Thanksgiving day conversation, okay?" said Marni. "Bill?"

Bea, at last, called them into the kitchen, where half a dozen pies were laid out on the long marble counter.

"What kind of pie would you want, Mr. Sir?" she asked softly. "Pecan? Pumpkin? Chocolate mousse? Lemon meringue? And we have five kinds of ice cream, including no-sugar and low-fat, although the no-sugar one is not low-fat." She shook her head apologetically.

"Hey, Reggie," called Einstein, muscling out some still-frozen pistachio ice cream, green as an alien. "Do you know why chefs are mean?"

Reggie looked at his father through hooded eyes.

Einstein grinned. "Because they beat eggs and whip cream!"

"Dad, I'm not ten." Reggie rolled his eyes. "Blargh."

"But you're not a teenager yet, either," added Young-ae. "No need to act like one."

Marni was hunched over the lemon pie; she was dissatisfied with the merengue and was administering a flame to it with a tiny torch. "Young-ae," she said, the tips of the whitecaps browning in the heat. "I'd appreciate you not disciplining my child."

"I'm not disciplining him, I'm stating a fact," she said. "Manny."

"You know," Yungman said, addressing his wife and daughter-in-law as Einstein handed him a glass of some kind of liqueur with a delightful licorice aroma. "This is the first Thanksgiving I don't have to worry about being called to the hospital." He took a satisfying gulp of the liqueur, which warmed his esophagus before sliding deliciously into his stomach, then into his legs. Ah, you know who else liked his after-dinner drinks? That made him think, a bit guiltily, of Ken.

"Your face is going to turn red," Young-ae said.

"I need the color!" He laughed a bit louder than was called for.

He took another gulp, which prompted another. He could feel a flush beginning. "Sir," said Einstein. "I actually wanted to talk to you about that."

Yungman was affronted. His "glow" was not the alcoholic's gin blossom. Surely Einstein knew about the ALDH2 heterozygote reaction that affected almost half of East Asians. "I think I took three drinks in my whole career. One of them was at your Harvard graduation."

Given that Young-ae flushed as well, Einstein had to be homozygous for this mutation, and, indeed, had round circles of pure red on each cheek, almost like a Korean shaman's mask.

"No, I'm talking why you *can* drink now—about Horse's Breath General's closure."

"Oh."

"It must have been strange to have that come on so suddenly," Einstein said. "I read that SANUS made the nation's biggest buys last year, something like a hundred hospitals. The rural ones, because they're so debt-laden, could be bought pretty cheaply, I would think."

"From my perspective, the hospital was running as well as it ever was, except for the glitches caused by Tinklenberg's cost cutting," Yungman said. "He got rid of my nurse-midwife. We no longer carry the TPA clotbusters—can you imagine? Ole Oleson had a post-op stroke because of that; half his face is paralyzed."

"Oh, what a nice man. That's too bad," Einstein said. "So where are your patients going?"

"I think the only local hospital with a doctor who can to do deliveries is Mahonen River General—but even that physician will be gone soon," Yungman said. "A young guy, Chad something, just out of residency. I met him at a regional Minnesota ACOG meeting. He's doing the rural debt forgiveness program: two years in exchange for your medical school debt."

"Ha! He better hurry," said Einstein. "I bet the president will get rid of that socialist program. *You* should have had your debt forgiven for working in Horse's Breath all these years."

"I didn't accumulate medical school debt," Yungman said. "Korea doesn't work that way."

*Of course, my brother had to work to pay for my tuition,* he did not say.

"How about Dieter?" asked Einstein. "How's he making out?"

Dieter Klaus was Yungman's colleague and friend, an OB at St. Luke's Hospital in Duluth. Yungman often envied his modernist apartment overlooking the aerial bridge. There were multiple OB-GYNs at his hospital, so he didn't have to be on call 24-7. *And* he didn't have kids, or even a wife. He took a lot of time off to go skiing in Colorado. When Yungman needed to take time off (proudly never a day for himself, even the day he passed a kidney stone)—to drive Einstein all the way to Minneapolis to take his SATs, for example—Dieter drove over and covered. Yungman would have to pay out of his own pocket, but it was worth it for the peace of mind.

When he returned, he'd take Dieter for a nice meal in the physicians' dining room, and they'd get to catch up. The pair had met at a regional ACOG meeting, Dieter was impressed when Yungman had correctly pronounced his name and didn't make a joke about "you don't *look* like a dieter, with that big belly." Yungman thought every doctor had to learn German, as they did in Korea, since so many medical texts were in German. The two men had bonded over being immigrants doing jobs regular Americans didn't want to do.

Dieter had also come to the US on a student visa and done an FTP repeat internship, just like Yungman. However, he became a "naturalized" American, while Yungman became "illegal."

"Dieter went back to Germany. He was going to retire here, but the election made him change his mind."

"I think we need to give our new president a chance," Einstein said, and Yungman wondered with horror: *Did he vote for that cretin? The one who wants to bomb North Korea? Who is beating the drum already to ban Muslims—like the quiet Bea who clearly would not harm a fly. (And what does her family do for Thanksgiving? Was she here in America on her own?)*

"Bill," Marni piped up, "you're way past retirement age. You should just enjoy your 'me' time."

Yungman took an energetic drink of his liquor, which tasted like medicine now. "My 'me' time is my work."

"'Workaholic' is what they're called. Einstein told me how you weren't home a lot when he was growing up."

"What?" said Yungman. "I was home all the time!"

"So now that you're retired, what *have* you been doing, Sir?"

"It hasn't even been a week," he said, even though, technically, it would be a week tomorrow. He didn't want to tell Einstein the truth: he actually sat in his chair most of the day. He hated the name La-Z-Boy, but where was the lie? "Ken and I went to see the Iron Tower Mining Museum."

"*That's* what you do when I'm gone?" exclaimed Young-ae. "Kwak-ssi, you were the top student at Seoul!"

Yungman didn't know what to say. He was supposed to have the career for both of them. It never reached the heights he'd imagined. In fact, on some level he was still waiting for it—something—to begin. He had never anticipated that it would end like this, his decades of accumulated experience rusting into oblivion.

"Interestingly, this is exactly where SANUS comes in," Einstein said excitedly. "Its whole mission is to help people navigate the gaping holes in our failing health care system. On the supply side, it provides a matching service for underutilized human resource medical capital."

"I haven't the slightest idea what you're talking about."

"That's you! Underutilized. If you want to keep working, there may be a place for you in Retailicine."

"Retailicine?"

"Retail plus medicine."

"Doing what?"

"Retailicine is a big umbrella."

Yungman paused. Something about Einstein's eagerness seemed rehearsed; he'd been planning this. He waited.

"I work at the luxury brand, the HoSPAtal. But would you ever consider working at what we call a Mall-Based Retail Outlet?"

"What, delivering babies at the Mall of America?"

"Ha ha, no—actually, that's what I do, at the Birth Boutique, which is technically 'mall-adjacent' as it's in a separate building," Einstein said. "But inside the Mall of America, we have dozens of Mall-Based Retail Outlets, or M-BROs."

"M-BROs?"

"Various primary- and specialty-care shops. It's all about bringing value-based medicine to optimize quality of life."

"But which ones?" Yungman asked. He threw out a random specialty: "Opthalmology."

"Yes! We have a walk-in store called For Eyes, where we do LASIK and rudimentary eye exams. Get it?"

"How about . . . kidney dialysis?"

Einstein paused, looked at Marni, who returned his look. "Yes, actually; it's called Speedee Dialysis."

"What would I do?"

"How about administering vaccinations?"

"Your company does that?"

"SANUS's *premier* M-BRO is Vaccines R Us. Makes them easy, affordable, and, can I say, fun."

"Hm." Humanitarian work that was just a drive away.

"There are five of them in the Mall of America alone, and one next to Nickelodeon Universe. The American Academy of Pediatrics has even praised SANUS for improving state booster compliance by fifty percent in just the last month!"

"Maybe I should look into it."

"One of the Vaccines R Us branches filled all its jobs within a day. All the hospital closures and mergers mean a lot of MDs are out of work."

"You don't say!" Yungman sat up.

"I *could* try to get you an interview." Einstein picked up his phone, that clear, palm-size pane of glass that occupied so many people's attention these days. He used his index finger, like a bird's beak, to peck at it. "Ah! Got one! Tomorrow."

"Tomorrow?"

"These interview spots aren't easy to get, but I have an in."

"You should go," said Young-ae. "You need something to do."

"Should I book it?" His son's finger-beak was poised. "We could drive to work together."

Oh, how Yungman hated these need-it-right-now decisions.

"Okay." He relinquished himself. "What do I have to lose?"

Yungman applied himself to carefully sponging away a gravy splotch from the lapel of his suit. In this unfamiliar room, it was easy for him to pretend he was a young father again, his son clasping a stuffed animal to his chest, wandering into the bathroom to stare worshipfully up at him as he readied himself for work.

"Excuse me, Sir—do you want to borrow a pair of my shoes?" Einstein said now. He was eyeing Yungman's white loafers, placed at the ready by the door.

"I just need to give them a quick wipe. Do you have a shoe cloth?"

"Sir, actually, how about a pair of my oxblood brogues?"

"Is it that disreputable to wear white after Labor Day?" Yungman asked, half joking. "Does this call into question my clinical decision-making?"

"Let's just say those shoes are a little . . . nonstandard. I mean, those chunky heels . . ." Einstein himself was wearing high leather sneakers that looked like dual Aircasts for his ankles. Again, inside the house!

Yungman liked his loafers. They slipped on and off easily. They had a gold ornament in the front, looking a little like the bit of a horse's bridle. The substantial heel gave him a nice lift. Overall, the shoe had a nice design, its tongue curved at the top like a gladiator's helmet. He'd been so proud buying these dressy shoes in Korea. White collar, white coat, white shoes. As close to being a white American as he could possibly get, he'd thought at the time.

However, come to think of it, he hadn't seen anyone else wear this kind of shoe here in the actual America.

Einstein handed him the oxblood brogues, redolent of pungent cedar shoe trees. He stood there while Yungman tried them on. Even though Einstein's feet were a half size bigger, the tapered style pinched. But now, his feet trussed by the skinny laces, he was committed. His son smiled approvingly as Yungman walked gingerly, unfamiliarly downstairs, where a delightful scent of batter was wafting up.

Marni was dressed in tight yoga clothes that gave off a kind of iridescent sheen. Their waffle maker was the kind they had at hotel buffets, an antigravity clamshell that dropped the finished product into the waiting plate, with no handling of hot objects needed. When Einstein was little, Yungman used to try to make waffles on Sunday mornings, establish a family tradition. Einstein would stand up on his chair and, in defiance of Yungman's warning to keep away, naughtily reach toward the waffle iron's outer surface. "Hot? Hot?" It became almost a game, one that Yungman didn't have the time or inclination to play. He had enough to worry about—getting the waffles done, the frozen sausages made, the Aunt Jemima on the table and everything done in time to hustle them off to church while wondering which one of his patients would be in labor by the end of the sermon. One day, when Einstein teasingly probed his chubby finger a little too close to the steaming lip of the iron, Yungman helped it along the rest of the way. The tiny finger had blistered immediately. Einstein screamed. "I said it's hot! This is what happens when you don't listen to your father!" Yungman had screamed back. His son wouldn't have lasted a day trekking on foot to Seoul during the war. And yet, Yungman felt the rebuke now, in the mere selection of their house appliances. Undoubtedly Einstein had told all this to Marni, probably characterizing it as a lasting "childhood trauma," language he'd learned from the therapist he'd been seeing since college.

"We'd better get going," Einstein said. The waffles weren't for Yungman anyway. He wondered about his breakfast, but wouldn't trouble them to ask.

Einstein's Military Utility Recreational Vehicle spanned almost a full highway lane. He seemed to enjoy the reactions—surprise, resentment, curiosity—from drivers and pedestrians alike at this ten-foot-tall armored vehicle with a rotating gun on top.

Despite the vehicle's size, its giant oblong gas reservoirs crowded the inside. Yungman felt something prodding his back. He fished out a bag of blackening pepperoni.

"Oh, that's Reggie's." Einstein threw it merrily out the window. "He likes to eat his 'roni in the car."

### THE MALL OF AMERICA
The Biggest Mall in the Nation!
Next Exit

It didn't look as imposing as Yungman remembered. What drew his attention now was the quartz-crystal-shaped spire seemingly growing out of the ground next to it. In gold letters across its base was written

~ The HoSPAtal ~ A Passion for Excellence ~

The road looked like it was going to run right through the quartz, but then a door opened. It shut after they'd driven through.

"Like the Bat Cave!" Einstein said with boyish glee.

~ MDiety PARKING~

"Isn't that cute?" said Einstein. "Here, physicians are 'MDieties'—get it?"

A young dark-eyed man took his keys. "Good morning, Dr. Kwak."

"Hey, thanks, José," Einstein said.

"It's Benedicto," the man said. "José left two weeks ago."

"Sorry."

They were in the basement. Einstein took Yungman to an elevator that said "To SUB Basement."

One door said:

~ Mall-Based Medical Retail Outlet Human Capital Department

The other:

~ *Caution: Ionizing Radiation in Use!*

"Ready to be a doctor of the future?" Einstein asked, thankfully taking him to the door that did not have the universal sign for radiation on it. It opened to a waiting room with a few dozen people seated on hard chairs. Facing them were an additional two doors: PRIMARY CARE PHYSICIANS and SPECIALISTS. A man poked his head out of PRIMARY CARE PHYSICIANS. "Nygaard? Dr. Soren Nygaard here?"

"Just answer to your name when you're called," Einstein said. "I called ahead and put you in the queue."

The SPECIALISTS door listed:

Nephrology
Radiology

Psychiatry

Ophthalmology

ENT

Oncology

Neurology

Urology

OB-GYN

Yungman was pleased—OB-GYN at Horse's Breath General was considered primary, not specialty, care, which he always thought was erroneous, as surgery went beyond primary care. He was every bit the surgeon Mitzner was.

"I have to get going; I'll call you later." Einstein's body was already facing away. He paused. "Oh, wait—you don't have a cell phone." For a moment a look of uncertainty, of dawning panic, crossed his face. "I won't know where you are."

Yungman and his son were separating in the same building, not on different sides of the ocean. "Hmm," Einstein said, that same troubled look from his Sears baby portrait. "Hmm." If his son blanched at the thought of being out of touch with his father for an hour, Yungman thought, could Einstein even begin to fathom what it was like to be one of the Korean "separated and scattered families" who were once each other's dearest hearts and now were on different sides of a military border, not even knowing who was alive and who was dead?

"Sir?" said Einstein. "Are you all right?"

Yungman blinked, the waiting room coming back into focus. "I'm fine. I was just thinking . . ."

"About what?"

"About . . . perhaps it's time to consider getting a cell phone."

"I've been telling you that for ages!" Einstein laughed cathartically. "I'll help you this weekend. Then you can also play games, like

Sudoku—neuroplasticity and all that. Anyway, once you're in the SANUS 'ecosystem,' you'll be easily trackable via my SANUSwatch."

"You're that confident I'll get the job?"

"Oh ya, you're my father." He beamed and popped the sleeve on his leather flight jacket to show Yungman a watch with a bunch of buttons on a camouflage band that echoed his tank-car.

"The customizing was a birthday splurge." At the top of the face, where Yungman's watch said "Elgin," Einstein's said "~SANUS~" and featured a background of a caduceus with the double snakes. "We can track the positions of Retailicinists in the mall. I think you get some kind of RFID chip like they use for pets in your watch. I don't think they'd chip you internally, ha ha. But take my card just in case. You can always call me."

---

**EINSTEIN ALBERT SCHWEITZER NOBEL KWAK**

MDiety

Chief of Aesthetic Vaginal Surgery

SANUS Global Health at The HoSPAtal

Twitter / Instagram / Facebook / SnapX

---

The SPECIALISTS door opened. A middle-aged woman, a swatch of her curly hair dyed a brilliant SeaWorld blue, looked with recognition at the two men. "Dr. Kwak, can I talk to you?" Maybe she was a colleague of Einstein's, Yungman thought.

"Which one?" Yungman said.

"How am I supposed to know?" she said. "Whichever one that's looking for a job."

Einstein gave him a thumbs-up and mouthed "You'll be great!" And then he disappeared.


Yungman had to take an employment test. He always did well on tests.

*Do you have any medical board violations or pending cases? Is your Minnesota license current?*

*Are there any arrest warrants out for you, or have you ever been convicted of a felony or spent any time in jail?*

*Are you certified by the American Board of Obstetrics & Gynecology?*

(What that had to do with administering vaccines he didn't know, but he obediently answered.)

The blue-haired lady "graded" his test and, apparently satisfied, sent him down the hall to another nondescript room with another middle-aged woman, with mouse-gray hair. He put his résumé down on the desk in front of her—Reggie had helped him put it together last night on the computer. She didn't even glance at it and instead asked to see his Minnesota license, his ACOG membership, and his ABOG certification.

"And you don't have any tremor conditions, like Parkinson's?"

"Of course not!" He was affronted. "I'm a surgeon!"

"No medical board or medical malpractice actions?"

"No!"

She took his fingerprints. Why, again, he didn't know.

Yungman was then given an address: a floor, a wing, a sector, a door number. He traversed a skyway to the Mall and walked for what seemed like miles past Earring Pagoda, Orange Julius, three GAPs, I Lefse My Heart in Minnesota, Victoria's Secret, Only in Minnesota,

Forever 21—all fronted with riot gates, oddly, like they had in Korea when demonstrations were commonplace. He saw no one as he strode past Nickelodeon Universe, manic characters frozen in midair, roller coasters eerily stilled on their tracks. Door 12-0003 was a dark storefront, barred gate also in place, across from a gaudy mega-restaurant, the Rainforest Cafe.

Through the ambient light, he spied a single counter, like the check-in at an airline's gate. Next to the counter, the letters A-T-M glowed. He rattled the gate and called hello. From behind the counter, a dark-haired young woman detached from the gloom and motioned for him to go down the side hall, where there was a small back door into the store.

"You're late," she said, exasperated. "You know it's Black Friday, right?"

She had a slight, unplaceable accent. Belarus? Moldova? Romania? She took his employment sheet and slipped it into a machine that sat behind the reception counter. Out popped a silicone wristband with a tiny holographic disc, which she then held underneath what looked like a supermarket price scanner.

Y KWAK read the LED display in cubular font.

"Scan in; it starts the clock." She gave him a clip-on badge that said TRAINEE (SANUSSEC LEVEL 0). Hers said TRAINER (SANUSSEC LEVEL 2).

In the very back of the place was a small storeroom, its shelves piled with inventory. In the middle, on a folding table, a woman lay naked from the waist down, in lithotomy position, her head propped up with one hand so she could check her phone. Yungman tried not to stare.

"Hi!" she chirped from the table.

"Er, hello," Yungman said back. "Nice to see you."

"This is Jenny, our standardized customer—they get one free treatment for volunteering."

"Why do we need a standardized patient?" he asked. True, normally Maude administered the flu vaccines, but intramuscular injection was hardly something he could forget how to do.

"You have run a Laser Defolliculator II before?" she said with surprise.

"No," said Yungman. Now they were using lasers for vaccines?

She turned to look at the clipboard she was carrying. "Just to confirm: Do you have a Minnesota State Medical License? Any pending malpractice lawsuits or medical board actions? Any felonies?"

"Yes, no, no, no," he said obediently. This was getting a bit annoying.

She handed him a white coat that said *SANUS Mall-Based Medicine* on the pocket. "It's ten dollars a day to rent."

"I have one back at home," he said. Paying for a coat?

"Consistency across the brand," she said. "We really have to hurry here." Yungman sighed as she left to go make a copy of his credit card.

While the trainer was gone, Yungman didn't know where to put his eyes, so he picked up a brochure from a pile.

MAKE MINE MEDICAL!! GRAND OPENING!!
Specialized medical retail puts the "treat" back into treatments:

Speedee Dialysis
In-and-Out Chemo
USA CancerCare
Depilation Nation
For Eyes LASIK and vision testing
Quik Vu MRI/Imaging
Barry's Bariatric (now with Barry's Jr. lap bands!)
Dome Depot Neurology & Psychopharmaceuticals
Faster Than the ER!

PharMACY's medicines, body care, clothes, appliances & gifts
    (check out our wedding registry!)
Vaccines R Us

"Keep this—this is your only receipt."

*White coat deposit plus $500 incidentals at Depilation Nation.*

"Depilation Nation?" he said, looking up.

"We really need to start your training. The store opens"—she checked her gadget-y SANUSwatch; hers was plain, with a black plastic strap that was cracked and whitened in a few places—"in fifteen minutes."

Yungman wanted to correct her, gently.

"I'm actually supposed to be administering vaccines—at Vaccines R Us."

"No, you're not."

"Yes, I am."

"Not according to your ID."

WELCOME TO DEPILATION NATION!
Where unwanted hair comes to die.
~ A SANUS Medical Retail Outlet ~
*Laser mustache/pubic hair depilation is:*
*LESS PAINFUL THAN WAXING OR TWEEZING*
*—NO ANNOYING STUBBLE*
*CLEANER SKIN WITH LESS CHANCE OF INFECTION*
*PHYSICIAN ADMINISTERED FOR*
*HIGHEST SAFETY STANDARDS*
*PERFECT SMOOTHNESS & PERMANENT RESULTS\*\**
*FINANCING AVAILABLE!!*
*\*\* your results may vary*

"They don't have doctors at Vaccines R Us. Just nurse's aides and nurses."

It was true that when in a hurry sometimes he got his annual flu shot at Walgreens. Some clerk did it; there was never a doctor in sight.

"OB-GYNs work *here*," she said in her accented voice.

"I don't mean to sound flippant," he said, "but depilation is even less of a medical procedure than vaccines."

"This is the exclusive FDA-approved machine for pubic hair depilation, and it requires a doctor to operate it."

"Pubic hair? Why would anyone want to depilate *that*?"

"It's an elective health therapeutic."

Yungman wanted to clutch his head. Health? Pubic hair cushioned and protected the sensitive skin of the area. Depilation was *unhealthy* for it. Folliculitis. Various infections. How did he end up in this absurd situation? Yes, it was Einstein!

"Doctors shouldn't disease-monger," he said. "Pubic hair is not a pathology and should be left alone. Here's your coat back." He could sit in some café somewhere and have a pretzel until the day was done.

"The store needs to open." She looked at him. "You know, I'm a physician, too."

"Excuse me?"

"I was an OB in my country."

"Then why are you—"

The trainer leaned over her electronic slate and typed furiously into it.

*I can't work here legally.*

Yungman stared. Was she perhaps "illegal" from a different country? Maybe South America? Or Muslim? She had pale skin, violet eyes, and, just underneath her curtain of black hair, a plum-size burn scar on the side of her face that looked like a second, smaller set of lips.

*If you leave, there'll be no one to work the shift. I'll be in trouble. Black Friday is one of the biggest days. Please don't leave. I need this job. My educational visa has expired. I can't go back to my country, for many reasons. I have a child. This job is what feeds us.*

Yungman paused. He knew the feeling.

"Hey," the standardized patient said, canting her head up to look at Yungman. "Can we get going here?"

"I'll be with you momentarily." Yungman smiled at her. A nice white lady. She couldn't even begin to fathom the life of the undocumented immigrant. Her fears would be along the lines of missing a good deal on a microwave at a Black Friday sale, not living with the icy fear of a hand on the shoulder (indeed, the INS was now called ICE). She probably envisioned "illegals" as dirty and scary and *not* the two doctors with her now.

He turned to the trainer. Might as well get her through the day, so she wouldn't get fired. "It says on the sign you also offer mustache hair removal. Can't I just do that?"

She shook her head and typed again:

*Mustache is on the menu solely to get around obscenity codes because we are within five hundred feet of a children's playground—Nickelodeon Universe.*

A beep from her SANUSwatch, followed by a misting sound. That smell of the air immediately after a violent August thunderstorm.

"Ozone," she explained. "The SANUSwatch comes with a SANUSwatch that deploys if it senses stress, to neutralize sweat odor from employees."

*Please.*

He recognized that hunted look. "All right," he said. Yungman tried to listen carefully as she explained how to use the Laser Defolliculator II on different kinds of pubic hair. The standardized patient was pleased to receive a double coupon.

The trainer lifted the metal gate at the entrance. *Clackclackclack-clackityclack!!* A twenty-one-gun salute going up and down the mall. She switched on the electric sign that ran in a banner, like a news feed:

BLACK FRIDAY SPECIAL: 5-session package only $800
~ Your operator today is Y. KWAK, MD, OB-GYN ~

The Defolliculator II was a waist-high beige plastic box on wheels, so the operator just had to move it from patient to patient. The treatment room held a circle of six beds facing the center like the spokes of a wheel. Same format the Russians used to mass-produce LASIK eye surgery to quickly standardize the vision of cosmonauts—no glasses in space! How strange to think that some of the most impressive achievements of Communism had been repackaged as consumer items in an American mall.

"Hello, I'm Dr. Kwak." He stood with the hose of the Defolliculator in his hand.

The patient was wearing headphones and what looked like ski goggles, but opaque. The trainer had disappeared.

"Don't bother, just get in there—she can't hear you through the audio on the SVRE," said a young woman, who appeared in the doorway to the treatment room. She said her name was Joelle and she was the receptionist. She wore a white SANUS coat like Yungman's.

"SVRE?"

"SANUS Virtual Reality Experience." She pronounced SANUS yet *another* way, as san-yoo-ess.

"So I should just start, with no introduction? Consent?"

"They sign all sorts of stuff; it's fine. By the way, SANUS is timing you. That chip in your wristband talks to the Defolliculator. I'd get going if I were you."

The patient giggled at something, then pawed at the air the way a kitten does at dust motes.

Yungman aimed the nozzle. He waited, as the trainer had shown him, for a circle of red, about the diameter of a quarter to illuminate "the target area," then pulled the trigger. He would repeat this action depending on "the density of follicular coverage on the labia majora and mons."

Yungman said goodbye to that inaugural customer. Would he remember her? He would never forget his very first patient. Cho Gunghae, annual exam. Curly perm; comma-shaped, kind eyes; almost the same age as his own dear mother. Yungman had at the beginning of the exam stuttered out orders to put her feet in the stirrups and she had jumped to comply, calling him *Respected Dr. Kwak*. Him, the third-year medical student! Yungman felt like he'd grown ten centimeters. He didn't know how he felt now, with the patients plugged in to some other world, not his. He moved on to number two, then numbers three and four. A strange relief, actually, to just put his head down and get the job done. He could do that.

Joelle reappeared in the doorway, frantically motioned to him to meet her in the back storeroom. "You're doing it wrong."

"The Defolliculator?"

"No."

"My bedside manner?"

"Is that what you call it?" She handed him a pair of black mesh panties out of a cardboard box, the same standard nonirritant panties Horse's Breath General gave to women postpartum. *Courtesy of Depilation Nation* it said across the gluteal section on the back.

"You forgot these. If the customer realizes she didn't get her free panties and makes noise about it, we have to give her a free treatment — that'll be taken out of your wages. As it is, you'll probably lose a customer service star right off."

Yungman paused, understanding that he was being scolded by a twenty-five-year-old. On the other hand, she was just trying to help him preserve his meager salary.

"Thank you, Joelle. I appreciate your advice."

She lifted what looked like a Kotex. "They can also buy this Chill-PAC—five dollars, and you get a fifty-cent royalty."

"Does it help?" Yungman had no idea what a laser-depilated vulva would feel like, but guessed it wouldn't be pleasant. Lasers *cut*.

"Who the heck knows?"

"You've never had it done?"

"What? Nah, I just work here. Before this I was a greeter at the Rainforest Cafe over yonder and saw the HELP WANTED sign and thought, *Why should I stand all day and get varicose veins at twenty-five? And watch little kids eat too much kukui ice cream and puke?* Oh, and you should keep this in your pocket for reference."

She handed him a card that looked like a grid of paint colors at Sherwin-Williams: (1) white school paste; (II) peaches; (III) ochres, burlap tans. (IV) was just a square of black with a big red X overlaid on top with an exclamation point.

"Why is category four crossed out?"

"That's the skin tone we can't do."

Yungman put the card to the back of his hand. If he didn't use sunscreen, his skin darkened to III easily. His mother, who had the kind of porcelain Korean skin whose color was as unchangeable as alabaster, used to tease Yungman, calling him a winter scholar, summer peasant.

Joelle flipped open the Employee Manual, and read:

NOTICE: Highly pigmented skin (skin gradient tints > III) CANNOT BE ACCOMMODATED per FDA regulations, as melanocytes pose risk of diversion of laser from hair to skin and burn risk. Operators should review proper legal language in Appendix 2(c) part iii and take proper caution for obtainment of liability insurance before operation.

"Miss Joelle, may I ask you something?"

"Sure."

"Why do people want to remove their pubic hair in the first place?"

"You've never heard of a Brazilian?"

"Of course I have! How about Pelé?"

"You're funny!"

A noise like a clanging school bell. It took Yungman a second to realize it was coming from his wristband.

"Oh, first time that went off it scared the bejeezus out of me, too. It can detect if you aren't moving; you'll get fined for 'wage theft.' It goes up every minute you're late."

Behind Joelle, the banner scrolled in an endless loop.

*LESS PAINFUL THAN WAXING OR TWEEZING . . . NO ANNOYING STUBBLE . . . CLEANER SKIN WITH LESS CHANCE OF INFECTION . . . PHYSICIAN ADMINIS- TERED FOR HIGHEST SAFETY STANDARDS . . . PER- FECT SMOOTHNESS & PERMANENT RESULTS\*\* . . . FINANCING AVAILABLE!! BLACK FRIDAY SALE BLACK FRIDAY SALE.*

Yungman got back to work.

Einstein came by at five. Yungman wanted to muster up some outrage, but he was too tired.

"So, how was it?"

"What do you *think*?"

"What do you mean?"

"You said vaccinations."

Einstein looked aggrieved. "*You* said vaccinations. Depilation Nation is one of the few M-BROs that still had positions open. I'm glad you got a position—congratulations."

"You knew in advance I wasn't going to work in vaccines? That I was going to end up here?"

Einstein smiled patiently, like he was talking to a child who was mad that a vaccine shot hurt. "It's all dependent on supply and demand. So, what do you think?"

"You can hardly call this medicine," Yungman sniffed. "It's actually kind of sordid." He spotted the tiniest twitch at the corner of his son's mouth. Einstein was just trying to help, of course—help his father avoid decomposing into a blithering pile of Alzheimer's.

Yungman made sure to remove his coat, fold it into quarters, then eighths, and tuck it under his arm. The material was flimsy and thin, no pockets; more like a butcher's coat than a doctor's lab coat. Traditionally, the more senior the physician, the longer the coat. This one, the same one Joelle wore, was comical. He didn't want to be walking around the Mall of America in a uniform like the teens in their Annie's Pretzels smocks. It was preferable to be an elderly immigrant man walking in the mall with his son, doing some useless shopping.

"Are you, Sir . . ." Einstein hesitated and winced a bit as if Yungman were going to hit him (and, truth be told, that tone made Yungman indeed feel like hitting him). "Going to go back on Monday?"

"Of course," Yungman said.

At 1 King Arthur's Court, Yungman walked into the spacious, turreted kitchen and noted the unusual smell of fermented garlic.

"Not a moment too soon," Marni remarked, a hand over her nose. Young-ae was back already. She sat, a cup of tea grown cold in front of her, with a trove of brown Cub Foods bag full of jars wrapped in plastic bags, each knotted tightly and neatly. Kimchi! He started to salivate.

"Kimchi," she confirmed, with a moderate level of distress. Yungman remembered his hunger to learn English, the enigma of Lieutenant Jarvis once describing kimchi as "sewage in a cocktail shaker" (What was a sue-wedge? A cock tail shaker?), plus the further mystery of why so many GIs refused to even sample the wonders of Koreans' most important food.

"You know," he said, "that one of the few things in the world that was shown to kill the dangerous SARS virus is kimchi. They ran a clinical trial on it in Korea at Yonsei University, the Yale of Korea."

"I believe it. Thank you for coming to visit," Marni said. "I need to get dinner ready for Reggie." She removed her hand to use a knife to poke open a package of hot dogs.

In the car, Yungman and Young-ae squabbled. Neither wanted the responsibility of being the captain. They were both tired.

Where were the self-driving cars when you needed them? "You're back a lot earlier than I expected," Yungman couldn't help saying, taking the wheel.

The church's Bible study group was, for whatever reason, undertaking to re-copy the Bible by hand. She was never home until well after dinnertime during these marathon sessions.

"Mrs. Kimm had to go out."

Yungman almost guffawed. "This Black Friday obsession is something else."

"No," Young-ae said coldly. "She had an emergency call at the hospital."

At last, the Hinckley exit was coming up. Yungman pulled off the highway and drove up to the particular Sinclair gas station. He did so because everyone did, for reasons that had become obscure. Horse's Breathers all drove to this station, even though there was an almost identical gas station, with the same price or even a few tempting cents lower, a hundred yards away. But they never stopped there. No one did.

The Hyundai Bongo got terrific gas mileage, so this was just a pit stop. As if choreographed, they switched sides. "Chinese fire drill," the kids used to call it. An alien observing them might think that this paired female and male of the human species were so intensely connected that their communication had taken on a form beyond spoken language. The alien might be right. And also wrong.

At home, Yungman eagerly unpacked the Cub Foods bag. The kimchi jar on top released a garlicky hiss as he opened it. He'd been bereft of kimchi for a few weeks, beholden to the church ladies and the kimchi-ripening cycles. He pincered out a piece with his fingers and deposited it in his mouth the way a magician swallows a goldfish. The heat from the pepper, the salt of the brine, the warmth of the ginger, the rounded ocean taste of shrimp paste wafted into the cavern at the back of his mouth, a place that was never stimulated by bland and fatty midwestern food. The fullness of this kimchi sensation was so familiar yet partially forgotten, it made him tear up unexpectedly.

He caught Young-ae glancing at him, one eyebrow raised. This batch was particularly spicy, with just the right amount of old-kimchi sour. See, the genius of it was, kimchi never went bad. It just ripened and ripened from fresh and salad-y to the concentrated, pungent stuff perfect for soup—his favorite stage. How stupid he'd been, all these years, to deprive himself of this just because he was so fearful of the smell sticking to him, of remembering how bitterly the GIs complained or joked about it. They hadn't even had the *option* to stink up the place because an "Oriental" grocery store hadn't opened in the Twin Cities until the 1970s.

Young-ae was making a face at his feast, a face closer to one he felt a white Horse's Breather would. "When I was very small," she said, a story she'd told many times before, but because it seemed so important, he treated it each time as if new, "Joongki, my brother, came home from his school in Tokyo. He'd missed kimchi so much that he ate it too fast and vomited. He almost died of a stomach ailment after that. Something about that happening when I was so young turned me off kimchi forever."

Back then, how could you even *have* copious amounts of kimchi? Yungman always wanted to ask, but did not. During the Japanese occupation, his mother made it mostly from her patch of water celery secretly sown at the hard-to-access bend in the river; Koreans were forbidden to grow anything for themselves—a crime against the Emperor—so they would have to count on the Japanese not knowing what minari was, should his mother be caught with it. He was always surprised by Young-ae's insouciance about her family's Japanese-friendly, pampered past.

"I remember you eating mostly Western foods in kindergarten, which was quite rare at the time," Yungman said.

"You have some memory."

"Hard to forget a little girl with biscuits. Remember how all the kids would pester you just to lick them?"

"The reason for that," she said slowly, "was that my father was put in charge of a factory that made hardtack and other military rations. It also made confections and pastries for the civilian market, like hodu gwaja. He brought back the rejects, so we ate those all the time."

"Ah, yes, hodu gwaja," said Yungman, remembering the brown cookies that looked like walnuts in the shell but were actually pressed wheat dough. He remembered the half dozen tongues stuck out obsequiously, longing to be blessed by a passing swipe of her cookie. "I remember when we started eating wheat when we moved to Seoul."

"We?"

"Oh, you know, people in the neighborhood. But I was about to say, it gives me diarrhea and cramps."

"You eat wheat fine, Kwak-ssi. You love pasta vongole."

"Well, yes; it's possible to grow out of allergies. But about the walnut cookies, remember how when we were in medical school every granny near the school gate was selling them? From treasure to, suddenly, you could get a dozen for just a few won!"

"I do. Nothing better than to get a bagful and go to Changgyeonggung Park."

Changgyeonggung Park was famous for its cherry blossoms. Yungman couldn't help wondering if she was remembering going there with him. Thinking of that day the blossoms peaked, that soft pink of that afternoon; he was always sent tumbling backward in time whenever he saw pink, even a bottle of Pepto-Bismol. He didn't dare ask, however, if he was in that picture in her mind. She hated anything that used the past to build a case for the present. "The past is past!" she would say. A forward-looker, she thought people who "lived in the past" were "pitiful." And if there was anything worse than her scorn, it was her pity.

"Speaking of Korean grannies," Yungman said instead. "Whatever granny made this kimchi, she must be from the south." He was speaking not of South Korea but of the southern end of the peninsula, where the food was extra salty and dank and fiery—and the people were, too. He wiped a spice-induced tear from his eye; it felt incredibly detoxifying. "I'm crying."

The rice, from yesterday's breakfast, was also perfect. Einstein had recently given them a new rice cooker, which had annoyed Yungman, since their 1970 Panasonic worked fine. This one could cook at lightning speed using a combination of convection and pressure, a technology that had, Einstein made sure to add, been invented to cook rice in space and could keep the rice at a perfect temperature and softness for up to four days. He had to admit that was convenient. Previously he ate old rice by softening it with boiling water, the rice ending up both dried and soupy.

Yungman's belly was half-full from this feast when he remembered. This was all new to him, calling his friend on the phone instead of just waiting to see him at work the next day.

"Ken! How was your Thanksgiving?"

"You don't want to know. Explosions, major and minor."

Frankly, he did not. Explosions could be a lot of things, given his cooking, his family situation, his irritable bowels. But what was the right thing to ask? To respect his privacy and pride?

"How's Einstein's new house?" Ken asked.

"It's really large. But there's an even larger house, the Taj Mahal, going up next door."

"The Taj Mahal? Didn't someone already do that?"

"The place where he lives encourages you to get creative about your dwelling, to live your fantasies. My daughter-in-law always wanted a castle. There was even a circus-themed house, a western sort of fort with a stockade fence, a giant teepee. A Paul Bunyan theme."

"Okay," said Ken. "Kind of like living in your bucket list."

"Exactly," Yungman said. As a thought exercise, he tried to imagine what a house physically embodying his aspirations would look like. And again: blank. It would look like an empty bucket. Yungman promised to check in on him again, "soon."

Young-ae had politely waited for him, even upended a saucer on his bowl of rice to keep it warm. Now they were eating together, and she picked delicately at the fern fronds, spinach, and fish cakes with her chopsticks while Yungman used a large spoon for Round Two: mixing the banchan into the rice, with a good dollop of fermented hot pepper sauce and a slug of roasted sesame oil. He paused to put a crinkle of seaweed on top, shoveled the whole combination into his mouth, and exhaled salty steam. This was eating.

There had been a period, when Einstein was maybe around seven, that was almost odd in its calmness. Einstein was receiving glowing teachers' reports ("Smart!" "He's no trouble at all!"), and Yungman and Young-ae were beyond the legal clutches of the Immigration and Naturalization Service; his job was secure. How swiftly the time had gone; he hadn't had time to savor these small, good moments, taking a pause to taste, to be with his wife, because he was always preparing for the next disaster. But as with the people in Horse's Breath who bought all those gallon buckets of dehydrated foods, the barrels of potable water, and generators in preparation for Y2K, the disaster didn't come. There had been 9/11, of course, but that had happened far away. Likewise, Einstein went to junior high, then high school, then Harvard, then Harvard Medical School. There had been nerve-wracking moments, but then it all turned out all right. The years were like waves, each erasing the one before it, the days quickly disappearing beneath the foam.

Those nights, he would pour boiling water into the rice cooker's battered pan, use a spatula to scrape the burned bits at the bottom, and decant the scorched rice water into teacups. This tradition of scorched rice tea continued beyond when finances made it unnecessary.

The KooKoo Outer Space Tech Kooker v. III was coated in Teflon; rice slid right off it — "Easy cleanup!" He boiled water separately and served Young-ae some Lipton's.

"How's the tea?" he asked.

"It's good," she said. He'd bobbed the Lipton's bag up and down, the water barely colored, the way she liked it. She stared into her cup like she was waiting for a message to appear. He was wondering if she, too, was thinking back to those nights, Einstein tucked in bed, dishes drying in the rack, no calls from the hospital. With the cold Minnesota dark pressing from the outside, they would sit at this kitchen table under the soft light of a single wicker-shaded bulb, warmed by the starchy rice tea, and feeling, maybe, just for a moment, that everything would be all right.

# BOOK II

## HORSE'S BREATH
### 20XX

In the half-light of Monday morning, Young-ae dug for her Hyundai keys in the bowl by the door, her fingers creating soothingly muffled clinks. Her arms were full of sheaves of paper, specially lined, punched with two holes so the pages could be sewn together to make a book.

Sunday, of course, was the biggest day of the church week; by Sunday night she was worn out from the preparation for the service, the two-hour service itself, running the church school classes with snacks (let her never, ever have to open another pouch of Capri Sun), then the socializing and lunch. But Mondays she liked for how they steadied her. She looked forward to seeing her friends, even though it was less than twenty-four hours since she'd last seen them: Mrs. Kimm, Mrs. Bae, Mrs. Lee, Ms. Yi, Mrs. Rhee-Sorenson, and Mrs. VandeHaar. Of them, the first three all had Grace as their American names. She was the only one who had continuously kept her Korean name, and this fact pleased her.

She looked up in surprise at the *flap-flap* of Yungman's slippers behind her.

"You're up early, Kwak-ssi," she said. Lately, instead of the usual slow erosion of feeling, she'd felt the tectonic plates of their marriage shift in a way that presaged imminent destruction—land grinding upon land with nowhere to go; something would have to buckle. That was how mountains were formed. She didn't know what would happen. At her age, she looked forward to it. What would happen next? Any change that wasn't death was worth attention and interest.

"Why, I have to get to work," he said, as if surprised she didn't remember. He opened the refrigerator and peered inside.

She wished he would ask what she was thinking, just once.

Yungman withdrew his head from the fridge. He smiled at his wife's back.

She looked like she was in a hurry. Very executive-like. He shouldn't needlessly delay her—her work, even if unpaid, was important, too.

"If you don't leave now, as in right now," Young-ae said, about as tenderly as she said anything, "the traffic around the Cities will be awful."

He gave her ten minutes to get ahead of him. He didn't want to be the pathetic husband trailing her like an imprinted duckling. Also, a ten-minute delay kept him within range of "right now"—or so he thought.

"Hey," said Joelle, when she saw him, red-faced, having been stuck in traffic for almost an hour, sprinting that last hundred feet, extending his wrist preemptively toward the scanner like a runner toward the finish tape. "You made it." She showed him her computer screen: 10:29.

He had fretted, bouncing uselessly in the car, then run the whole way. And for what? What was so important here? What if he'd had an infarction just for being late to depilate women's genitalia?

But as Yungman made his way to the back to change into his coat, he saw a youngish man approach the desk and mumble, "I'm looking for a job. I'm an OB-GYN." He was red-eyed, slump-shouldered.

Attending a long labor? Economic stress? Who knew? "I can start right away."

"Dude, I'm just the receptionist," Joelle said. "The department in charge of hiring is in the other building." She handed him a map. "See that crystal thing? Take the skyway across, find the elevator. Ask for the sub-basement."

What kind of person was this young man, Yungman wondered. He looked so clean-cut. And so young. Who wouldn't find this sordid and distasteful and something only for an extreme last resort?

Joelle saw him looking. "I know, right? We get a dude like every day. I never thought about doctors needing *jobs*. I thought you were, like, automatically assigned them after med school or something."

"Hey," said one of the customers, writing on a clipboard, using her arms to keep her paper kimono closed. "Why do you need our blood types? I'm not even sure I know mine."

"Probably something with the laser," said Joelle. "Plus, you can get a free blood typing test, takes two seconds. Everyone should know their blood type. Like if you get in a car accident or something."

"It's free?"

"Yes, free."

"Sure!"

Joelle got out a tiny spring-loaded plastic pipette that expertly took a drop of blood out of the customer's fingertip. It didn't even look like it hurt. Not like those crude metal styluses that looked like razor blades that they used to use.

"Data mining," she told Yungman later. He wondered how that was different from normal mining.

As Yungman was getting off his shift, there was the young man he'd seen earlier.

"Hi, I'm Chad." To Yungman he looked barely older than his grandson. "You look familiar."

"You saw me here this a.m."

"No, before that." He snapped his fingers. "Oh yes, I met you at the ACOG meeting in Chicago. I'm Chad Martin, remember? From Tacoma."

"Ah," said Yungman, remembering. "You're the OB at Mahonen River Hospital."

"That's correct. *Was.*"

"What happened?"

"Consolidation. Mergers and acquisitions. But that also terminated my debt forgiveness. The interest and penalties are accruing as we speak. Apparently, when something like this happens you can theoretically end up owing *more* than you paid for med school. So I need to work and get some inflow, like right away."

One of the customers, just arriving, eyed them. She was wearing khaki and a pith helmet as if she'd just been on safari. Her badge said, "KELLY—Rainforest Cafe." "Can I have *him*?" she asked Joelle, pointing at Yungman.

"He's done," said Joelle, bored. "Dr. Martin is just as awesome."

. . . YOUR OPERATOR TODAY . . . ! Chad Martin, MD . . . !

"You don't have any lady doctors? What is this bullshit?"

Joelle shook her head. "So far, all dudes. Soh-rry."

"Can I make an appointment?" she asked Joelle. "For him, the old guy?"

"Absolutely."

"See you around," Chad said to Yungman, clocking himself in with his SANUSwatch.

✻    ✻    ✻

Oddly enough, Yungman began to enjoy his work at Depilation Nation. Not the content of it but its steady routine, its clear beginning and end, saying hello to his coworkers. The trainer was sometimes there, and she thanked him warmly each time he showed up for his shift. She gave him a colorful bead bracelet that she said had been made by her daughter. The beads were rolled-up pieces of magazine paper that had been lacquered and strung on an elastic. He carried it in his SANUS lab coat pocket as a kind of talisman. It would be silly to wear. One day, he put it on. It did look silly, especially on a man. The lacquer was globbed on lumpily. He wore it.

One day, the trainer offered to transfer him to a new Mall-Based Retail Outlet, At Your Cervix. "Probably the closest thing we have to what you were doing. It offers basic GYN care: Pap smears, STD tests, birth control and even HPV vaccines. Conveniently located next to Victoria's Secret."

Yungman considered it for a moment. He was trained in the use of the Defolliculator. He wasn't bad at what he did; he zoned out pleasantly while he did it, sort of like mowing the lawn: one row, then another. Next thing he knew, three months had gone by, and he always had a room full of customers waiting for him, a job to do. Some of them even smiled at him; some even said thank you. For now, that was enough.

Then one day, at the end of his shift, Yungman replaced the nozzle of the Defolliculator in its stand, passed his SANUSwatch under the barcode reader, and stretched.

His right wrist stayed frozen. At first he assumed it had fallen asleep in this pronated position, but he couldn't unbend it, even if he used his other hand to forcibly straighten it. For a physician, any kind of infirmity always felt embarrassing, akin to a moral failing; certainly a hand at a right angle to its wrist fell into that category. He left-handedly waved to Joelle, then tried to slip his right into his white coat pocket to hide it, only to find the pocket was a faux pocket, sewn shut.

As he struggled into his car, an image came to him of—of all people—Rosemary Mitzner. She had had terrible arthritis her whole life, and drove by pushing the heels of her hands on the steering wheel. Which is how Yungman drove home now, his left hand normal, his right like Rosemary's. It wasn't the best driving he'd ever done. It wasn't until he'd pulled into their driveway that he supposed it might not have been the safest course of action.

He iced his wrist, shook out a few prescription Motrin, and waited. Ugh, would it heal over the weekend? He kept twisting it to see if it still hurt, and it did. It reminded him of when he and Yung-sik were first living in Seoul right after the war and Yung-sik had gotten punched in the head fighting at the US Army dump (but had emerged victorious, with an entire can of Spam). He'd wrenched his neck, which clicked when he turned his head, which he kept doing—*click, click, click*—driving Yungman crazy.

"Why are you doing that?"

"It hurts when I do that."

"So *why are you doing that?*"

"I want to see if it still hurts."

"The wise thing to do," said Yungman, "would be to stop *doing* that." He needed to take his own advice right now. Aigu! Still hurt.

Young-ae emerged through the flimsy door that connected to the garage. Yungman had read in the local paper that that was the weak spot in a house, and people needed to fortify that door against burglars. But they were forty years in—did it make sense to secure it now?

"Another letter came for you," she said.

"What do you mean?" said Yungman.

She handed him an envelope that said *It's a boy*! It had one of those free return-address labels, stacks of which the Kwaks had as well and wouldn't be able to "spend" in their lifetimes. It was from Mrs. Robert Maki. Which Maki *was* that? Let's see—was that Lorraine? Ashley? Gail? Carol?

*Beyoncé Maki*. What a tiny baby. Four pounds and six ounces. This sounded silly, but Yungman never forgot a baby's face. It was an unearned honor that he, not the mother, was the first to see the newborn's face, so he always took a moment to look, appreciate, whisper, "Welcome to the world, little one!" This baby's face was round as an apple and blushing like one. Ah—young Mrs. Asia Maki. Placental abruption. Despite all the trauma, the medevac, the baby looked perfect, no worse for wear, and four pounds was actually quite good for a slightly preterm baby. Also, without being squished in the birth canal, the C-section premies tended to come out looking exquisite. The baby was slightly older here, and still beautiful. Yungman guessed they had treated her well at UMD Hospital.

*Thank you, Dr. Kwak, for saving my life and Beyoncé's. With love and gratitude, Asia Suhonen Maki.*

Yungman smiled and put the card faceup on the counter. Was he that vain that he should hope Young-ae would see it and admire him? That had been such a tricky emergency surgery—so much blood, he'd placed the clips on the arteries blind but nailed it, each time. She was looking! His heart leapt.

"What's wrong with your hand?" Young-ae cried. Her eyes were on his hand, not the card.

Try as he could to unbend it, his wrist stayed at a rather acute angle. "Just a cramp. I'm probably low in magnesium from drinking too much coffee at work."

"That looks more worrisome than a cramp, Kwak-ssi."

"*You* have a similar problem," Yungman reminded her. The transcribing of the words of the Bible. Word. By. Word. He reminded

111

her that last week she'd had to ice her wrist, but she'd stated stopping wasn't in the equation; the whole point was the devotion.

"Repetitive motion stress from overwork is what we *both* have," he said. "Do you remember in medical school how steeply we had to pronate our wrists? Even outside school, I would practice another thousand incisions on whatever cheap organ carcass I could find at the butcher's. My wrist froze just like this. I just had to rest it."

"Aigu, cham," Young-ae said, smiling despite herself. "You're impossible. Use a muscle relaxant if you have to."

Yungman was touched by her alarm. He was more interested, however, in the fact that she'd returned bearing more Cub Foods bags. Today: egg-battered hot peppers and egg-battered bite-size hamburgers.

"These are good," he said, inserting two peppers and one hamburger into his mouth at the same time. "Was it someone's birthday? This is fancy food."

"We went to the Edina CareAway nursing home. We keep telling the nursing home people the elderlies are lactose intolerant and can't eat all that pudding and macaroni and cheese they give them; that's why they're getting so skinny. And they're getting diabetes. One of the elderlies said the desserts were so sweet they made her dentures hurt. Ha! Do those people know that for us, red beans are our sweets?"

"Wait," said Yungman. "Korean kids put their parents in homes?"

Young-ae nodded. "On Saturdays and Sundays you should see the guilty-faced kids. The parking lot is crammed with Mercedes and BMWs."

"Shameful," said Yungman.

"If we were in Korea, *I'd* be taking care of your parents, Kwak-ssi, wiping their ongdongis."

"Sure, if we still lived in the village."

"Urban women face the same pressures. Apparently, the birth rate in Korea is going down precipitously because young women are just deciding that they don't want to enter into this life of servitude—serving the kids when they're young, serving the in-laws, no rest ever. Even though we had servants I still remember my mother cleaning when Grandmother started smearing her feces near the end—all that bedding, all those white clothes." Young-ae paused. "But this American ease with warehousing the old is a bit much. At least Einstein would never do that."

Yungman snorted. "Einstein, no. Marni would do it in a heartbeat. That rotten Reggie, too." Young-ae giggled. Yungman hadn't heard that giggle since they were in medical school.

Her visage had perked up some since she started going to the Korean church, but at home, mostly, she looked the same: mentally tired, her shoulders slightly slumped with an invisible burden. He used to get a bit impatient at that—what did she have to be so weary about? She didn't work!

"The elderlies are lucky, though," said Yungman, chewing another pepper—ah! This one was really spicy. "This is party food."

"Oh, you should see what the church does for birthdays. Mrs. Kimm—Kimm with two Ms—even made a parishioner a whole pan of nurunji."

In any normal conversation with Young-ae these days, he heard "Mrs. Kimm" twenty, thirty times, he reckoned. Mrs. Kimm was at the top of her class at Seoul-dae. She played golf like Tiger Woods. She was a great cook, wife, mother. Their filial children had never received birthday presents because Mrs. Kimm used that money to make donations to the poor. The Bible copying gave them hours to chat, as did the days of preparing the church for service, the cleanup after, the prayer meetings. Young-ae had a crop of fresh stories every day.

"Mrs. Kimm said in Korea they now have restaurants where they just serve nurunji in hot water. Can you believe it?"

"Making money off scorched rice tea," he marveled. "When I was living with the monks, that was a task the apprentices had to do—clean the gamasot by pouring in hot water and letting it steam. My br—I mean, the other apprentices hated that job because it was long and tedious, hauling the water, heating the water, waiting for it to soften the rice at the bottom. I secretly loved it. I'd get a few minutes to myself, waiting for the tea to steep. There was this one kid we called Green Vegetable—he would even trade me a latrine assignment."

"It sounds like even you monks in training had American-style ADHD."

"We—I wasn't really an apprentice, I just went along with it for a place to live. I left before I would be required to shave my head. And the food wasn't bad, just very plain, but we always had rice."

"It must have been so lonely being in Seoul all by yourself."

Yungman's throat constricted. *Be a cat*, he reminded himself. Cats are so good at evading obstacles around them because they carefully place their back paws only where their front paws have already been, avoiding breaking new ground to stumble into. He gave himself a moment to let the convulsion pass. "Yes, those first years in Seoul were awful—I was actually lucky the monks took me in. There were a few other family-less boys there."

"I suppose they needed to replenish their ranks."

"How else are they going to do it if they don't reproduce?"

"You had a brother, right?"

"Yes," he said, more smoothly now, carefully picking his way among his memories. "My parents just called him Mangnae, even though there were just two of us. He didn't like that, as he was only a year younger. But I'm the seventh-generation first son; you know that."

Young-ae paused. "But you know what? You don't talk about your past much, Kwak-ssi. You never have."

"Why? What is there to talk about? You and I met when we were young. We're from the same tiny village. My past is your past, too."

"My family lived behind a stone wall. I went to high school in Seoul. Honestly, I don't think I could identify your family members if I saw them."

*Thank goodness for that*, Yungman thought.

She motioned to the fireplace mantel, where there were not only contemporary pictures of her sister Youngja and her family, her sisters back in North Korea, Joongki, her mother, her father, but also carefully framed pictures of her grandparents sitting in Western-style wooden chairs. Only the rich, of course, had the money and inclination to pose for such portraits.

"I always felt it sad you didn't have any family pictures, Kwak-ssi. Mine so far outnumber yours."

"I told you," Yungman said. "What photos we had, we lost when we evacuated to Seoul."

"What do you mean, 'we'?"

Ugh. He had to stop doing that! "I, er, mean the colloquial 'we' . . ." Yungman's mind scrambled for the right believable answer. "The collective 'we,' woori. Like how we say in Korean, 'our wife.' That always used to mix up the missionaries, remember? They thought the village elders all had the same wife!" Yungman laughed, authentically, he hoped. It *had* been funny. Like when the American soldiers were trying to get kids to rat on their parents as Commies in exchange for Hershey's chocolate bars. Some kids named "our mother" as a Communist when American kids would have said "my mother," and the translators' word-for-word translations—plus the fact that most of the people in the village were named Park—made it seem like there was one mother for all the kids. In their confusion, the soldiers left the mothers alone, and the kids got the Hershey's.

"Kwak-ssi, how strange that you're thinking in Korean when you haven't spoken Korean in . . . I don't know. Maybe since we moved to Horse's Breath?"

That was probably true. After seeing how terribly the Black people were treated in Birmingham, Yungman had decided being as "American" as possible was their only chance at assimilation. He purged all urges to speak Korean and spoke only English. He constructed an English-only home to keep any linguistic contamination away from Einstein. How could Yungman forget how eager he'd been to show off his perfect English when they'd docked at the Port of San Francisco? The official squinting at him, his obvious contempt. "Vely nice," the man had said, and made buckteeth at Yungman.

Yungman remembered making sure he and Young-ae spoke only English in the house. Even when saying it in English was more awkward and imprecise and did not have Korean sound effects—poogool, poogool for boiling—that made such satisfying physical punctuation to words. But they'd stuck with it, and over the years the habit had become fixed—so fixed that during the 1988 Olympics, seeing the red-white-and-blue-garbed pungmul dancers with their drums and propellers atop their heads, catching bits of Korean, it had struck Yungman first as foreign, then, at best, as something dimly remembered, like in a dream. He'd felt no sadness at that, actually; only a sense of completion.

So, now, Yungman dissembled along a path that was still there. "It's not that strange. Even if I'm not using it, that doesn't mean the grammar and everything isn't there. For instance, when I have to count something, I still start with my pinky first. And in my head I count in Korean. Occasionally, even Japanese—*ichi, ni, san*—because that's what was drilled into me when I was young." Yungman ate another pepper and found himself getting a bit sweaty.

She peered at him.

"I ate too close to the stem," he coughed.

Young-ae got up from the table. She returned with a glass of milk in one hand, a basket of steamy white dinner rolls in the other.

"Here," she said, offering him the glass. "You must be losing your tolerance for spicy foods." The dinner rolls were for her. While she had eaten a few of the tiny egg-battered hamburgers, she'd skipped the peppers entirely. On the rare occasions when she ate kimchi, she put a bowl of water beside her and rinsed each piece. When they were in med school, after one of their clandestine nights together, they'd sneaked out to one of the cheap all-night restaurants in "student row." On fire with sensuality, Yungman had consumed a steaming bowl of chunky cod and egg sac stew, washed down with boiling hot cups of beef tea and chasers of garlic pickles. As the sun had begun to rise, Young-ae had sat, almost primly, and declared she ate only bread for breakfast. That had been one of their first discordances, which Yungman had easily batted away as an irrelevance.

"By the way, Dr. Kimm has started an 'Unforgotten War' speaker's project—you know how Americans call 6.25 the 'forgotten war.' "

"You don't consider yourself American?"

"Kwak-ssi, you know very well what I'm saying. Anyway, the first Sunday of each month, he invites a speaker to talk about their experience. Last week, Mr. Chae talked about being kidnapped by the North Korean army when he was seventeen and then by the South when he was eighteen, and then the North again! He now has fifteen grandchildren and a great-grandchild, can you believe it? And lives in Edina after owning a successful car dealership."

"That sounds so interesting," he said, relieved to finally steer the conversation to a different path that wouldn't lead to his brother, even if it did lead to a guy exploiting his ethnicity to sell Young-ae a new, as in new-car-smell new, Hyundai.

"So maybe it would be good for you to attend one sometime. I think everyone at church has lost someone to the war."

Yungman was not a big fan of therapy, but he said, "All right," because he realized there were a good three weeks to go to the first of the month. So many things could change by then, including Young-ae's forgetting she'd elicited this promise from him.

"The Kimms have a wonderful house in Edina, big enough that we can have these kinds of meetings there."

Yungman could stand it no longer. Young-ae barely talked to him after decades of marriage but had fallen into some kind of friendship-love with these Korean strangers after only a few months! "So, what's so great about them?"

"About what?"

"About the Kimms-with-two-Ms. Their gigantic house in Edina. And why do they spell their name like that? You don't remember that Korean proverb—coals to Newcastle is 'like trying to find a Mr. Kim in Seoul'? Is this so they can say they're different from the other million Koreans named Kim? How does that make Mrs. Kimmmmmmmmmm so very special? Or Dr.Kimmmmmmmmmm?"

"Mrs. Kimm is *also* a doctor," she reminded him. "They came here, just like we did, with nothing and made it into something, and share it with the church—what's so terrible about that? The extra *M* comes from when their visa application to come here was denied. It was Dr.—Mrs.—Kimm's idea to add the extra *M* to have another shot in the lottery—and it worked."

"So . . . by cheating?" Yungman said. But then was relieved when Young-ae didn't respond. His record, of course, was not the cleanest, either.

"Spelling your name oddly isn't so original anyway," he grumbled, secretly annoyed at himself for his juvenile need to justify his pique. "Look at Syngman Rhee"—the American-installed president, dictator number one—"spelling 'Lee' so ridiculously. Also, 'Syngman' could also just be 'Sungman'—like Yungman. That's the sign of an overinflated ego."

Young-ae, wisely, ignored him. "You know, the Good News Church is a 'megachurch' with over two hundred members. There's got to be a hundred Kims there, so even in just that limited context it makes sense."

"Huh," said Yungman. "I'm thinking how in our village it was all Parks." Indeed, of the twenty or so families in Water Project Village, most of them were Parks, most from the same natal clan; spelling their name differently would have been strange, to say the least. The Kwak line in the village was an old one, but very small. And Yungman's mother, a Mo, was from an even smaller outlying village. Mo, along with some of the two-syllable Korean names like Sunoo, was one of the rarest. Villagers sometimes referred to her as "Tofu" because "Mo" was less familiar as a surname and more familiar as a counting unit for things that came in blocks. Yungman always wondered if she regretted leaving her village with its own familiar hierarchy of names. His parents never talked about it, but it was clear that theirs was some kind of love marriage. At the time, a non-arranged marriage was rare, and even rebellious. Yungman wondered what Grandfather thought of his son marrying someone he did not choose, had not chosen with an advantageous linking of families in mind; to marry someone from outside the village was to confer no social advantage by the union. This brought Yungman's thoughts to *his* father-in-law, with whom he hadn't spoken since the day he'd been beaten by him. Yungman shuddered with residual fear, even though the man hadn't walked the earth in more than forty years.

Yungman reached to chopstick out another batter-coated pepper; he almost gasped in pain, and bit into the hot pepper quickly to cover it up. "Gosh, that's a hot one, whew!"

"Maybe," said Young-ae, "when you accompany me to church, you should approach Dr. Kimm. He's an acupuncturist who also does hanyak, moxa, the cups."

Ah, *that* made sense. "Dr." Kimm made big money by snookering white people who loved their "alternative medicine." Koreans went to the acupuncturist only if they couldn't afford a Western doctor.

"Remember Hwang the acupuncturist?" Yungman reminded her. "He almost killed me when I was young. He thought I had a tummy ache when I had appendicitis. Talk about a tolpari doctor. My mother brought me to the base, where I had proper surgery and they saved my life." When he thought of himself, a Western-trained physician, stuck with needles, the herbal moxa burning in the background, his back covered in those medieval cups, he almost guffawed. He looked up to see if Young-ae had noticed.

"I just remembered: no need to wait until next month—see, the Kimms are having a New Year's party this Saturday. You can come with me."

"New Year's?" said Yungman. It was March. "Ah, you must mean Lunar New Year."

Young-ae made a face. "Just a late New Year's party. Our church doesn't follow any of the lunar calendar—it's superstitious."

"What do you mean?" said Yungman. "The moon sets the planting cycles—my father taught me all about it. Crops don't care what the Gregorian calendar says—that's not superstition, that's agronomy."

"Are you coming or not? It's in the evening, so you won't have work."

Yungman made grumbling noises about checking his calendar, but he was licked. He also didn't want her to know, even after all this time, how delighted the invitation to do something together with her had made him. He carefully tucked away his reaction under an expression of slight harassment. One thing he had learned over all these years is knowing how much he loved her only irritated her.

\*     \*     \*

Yungman's wrist was still throbbing, but better. The trainer had noted his wrist and sent him to Operator Optimization, also housed in the sub-basement, where a cortisone shot had increased his mobility by a good 60 percent. He was glad he hadn't immediately ingested the offered anti-inflammatories, which he socked away in the medicine cabinet. This was his habit. He couldn't even eat an instant ramen without using only half the flavor packet; he was so used to splitting everything half and half with his brother. These early habits stayed ingrained forever, he supposed. He noticed even more improved wrist articulation as he dug out his sharkskin suit. Young-ae wore a red dress, a cardigan, and understated gold earrings that were whorled like seashells. This was Saturday night at the Kwak household, the retirement version.

"You look nice," Yungman said.

"Thank you," she said, scooping up her keys. "I'll drive."

"I can drive," he said.

"No, *I'll* drive. I know the way."

Yungman was a bit chagrined. What it would look like when they pulled up to "Dr." Kimm's house, his wife at the wheel? He wasn't hung up on gender roles, but this would be unmanly, at minimum, and first impressions were first impressions. But he didn't argue. This was her show, and he was just tagging along.

"Now I'll get to see where you spend all your time," he said as they finally got underway. He hadn't meant to say it with an edge, as if he were a snotty-nosed child. He was grateful when Young-ae had the grace not to respond. Instead, she nodded toward her purse, from which Yungman obediently extracted a Tums.

"The Kimms are impressive people," she said. "They're always thinking about the less fortunate. On Saturdays they go work in a soup kitchen. Even the grandkids."

The Imp of the Wrong Thing to Say moved inside him, then slipped out of his mouth. "Ah, so is it the church you're interested in, or just a reason to be the president of the Kimms' fan club? I don't remember you going to church when we were in school."

"The boarding school in Seoul where I learned English was run by missionaries," Young-ae said. "I *grew up* steeped in Christian instruction." This was also why, even though they lived in a small village, Yungman had rarely ever seen this person who lived behind high walls: she had a rarified education that kept her living in Seoul during the week. Also: the eldest brother had been sent to Tokyo for his schooling, which was saved for the elite of the elite. But this of course meant some kind of relationship with the Japanese. Again, this was what high walls were for.

"—And don't forget we attended First Presbyterian for almost forty years," she reminded him.

America was a Christian nation. That's what the Founding Fathers talked about. American currency said IN GOD WE TRUST, while the Korean fifty-won piece said only "50 won" and "Bank of Korea" with a picture of a rice seedling.

"I don't understand," Young-ae said. "If you abhor being around Christians so much, why come with me?"

Yungman thought: *Because I'm delighted by any minute in your company.* But how could he say this? Or admit that his attendance at the First Presbyterian Church was part of the motions of life, tending a personal portfolio that marked him as an upstanding member of the town?

So instead, he growled, "Don't tell me you believe that Jesus rose from the dead after his corpse rotted for three days, and that we're supposed to eat his body and *drink his blood*?" And Westerners thought burying kimchi in the ground was strange.

"That's what faith is. Our church is composed of educated people, doctors and professors."

"And Kimmmmm the acupuncturist," Yungman reminded her. "Medical science thinks of acupuncture as little more than folklore."

His wife looked at him and laughed. And laughed some more. He hadn't seen her so unrestrained since he didn't know when.

Yungman, all his life, set certain poles by which to map his self-esteem. He could use these poles to orient himself if he was ever lost to himself. Despite his shabby background as a North Korean refugee, son of a Commie, Dr. "Quack," and now an "operator" at a store at the Mall of America, he was still and would always be a graduate of Seoul National University College of Medicine. A medical doctor. A man of science.

"Dr. Kimm practices acupuncture as a *hobby*," Young-ae explained. "He works as a radiologist. He's the chair of his department at Snowview."

These poles were collapsing now.

A radiologist (one of the highest-paying specialties!), and at Snowview, one of the best hospitals in the Cities, where politicians and the WCCO anchors went—*that* hospital would never go out of business.

Kimm was also, Young-ae added, "The head of the state medical board. Can you imagine, a Korean in such a prestigious position!"

Yungman ate three more Tums over the course of the ride to Edina.

A handsome man in his thirties opened the majestic door to the Kimms' huge house. "Hello," he said, using maximally polite Korean and bowing. He kept his eyes averted, which inexplicably rankled Yungman, even as he knew it was a sign of deference.

A man about Yungman's age hurried toward them. "Aigu, there she is!" said the man in Korean.

Yungman blinked. Sticking out of the man's face like a cat's whiskers were extra-long needles, the kind an acupuncturist would normally use to stab deep into your abdomen. The kind he remembered only too well.

"My name is Dong-woo, family name Kimm," Kimm said in silky Korean. "That's Kimm with two Ms. You can also call me Don, if you need to," he said in English. He began pulling out the acupuncture needles, placing them unhurriedly in a long silver case. "Every free minute I have, I stimulate these points, keep my hair black—heh."

Yungman was aghast at Kimm's vanity, but he also couldn't help comparing Kimm's lush black pelt to his own thinning hair and his $3.99 Grecian Formula for men from Walgreens, which left his hair a penguin color—matte black, but also flecked with white on the underside.

"This way!" Kimm trailed a spicy, flowery smell. Aramis? Frankincense and myrrh? His face and hands were brown as a piece of old bamboo.

As governed by Korean politeness, Yungman had shucked off his shoes before entering. He placed them next to an odd black pair, bulbous at the toe, slightly clownish. However, he eschewed the guest slippers neatly stacked on a wooden shelf by the door. Footwear should be a private, monogamous affair. A string dangled off the big toe of his left sock.

"Our last guests have arrived—finally." Kimm said in Korean, ushering the Kwaks into a "great room," just like in Einstein's house. This one had an expansively marbled fireplace in which a fire glowed and crackled like in a Riunite commercial. Stately high-backed chairs were arranged along the perimeter, ballroom-style. In the middle sat an ebony Steinway piano, on top of which were so many framed pictures of the kids and the grandkids that it looked like Kimm was farming a crop of photos. The largest one was of Kimm shaking hands with George W. Bush. Another was an X-ray of lungs, identified as former governor Rudy Perpich's.

"That's Angelina's childhood piano—she went to Juilliard," Kimm explained, turning toward Yungman. "She's upstairs tutoring the grandchildren. I apologize for her rudeness in not coming out to say hello—the children have a big test at school tomorrow. Can't waste a minute!"

*Hmmph*, thought Yungman. Kimm's fulsome voice suggested that he believed he was getting away with using the humble apology as cover to brag about his studious grandchildren and daughter. However, to make Young-ae happy, he would be amiable, and act as if Kimm were a patient: "Your grandchildren live in Minneapolis?" he asked. "How nice to have family so close by."

Kimm seemed not to hear him. Was it because he wasn't speaking in Korean?

"Oho! Not only that, they live here!" A white-haired man butted in. He spoke English at a rapid clip, but with a strong Korean accent: "Not-tu on-u-ry that-u, dey lib-u he-are." He introduced himself a bit self-importantly as a tenured professor of astrophysics at the U. He must have been the oldest one at the gathering, because when he spoke Korean, he used the most casual form for everyone: "Guys, this place is a compound—like the Kennedys'. Ha! Ha! Ha!" It would turn out that he was the owner of the clownish black shoes. Yungman presumed they were orthopedic, but Young-ae told him later that they were just fashionable—some Japanese designer. Japanese! That guy was certainly old enough to remember their colonial oppressors!

"Ah, here they are!" cried Kimm in Korean.

A wizened old woman appeared, bending like a branch under the weight of a platter filled with dumplings. Kimm went to her, arms extended not to greet or assist but as an expansive gesture to his guests: "Sorry we missed having these at Christmas, but the kids sent us on a combined cruise and tour of Fiji, Bali, and the Faroe Islands. How could we say no to that?"

"Happy belated Year of the Pig!" cried the wife of the professor, but the professor glared at her and she quieted, but muttered, "I thought this was a Lunar New Year celebration."

Kimm's wife, elegantly coiffed, strode in, making micro-adjustments to the tablecloth covering a long banquet table. "Clean this up, would you?" she said in casual Korean to the wizened woman, who must have been their ajuhma, a live-in worker for whom living in America with another family was preferable to whatever her situation was in Korea. Her hands, bent like sickles, had somehow produced enormous quantities of songpyeon, the traditional rice cakes—a common offering, actually, for ancestor worship. Here they had been arranged into a gigantic pyramid.

Yungman ate a rice cake, speckled decoratively with roasted black sesame. So good; he immediately snatched up another. Then another. There was nothing in American food that even vaguely resembled the soft but springy texture of ddeok.

"Are you liking these?" The ajuhma's Korean was thick with dialect.

"Oh, they're delicious!" Yungman said, hoping to perk her up. "It's very nice to meet you, Miss . . . ?"

He thrust his hand forward. She stared at it with alarm and scurried back into the kitchen.

"She doesn't speak English," said Mrs. Kimm, coming up behind him. She was tall, with a graceful slouch like an orchid. The fancy Seoul accent of someone who was born there. "She was our family's maid. We brought her here so the children—and now the grandchildren—could learn Korean."

"Ah," said Yungman. "Ah" could be either Korean or English. This crowd seemed to use Korean as their lingua franca, thereby adding to the stereotype of the clannish Asians who can't be bothered to assimilate. You can only do that with critical mass—in Horse's

Breath, everyone except the Native Americans was descended from immigrants, and yet people hated "immigrants"—even the word, now synonymous with dusky people sneaking over the border to murder "real" Americans, was spat, not pronounced. The prevailing attitude had actually gotten worse over the years, not better; a teacher who was Hmong and had been recruited to teach special education had lasted only a month. The ENT physician of Indian descent had been driven out by an anonymous group, "the Dot Busters," as his wife wore a traditional red bindi on her forehead. Most recently, there had been a protest over refugee resettlement that people had stood out in the freezing rain for. At first, Yungman, reading this in the paper, was inspired—people fighting for refugees! But then he saw the pictures.

## AMERICA FIRST NO REFUGEES IN HORSE'S BREATH
## AMERICA FOR AMERICANS

Hardly a righteous protest like the Boston Tea Party or a civil rights march. There weren't even actual refugees looming. This was just a vote to preemptively reject *any* refugees. It wasn't like the area had been overly friendly at all, but at least in the 1970s, Horse's Breath had taken in two "boat people," Phan and Van Phuong. Einstein had been assigned to show them around; the administrators of the program seemed to think Yungman and Young-ae should be able to translate at home, which was absurd. Still, even not being able to communicate what they wanted to eat or do, the two kids had been impossibly cheerful for what they must have been through—losing their parents, grandparents, and five other siblings in an American bombing; months at sea; cigarette burns on their arms from pirates; years in a refugee camp in Thailand. Yungman had fed them sticky Korean rice, which they ate carefully and neatly and thanked him for, and felt humbled. Van and Phan were gone within two weeks, and the administrators did not tell them where. Then, everything went back to "normal" in Horse's Breath. As long as there was only one family, they would get to be The Kwaks and not "immigrants."

The handsome young man who opened the door—one of the sons, Yungman presumed—now replaced his mother. He asked Yungman in Korean: "May I get you a bee-air?"

Yungman wondered aloud, "What in the world is that?" The young man smiled and handed him a Budweiser.

"Mek-ju," said Yungman. *That* was the proper Korean word for beer. Yungman was also reminded how slavishly Koreans exoticized quotidian American things that a simple working man like Clyde Lungquist loved: Spam, Budweiser, penicillin.

Mrs. Kimm began herding the guests to the middle of the room in anticipation of some group activity (a sermon? A round of flower cards?). The boys had arranged the chairs in a circle. Yungman made sure to replenish his supply of songpyeon.

When they were all seated in the stiff-backed chairs, Dr. Kimm emerged from a book-lined study carrying a glass specimen bottle the size of a Wiffle ball bat.

"The ginseng!" cried the professor's wife.

Kimm nodded happily. "Korea's National Treasure number five," he said. "I'm applying to have it recognized as a world treasure by UNESCO." He started passing the bottle around. "The honey is as old as the root—itself a treasure of antiquity. No need to crowd. I'll give you each a turn."

When Young-ae passed the bottle to Yungman, Kimm hovered. Yungman tipped the bottle upside down to watch the air bubble trapped in the honey rise.

"Be careful! This isn't a toy. It's a five-hundred-year-old ginseng. Undisturbed for five hundred years!" Yungman had to admit this was no ordinary ginseng. When Yung-sik was beset by a terrible ailment in his early years—probably some combination of rheumatic fever, measles, tuberculosis, pertussis, scarlet fever, maybe even diphtheria— their mother spent so much of their scarce money on ginseng. But for all the money that she gave Hwang the acupuncturist, she returned with nubs the size of acorns. *This* ginseng was a foot long, maybe even more.

"How did it get so big?" Yungman couldn't help asking. Heads swiveled toward him for speaking English.

"It happened to grow in the crevice between two huge boulders," Kimm said. "Generations of the best ginseng hunters missed it!" Kimm repatriated the bottle with a gentle yank and handed it off to the astrophysics professor.

"My hometown, Kaesong, is, as you know, famous for ginseng," said the professor.

"I do know," said Kimm in his elegant Seoul accent. "At university, we always thought the guys from Kaesong were the super hicks."

The professor reddened. "But isn't this where the ginseng is from?"

"No, no, no. Cultivated insam ginseng is not half as rare as wild sansam."

"Where do you think the 'in' in 'insam' comes from?" chided his wife. "It comes from 'man,' as in 'man-made' versus 'mountain-made.'"

The professor ignored her.

"It was found on Palgong Mountain, in Daegu," Kimm said primly. "By a very skilled, very skinny ginseng hunter."

"Well, I've said it before, but I'll say it again: This is the only time in my fairly long life that I've seen a ginseng root with two arms, two legs, and a gen-u-ine hot pepper!" The more human the shape of the root, the higher its medicinal value. This root even had dried fruit stalks on it that looked like bushy hair, and in the leglike fork, a peanut-shaped protuberance stuck out at a ninety-degree angle, making the ginseng-man look like he had an enormous erection.

"A corpse could regain his vigor by eating this," Dr. Kimm concurred.

"Hey, guys, have you ever had snake whiskey?" asked the professor. "Popular rheumatism and cancer cure, but my father used to swear by it for getting the old wacka-wacka back."

Dr. Kimm disappeared back into the book-lined room and returned with a large, clear liquor bottle, the kind they sell to drunks or people having a party; at the bottom, pickled in some kind of pinkish fluid, was a big black snake.

"When the kids were little, they were always trying to steal this to take it to show-and-tell." Kimm laughed. He shook the bottle violently, which made the snake undulate. Then he became solemn. "In North Korea now, I bet this is what passes for medicine. It's all they can afford."

The professor spoke up: "That is, if they can even *find* a snake. I heard there aren't even trees left in the Diamond Mountains because people have stripped them bare of leaves and bark. Those heathens are killing our country's sacred trees!"

Kimm nodded solemnly. "The famine keeps happening over and over, but the country's leadership is interested only in retaining power. I heard that Supreme Leader Kim sentenced his uncle to death by being eaten by a pack starving dogs."

"No, I heard he ordered him shot from a cannon," said the professor's wife. Everyone ignored her, including her husband, who mused, "You know, with snake whiskey, you don't want to keep it too long—the snake will dissolve. Look: all the scales floating in there. Better drink it soon," he hinted.

"Such a pretty pink color," said the professor's wife, then switched to English and French: "Almost like a rosé wine."

Kimm explained that the pink color was from blood. It showed it was authentic, he said. Instead of using a dead snake, like the cheap places did, this one was made from a live snake frozen into a stupor, slit open, insides punctured, and loosely sewn shut again. Then, when submerged, it would start thrashing as it was drowning and spew blood into the alcohol.

"That's terrible!" Yungman blurted, so shocked, he reverted to English. Young-ae pinched his arm, but he ignored it. What kind of Christians were these people? "You don't think that's terrible?" he whispered to his wife, not quietly enough because she pinched his arm again.

"Respected Uncle, please receive this." The handsome son was back. Oh! Yungman had crushed the songpyeon he'd been holding in his hand, a stalactite of red bean filling threatening to drip onto the snowy white carpet below. The proto-Kimm passed him a napkin. Cloth-like, thicker than a paper towel but somehow luxuriously disposable.

This was the first son: Dante. Joyce, the younger and less good-looking, was not a girl but a boy. Kimm had proudly shown off his library of English-language literature, "my college hobby."

"Thanks, child." He whisked away the mess with the legerdemain of Houdini.

Yungman heard him in the kitchen, instructing his son in Korean: "Hyun-suk-ah! If you're done studying for your test, then go make Grandfather a plate of food—quickly!" Dante even used the complicated sino-Korean honorific for an elder's food, jjinjji, instead of calling it just "rice," the common word for food. And the boy, younger than Reggie, instead of making a sulky face as Reggie would have, ran to carry out his father's orders. As the boy walked into the great room, Yungman noticed the deep epicanthal fold in his eyelids, making him look almost like a Westerner.

"Ah, what a good boy you are, our Hyun-suk-ah!" exclaimed Kimm, clapping his hands in delight.

"Oh goodness," cried the professor's wife. "How your grandson resembles you! His face!"

"He looks just like Dante did when he was that age," Kimm said.

"His eyes," the professor mused. "So round. They look like headlights."

Kimm looked pleased. "Our family has been so proud of the double-eyelids, passed down from firstborn Kimm son to firstborn Kimm son for generations."

"Ha ha, you can save all your money on the surgery—in Korea everyone's getting it these days. Even the boys!"

"Oh yes, have you seen the Miss Korea pageants? They all look the same. The eyes, the jaw. The perfect tiny little heart-shaped face."

"Ah, that's Dr. Mandible's work. Choi Suk-Hong."

"Yes, Dr. Mandible! His work is magnificent. He's the one to blame when your son marries a Miss Korea and their kids turn out ugly!"

The Korean was whizzing too fast over Yungman's head, like bullets. He searched for his wife, who was no longer beside him. She must have gone to the restroom. Yungman sat, all by himself, an empty seat on each side, as he watched the congregants of the Good News Korean Church perform for one another.

He got up and wandered around the great room, pretending to look at the art to distract himself. There were giant wedding pictures of each of the kids, taken against stark white backgrounds that made it look like they were floating. A striking aerial photo of glowing red neon crosses scattered across South Mountain at night—"Seoul 1990"— looking at first like a carpeting of red stars, but then, upon further contemplation, unambiguously like a graveyard.

Next to a reproduction of Vermeer's *Girl With a Pearl Earring* was, framed and hung in a place of honor, a poem.


My Hall-ah-buhjji—할아버지


I love my Hall-ah-buhjji because he takes me fishing
He gives me things I am wishing

132

I love him so
He lets me open the car window with my toe
My Hall-ah-buhjji
    Love,

Brandon Kimm,
aka Hyun-suk, aka 현숙
seven years old

Yungman read the poem again.

*He lets me open the car window with my toe*

He swallowed—was that a bite of songpyeon in his throat? He didn't know why that particular line moved him. Maybe because it made him think there was something more he could have given Einstein as a father. He'd overseen Einstein's studies but had had no time to be silly. He wouldn't have encouraged Einstein to write poetry. He would certainly have spanked him for opening a car window with his foot.

Yungman's own halaboji had often delighted in telling Yungman that his first word was not the expected "ummah" or "ah-pah" but "to study." "Even three feet tall and in short pants, you did our family proud," he'd say.

In turn, Yungman had trained his son to ignore his peers' jeers that studying was for "nerds." Christmas gifts were *1001 SAT Vocabulary Words* and his old *Merck Manual*. He made Einstein learn how to read before kindergarten. He had Einstein catalog the books he completed (every year, he easily won the public library's summer reading competition). As Einstein grew older, Yungman had him do extra homework, write essays that Yungman corrected. Yungman did some research and learned that there was no reason Einstein couldn't take the SAT twice, and so he had him take it during his junior year for practice (Yungman paid Dieter out of pocket while he drove Einstein to Minneapolis—the closest place that even offered the yearly SAT—to take the test).

Yungman also forbade excessive socialization.

When Einstein complained that the kids thought he was strange for his antisocial habits, that bullies beat him up, Yungman only said, "Just wait. At the end of secondary school, when their lives will end, yours will just be beginning." And he had thus given his son Harvard.

A child can't see what's over the mountain. But a parent, who has already been there, can.

Kimm's daughter did go to Juilliard. But none of his sons did any better than St. Olaf.

Yungman stared at the poem again, searching for triteness or grammar mistakes unbefitting a seven-year-old.

"Gurae, gurae!—All right!" Kimm's laugh was an irritating whinny. The professor was conspiratorially whispering into his ear. "Time to break open the snake whiskey!"

"Dante's mother: Get me a bottle opener," Kimm commanded in Korean. His wife glided into the kitchen. If Yungman ever spoke to Young-ae like that, she would scream at him, "Don't you have legs?"

Yungman salvaged his night with more songpyeon. The ajuhma must have made a thousand of them! All the plates had been soiled, however. He calculated that he could probably fit three comfortably in a hand, two for Young-ae and one for him. They tasted so similar to the ones he remembered from their village. Had Kimm imported some of Water Project Village's special water? Did the ajuhma run into the woods to find some pine needles to steam them on? When he looked for Young-ae, he found her talking to Kimm and the professor.

"Sister Kwak," said the professor, "going back to what you said earlier, you actually know the singer called Lark?"

"Yes—we were classmates at medical college."

Kimm clapped his hands. "Ha! Seoul National University College of Medicine, our humble sister neglects to mention," he said.

"And Lee JongDal a friend of yours. How impressive!" said the professor. "And that this famous singer was once a medical student—who would have known?"

Yungman waited to see when she would mention that *he* was her classmate as well. They were all the same age, same class, they three.

"Actually, he was already writing poetry and lyrics while we were in school."

"Doubly impressive! Who would have the time? Medical college is no joke."

"He was a very strong student," she averred. "But quite socially conscious. His singing actually came out of setting his poetry to music for the protests that eventually ejected Rhee from office." Yungman admired his wife's fluency—she sounded so learned.

"Music is supposed to soothe the heart of the savage beast," said the professor. "Not inflame it."

"He did it deliberately so the words would be easier to remember. So people could sing it together."

"Actually, I had no idea he had such a radical past. Gosh. Today, the colleges know to just give the kids more homework. Ha, ha, ha!"

"Ah, the Lark," said Kimm. "It was my parents who liked his music, that old-fashioned folk stuff. I was never a fan."

"I think embracing and remaking what people dismiss as past its time is quite revolutionary," Young-ae spoke slowly, deliberately, not smiling. Yungman blinked. This was the first time he'd seen Young-ae train her Young-ae fire on someone not named Yungman. And on a Kimm, no less. He was so startled that he almost forgot his primary emotion: dismay to find the man who'd been his number-one rival apparently still was.

Yungman had tried to forget about JongDal. Yet still Lark found him. He always did.

The day thirty or so years ago when Yungman had learned his luck with his student visa had run out, when his so-called immigration lawyer (found in the Yellow Pages) pocketed that last check, shrugged, and sent Yungman off into the wild as a newly confirmed "illegal alien," Yungman had gotten into his car only to find the gas needle was in the red. A kind passerby informed him there was a gas station on Grand Avenue, maybe a mile away.

As Yungman continued down Grand Avenue, his eye was caught by a tiny sign in a nondescript shopping center.

Did it really say Kim's Oriental?

He slammed on the brakes.

Kim's Oriental Foods had only two painted parking spaces in front of it, one already occupied by a low-riding station wagon. The front window was obscured with stacked bags of rice and a sun-scorched jade plant and a sign in Korean that said HIRING AN ASSISTANT. Just seeing the letters of their language suddenly made him tear up. He walked in, a bell tinkling dully as the door opened. He roamed the cramped aisles in a daze, noting the familiar sights of flattened squid and tilefish, greasy bags of red pepper flakes, black seaweed wrapped in clear plastic. So ironic, he was thinking, to be greeting these dusty foodstuffs like long-lost friends when he'd soon have all the fresh Korean food he could ever want. Deportation meant he, Young-ae, and Einstein would get on a plane; it was hardly brutal. It was not war. Einstein was young enough that he could probably adapt seamlessly.

But Yungman had given his all to this country; was it that outrageous to want to stay? Dieter had been naturalized even after his student visa ran out; you also never saw someone getting deported to, say, the UK. Yungman's son was a US citizen, so why deny his parents the ability to raise him in his natal country?

Yungman realized he had a pounding headache, at least partially due to the screechy Korean folk music the proprietor (the putative Mr. Kim) was playing on a rickety record player. But the voice sounded oddly familiar, hitting all the high notes in a plaintive mourner's wail.

*. . . beautiful rivers and mountains surround me.*
*Hello, Mr. Sun. I want to go where I will feel your warm rays . . .*

The proprietor, hands and voice rough, had been cranky when Yungman approached the counter. Yungman thought he'd be overjoyed to meet another countryman, but that was not the case. He supposed, in Korea, Koreans aren't overjoyed to see each other, either—only exile makes the heart grow fonder, heart beaten and softened by nostalgia. Yungman was almost scared to ask him who that was on the record player, but when he did, the man's tired face lit up; his wrinkles of anxiety seemed less deep.

"It's Lark," he'd said in guttural Korean. "Gosh, but he's so much better than the rock and roll nonsense the kids listen to these days."

Yungman's eyes must have gotten so big that the man chuckled. "You're a fan, too, I see." Yungman excused himself to take a tour of whatever was in the back of the store: the kimchi section. A dozen jars, chopped cabbage kimchi and one of daikon cubes. Because of the fermentation that caused the kimchi liquid to rise, they couldn't be filled to the top. The partially filled jars looked dubious, rotten. He picked one up. It was three dollars, and he had two dollars left.

He also noticed a row of round appliances with lids shaped almost like faces with hats.

"Automatic rice cookers," the man said. "The newest-fangled thing."

Young-ae's birthday was coming up. Not like she did any cooking, but they rarely ate rice because minding it was so much trouble; plus the grocery store only carried that non-sticky Uncle Ben's, which was definitely not worth it. But with this they could have rice all the time. Three, four, five times a day, until they had to leave the country.

You see: Yungman had a credit card.

"I'll take it," he said extravagantly. "And a bag of the Kokohu Rose." It was clearly Japanese, but it was going to be better than Uncle Ben's.

At home, he had been so preoccupied with the deportation hearings that he'd put the giant bag of rice and the rice cooker in the downstairs closet and forgotten all about them.

By the time Young-ae's birthday came around, they'd learned that Horse's Breath General Hospital had helped arrange for them to stay by urging the townsfolk to sign a petition (they had open hours at the Armory), which they brought to their local congressman.

"Ha!" he'd overheard Mitzner say in the physicians' lounge. "It was actually easier to sponsor Kwak for citizenship than to try to get a young doc to move up to this godforsaken place." Yungman had been furious and thought to accost Mitzner over it, but he didn't, because, unfortunately, it was true.

The hospital had a big party for them. "I thought you already were a citizen!" Marge Rasmussen exclaimed. "Now you're one of us," cooed Rose. "Welcome to America!" said Rodney, the respiratory tech, handing Yungman a tiny American flag on a stick.

Whilst searching for a dimly remembered bag of art supplies for Einstein, Yungman found the rice and cooker just in time for Young-ae's birthday. Lark, he'd left in the closet, so to speak. Young-ae never spoke of him. Yungman hoped she had forgotten.

The conversation had moved on: "—Rhee was a refined yangban with a PhD who spoke perfect English, while Park was a brute; the military coup and all that," said Kimm in his silky Seoul accent.

"However, it's indisputable: Park Chung-hee made the trains run on time, so to speak."

"Having a dictator in power can be helpful for stuff like that," the professor agreed. "Double-digit growth. Pulled us out of the muck. He'd also been some high-up muckety-muck with the Japanese police, so he also had an inside view of how things worked."

"In an odd turn of events," Young-ae interjected, and unlike with the professor's wife, the men all stepped back and yielded the floor, "it turned out that even President Park was mesmerized by Lark's revolutionary poetry-music. See, Park was from a small village, and the folk songs spoke to him on some heart level, the big general, even though maybe he was too dense and uneducated to apprehend their actual message. President Park summoned Lark to the Blue House, demanding he compose a special folk ballad for him."

"I didn't know this," said Kimm, leaning in. They all waited. Even Yungman, who knew what had happened.

"He refused, of course. He even released a new song, 'Beautiful Rivers and Mountains,' which he announced he wrote for the people to give them strength to overcome oppression."

"And then?"

"Lark was jailed by Park and tortured," she said. "They broke all his fingers, pulled out his nails. He was in prison for almost a decade. Park made sure all record companies blacklisted him, just to be sure."

"Ah," said the professor. "That's why it seemed like he just faded away, crumbled to dust. Sadly, I barely noticed. It was like one day he just stopped appearing on the airwaves, and that kind of music fell out of fashion anyway."

"Through all those years in prison, he never gave up a single name of his compatriots. And you know how brutal the police can be—the Japanese system, with the electric shocks and all."

"Is he still alive?"

"Oh yes, he's very alive. He never stopped making music, despite it all. You know 'The Eagle's Wings' was written by him."

"Ah ah ah!" said the professor. "That saucy girl with the pigtails sings it. It was a favorite of the Korean students at the U, mostly because that girl was so cute."

"You've followed Lark's career all this time," Yungman said, a bit sourly, to his wife. Those years he had tried to completely forget that the country of Korea and all the people in it existed, Young-ae had, obviously, kept it alive in her heart.

"My sister sends me pages of the Korean newspaper," she said. "You know that."

Lark had been *his* friend. Yet Young-ae had never mentioned that his name had been in the papers; was she trying to spare Yungman, or just keep Lark for herself? Being reminded of his imprisonment made Yungman shudder. Lark was the most physically delicate of all of them; his wrists were so slender that Yungman had often joked about breaking them when he was mad.

"Sounds like a first love," said the professor impishly.

"We went on a few soen," Young-ae confirmed.

The professor's wife clapped her hands like a schoolgirl. "A date with the singing Lark Bird!"

It wasn't like Yungman didn't know about those meetings, but still, his bile rose. "Chaste soen," she had said back then. "That's all they are. At a teahouse," she added. "To ease the mind of my father that I'm not dating *you*."

But a soen was serious. It meant there were expectations that it would proceed to marriage.

"You can't just go playing with men's hearts like you're a schoolgirl picking jacks up off the ground!" Yungman had yelled at one point. But Young-ae was also like a bird: she would fly away if you tried to control her. Yungman learned to tamp down his peevishness, pretend he didn't care. He was a rogue! But inside, he seethed and quaked with fear—he couldn't compete with his friend's money, talent, and refined looks. Lark was even one of the top students in their medical college class. He was a living angel *and* a genius, apparently.

Yungman could feel his pulse beating in the tips of his fingers, a glob of red-bean filling sliding down his hand. Not again!

"Could I have a napkin, please?" Yungman called.

Kimm was talking to someone over his shoulder, holding the uncapped bottle of snake whiskey. He placed something in Yungman's free hand. Instead of the softness of napkin, it was cold, hard glass.

"Let's have our Brother Kwak start us off!" Kimm, distracted by his other conversation, seemed blind to the leaking dumpling, so Yungman pointedly handed the glass back to him. Kimm then mistook this gesture as Yungman rudely demanding to have the glass filled. Kimm bowed slightly, perhaps faux-obsequiously, and filled the glass. As he did so, the snake's head bobbed and turned as if to stare accusingly at Yungman, although its eyes were two empty holes, eyeballs dissolved by the alcohol long ago.

"Drink! Drink! Drink!" the guests shouted.

Yungman, now stuck, looked at his glass, bits of scale floating. "Is the snake venomous?"

"I hope so," said Kimm. "That makes for the most potent brew."

"Don't worry," said the professor. "The toxic nature of the venom will be denatured by the ethanol. I think."

"Let's have our honored guest, Kwak Yungman, start us off with a toast. The Bible says God gave Adam dominion over animals—thus we thank our Heavenly Father for giving us this snake to make this snake whiskey. Glory be to God in the highest, and his will be done."

"Ah-mehn," said the parishioners. Everyone was watching Yungman. *Heck with it*, he thought.

"*Cccccccccckkkkkk!*" The liquor-pleasure noise cracked from his throat even as he felt, or thought he felt, bits of scales flexing between his teeth. Dr. Kimm smiled as he refilled Yungman's glass. "To your health! May Korea live ten thousand years!"

"Over here!" shouted the professor. "Fill mine to the top, too!"

"Lark was his class banjang," Young-ae was saying to the professor's wife. Apparently, snake whiskey was only for men.

"I have no doubt," she replied. "So was our Dr. Kimm, naturally. Even kids can easily tell the leaders early on."

This was true, Yungman thought: there were certain people who had this recognizable trait. With this confidence, they thus got to organize the world to their will instead of the opposite. Mitzner the surgeon was like that, for instance. He set the social order in the hospital—and town—and people followed. But why? Because he was rich? Because he looked like Charles Lindbergh? Despite his dislike of the man, Yungman had yearned to break into his circle. However, the more he tried, the more he was rebuffed as an irritant. Whenever Yungman tried to engage the surgeon in conversation, he always preemptively squinted and sometimes even said, "What?" as if he couldn't understand what Yungman was saying, before Yungman had even opened his mouth.

Yungman stood slightly apart from his fellow Koreans, feeling similarly expelled now.

"It's getting late," he said to Young-ae, making a show of checking his watch. The battery must have been dead, so he guessed: "It's almost ten."

"In just a moment, we'll go," she said. She said it again five minutes later. And again. It was like announcing a five-minute train delay that gets extended, minute by excruciating minute, so that what could have been a comfortably passed hour instead is shattered into broken-glass bits of disappointment. Yungman was thus in a foul mood when they finally left probably near midnight, Kimm looping the handles of a sparkly gift bag onto Yungman's arm as if hanging merchandise on a rack.

"Go safely!" chorused the sons, bowing in perfect synchrony, each at the same angle, their pomade, like their father's, reflecting in the outdoor porch light. The grandchildren had gone to bed hours ago, resting their brains for their upcoming test—Dante had mentioned to Yungman how important theta-wave REM sleep was for the brain. He was a PhD neuroscientist *and* an MD.

Thankfully, Young-ae drove. At least she didn't say anything more about the Kimms. What more was there to be said? They exceeded expectations in every way. A supernova of Kimmmmmmm-ness.

"We need to talk," she said ominously.

"About what?" Yungman started to panic. Having been reminded of Lark, did she finally realize she should dump him once and for all? How could he even compete with a man who'd been tortured for standing up to a dictator and still smuggled out protest songs?

"About anything. I'm getting sleepy."

"Oh," he said. "Ken said he heard a new hospital might be doing a feasibility assessment."

"That's exciting."

"I just worry it's more like how every month some music man comes to Horse's Breath to say he's going to open up a chopstick factory or another mine that's going to save the town." In fact, none of the businesses, including a Delta call center, where prospective employees had to pay for their own provisional training, proved viable. Hundreds of people showed up to apply for a job that at best had twenty-five slots. The lucky twenty-five had only worked a week before a comedy show (one of the "Jimmy"s) played a tape of the distinct Scandinavian-Canadian accent made infamous by the movie *Fargo*, and Delta shuttered the operation, even while saying the Jimmy show had nothing to do with it.

"It's just so strange knowing there's not even an emergency room nearby."

He was thinking of how Ken had called him this week to tell him about Carol Maki, Elmer's daughter.

"Is something wrong with her?" Yungman had said. He'd remembered how Patsy had, a bit snidely, labeled her a "frequent flier."

"Cancer," Ken had said. "I'm reading her obit. Didn't she come into the ER?"

The backache. The spotting. The fatigue. Just as Yungman clawed his way to a realization, Ken said it: "HPV." Human papillomavirus. A preventable cancer of the cervix—there was both a test *and* a vaccine, and between the two of them, no woman should die of cervical cancer.

"She *confirmed* she'd had a recent Pap smear!" Yungman almost yelped in disbelief. "I remember asking."

"You're very thorough, Yungman," Ken said. "Everyone in the hospital knows that."

Even though it would change nothing, he couldn't help mentally combing over that visit. He realized that when he'd asked if she'd had a Pap smear and she'd asked, "Where they stick that thing up your vagina?" he'd assumed she was confirming the swab to collect the tissue, but in hindsight, perhaps she was talking about a vaginal speculum—"that thing" Yungman had just used—and what also could have been a mere cursory internal exam in an ER. Without a primary care doctor, there was no one keeping track, double-checking.

Yungman was thinking that, instead of depilating women's genitals for money, why didn't he spend the last of his life doing things like checking up on Carol?

But running after his old patients didn't seem right, either.

Of course, then what was his reason for not seeing Ken in probably a month? Sure, the days went by like beads pushed on an abacus. Weekday. Weekend. He was tired from work. But wasn't his "work" supposed to be a stopgap, mortar wedged into the bricks of what his actual life was?

He thought of how he'd finally put something on his bucket list: "Go off somewhere and think." But he couldn't even think of a somewhere he'd like to go.

"Where would you like to go?" he asked Young-ae now. "If you could go anywhere?"

"Where wouldn't I like to go, Kwak-ssi?" He could almost hear her rolling her eyes in the dark. "I just fear for some places, it's too late."

At home, the answering machine was blinking. Ken again. A patient of theirs with a headache had tried to tough it out at home, taking an aspirin. She'd had an undiagnosed pregnancy, an ectopic on her fallopian tube, and it ruptured, the aspirin making her bleed out faster. She died in the ambulance. Yungman couldn't help wondering if she was still charged the $800. Most likely, yes.

Yungman opened the cupboard. Maybe he should tell Ken to stop informing him about these bad outcomes. They weren't his patients anymore, and he couldn't do anything about it except become needlessly upset. He found what he needed—the Johnnie Walker Black—next to the unopened but strangely sticky bottle of Midori that Duckie and Clyde had given them a decade ago. He poured his drink into the Flintstones jelly jar (free from the gas station) that he placed next to the sparkly gift bag from the Kimms. Inside there had been a notebook with a rabbit waving from the moon. While Americans saw a man in the moon, Koreans saw a rabbit pounding ddeok. Also included was a slim book, *The Real History of the Korean War*, which had been wrapped in gilt paper announcing THE EDINA GALLERIA: WHERE LUXURY MEETS LIFESTYLE.

He idly flipped to a random page. He thought about how people didn't stop being human when they weren't his patients anymore. And some, like Duckie, were also his friends.

*. . . This war took the lives of at least three million people, mostly Korean civilians, twenty percent of its prewar population. Property damage was unparalleled: 612,000 civilian homes were destroyed, countless families were separated. The orders from MacArthur had been "bomb every village" (North and South).*

*Life is cheap in the Orient.*
*—General William Westmoreland*

The earthy taste of peat mingled uneasily with the acid of the snake whiskey, just like his memories now mingled uneasily with one another. You weren't supposed to daintily sip liquor, a man downed it in a shot, like from a gun.

> Yung-sik
> Tadpole
> Lieutenant Jarvis
> The Lark Bird
> Young-ae
> His father's beaten face. Halaboji's, too
> His mother running away

There was a golden scrim of alcohol left. One finger, maybe two. To not waste it, he took it like medicine.

In bed, he reached across the invisible border that divided him from his wife. Maybe she had loved Lark, and still did. He didn't want to know. But he couldn't help parsing their date nights. Thursdays with Ken and Myrtle when the kids were young.

There wasn't a lot to do in Horse's Breath. Myrtle was a movie buff, so mostly they defaulted to that. Either the North Star Theater downtown or the drive-in in the summer.

Yungman liked the drive-in. There was something so wildly optimistic about it's being called the French Village—so sophisticated! They served croissants there before anyone knew what they were. Being out under the stars in the summer. The French coffee (whatever that was) with the hint of orange. On two-dollars-per-car night it was so cheap, and the three kids could run around and then crash in a nest of blankets in the back of the Hokkanens' station wagon.

Myrtle and Ken were always holding hands. They also hugged, joshed, and crunched popcorn with such a greedy ferocity that Yungman involuntarily wondered what went on in their bedroom.

In the North Star once, sharing an armrest (precisely fifty-fifty), Yungman had attempted to hold Young-ae's hand. She didn't snatch it away with an *Are you crazy?* look as she had at Einstein's wedding, but instead let her hand go dead and unresponsive, even as he clung to it.

One Thursday, it was "classic night" at the drive-in. *The Great Escape.*

Yungman thought: *At last.* Young-ae could not *not* think about having seen it at the Changchoon Theater. One of their first dates! Did she at least remember the novelty of watching a Western movie? How they made fun of how funny and pasty the white people on screen looked?

In the dark, where it wouldn't have mattered to anyone else, or seemed performative or embarrassing, Yungman reached for her hand during the same scene where, decades ago, their hands had come together as if magnetized. She pulled hers back so quickly that

Yungman was left grasping air, and he wondered if Ken and Myrtle, squished in the bench seat beside them, had noticed.

Tonight, Yungman's desire was greater than his fear. He rolled over to her side to kiss her.

Her noises of protest (*aigu, ya!* . . . *Omuhna* . . .) faded. Eventually she kissed him back; at first tentatively, and then with earnest ardor. JongDal loved his whiskey, and because he could afford it, only drank the best. Yungman's hot whiskey breath inflamed them both.

In the morning they were as shy as newlyweds. Yungman was wearing the terry cloth robe with the embroidered BILL that hung on the bathroom door—a long-ago Christmas present from Einstein and Marni—but had never been used. Who *wears* a towel with sleeves? It was easier to just go naked and air-dry. He felt faintly ridiculous—who did he think he was, Hugh Hefner? He made sure to wear his briefs underneath, because that thing swung open alarmingly when he sat down.

Yungman was touched that Young-ae had not abandoned him for church today. She didn't say why. He made two cups of coffee and set them on the table just as she came down the stairs, rubbing her eyes. He didn't talk. He wanted to enjoy this moment.

"So, the Kimms," Young-ae said, sitting down.

*Oh no*, Yungman groaned inwardly. The last vestige of the night's tenderness was now thoroughly scrubbed away.

"I was thinking, hearing the Kimms talk about Korea, how we haven't been back, how it's changed so much."

"I don't want to go back—ever," said Yungman. "Do you think people in Horse's Breath are always wanting to back to Sweden or Finland? Ken still has relatives in Finland, and he's never been!"

"I *want* to go back. And, actually, lots of people do: that's why the library has the Sons of Norway and Scandinavian Club nights—so people can show their pictures from their trips."

"What's stopping you, then? Perhaps Mrs. Kimmmmmm"—he added a few extra *M*s for emphasis—"would like to accompany you."

"Mrs. Kimm, the doctor, was born and raised in Seoul. I'm talking about back to Water Project Village."

"How's that going to happen?" he yelped.

"Well, I'd go with you, if we can find a way to go."

The "with you" reverberated around his head.

"You asked me where I would want to go, and that's where. You and Ken are always chattering about your bucket lists; well, here's mine."

"It's very hard to get into North Korea, you know."

"It's not North Korea. It's our home. You'll figure it out. You're the Evening Hero, after all."

# BOOK III

# Kwak Yungman

Nine-year-old Yungman and Halaboji both panted, having walked to the top of the hill on an unusually warm spring day—it was early enough in the season that the wild azaleas were still blooming. From a stagnant pond nearby arose the sweet sound of spring peepers. They'd made it to their objective: Cosmos House. It was also just known as "the big house on the hill," but got the name Cosmos House from the imprints of flowers pressed into the end tiles.

His paternal grandfather, his halaboji, in place of his absent father, took on the task of teaching Yungman his duties as First Son. About the land he would inherit one day, along with his responsibilities to it, including conducting the ancestor worship to everyone who was buried there.

Halaboji did not always explain exactly what the lesson was; like today, he just told Yungman to follow him. That was the best way, he said, for Yungman to learn how to make his own judgments and decisions. "And to know," Halaboji said, "that these judgments may change over time, even if the facts and events do not."

Yung-sik was upset when he was so obviously left behind.

Grandfather and grandson took a rest in the shade of the seven-foot wall made of smooth gray stones mortared together. The roof of the Kwak home was made of simple thatch that collected bugs and rot and from which, in the summer, insects and baby snakes fell, sometimes right into their rice bowls, but here, even this fence had its own roof made of expensive slate, the same imprints of flowers pressed into the end tiles.

"Why is the wall around this house so high?" Yungman asked. It was even higher than the tallest man in the village, who happened to be Rhim, who owned this place.

Halaboji, leaning on his walking stick, put his other hand on Yungman's shoulder. "No questions for right now."

He knocked on the gate next to the burned-in sign that read THE HOUSE OF RHIM in exquisite Chinese calligraphy.

"Rhim" meant "forest." Its Chinese ideograph was two trees, one larger, one smaller, nestled next to each other. That was another purpose of Halaboji's stick: he used it to write characters in the dirt, quizzing Yungman and Yung-sik. Thanks to Halaboji's tutoring, Yungman could already read and write ten thousand Chinese characters.

A guard opened a small cutout in the gate in response to Halaboji's sharp rap. Halaboji politely asked the man his name.

"Choy," he grumbled. "What business do you have in the House of Rhim?"

"You know who I am." Halaboji was, after all, a village elder. "I would like to speak to the household head, Rhim Sajang-nim."

Halaboji cut a nice figure. His hanbok was as spotlessly white as his beard. He wore a black horsehair stovepipe hat that spoke of his long lineage as a scholar. Water Project Village had had a municipal structure imposed on it by the Japanese government during the colonization, but the village retained perhaps more strongly the age-old Confucian structure in which issues were resolved via a meeting of the elders, who sat and smoked pipes and were given ultimate authority. Yungman knew that Rhim had also been admitted to their circle as a council member, but mostly on account of his fabulous wealth and power.

The cutout, which only showed Choy's eyes, was rudely shut. Out of respect for Halaboji's stature as a village elder, Choy should have invited him in for tea while he waited. At least he should have used the "high" language. At the very least he should have said, nicely, "Please wait." Was he going to come back?

Halaboji waited uncomplainingly. With a twinkle in his eye, he put a finger to his lips and motioned to Yungman to come closer.

For all of Choy's fussing with the tiny cutout in the door, the gate itself was ajar.

Yungman peered through the opening.

He saw a wood-frame house with a traditional tiled roof right inside the gate. He looked back at his grandfather with awe. The Kwak house was a common village choka house, mud-plastered, with two rooms—no bigger or smaller than the other houses.

"What a beautiful house!" This one had at least three rooms.

"On-nya, that house you see is just the one of the guardsman's family! Look up on the top of the hill."

Seemingly floating among the clouds, like an ancient Korean painting of heaven, was a majestic manor. The house was a traditional hanok, exemplifying the beauty of Korean architecture, Halaboji explained. It would have a large receiving room for guests with a maru wooden floor that would stay cool in the summer. Maru would also connect this main part of the house with the inside wings, where the women and servants would be.

Yungman also glimpsed an outdoor pavilion with a raised wooden platform for eating. It was surrounded by a flower garden bright with cosmos and rose of Sharon—a garden with no other apparent purpose than to be beautiful. (Yungman's mother grew bellflowers, various white-petaled alliums, and ginger for their tasty roots.)

Unbelievably, a slender spider-leg of a creek also ran right through the place. Their hamlet was called Water Project Village, but it was actually arid here in the mountains, especially after the Japanese had cut down so many of the trees for their war effort that crops had difficulty growing. The primary source of fresh water for the twenty or so families in the hamlet was the well. The steep-banked river went untouched by most, although Yungman and his family would on occasion brave the brambles in order to fish and pick the blackberries that grew there.

It was unimaginable that these people, the House of Rhim, had fresh water to scoop out at will instead of having to haul it from the well in town. Yungman's mother washed dishes using very little water, putting it in her mouth to create a spray and slurping it up again, over and over.

On the guardsman's side were the pigsty, the storage bins, the compost. All that unpleasantness away from the main house. At Yungman's house, their outhouse and the sewers stunk up the place day and night. The less mannered types thought nothing of taking a shit in the gutter in the middle of the day.

"Why do they need a wall?" Yungman inquired again. The House of Kwak had no wall. The entrance to the house was a raised porch with a sliding rice paper door that anyone could open. The next house over had only a mass of bundled twigs for a door.

"Perhaps they feel safe this way," Halaboji said. "Perhaps they feel they can protect their wealth and their womenfolk, keeping them all inside this compound."

After age seven, schools split by sex. Yungman and his friends gathered to play jegi-chagi, to catch frogs, to go to the comic book seller's and sit and read until the owner yelled at them. There were never any girls to join them. Their school was on the other side of the village. "Why would girls be safe inside the wall?"

"I did not say they are safe—I said the walls make them feel safe," Halaboji said. "The rich just do things the way rich people tend to do. They think their wealth and connections can fix everything." He paused, his eyes focused on some point in the distance. "Your grandmother was quite clever. She would have loved her two fine grandsons."

Yungman always tried to picture his grandmother. She would have a wise, kind face like Halaboji's. She would put a hand to his cheek and say "On-nya" when she was pleased with something he did. Beyond that, he couldn't picture her. Yungman's mother had told him she had died in childbirth; the son she was carrying had died with her.

His father had been gone for two years by then. Yungman worried he would one day fail to picture him, too. He had tried to remember the cleft in his chin, the long, distinct philtrum from his nose to his upper lip, his wavy hair, unusual for a Korean, much like a movie star's. More and more, the image of his father's face was replaced by that of his silver chopsticks and spoon, which his mother set out at his place at the table along with everyone's else's, as if he might walk in at any time.

"Do these people know where Father is?" Yungman said suddenly. Was *that* what today's lesson was? But at that moment, Halaboji stepped back as the gate swung open, revealing the flat eyes of Choy set in a pumpkin-shaped head. Yungman was careful to stay quiet. But he still had ears.

Choy said: "The master says we know nothing."

". . . Kang the policeman . . ."

". . . disappeared . . ."

". . . just know we don't take kindly to Communists."

Halaboji stepped slightly back. "That is a fancy word, 'Communist.' Do you know what a Communist actually is, or do you just accept the idea that someone's enemy calls him that?" Halaboji said mildly. "They are called 'palgye,' as if they are monsters with red skin. I am not looking for a palgye. I am looking for my only son, who did nothing more subversive than teaching farmers how they deserved the land the Japanese took away from them."

Choy stared dumbly at him.

"Look around you," Halaboji continued. "The Japanese oppressed us for so many years. They made us learn Japanese. They changed our names. They forced the farmers to grow rice and took it away, gave us animal feed to eat instead. And while Koreans who dared fight back were being tortured and murdered by the police, those who collaborated with the Japanese did quite nicely."

"What are you trying to say?" Choy's speech was grooved deeply with the Gold Sea dialect.

"Liberation from Japan was called the 'Day of Return of the Light.' Do you remember how good it felt to drive the Japanese off our land? And how we elders promised land reform so that the people — like you — who did all the rice farming would get a piece of land for themselves? But *some people* made way for the Yankees to split our country and rule over us, instead of trying to fight off the American occupation, allied themselves with them — and, since they profited, largely allowed a continuation of our oppression by another nation. If you don't believe my words, consider who was the police chief during colonial times. It was Commander Ugimoto. And after? Still the same person, even though he is back to being called Kang, is he not? Did your master also give up being Korean a little too easily, first to the Japanese and now doing the bidding for Americans?"

Choy's flapping mouth suddenly grew silent. He shut the gate, but it made hardly a sound.

"You are too young to remember the thick forests," Halaboji said to Yungman. "During the occupation, the Japanese made all us men go out and chop down the trees. With their roots no longer in the soil, all the water ran off. That is why the villages on this mountain, even Water Project Village, are turning dry. The vast coniferous forests were suddenly gone, and the monsoon rains washed away so much soil and nutrients. Your father spent his life trying to breed special drought-resistant seeds, including rice, that could still grow here. That's all he did—that, and wanting to return the land to those who would no longer harm it."

The beautiful, grassy spot where Grandmother's grave was placed, apparently, was once surrounded by delightfully shady trees, so his father had planted new ones. One of Yungman's first lessons from Halaboji was how to care for these saplings. He would also from now on be responsible for the family burials, protecting the bones of the dead. "When the Japanese came, they started forcing us to burn the dead; they said it was for public hygiene. But it was to attack our spirit with their Shinto beliefs. We don't burn our bodies in death. We keep our bones together, every last one, and place them back in the earth, for the spirits to return to, and where the living will know where to find them."

"So will the House of Rhim people burn their bodies, like the Japanese?"

Halaboji looked thoughtful. "It depends on whether their minds and hearts remain more Korean or not."

Halaboji would never take him there again. Yungman would still often gaze at this manse, the tip of the slanted roof visible from the train station, wondering who was so special that they got to live in the clouds, halfway to heaven. All Yungman knew was that a daughter of the House of Rhim later left the village to attend middle school in Seoul.

As they walked down the hill, Halaboji pushing aside the tall grasses with his stick, they heard a soft *shushhhhhh* sound that could be mistaken for snakes, but they both looked up because they had heard this sound before. Over the mountains came some shiny silver planes in a diamond formation, heading north, so fast and so close that, in a blink, they were gone.

Sometimes from the bellies of the planes came dark objects like the pellets rabbits drop. Other times, from far off, they could hear what sounded like a *pooof!* accompanied by a puff of white smoke, visible for minutes if it was a clear, still day. There had been rumors of military activity on the 38th Parallel—specifically that President Rhee, the American-installed leader, was provoking the North, deliberately trying to draw fire. "If so, he's a megalomaniacal fool," Yungman had heard Halaboji say to another village council leader. "They say he's trying to draw the North into a war so he can reunite the country, with the American troops at his back." The old men all shook their heads and clicked their tongues. But as long as there was quiet and relative harmony in the village, none of this concerned them.

There was no gate and certainly no wall around their house, but if there had been, Yungman supposed the men would have broken it down. Halaboji had been up reading by the kerosene lamp, the rest of them sleeping, when police in uniform stormed their house, broke things, kicked over the brazier in the scuffle, and dragged him out without even his shoes. Yungman saw only the white of his socks and the lavender of his silk pants as he was pulled out into the night. Yung-sik and their mother busily chased after the coals that had been spilled from the brazier lest their hut catch on fire.

The next morning, there was a rap on the door. Yungman slid it open and saw no one. Then he looked to the gutter. Halaboji was lying in it, an abrasion on his head, a red rusty stain on his silk pants. He could not get up without his walking stick, so he just lay there, humiliated. He was missing his snowy white socks as well. Yungman had never seen his bare feet. They were like a child's feet, strangely unmarked—except for the purple bruises.

Yungman's mother helped him in, crying quietly. Halaboji shushed her with a little impatience. "On-nya, Daughter. I'm just a little scratched up from when I fell. But can you believe they could treat the old village head like this?"

His mother sponged Halaboji's bony knee and sent Yung-sik out to the mountain to find some plantain leaf that she could chew to make a poultice.

"Is this because of when we went up the hill?" Yungman couldn't help asking. Halaboji looked at Yungman sharply. "It has nothing to do with our hike to go fishing," he said. And suddenly Yungman understood. He wasn't to talk about visiting the House of Rhim. He supposed Halaboji didn't want to give Mother false hope about their ever finding Father again.

SUMMER 1950

In the lotus-blooming month of June, Yungman turned ten. A week later, on a date all Koreans would remember as 6.25, the Communist Korean People's Army, led by Kim Il-sung, crossed the 38th Parallel and headed south.

Halaboji often said, wars do not start, they come.

Over the past year, for people who lived around "the line" the Americans had drawn, it was impossible to miss the flare-ups: small arms fire, air force flyovers, an occasional bombing. Ironically, Water Project Village was so remote, tucked away in its valley between two steep mountains, that while it saw many of the worrisome exchanges, it remained unaware of this newest activity. Only the Catholic priest, a Korean who went by Father Andrea, had a Philco radio the Maryknoll Sisters had given him. He alone received the strange news of a supposed North Korean troop movement over the line, but did not know what to do.

A mere fifty kilometers south, in Seoul, civilians first heard then saw the artillery and rolling tanks. A few saw some Republic of Korea soldiers running pell-mell through the streets, discarding their rifles and tearing off their uniforms as they fled, screaming that people needed to save themselves, the Reds were coming. They ran so fast and were gone in a blink—had they been real? Was this a trick of some sort?

On the radio, President Syngman Rhee calmly and bravely informed the people that there was nothing wrong and they should stay home.

> *Every Cabinet member, including myself, will protect the govern-*
> *ment. Citizens should not worry and remain in their workplaces*
> *and homes.*

Rhee had left at the first rumble of a tank, secretly escorted by the US military. After he'd crossed the only means of egress out of the city, he'd had the bridge over the river Han blown up—with many people still on it. The next morning, the trapped citizens of Seoul awoke to the one-star flag of the Democratic People's Republic of Korea flapping from the flagpoles. The invading army opened the prisons, full of partisans and suspected partisans. Many were joyfully reuniting with their families, dazed from their confinement and torture; others were out for revenge. There was a rumor that the North Korean soldiers had even entered Seoul National University Hospital, which had been turned into a kind of field hospital, and slaughtered the injured ROK soldiers in their beds, as well as the doctors and nurses attending to them.

America liked to portray itself as the savior of Korea, but it had also created the very conditions—the divided state, the proxy war with Russia—that it itself had to step in to salvage if South Korea was to remain a beacon against Communism in the Orient. Back home, there was the idea that America's superior air power—North Korea did not have an air force to speak of—would make this a quick victory, and thus the president never bothered to gain Congressional approval for war but went in as a "police action."

By fall, the North Korean People's Army had overrun the entire peninsula except for Pusan on the very southern tip, separated from the rest by a natural water border, but it looked soon to be overcome as well.

Before a humiliating withdrawal for the US—never mind what such an abandonment would mean for Koreans—General Douglas MacArthur, fresh off his triumphal slaughter in the Philippines, hatched a last-ditch tactical plan to land in Inchon, its bay so shallow and its tides so unpredictable that the Korean People's Army wouldn't expect such a foolhardy attack. First, he cleared nearby Kanghwa Island with an aerial bombing of napalm (hitting housewives hanging laundry, children playing, a farmer in the fields irrigating her famous scarlet kohlrabi—all killed in a macabre frieze to rival Pompeii's).

"There had to be a Korea somewhere in the world," a Texas congressman told the newspapers, referring to its place in geopolitics, not to its people. "We had to show those bastards we would fight."

For MacArthur, the Inchon landing was his Normandy. Soon, the clean, white South Korean taegukgi—which, before the Americans split the country, was the flag of a whole Korea—flew from the flagpoles in Seoul again, and the "General Megadoo" joined the pantheon of deities that Korean shamans called up in times of trouble.

Megadoo and the UN troops under his command punished the North Korean People's Army by chasing them north, continuing the bombardment (eventually, more bombs and napalm fell upon the tiny country of Korea than in the entire Pacific Theater during

World War II). Immolating homes with people inside was easier than having to decide who was friend or foe.

Allied forces captured Pyongyang by the end of fall. Megadoo told the American president Truman that the US would show the world who was boss *and* be home by Christmas. He had ambitions for the presidency.

North of the line, where the winds from Siberia come howling off the mountains, it was one of the coldest winters in Korea's history. Megadoo had already decided the Allies would push the Commies over the Yalu River and into China, reuniting the two halves of Korea and also establishing his platform for the presidency.

Take that!

By Thanksgiving, US troops had emplaced themselves at the Yalu, easily defeating scattered NKPA and trouncing the desultory pockets of Chinese troops—so poorly equipped that some were carrying only wooden sticks carved to look like rifles.

MacArthur flew up to the border for a victory photo. Padded against the cold, with aviator sunglasses and corncob pipe, he posed with the troops who clutched their tin mess cups and grinned over the vats of steaming mashed potatoes and turkey. The general waved to the troops (holding the motion an extra few seconds so it would look good on tomorrow's front page), and reboarded the *Bataan*. He went to sleep that night, heart full, thinking of his victories as the leader of the Pacific command: Japan, of course, but also Leyte in the Philippines (where he'd met his sixteen-year-old mistress) and what everyone would remember as the Inchon Landing and Home by Christmas push, which won Korea and would result in his canonization.

It had never occurred to the general that the scattered, poorly coordinated resistance from the NKPA and the Chinese that they'd easily and happily quashed on their rush to the Yalu could have been mere decoys for a trap.


A pounding at the door, so hard Yungman feared the rice paper would tear from its wooden frame.

Yungman's mother looked at an ashy-faced white man in an Allied uniform, warm parka, winter military gear. His eyes bugged out of his head; he was shouting gibberish and waving his rifle as his translator, protected from the cold by a single layer of hemp linen (Koreans accepted cold, while white people seemed to shiver and fight it), and said, only once: "The Chinese are coming—evacuate to Seoul!"

Yungman's mother packed a bag of rice and some utensils. Yungman was going to have to carry one of the cast-iron cooking gamasot.

He tried to hold it on his back. "It's so heavy!" he wanted to say. But he didn't. The largest one sat in a cutout on the counter, so heavy it was fixed as if glued, and pure iron, blackened over thousands of fires. At almost a hundred years old, it was one of the most expensive items they owned. The gamasot Yungman was assigned to carry was one of the two smaller ones. Maybe he wouldn't have to carry it far, since the train station was just outside the village gates.

He went with Yung-sik to find their warmest hanbok and layers of underwear. His father had a beautiful quilted cotton coat that he didn't dare touch. He noticed his mother glancing at the framed print on the wall, a dreamy painting of women in a field by Pierre Bonnard; also, the antique celadon vase on the shelf—two precious possessions that would have to be left behind in a home that had no locks.

Their father's silver spoon and chopsticks she tucked into a bag that she wore under her voluminous skirt. She rolled blankets tightly into rolls, used the largest one to wrap a bundle she carried on her head. Halaboji insisted on wearing a workingman's A-frame on his back to hold the small bag of rice and dried vegetables.

Yung-sik had been running another of his fevers. Yungman feared they would have to rig up a way to carry him—a cart? But what if they missed the train? He was relieved when Yung-sik, glassy-eyed, rose from his mat. Yungman stuck his straw shoes on his feet and gave him a small bundle to carry.

Yungman felt his back would break in two from the weight of the gamasot. His mother tapped him on the shoulder and moved his arms like a doll's. She was putting on his father's jacket over everything. His father had broad shoulders; the coat fit over the bundle and Yungman. They could hear bursts of cannon fire in the distance. Walking out the village gates they began traveling south, puzzlingly away from the train station, which sat slightly to the east.

"Why aren't we going to the train?" asked Yungman.

Halaboji shook his head. He was wearing only a light topcoat over his hanbok and looked like a wraith next to the bundled American soldiers, a few of whom themselves were using Korean A-frames to carry their gear. "Ah, no train has come here from the south for months. I reckon we must head on to Seoul."

To Seoul! That was a long way! But Yungman ducked his head and walked on, humping the heavy pot, encouraging his feverish little brother. When they stopped to rest, he melted snow for him to drink—Chinese medicine said it was bad to chill one internally—but he also rubbed Yung-sik's little hands with snow to slow the fever.

Lines of other villagers streamed down the mountain join them. The refugees walked where they could on the frozen roads, close but not too close to the soldiers and the occasional tank taking up the road. Their procession passed burned-out tanks that lay in ditches. Yungman thought they had been bombed, but they had merely run out of gas and been set on fire so they wouldn't help the Communists.

As they passed Bush Clover Village, the thatch of the houses' roofs visible along a ridge, they heard a mosquito buzz and looked up to see the star emblem of an American plane, a series of those dark bombs falling from its belly. The noise was immense; the vibrations passed through their bones. One errant bomb hit very close to their line. Yungman saw, or thought he saw, scraps of white hanbok dancing in the dark smoke. Why? Bush Clover Village was a nothing village, even more nothing than theirs; they could sell their water, but bush clover was useless. Their mother hissed at him to walk on.

Yungman and his family made the entire fifty-kilometer journey to Seoul on foot. A unit of ROK soldiers coming down from the Chosin Reservoir had marched with them for a while. One ROK spoke in a low voice to Halaboji. He explained how, on their retreat, the Americans—the mighty Americans!—had bombed even their own troops because of faulty communications—not once but several times.

One morning they spied another plane overhead. It, too, sported American markings. The refugees scattered: some ran; some jumped in a ditch. Others, weary, just sat down and waited to die.

A silky white powder fell from the plane like snow. It landed on some people and not others, depending on the wind. There were no explosions. A few minutes later, however, some people fell to the ground, seizing. A few, including some American soldiers, died, foam pouring out of their mouths.

They walked on.

Later, along the road, a British tank rider peered over and stared hard at Yungman. Then he tossed a round white object toward him.

Yungman grabbed Yung-sik and huddled over him. The white ball sat in the road and never exploded.

The soldier had seen his disintegrating straw shoes, the frozen blood on his ankles, and tossed him a clean roll of bandages. Yungman used the bandages to warmly wrap Yung-sik's head; he hoped to signal of how sick he was.

Not too long after, another Allied soldier stopped for a baby that was crying on the road, prying it out of its dead mother's arms. Yungman feared some mischief until he saw the man was carrying it tenderly, a hand like a visor protecting the baby from the snow as he marched.

Another soldier took a baby from its dead mother's teat, twirled it around his head by its arm yelling "Yee-haaaaaahh!" and let the baby fly into a field. They could all hear it faintly crying. Yungman's mother wept. But they walked on.

Along the way, the refugees took shelter in whatever abandoned structures they could find—houses, sheds, barns, caves. Some houses still had people in them—mostly the elderly who had refused to move. These people wearily let them in, knowing the soldiers would break in and take what they wanted anyway. One time Yungman and Yung-sik were fed a delicious pumpkin porridge. It was so good that the boys immediately exhorted their mother to eat, but she said she was suffering from a stomach ailment and smiled and said she was going to take a quick nap instead. Even through all this hardship, she still looked young and pretty, and Yungman could see so easily how his father, studying a rice field in another village, had fallen in love with her, a tailor's daughter whom he saw from afar as she pedaled her bicycle— the picture of balance and grace, he'd said. The back of her well-oiled bicycle had been piled high with colorful fabrics that fluttered behind her like the flags of happy nations. Her skin was so paper-white that the aunties of Water Project Village often referred to her as "Narcissus Maiden," even after she was a married woman, like them.

One night, as they all huddled together sleeping in the luxurious comfort of straw in a barn, an Allied soldier came in—slinked in—with his friend. Yungman's mother was alert like a deer and sat up, quickly nodding yes, but Halaboji started to yell, and the friend hit him in the jaw with the butt of his rifle. They saw a tooth go flying. Yungman and Yung-sik cowered in the straw all night, eyes shut tight, hoping everything was a dream.

As they trekked south, it became harder and harder to find shelter. Allied troops with their great guns that shot napalm, the fire jelly, set everything ablaze—houses, gardens, army jeeps, ammunition. Yungman saw up ahead an American soldier about to destroy a rice seed storage hut. An ROK soldier pointed out the chimney smoke from the farmer's thatched choka; he had chosen not to flee, for who would grow the rice for the people?

The American shoved him aside and set the house and hut on fire. The old farmer crawled out dazedly from the blast.

Yungman and his family had to walk past. Past the old farmer, now screaming in pain as his skin slowly cooked to the bone, past the heat. They were spooked by a sudden pop-pop-pop sound; they thought it was small arms gunfire, but it was the seed rice exploding. Yungman's mother didn't forbid their grabbing handfuls as long as they didn't slow. Yung-sik went by with his mouth open in hopes an errant kernel would land in it, like how they used to toss grapes at each other during a happier time.

When they made it to Seoul Station, they had to wait. Many people were crowded into the space, but the ticket stations were empty. It was impossible to tell if the trains were running.

Halaboji's jaw was still swollen, making it difficult for him to talk or eat, so he didn't do much of either.

Father Andrea, the Catholic priest, approached them. "They said there will be one last train," he said, "so you should wait. Even if others tell you not to." He was traveling alone. Yungman's mother had used melted snow to rehydrate some of dried dandelion greens they carried; she added a pinch of salt and gave a handful to the priest.

"I can't take your food." He recoiled as if she had hit him.

"Too fibrous for Grandfather to chew," she said, pushing it back. "After my husband was taken, we ran out of food, and your Catholic church gave us a bag of rice. We feasted on that for a glorious month. I will never forget." Father Andrea thanked her, made his strange motions over the food, and ate.

They waited. Some refugees debated whether it was too dangerous to stay; the North Koreans and the Chinese were coming down in waves from the Chosin Reservoir. Yungman's family decided to believe their friend the priest and watched as more than half of the group got up and continued the trek south.

"Why wait for certain death?" the leavers admonished the ones who stayed.

Eighteen hours later, the family awoke to the sound of screeches and a belch. A coal-fired train was pulling in, with only three passenger cars attached. But a train! The refugees roused and began to run toward it, bundles in their hands. As it came closer, Yungman could see most of the windows were smashed, the frames gaping holes. There was no kind of order, no one directing them, so they pushed their way on even before the train had stopped. Inside, the train seats looked like a giant had tried to rip them up by their roots; they were missing their cushions, frames bent, some with no seat at all. With the desperate pushing and shoving as more tried to board, Yung-sik, Yungman, their mother, and the priest protected Halaboji so he could lie down. People were still worming in through the doors and unglassed windows. The train was so laden that some climbed on top. They tied their children to whatever protruding metal there was on the roof.

The train stopped and started. Faster than walking, but not by much. A whole cold day passed. Then it was night again. Someone had vomited, and the stench was sour and cut through the frigid air pouring through the holes where windows used to be. Yungman did not know how the people riding on top would be able to hold out, and indeed, he winced every time he heard the thump of a frozen body rolling off, or pushed off, the roof of the train. A few times when it stopped, people got off and didn't get back on, seemingly driven out of their minds by the cold.

Halaboji noticed little. He was barely awake. Saliva leaked out the corner of his mouth where the missing tooth was, and froze. Their mother worried his jaw was infected. They all, including Father Andrea, took turns massaging his limbs to keep him warm. Yungman's mother took out more herbs and made a poultice, applying it as a paste to the abrasion on his face. She took out a small, precious ball of rice wrapped in seaweed that a farmer's wife had cooked for them, unwrapped the seaweed, and chewed up the rice for her father-in-law. Much of it leaked back out of his injured jaw. She handed the seaweed to Yung-sik to eat.

Yungman suddenly thought of the puffed rice in his pocket. It was dry and soft. He poked it through the O of his grandfather's mouth, where it slowly softened and dissolved. He swallowed it without problem. Their mother nodded at him in approval.

"Am I dead?" Halaboji cried in his delirium. "Let me die."

In the corner near them, a man grumbled at the noise. "You should fend for yourselves. Why are you wasting your energy and your food? The old man—clearly, he will die soon."

Yungman, his brother, his mother, and Father Andrea rubbed and massaged Halaboji's limbs, one taking over when the other tired, all through the night.

They finally reached Pusan at dawn. Halaboji's breathing was easier. How pleased they were to see the puffs of breath in the cold as he slept the sleep of the weary. The man in the corner didn't stir. He had fallen asleep and been taken by exposure during the night.

PUSAN

1950

Pusan was the only city that had remained consistently in Allied hands. It grew ever more unwieldy as the war went on. Those who didn't have kin in the city made homes in shacks clinging lawlessly to the hillside, in the pews of churches, in livestock paddocks constructed by the Japanese, on the floors of factories.

Father Andrea went in search of his church. Not knowing where else to go, their mother led them toward the shacks, higher and higher up the hillside, until they found an unoccupied space, barely three meters across, an accidental gap between other lean-tos.

While Halaboji rested, their mother fashioned a hut with wooden pallets Yung-sik and Yungman carried over from a pile on the docks, discards from the American Navy LST ships. Their mother was intent but unhurried. A surprisingly large man poked his head out of the adjacent Lilliputian shack, and offered to share his cardboard wall. He helped their mother hang one of their blankets—all they had for a roof. In thanks, their mother offered him some of their food. But the thirtyish man, his hair thick as an otter's, who would have been handsome except for all the dirt on his face and how he—like Halaboji—had a missing tooth, said he was just glad for the company.

The next day, Halaboji said he wanted to see the ocean. The swelling in his jaw had gone down considerably, and his eyes looked clear. His walking stick fit into the grooves of his hand again like an old friend. Their mother fussed, saying he was too weak to walk down the hill, the shore would be too cold. But Yungman and Yung-sik clamored to join him, desperate to escape the hovel. Through the night they had also noted coming from somewhere in the west an unrelenting smell of burning fat, both sweetish and repugnant, that clung to their nostrils.

"Let the children accompany me, Daughter," Halaboji said. "My mother came to me in my dream last night."

Yungman's mother looked, momentarily, alarmed. But when she turned to Yungman and Yung-sik, she was smiling again. "All right. Go sightsee a bit."

"On-nya, so glad I brought my walking stick," Halaboji said, brandishing the polished wood that had accompanied them all around the mountains and would now see the ocean. On his head, instead of the bulky black stovepipe hat, he wore a fedora, which gave him a dignified but also dashing air. For someone who had seemed on the brink of death just a day or two ago, he stepped down the hill almost as nimbly as his grandsons. He turned his face toward the sea, eager to smell the salt.

They threaded their way through the city streets, dense with refugees and troops pouring off the ships docked at the port. They walked past and into and through the human hubbub until they came to a steep path that led down to the beach, rocky with black volcanic formations, lava frozen mid-eruption, some as tall as a man. The sand was also black.

"Wah . . ." Yungman couldn't help himself as his gaze swung away from land. So this was the sea: an endless plain of water that could swallow him up without a second thought.

Yung-sik made his way to the beach's edge, delighting at jumping back as the waves foamed toward him. Halaboji looked on, a slight, wistful smile on his face.

There was no one else on the beach except for a man stirring a fire a hundred meters away. When they passed him and Yungman looked closer, he saw that what he'd thought was white driftwood in the fire was actually bones.

Halaboji stared at the bones serenely and then turned to the boys. "My dream last night," he started.

"Your mother!" Yung-sik almost screeched. "She was in it."

"On-nya, you listen well," he said. "You want to know what she said?"

Both boys nodded. Halaboji beckoned them to come close. "It's not frightening. So don't be frightened."

"I can't be scared," boasted Yung-sik. Then he ran away from a particularly large wave and Yungman laughed.

"Good. Now shush so I can tell you. In my dream my beloved mother said I would die as a stranger in a strange place."

"No, you will live for a long time," Yungman said.

"That may be, but I heard those words so clearly. So I want to tell you, my two grandsons who are the most trustworthy boys in the world: when I die, I want to return to rest near my long-gone wife."

Yungman thought of the place where Grandmother was buried. At the lip of the mountain, the breeze would be cool, the view magnificent: without trees, one could even see the tip of Kanghwa Island floating atop a finger's-width scrim of azure sea.

In spring, mountainsides blazed yellow and pink, or white with the small dandelions that carpeted the grass like stars. This particular mountain was special, Halaboji said, pointing to what Yungman thought was the pheasant's eye flower, but it was the spotty-petal lily. Rovers and mushroom hunters and picnickers alike cried out in delight to come upon these flowers poking out of the rock, as they were thought to be lucky. The spotted bud is delightful; then, when the flower blooms, the petals swoop majestically back on themselves until the blossom looks like the round chignon in a newly married woman's hair.

It was as if she came back every year as a flower, he said.

That night, Yungman put a hand to Halaboji's forehead. It radiated heat even though the shack was cold. There had been a few deadly infernos in the cramped encampments, so the city had prohibited fire of any kind. At the base of the hill, people had set up makeshift stoves using piled-up circles of bricks and stones to hold a can or a gamasot. Halaboji never complained about the cold; however, in their house in the village, he was fond of his brazier, which his mother always kept glowing with hot coals in the winter. Poor Halaboji must have missed it.

Yungman slept the kind of sleep where you can't tell if you're awake or dreaming. He thought he saw his mother step to the threshold of their hovel, flutter Halaboji's linen hanbok three times, and call his name, as they do for the dead. In his dream, the white fabric rose and fell, looking like the petals of the spotted lily in the wind.

Their mother spent the day washing Halaboji's body. Pusan's water system, already forty years decrepit, couldn't handle the additional burden of hundreds of thousands of refugees. There was a single pump at the base of their hovel city, and the municipal water came on only once every three days. Families were allowed two buckets a day.

Thankfully, the water was running. Yungman and Yung-sik waited hours, never budging, fearing the flow would stop. When it was their turn, they each filled a bucket. Neighbor Uncle came down and filled a bucket as well. Even though their hovels shared a wall, he always kept a respectful distance from their mother. Yungman was grateful for this. They knew nothing about him except that he was from Sokcho, a South Korean town near the sacred Diamond Mountain, part of the long Taebaek range the American 38th Parallel had also chopped in two, leaving Diamond Mountain and its twelve thousand peaks north of the line. His untamed whiskers and sloping shoulders caused Yungman and Yung-sik to secretly call him Bear Uncle. He was the sole son in his family, so his mother had sent him south rather than allow him to be forced into the North Korean army, which had stripped their town of all males over ten. Bear Uncle had thought he would hide in Seoul for a few weeks and then return, but the same evacuation that propelled Yungman's family had sent him to Pusan. He hadn't heard about what happened to his family, and so most days when he wasn't working at the docks, he roamed the center of the city, reading the newspapers pasted on the telephone poles and trying to find news from his hometown.

Bear Uncle carried his and Yung-sik's buckets up the hill, careful to not spill a drop. It was a clear day and the three could see the blackened smokestack that the sick-sweet smell came from. "Some kind of factory," Bear Uncle surmised. "Maybe an animal-fat rendering plant." On some days, smoke and ash belched out of it like a volcano, leaving clouds around the shantytown that made their mother wipe their floor more than twice a day. Right now, it was still.

By the time they reached their shack near the apex of the hill, both boys were murderously thirsty. Their tongues felt huge and swollen. Bear Uncle bowed to their mother and left his entire ration of water, retreating like a hermit crab back into his hovel.

Both boys watched their mother dip a cloth in the water and wash Halaboji, beginning at the crown of his head. She dipped, wrung, washed. Each finger got careful attention, as well as the crevices between them, behind his ears, the crook of his elbows, between his toes.

After she dried him, she unraveled part of Yungman's father's jacket and extracted some of the cotton batting to pad Halaboji's ears. She wrapped his corpse carefully in a ramie cloth that she tied with twine. He should have had coins for his eyes, but coins, even if they had them, would be Japanese jeon, and Halaboji would not have liked that touching him. He also needed a mouthful of rice.

Yungman had another pocketful of the puffed rice. Halaboji's jaw was not yet set with rigor mortis, and they could see now how badly it had been knocked askew by the white soldier. Yungman carefully, gently slipped in the rice, food for his journey to the next place.

"I need your help to carry Halaboji," she told the boys. They lifted him up.

Bystanders gossiped at the sight of the young boys carrying their grandfather's wrapped body through the twisty alleyways of the city and down the hill toward the public cemetery. "What a sad lot to be buried so far from home," one clucked. "Do these refugees not care about proper ancestor worship? They should find a way to get the body home. Aigu, shame."

Yungman was surprised when their mother directed them around the cemetery and back up the hill on a lateral path that led toward the smokestack, where Yungman could hear the roar of a fire. She hailed a man in a green uniform leaning against a stone wall. He looked like he was chewing on something, but he wasn't eating. His skin was nut brown like a peasant's. He had black hair but his face, wider than it was long, with a runny, rubbery-looking triangular nose, was foreign. That face split into a smile as he looked at Yungman's mother, up and then down.

Yungman, at eleven, didn't have much of an inkling of what the smokestack was for. If he had, he would have said, "Halaboji said we Koreans don't burn our bodies in death; only the Japanese do such a thing. Just like the Japanese have the one Mount Fuji that looks the same to everyone, but Diamond Mountain actually encompasses twelve thousand peaks. Halaboji said we think differently than our so-called Japanese masters. We Koreans keep our bones together, every last one, and place them back in the earth where the living will return to until it is also their turn."

Their mother moved a strand of hair out of her eyes with the back of a wrist. It had been cold when they left the hovel, but near the smokestack, it was sweltering, heat radiating off it like Yung-sik when he had a bad fever. "Go now," she told her sons. "Go straight home. Do not speak to anyone; do not let anyone in, even Neighbor Uncle. Stay and wait for me."

Yungman didn't want to leave his grandfather. His grandfather should have a funeral with a long procession, flanked by the people of the village. He, as first son, would carry a portrait of Halaboji, banded in black. Actually, it was his father who should be doing all that. He should wear the woven hemp crown of a mourner and light the incense at Halaboji's altar. He should be the one to send his father on his next journey. Yungman obeyed his mother.

His mother returned hours later. She didn't speak. Her hair was mussed, chunks of it falling out of her chignon. Yungman remembered the one time he had seen her removing the bone hairpin that held it in place, how it fell to her waist in waves and how reverently his father looked at it. Now she kept it tightly coiled and rarely took it down. Her face looked bruised. In her chapped hands she held a gray cardboard box.

It was a month after Halaboji died when, on the way to the water pump line, Yungman saw the sign. He often stopped to read the papers pasted on the telephone poles. Fighting here, fighting there. Seoul had been bombed into rubble. So had Pyongyang. Were the Americans getting tired of the war? Some American general had been triumphantly quoted saying that the Allies had bombed Korea into a series of bare chimneys. Were they planning to drop a nuclear bomb, the way they had in Japan—killing not just Japanese civilians but also Korean forced labor, POWs that included white people from other nations, American GIs? If a country could do *that* to its own people, no doubt it could do the same to them. Megadoo, mysteriously, had been fired by the president. Americans just couldn't be understood, and Koreans were realizing that they wouldn't keep them safe. Even in the quiet of Pusan, isolated from the fighting, the whine of a plane overhead caused anxiety.

Sometimes there were LOCAL NOTICES. He stopped to read:

Hanyang Middle School—meet at the foot of Kudok Mountain.
Kyunghee High School—meet in the Pu'yong Pottery Factory.
Hongdae Girls' Middle School—meet at the Pumil streetcar stop.

These weren't small village schools but elite Seoul schools, including Doksuri—Eagle—High School, one of the best in Korea.

On that walk to the sea, Halaboji had taken Yungman aside, put two hands on his shoulders, and said, "You will soon be the eldest male in the family—"

Yungman wanted to blurt *Please! Live a long time!* to his grandfather, but he stayed respectfully silent.

"Your father was a brilliant man. He also kept to his principles. Under the occupation, he did not get to do what he would have liked to do, what could have fulfilled a very strong ambition in him. Thus it's the duty of the children to go forth and continue what the parents started."

He explained that as a boy, his father had scored so high on an intelligence test that at first the Japanese were skeptical—how could a Korean overtake the Japanese? They forced him to retake the test; he scored a few points higher. He was then one of the few Koreans offered a place at Pyongyang High School, which was established for the occupying Japanese elite. Yungman's father understood that all the Japanese wanted was loyal bureaucrat, a Korean given a few treats and trained to keep the colonial system in place. He refused.

When it was time for college, he wanted to study botany. But what had been the Great Han Empire's crown jewel of higher education, Seoul National University, had been turned into Keijō Imperial University, and so he chose instead to stay home and attend a nearby technical college and become an agronomist.

Yungman knew that it was his father's dream that his sons, after liberation, would attend Seoul National University and become credentialed — doctors or professors. Even when Yungman was five, he remembered his father saying to him, "When you go to college . . ."

He also understood that in order to do that, he had to enter a proper high school. The exams for the good high schools in Seoul were coming up in the late summer.

"The Water Project Village That Sold Its Water So Its Children Could Attend School" was a local Gold Sea Province song that drinkers and itinerant peddlers liked to sing when they wanted something peppy. The song evoked a picturesque village with special, magical water. The village was in fact no different from a dozen others within the valley, except that water from its well carried a musty sulfur odor that Yungman found off-putting, like opening an old trunk. The water was so laden with minerals that it left spots when it dried on metal or stone. Supposedly this made it a special Medicine Water that could cure ailments, even cancer, some said. Because their village was so remote, the villagers had Choi the master potter create special vials so they could bring the water to markets in Songdo or even to Seoul to sell.

A famous young poet in Seoul who claimed his arthritis was cured by this water stole the song and wrote the poem "The Water Project

Village That Sold Its Water So Its Children Could Attend School."
This poem was integrated into the South Korean elementary school
curriculum as a "classical poem" extolling the virtues of hard work,
the devotion of parents, and the prizing of education.

Of course, now, far, far away from the village and its fee-paying
water, Yungman had to wonder what to do next.

Children needed to continue where their parents had left off,
Halaboji had said. You need to live your father's dream for you.

And, as if—indeed—in a dream:

*Eagle High School—meet at the east end of the train station*

Eagle High School was famous for having the most alumni admitted to Seoul National University. Yungman wasn't even yet of age to
be admitted. But here in the topsy-turvy world of Pusan, maybe he
could use the wartime chaos to his advantage.

He walked the hundred meters to the Pusan train station. There
were two groups sitting outside, unshielded from the elements. Both
were groups of boys with close-shorn hair, but at the east end, instead
of tattered refugee rags, many were dressed in navy jackets with white
shirts.

The teacher wore a Western suit and tie, the first yangbok Yungman
had ever seen. But the teacher stood in the same beating sun, the same
clouds of dust and exhaust from the train, as the students. There were
maybe forty students—not an anonymous crowd but not an intimate
handful, either. There was even a blackboard. The students used the
respectful "sir," as they would if they were back in their classroom.

Yungman had no idea what was going to happen next. If he entered
the group from the back, the teacher might not see him. Then again,
he might. The students would surely know he didn't belong. What
would happen? Would he be beaten?

He took a breath and slid into the group. A boy immediately turned and glared, mouthing, "Scram!" But Yungman stood still, holding his gaze. The boy scowled and *hmmph*ed, but then actually made room for him to sit.

Yungman returned the next day. A few boys stared, but he stared haughtily back like fallen royalty, with a confidence he hadn't known he had. On the first rainy day (of which there would be many, during monsoon season), they moved to a church. Yungman walked in to find every inch of the vestry filled, the pews (first rule: no one was allowed to lie on the altar) dense with refugees, the air humid with human sweat-stink, hair oil, and farts. In this limited space, the boys noticed and grumbled when Yungman pushed in. "That one is not a class-mate!" Once, during math, a teacher threw him out as an impostor.

But most were too careworn to notice, five at a time crowded around a single slate or textbook; as the days wore on, fewer bothered to wear a uniform. One boy even had a younger sibling strapped to his back who was always crying or shitting his diaper; he drew more ire than Yungman. Many were malnourished and small, all of them straining to hear the English teacher over the din of the train.

"Hello, how are you?" the teacher said, and put his hand to his ear, waiting for a reply.

Yungman couldn't help himself. Halaboji had made him learn some English "because it may be useful one day." He stood up.

"I am fine, and you?" he practically shouted. The boys all laughed derisively. He was supposed to have repeated "Hello, how are you?" Yungman reddened and sat down.

"Student, what is your name?" said the teacher, looking at him hard.

"Kwak, Yungman, Teacher Sir!"

The man frowned, puzzled, but then turned back to the makeshift blackboard as he said, "Good job," and no one questioned Yungman after that.

WATER PROJECT VILLAGE
1952

The 6.25 war turned two, and Yungman turned twelve. He had trouble remembering how many months it had been since they had arrived in Pusan, or how long it had been since he last saw his father. Living in their hovel in Pusan had been hard. Some nights, as they huddled together for warmth, he feared they would freeze to death, just like that mouthy chap on the train. But so many living humans crammed together, breathing, warmed one another. Yung-sik swore the wall of the hovel they shared with Bear Uncle was much warmer.

The second winter turned to spring. The influx of refugees dropped off. Their mother took in sewing while Yungman went to school for free, and resourceful Yung-sik scampered upon the beach, gathering driftwood to sell for fuel, sometimes accompanied by Bear Uncle, who would help him lay out the wood on top of his tin roof to dry in the sun.

Bear Uncle had become a quiet and helpful presence, always on guard at night for intruders at the hovel of their pretty mother. The soughing of the sea was soothing, and thanks to Bear Uncle, who was one of the largest men he'd ever seen, Yungman gratefully, deeply slept. Even Yung-sik's constant ailments seemed to be washed clear by the sea air. Yungman was almost disappointed when the news came that Korea below the line was once again in Allied hands. The schools packed up. So did Yungman and his mother and Yung-sik. Bear Uncle bowed deeply to their mother. He gave a piece of rice taffy candy to each of the boys. Seeing a tear that Bear Uncle was quick to rub away before it fell, Yungman wondered if the man had secretly been in love with his mother. Who wouldn't be?

"If you ever find yourselves in Sokcho, look for Halmae's Place," he said. "My grandmother makes the best mountain vegetable mixed rice. If the Buddha allows, I will be there."

Yungman wondered if they would ever see him again.

Water Project Village had been waiting to be inhabited again. Except for the pile of twisted metal that was the train tracks, bombed even with no trains, the village was untouched. There were fewer people, of course, but that couldn't be helped.

The Pierre Bonnard painting and the celadon vase welcomed them home, vivid again when cleaned of their dust. Yungman saw his mother check a little pocket behind a beam in the wall where their father often left her little treasures from his walks in the fields: a buckeye, dried flowers, seeds that he strung into bracelets. Yungman could tell from her stricken face that the note she had left telling him that they had gone south was untouched, unread.

Even though they were home again, the war had ripped up the fabric of their old life, and this new one would turn out to be even more of a struggle. In Pusan, as refugees, they had received small but steady rations from the government. The priest had found the Maryknoll order, who had helped them with rice, and the Yankees distributed dried milk. They were sent off with one last bag of rice, one last bag of dried milk, which they brought back to the village. But after that, who knew what would happen?

Everyone was so traumatized from the war that they hardly registered the woman without a husband who was struggling to support her children—there were many people in that situation. Another disadvantage: Yungman's mother was without her clan. She came from "outside" and wasn't of the village, and most had forgotten that she was Narcissus Maiden before the war. Her sewing skills were of little use in a place where each housewife already sewed her family's clothes. She did some laundry for some kisaeng from another village where there was an entertainment house. She also sewed for Hana, the young girl who'd been brought to the village for one of the oldest families of Parks, in which the wife hadn't been able to give the old patriarch a son, even after twenty pregnancies that had produced five living daughters. Nineteen-year-old Hana had rapidly become pregnant and shrewdly used this time to ask for a set of new clothes for herself and the baby on the way. But even with all this, they were short on money to survive.

Yungman came up with the idea of selling metal, which every household needed. Yung-sik was a master at sniffing out an old pot or some wire. He was able to scrounge bullet casings, bits of exploded mortars, and other scraps to add to the pots and pans. Yungman went door-to-door before his last stop, the junk man, who barely paid him anything. Luckily, a good housewife always needed something.

He knocked on the door of the gate of the house that touched the clouds, the House of Rhim.

No answer. He knocked again.

"Who do you think you are?" roared Choy the guardsman before he even opened the gate. Choy's head, which used to look round as a pumpkin, had somehow deflated from the war. Now his face looked as long as a horse's, with two sagging bags, one for each cheek. "Making so much noise." Yungman stood fast, though his legs were curved with rickets, making him seem even younger than his age. He had pots and pans strapped to his body as though he were a small, armored animal. In his hand he held a bouquet of random pieces of wire.

Yungman never sold anything here. Instead, because of Choy's sloppy gatekeeping, it had become a game to try to catch a glimpse through the gate to collect as many details as he could about the wealthy people who lived inside.

So far, Yungman had told his little brother, he had seen a pigsty, a grape tree, and a root cellar.

Even if he didn't get a peek inside, he could note that, over the high wall, smoke rose from the kitchen day and night. This family never got cold or hungry. He once heard the *thump-thump* of a servant pounding rice for cakes.

"I have pots and pans!" Yungman said. "And scissors," though he failed to mention that they were rusted shut.

"You made me open the gate for this? Why didn't you just yell out what you have, like everyone else?"

That's what the onion seller, the charcoal peddler, and the shit-wagon man did, it's true. The taffy man clacked his scissors. You could hear them coming long before they arrived. But Yungman knew better than to announce his presence. It didn't matter whether above the line or below the line: the war had made the village conspicuously bereft of men of all ages, and anyone who was left was a tempting target for recruiters, who snatched boys and handed them off to the military—north and south—for a fee. They were no longer teaching at the middle school lest a whole class of boys be abducted at once.

Choy, as he continued to scold, spittle flying from his mouth, inadvertently let go of the gate. This angle was unexpectedly splendid: grain storage bins for the livestock, a maid sticking her arm elbow-deep into a kimchi urn. Yungman even spied a girl with a thick braid down her back loping past, wearing boys' silk pants instead of a hanbok or a Western skirt.

The wall around this house looked like it encompassed its own country. Apparently, during the colonial period, this place was a favorite for the Japanese to come pheasant hunting, and they even once caught a leopard on the grounds. Yungman imagined being able to wander this compound, the seemingly endless land. What did the people inside the house do all day? He knew Rhim had many daughters and one son, Joongki, who had gone missing during the winter of 1950.

With an active imagination but no sisters, Yungman had little idea what went on in the house. Did the sisters learn the delicate arts of embroidering on cambric fabric, of pressing designs into rice cakes to match the sweeping decorative terra-cotta tiles of the house's roof? The mother would undoubtedly cosset her children. Maybe she would line them up like baby birds and pipe golden drops of cod liver oil into their mouths so that they could stay strong through the winter. Halaboji had told Yungman about the cod, how you had to squeeze their slippery livers to yield a few drops, which is why it was so dear. The rice cakes would undoubtedly be dipped in the expensive black sesame that, when roasted, smelled like heaven.

Choy squinted at Yungman. "Close your mouth, you drooling fool!" He stepped forward and boxed Yungman's ears, sending his pots crashing.

"Do you think the wife of Rhim Sajang-nim needs an old pot from a dirty beggar like you? And with a palgye father and a mother who washes the underclothes of whores?" He kicked Yungman in the ongdongi, sending him sprawling further into the dirt. As Yungman rose, groaning, he swore he saw the figure of the girl rush past.

The gate shut with a bang, followed by the thunk of the bolt being laid crosswise.

Yungman picked himself up. His most salable pot, a fire-blackened but usable brass kettle, was now dented. But no matter; he had a good story to bring back.

As Yungman walked all the way down the hill, he amused himself by memorizing all the wondrous things he had seen, the shiny details of the House of Rhim that he would, like a mama bird, bring back to the nest to share with his little brother and mother. The three of them kept one another company at night, gathering about a single kerosene lamp to save money, while their mother mended.

He should ask his mother what the word "whores" meant.


The fighting continued around the line where it began. One hill would be won by one side. The next day, the other's flag would be flying. It became clear that neither the Reds nor the Allies—despite MacArthur's entreaty to Truman to drop atomic bombs (thirty-four bombs, to be exact) on the North—were going to be able to claim victory, and victory is all that counts in war. Both the US and Russia were starting to look elsewhere for their empires. Talks of a cease-fire tentatively began. They stopped, then started again. Each side had all the time in the world to wait the other out.

On the ground, soldiers died.

So did a boy fishing near Chestnut Village, killed in a strafing attack by three American jets. At first, the Americans said they hadn't done it. Then they said enemy planes did it, and they saw it. Then they admitted they had done it, and the pilots had been punished. But they wanted peace talks to resume.

When Yungman heard that, he couldn't help wondering if it had happened in the fishing spot Halaboji used to take them to. Steep to get down to, but due to the bend in the river, there was a sandy beach, with shade provided by the copse of overhanging willow trees. The path to the river was also impeded by wild blackberry canes whose thorns could tear your clothes. But they also produced the sweetest, juiciest berries in the summer. Yungman couldn't get the image of bursting berries—and bursting skin—out of his mind.

In Water Project Village, from time to time, villagers could see a puff of white phosphorus from artillery, an earthbound cloud. The radio warnings forbade any civilians moving north of the 38th

Parallel; sometimes a B-29 bomber would shower them with leaflets: NO MOVEMENT NORTH OF THE 38TH PARALLEL IS ALLOWED. Many of the flyers were written only in English, the official language of the US Army occupation. The Koreans shrugged, then duly recycled them as toilet paper, impaling piles of them on nails sticking out of the sides of privies.

At a long table in a Quonset hut on the 38th Parallel, government representatives from each side fought over the respective heights of decorative table flags the size of chopsticks. Each side needed to show the other how obdurate they were.

Syngman Rhee was set on continuing the war, unifying the country by force. He railed at his American protectors, who denied him the weapons he wanted. He considered a cease-fire a defeat, to walk away sniveling. Kim Il-sung, a hero of the anti-Japanese resistance, felt the same. So on faraway mountain peaks that were sacred to the Koreans but to the Americans were "Pork Chop Hill," "Bloody Ridge," or, most often, merely a number, these beautiful places with their painted shrines to the Mountain God and Goddess were blasted with munitions and stained with blood. Brother was still fighting against brother, hardly remembering why, mixing in the Chinese, the Americans, the Colombians, the Turks, the British, the Australians, the Ethiopians—sixteen Allied countries in all.

Sometimes, the Allies succeeded in routing a bunch of Chinese or North Koreans. But by the next day, partisans would crawl back into positions in bunker-like spaces dug deep into the mountains. In these human-size pockets protected by shelves of rock were tucked away things the Korean soldiers left for one another: dried skate jerky from the North; a jar of hot pepper paste from the South; a Buddhist amulet for safety; notes from home; reminiscences about a sweetheart;

persimmon candies. For, because of the kidnappings and the con-
scriptions and the haphazardness of the way the line had been drawn,
one never knew if a brother might be fighting a brother, finding him
again on the same side, as brothers, in nature's bunker, embraced in
the arms of, say, Holy Mother Peak.

Similarly, not even a mile away from Water Project Village sat a
long, curiously pristine strip south of the 38th Parallel that glittered
white from the local rocks. Because American bombs had destroyed
the village that had once been there, and because it was too remote
for the North Koreans to bother with, this strip, like the first seedlings
that sprout after the devastation of a forest fire, had become a place
where Koreans could be Koreans again, People of the Choson. The
White-Clad People, which was what foreigners who visited Korea
called Koreans. There was no North Korean or South Korean, Commie or Rightist. The snowy-white roads led to here.

It became known as the Exchange Zone Market. This odd place
of commerce and sociability had begun with a single seller, an aunty
selling canoe-shaped rubber gomushin, squatting right there on a
dusty path. She was joined the next day by a wizened old woman who
collected mountain herbs; she spread them out on a dusty tarp that
looked like US Army surplus. At first people passed by, looking pity-
ingly at the women, who must have been widows from the destroyed
village. Then a man set up a nice-looking shop on the other side of
the strip, with four posts and a tented canopy roof, to sell steel rice
bowls and repurposed artillery shells (he and the shoe aunty would
later marry).

The Exchange Zone Market became a real, living market when
the silkworm larvae seller set up a smoking wok—at last! There was
also a rice-syrup taffy man who enticed marketgoers by clacking his
rectangular scissors. A woman trekked in from the coastal plain with
dried shrimp and seaweed, as well as the tiny dart-shaped fish and

scarlet kohlrabi native to Kanghwa Island. Pyramids of dusky purple grapes with bitter skins but the sweetest insides appeared.

Popcorn Uncle brought a cylinder of thick steel with a raging fire behind, a cannon that went off with a *boom!* and spilled out white kernels of puffed feed corn, so chewy it squeaked in your teeth. The children who gathered around the cannon were all trained to duck and cover their ears, for they had heard the warnings from their mothers that a homeless child had once gone deaf from the noise.

A man in a dignified horsehair hat took up a beautiful brush and mulberry paper to write letters for the illiterate. Shoe Aunty, as she was now known, welcomed her compadres with a gap-toothed smile that she shockingly didn't cover with a hand. "I'm a war widow!" she cried. "I'll never lie with a man again, so what do I care?"

She, too, could not see the disappearing future that lay ahead of them. None of them could. They couldn't even guess. They were just here to celebrate the day.

Soon, there were also books, cosmetics, a black market stall with American Spam, antibiotics, and powdered milk, as well as uniforms from both sides. Anyone who sought news came here first. As had been done in Pusan, the pages of the newspaper were posted on telephone poles; people chattered among themselves as they gathered to read. The rice bowl man had a tiny radio that he played from his stall for anyone to listen. The Exchange Zone Market became a liminal space, swollen with refugees from both south and north trying to find a familiar face from home, to hear the curl of a regional dialect, waiting for word of when they could return home once again.

Here, young men in red-starred uniforms walked hand in hand with those in ROK uniforms. The young men carried rifles slung over their shoulders like journeymen's bags. No shots were ever fired.

Yungman's mother continued to look for ways to earn money. She often brought in silks that she had to wash carefully and press with various iron rods. When Yungman asked whose they were, she said they belonged to the consorts of the House of Rhim.

"Consorts?" said Yungman.

"Yes, sort of like kisaeng. Some consorts are for when a wife can't bear a son. Some patriarchs take more educated consorts for entertainment. Some, I guess, just want to feel young again."

"Is that what they mean by 'whore'?"

"Where did you hear that?" his mother said sharply. Then she softened and smiled sadly. "Actually, don't tell me. I don't want to know. You need to know that that is a word men made to talk badly about women. No woman is really a whore."

"What does it *mean*?"

"It's a loose term for women who make money from favors they get from men."

"Favors? Like men being nice to them?"

"Of a sort, yes. There aren't many ways for women to get things, especially for unmarried women. So some turn to the things they do have, like their prettiness. Every woman has a story, one that she doesn't show to the outside, so we can't judge because we don't know what's in her heart. Just know that that's not a nice word. Don't use it, ever. There are women who work not just for favors but openly for pay. I'd use the word 'harlot,' I guess."

"These are pretty," Yungman said, gesturing at the silks.

"They can't get any women in the village to launder or sew," she said. "They need to preserve their hands so they're nice and soft for the men. And that has been lucky for us; you and Yung-sik will need your school fees. We will need more money."

Yungman's mother augmented their food with a garden, even as the rocky soil and lack of water made it almost impossible—she could do the impossible. Once, she fermented fish tails with straw and created a cupful of compost that she grew a strawberry plant on. She watered it with gathered rainwater and her own urine until one day it yielded a single strawberry, which she vigilantly guarded from birds by putting a rattan basket over it. When it was ripe, fitting snugly in her palm, she carefully cut it into fourths, one fourth saved for Yungman's father, always—as if he might walk in the door at any minute. She also said her stomach hurt and gave her portion to Yung-sik; he and Yungman ate their portions slowly, savoring the warmth in them of the sun and their mother's hand.

One day, she took note of the figure-eight-shaped gourds that grew wild all around them, even amid the thatch of their roof. These kinds of gourds had bitter, seedy inner flesh that could make you sick if you ate too much at once. For the past few months she'd harvested one or two, scraped out the flesh, cleaned it of its numerous seeds and stringy bits, soaked it overnight in salt to draw out the moisture and some of the poison, and created a vegetable side dish. Their resourceful mother had created food without money, and they ate with relish, their smiles masking the acrid bitterness still left in the flesh. The shell of one of the gourds she dried to make a dipper for their rice.

With the gourds so abundant, she dried a heap of the flesh to make a kind of salted jerky, as well as a dozen dippers with the shells. She set up a small shop next to Shoe Aunty in the Exchange Zone Market and did a modest trade, especially among the wandering peddlers who wanted a dipper to sample the famous local water of their village. At night she mended and pressed delicately embroidered underclothes using wooden bats and heated iron rods while Yungman and Yung-sik cleaned endless gourds and put them by the stove to dry, with a separate basket for the golden strips of gourd meat. Next to them, on the low rice table that had become an altar of sorts, their father's silver chopsticks and spoon lay faithfully waiting for him to return.

\*     \*     \*

"Miss, pay me just one won more," said Yungman's mother in her sweet but shrewd market voice. "I'll give you two dippers."

A girl stood before her, in Western dress down to her snowy-white ankle socks and black patent-leather shoes. As Yungman approached, he could smell her soap, a fragrance of flowers and aloe. He was most familiar with the green alkali soap they used at the bathhouse, with its sharp scent of indefinable chemicals.

"Ajuhma, I need only one."

The girl didn't pay a second of attention to Yungman, who had walked up to stand beside his mother. Yungman's fists balled. She should at least call his mother "Aunt," not "Aunty," and why not "Madam," as she was clearly a proprietor? As the girl continued to argue, her scorching Seoul accent made Yungman feel like he had dirt on his face. How could this insolent and scornful young girl address his mother as if she were her servant, here to do her bidding?

He looked at her slantwise, so she wouldn't know he was looking. What was in his line of vision: a dark skirt that went past the knees, a flash of muscled calf.

"A pretty girl like you must have lots of boyfriends," his mother gently teased, in an effort to cajole out another won.

"I'm only in middle school."

"In the Choson dynasty, girls were married off at nine, ten."

"This isn't the Choson dynasty."

It was an impertinent remark, in the voice of a person impatient to make her own destiny. A person who threw inconvenient others away. She handed Yungman's mother a single won.

"Goodbye, then, Aunty." Nodding to the neat pile of dried gourds, she acknowledged, "You worked hard." Not even a glance Yungman's way as she left. Her thick hair was shorn surprisingly high in the back, exposing a sliver of nape. Yungman didn't know it yet, but that was the regulation haircut for girls at schools in Seoul.

"Ungh. Come back again." Yungman's mother waved her off.

"Aigu, those yangban." She sighed. She helped Yungman take off his clanky yoke of pots and pans and handed him a jumok-bap, in the center of which, he noted with delight, she'd pressed a strip of seaweed. It reminded him of how in Pusan they often didn't have salt for seasoning, so she would slip her hands into a bucket of seawater before she molded the balls, imparting an essence of salt and sea in the grains that made it, even though it wasn't always rice, indescribably delicious.

Now, in the mountains again, Yungman missed the East Sea, missed its tastes. It was amazing to him the things you could find yourself yearning for, even things that reminded you of a miserable time.

"That girl," his mother went on, nudging her chin in the direction she had taken. "All that haggling—for a single dipper! She just wanted it to hang it on a wall."

"On a wall?" said Yungman, confused. "As they do at the well?" At their village's well, a tin cup hung by a wire, welcoming all.

"As decoration, it seems. Those yangban!"

"But she wanted it," interjected Yung-sik, uncurling his neck and detaching his shape from the shade. He had been napping, fitting his limbs into the varied bits of shade from a single scraggly gingko tree. "I bet she would have paid more."

"My son knows the yangban mind," she teased.

"I think I do," said Yung-sik. "And after all, Halaboji was a yangban. He wore the tall hat."

"That's true," their mother agreed, sounding wistful.

Yungman thought of how she had kept one of Halaboji's white hanbok collars, clean and yet slightly sour with his saliva; after the accident he'd had trouble controlling his drool. She kept the collar on top of a pile of scraps. Yungman noticed that she never used it but would touch it when she reached for a different piece of fabric.

Yungman woke up in the night with indigestion. He'd eaten too much gourd flesh, and his belly was swollen. He shifted, contemplating whether he should get up and go to the outhouse to wait out the inevitable gastric explosion.

His mother's eyes were open. Staring.

"Mother, are you all right?" She was gazing at the dippers drying by the stove. "My son," she said. "We have to sell so many of these. I feel terrible that you and your brother have to work day and night."

Yungman didn't know what to say. His mother was basically a widow, someone people should look kindly upon, but the villagers seemed loath to admit she existed, afraid to help. Guilt by association was now a real legal term; their family, he understood, was Red by association. But Yungman's father didn't support the North Korean or Russian regimes—or the Americans. He only wanted land returned to the farmers and to help them to grow more crops. The villagers must know that, as his family had lived in the village for generations.

The rejection from the villagers made Yungman angry. His father had always helped and never harmed. He was always rushing to set the rice table before his mother stooped to it. He cleaned and seasoned the vegetables, even doing the nitpicky work of pinching off the tails from soybean sprouts, something only women did.

On Arbor Day, he always led a phalanx of men, women, and children into the mountains to replant hundreds of trees. Yungman was so young then that he had never gotten to go on the daylong journey.

Their father packed a box full of soil and turned a corner of the house into a germination station for his thremmatology crossbreeding experiments. He had dreams of taking indigenous Korean rice, whose grains were tiny as sand, and crossing it with the familiar Japonica rice, whose grains were fat and easy to polish but bland, to make a grain sturdy enough for export, with enough of a roundish size for chewing—but also, more important, drought-resistant enough that it could even grow in their nearly treeless valley, a dearth that had grown worse with the relentless Allied bombing in the years he'd been gone.

Kwak Gwan-su was someone people respectfully called "teacher," because even though he was not credentialed, he helped the other farmers in the village diagnose insect or fungal problems with their crops. In thanks, he was almost always sent home with a bag of grain or sweet potatoes as a gift. Yungman, in his short life with his father, had never remembered being hungry, because there was always something growing or something traded for his father's knowledge and care.

Now, their mother hiked deep into the mountains to look for pine mushrooms or codonopsis roots, but those forays yielded little more than a handful or two of food. Their favorite was springtime, when many of the edible flowers, like the abundant azalea, were in bloom. But they could have starved behind their walls and no one would have looked in on them. Only Father Andrea stopped by, bringing a rice donation when he could. Yungman often saw him early in the mornings, on the rickety bicycle that he was immensely proud of, pedaling on the dirt path to the Maryknoll Sisters.

If not for the rice from Father Andrea and the leavings the other vendors in the market slipped them—fish tails, vegetable peels, and seeds—they indeed would be starving, maybe forced to eat the insides of gourds until their bellies swelled up and they died. Yungman leaned over to pull the bedcovers up to his mother's shoulders.

"I'll work harder," he whispered over Yung-sik's snores. The gut pains became an alarm. There was a ripping sound as he frantically freed his legs and jammed his feet into his shoes in the scramble to the outhouse. After he returned, he realized his toe had gotten caught in a hole in the blanket cover and ripped it cleanly to the end.

Fabrics in their house wore out quickly because their mother kept them spotless: the bedclothes, the hanbok, Halaboji's white collars. Once a week, Yungman and Yung-sik hauled extra water. She beat out all the dirt with sticks, gave the fabric a quick, spare rinse, and whitened it with the bleaching power of the sun. The bedcovers then had to be resewn by hand with a thick needle. The fabrics thinned more each time.

"Remove it; it's ruined beyond repair." She wasn't angry, just tired. Yungman peeled the cover off gently to not disturb Yung-sik.

He heard their mother rustling about, snipping into the night, and the *whoosh-pump* of the pedal on the sewing machine, the oiled whirr of its motor.

In the morning, the boys gazed in amazement at how, with the cover and silk scraps, she'd turned out a slew of tiny stuffed ornaments—canoe-shaped shoes, chili peppers, the sign of the dao. These she attached with hemp string to the holes in the handles of the dippers where she normally attached knotted loops of hemp to hang them from an A-frame backpack or a belt to keep them handy for drinking water or rice wine. She knotted the string in the elaborate shape of a flower. There are certain knots Koreans believe bring good fortune, and as a girl, she had made such decorations to bedeck her Lunar New Year's hanbok, freshly made for her by her father the tailor.

At the market, Shoe Aunty admired the ornaments. "Wha!" She moved her army of canoe-shaped shoes over so Yungman's mother could set up Boon-Yi's Lucky Gourd Dippers, announced with a sign that Yungman had written in charcoal on a wooden plank in the elegant handwriting that had even been praised by the teachers at the outdoor school in Pusan. Yung-sik made a wire stand with parts scavenged from Yungman's junk to attractively hang her wares.

Soon, people in the market chattered about the "lucky" gourd dippers. One rich woman, who'd come to the market from Songdo to find some special herbs to help her conceive, stopped at his mother's stall. She had noticed the dipper with a chili pepper: dried chilies were strung outside a house to announce that a son had been born. Half jokingly, Yungman's mother claimed the gourd dipper ornament represented luck and fertility, and so the woman bought it, eschewing the herbs. Not a month later, the woman became pregnant.

Crowds of infertile women who used to climb mountains to get to a Buddhist temple to pay monks to pray for their fertility went instead, to the chagrin of the monks, to find the Lucky Gourd Dipper seller at the market.

Yungman's mother now made as much money in an hour as she used to make in a day. To Yungman and Yung-sik's relief, a single decorative gourd could buy heaps of shepherd's purse, watercress, chrysanthemum, young garlic, and other tasty greens for side dishes, an occasional meaty oxtail for soup.

Lee, the dignified gentleman who wrote letters in the market, stopped to read the notice on one of the poles. "Oh no!" he cried. "The Yankees are coming!" People clustered around him. What did this mean?

"It says here they plan to build an air base a few kilometers from here."

"An air base!" exclaimed the brass seller. His new stall, everyone noticed, was set up next to Shoe Aunty's. He'd even considerately extended his tent so it provided shade for her and Boon-Yi's Lucky Gourd Dippers. "With all these mountains? How can they fly?"

"The Yankees' flying machines are marvelous," Lee said thoughtfully. "I was out walking on the path going to visit my son in the administrative office, and when I was on that part of the path that's out in the open a plane swooped down on me. I swear it came so close I could see the pupils in the pilot's eyes."

"Maybe he thought you were a North Korean infiltrator," the brass seller joked.

"Even he could see from my clothes that I was just an old man walking to town," Lee said. "But what will happen when there are many Yankees here?"

"Will they rape?" asked Shoe Aunty. She was from farther north: "When the Russians came in, they were complete barbarians. They didn't leave old grannies or young girls or the sick and the lame alone."

Yungman could feel his mother cringing near him.

"I don't think the American and British Yankees are so much like that," said Lee, as he carefully addressed an envelope for a customer. "Or not as *much* like that anymore. They've been at war long enough that the Western Princess corps have had time to assemble. They go where the soldiers go; it's their patriotic duty to keep the big-noses happy and fighting. And then also they won't bother the village women. But honestly, if I had a young daughter, I might blacken her teeth with some charcoal, as I've heard the appetites of some of the blackie soldiers can be insatiable."

"What's a Western Princess?" Yungman asked his mother. "What's a blackie?" She shook her head. "Sounds exotic," was her nonanswer.


Near the village of Chilpal, the Seven Arms of Mother Mountain, giant clanking earthmovers flattened the ground for a runway. The Americans hired scores of hardworking Koreans to haul away rocks by hand. It was monsoon season, the one chance for the rice paddy to soak up the rain, but it fouled the construction. The hired Koreans had to work around the clock to create a concrete runway, a command center, and a city. Barbed wire was unfurled from a giant spool to create a fence, which heedlessly enclosed part of their hamlet. The villagers gasped as their 1,500-year-old gingko tree, carefully tended throughout the generations by a single family and their descendants, was casually chopped down for the eighteenth hole of a golf course.

Soon, the half-ton trucks and personnel carriers brought hundreds of soldiers. Outside the base's rear gates, another small city began to form — not as nice, even more temporary, with shacks reminiscent of those they'd lived in in Pusan, made out of whatever items were at hand. This time their construction was commandeered by youngish women decked out in tropical-bird colors. They had cash and goods, and soon assembled a number of Korean men to help construct their dwellings and something called the Club.

Yungman finally understood what a harlot was.

Unlike the kisaeng at the wine house or the consorts in the village, these harlots laughed without covering their mouths, swore like men, and somehow made their hair into frizzy bushes, uncontained in a chignon or unmarried woman's braid. These harlots also preferred Western things, including high-heeled shoes, makeup, and pama — what made their hair so bushy. The market expanded to suit all their needs and those of the soldiers. The black-market stall began to carry the American things the men missed from back home, as well as lipsticks and other trinkets they could give their Western Princesses, as the other Koreans called, sometimes derisively, these women.

An art teacher set up a stall where a GI could have a portrait painted on a silk scarf from a photo of his inevitably smiling American sweetheart to send back home; the GI often grinningly watched the painting process with a brassy harlot on his arm. The rice bowl seller enticed the GI trade by selling brass bowls and vases made of old artillery shells etched with beautiful designs — cranes, dragons, peonies. He enlisted the sign painter to make a giant billboard on a piece of scrap lumber:

- WASHINGTON -
Welcome US Army
Here ARE Better Best Souve Venirs for your
DAD MAM SISTER SWEET HOT

American soldiers started visiting the Exchange Zone Market not just to shop but also for entertainment: to gaze in puzzlement at the sight of Korean soldiers walking arm in arm like couples on a date, giggling like the schoolboys many of them were. The Americans tried to haggle, to get them to sell for almost nothing or accept worthless Japanese scrip, then shouted in frustration because "No one in this got-tam place speaks eny English!" Yungman often whispered "got-tam" to himself, burning to understand the meaning, the tantalizing sounds of English.

One day, Yungman and Yung-sik had been hounding the taffy seller, trying to get him to accept a battered pot in exchange for a piece of taffy, when they heard a familiar rumble. They began to run toward the road. It wasn't a real road but one the Americans had established by running the earthmovers through, heedless that it bulldozed into the center of the Exchange Zone Market. The sellers had to take it upon themselves not to set up shop; everyone knew not to take a nap in the space or be run over.

Right now, a half-ton army truck was bearing down on them, its open back full of men in their moss-colored uniforms. They were laughing and hooting, mouths wide open as Westerners tended to do. The truck stopped in the middle of the crowded market, and then children converged on it like iron filings to a magnet, yelling, "Cho-co-lah! Cho-co-lah!" American GIs in the cargo area would often throw them chocolate and things from their meals if they were amused enough. Jae-hak, the illiterate farmboy who always had a belly distended by worms, yelled, "Yankee! Yankee!" and did a kind of shuffling two-step. One of the men laughed and tossed him a mud-colored rectangle:

HERSHEY'S
*Tropical*
CHOCOLATE

Yungman hadn't been lucky enough yet to get any chocolate and existed only on Jae-hak's descriptions of it as ambrosia. *Hiroshi's* sounded Japanese, but he knew it wasn't. In fact, during the Japanese colonial period, while so few Koreans even enjoyed the taste of rice, it was the richest chinilpa who were the first to taste actual sugar, the kind that this chocolate was made from; the taffy Yungman and Yung-sik were clamoring for was made of brown rice and sorghum syrup, which was sweet to them compared to other Korean foods.

The GIs were tossing cans of C-rations into the street—even better. The men laughed as they watched the street urchins and beggar kids swarm first, viciously fighting one another. Yungman recalled how lucky he'd been that time when he found the old oil can in the alley in Pusan; they could finally cook rice. Here he was, a future college student, but he bit and scratched and received his own black eye fighting with another boy for it, so they could have warm rice and barley that night. Their mother made Yungman bring a bowl to Bear Uncle, who in turn had given him an egg to roll on his black eye.

Yungman and Yung-sik pushed into the crowd with fortified vigor. The cans reliably brought good prices at the Exchange Zone Market because they contained cigarettes, which were better than money, which was always losing its value.

Yungman was so focused on fending off the other grubby hands that he did not see a large, hairy, freckled one reaching to grab his hanbok's collar, pulling him into the air.

"Kid," the man said, dangling him like a fish. His face was dotted as if splashed with paint, his hair an unearthly color, almost the orange of a Cheju Island tangerine. Yungman was so terrified he almost shat his white farmers' pants. "Today is your got-tam lucky day."

This is how Yungman became a houseboy at Chilpal Air Base, its location chosen solely because the name was easy to pronounce in English. When the freckled man "gave" him to Bunk Sixteen, a group of a dozen toothy, boisterous men who called him over with an upward sweep of their palms—the same way you call a dog—Yungman feared that he'd become a slave and immediately began looking for ways to escape.

He learned, however, that "houseboy" was a coveted job. Another Korean boy, who told Yungman to call him Tadpole, showed him the ropes. Today was shower day. The GIs lined up and walked through a series of outdoor tents: disrobe, soap up, wash, rinse, dry. However, Tadpole explained, unguarded clothes were known to disappear by the time the wearer came back to retrieve them. The houseboys would carry them and have them waiting when their GIs stepped out.

Yungman was terrified and repulsed by his GI, Red, and his hairy naked body, including the enormous bearded sac that lay under his "pepper." But he remained brave and did his best to act cool, as if he saw a man whose skin had more spots than the spotted lily every day. The boys would also bring the men's dirty socks to the aunties, because otherwise they would rarely be laundered. The aunties beat the dirt out at the stream and ironed them by smoothing them with wooden bats. Sometimes the boys would regale them with tales of the strange things these men did, like not washing their feet before bed, to try to make the aunties laugh and see if they'd uncover their mouths with their arms full of laundry.

Jae-hak liked to compare them unfavorably to barnyard animals. "Our ox is sweet-smelling next to these chaps!" He had a fascination with the Americans and hung around the periphery of the base as much as possible. He wasn't a houseboy—mother dead since he was two, he'd had to drop out of elementary school to tend to his crippled father, blinded and de-limbed by a mine that had been planted in his field, along with corn—but he never dwelled on hardship, the impossible task of one little boy continuing to farm with only the occasional help of a badly concussed uncle. Jae-hak only liked to laugh and make others laugh. Yungman supposed that if he'd gone on in school, he would have been the class clown. "Can't they smell themselves through those big noses? *Pi-yoo!*"

Yungman got along well with the other houseboys—Tadpole, Sparrow, Rotten Melon, and the Professor—who formed a merry band. Tadpole, their leader, was the height of a child but was actually in his twenties. He handed out the nicknames as if he were a family patriarch. Yungman, for no particular reason, he nicknamed Hong Kil-dong, aka Robin Hood. The GIs—Red the freckle man, Ray, Hal, and Adam—called them all "Charlie."

It took Yungman time to acclimate to their varied accents; only the Professor was from Gold Sea County. They were also all orphans: the Professor's entire Chestnut Village family was killed in an Allied bombing. Rotten Melon and the Professor had escaped from an orphanage farther south, where the director barely fed them, beat them when they tried to escape, and basically used them as a way to get Western humanitarian aid that he would pocket for his own family.

Tadpole had slick black hair and tadpole-shaped eyes that glittered with a kind of unearthly energy. He seemed to never need sleep, and even though he was one of the smaller of them, he was by far the strongest and hardiest. He told Yungman he came from a small northern village on the Taedong River near Namp'o on the coast. During that same winter retreat in 1950, some American soldiers ordered the villagers to cross the freezing-cold Taedong to escape the oncoming Communists. The two dozen or so villagers—old ladies, children, a few men heavily laden with burdens—had huddled on the banks, unsure of what to do. On the other side, there were more Allied soldiers standing with machine guns and artillery pointed at them.

"They are there to protect you, so you have to cross now. Hurry, because the Chinese are coming!"

The soldiers took out their guns and pointed them. "If you don't, we'll have to assume you are Communist infiltrators." Everyone eventually began to wade into the icy river, even the grannies. Tadpole had had a cooking pot strapped to his back, and his younger brother clung to it, head above water. A few people began to shout and cry as they were carried off their feet by the current. Inexplicably, the soldiers on the opposite shore opened fire. The refugees all died, except for Tadpole. His little brother, shot in the head, covered them both in his warm, comforting blood. Thanks to an air bubble trapped in the pot, Tadpole, still holding the small hands of his brother turtled atop him, floated like a corpse past the soldiers downstream for miles until he hit a sandbar. His brother had lost so much blood that he was pale, like an eel, and beautiful. Tadpole took some hemp cloth from his bundle, closed his brown eyes, place a jeon coin over each, and covered his tender face before continuing to trudge on south.

"You're not mad at the Yankees?" Yungman asked his new friends. How could they so easily work for the people who may have killed their families? Tadpole shrugged. "My mother made us flee because of what she heard the Commies did to people, and also that I might be snatched into their army. Who knows who was better? And after I got out of the river, it was a Yankee driving one of those big trucks who saw me and opened the door. I had nothing to lose by then, so I jumped in, and here I am."

"Lucky you're a midget," said Rotten Melon. Tadpole looked at him as if amiably absorbing the humor, then struck him, fist in face.

"Tadpole has a fiery temper; be forewarned," said the Professor, who, like Yungman, was still attending school. The two of them sometimes took breaks together. "But it's a righteous fire. He doesn't do it rashly or in the heat of passion."

The other houseboys slept on the floor between the bunks, except for the Professor. He came to the base only when he didn't have to go to school. A friendly teacher at his school left his classroom unlocked and let him sleep there.

"Our orphanage was called Heavenly Angels Orphanage, and it was absolute hell," said Rotten Melon. "One day, the director brought in these white people looking for a son to adopt. The director showed off the Professor, because he's so light-skinned, and told them he was age seven, not twelve—and those big noses didn't know any better. That's when we decided to escape for real. The only thing worse than being a servant in Korea would be being a houseboy in America."

Rotten Melon showed Yungman a burn on his arm, puckered like a kiss. "That's from the first time I tried to run away. The director said he'd break my legs, but instead he just burned me. I think he was hoping to sell all of us if he could find enough Westerners, maybe when the war was over. Apparently, lots of Western women have trouble getting pregnant, and they don't have concubines in the West, so they adopt. Ha, the joke was on him when I took the Professor with me the second time."

Yungman soon caught the notice of the GIs, because, as they said, "That one seems intelligent, at least." The Professor, of course, was smart, but the GIs were judging only by their spoken English. Yungman had already studied it at the fancy Eagle High School for almost two years in Pusan. When a job selling doughnuts opened up at the base's commissary, Yungman volunteered. He kept his receipts nice and neat, his name—YUNGMAN KWAK—spelled out in perfect English letters on top. He spoke English every day.

Yungman studied extra in the mornings. Evenings, he spoke—*Hello, how are you?*—to his mother and Yung-sik, even though they didn't know what he was saying and sometimes laughed at the weird sounds coming out of his mouth, especially when he imitated the way Red spoke. "Hoo-ahhhh!" "Got-tam it!" And perhaps his favorite, because it sounded almost exactly like "let's go home," jip ae carl rlae—" Yippe-cay-yay!" He was so happy to find a phrase that easy to remember.

In another month, he'd outpaced the Professor by a safe margin. In fact, Yungman spoke English better even than the handful of KATUSA—Korean Augmentation to the United States Army—soldiers attached to the regiment, whose job it was to be fluent in English. Yungman shamelessly bugged the GIs for reading material, and they gave him *TIME* and *Life*, the Sears catalog. It made him dizzy to picture all the American *things* there were to buy, things to have in your house, like clothes that you didn't make yourself.

One GI had a Bible that he loaned to Yungman. Yungman carried it around everywhere and tried to decipher words. He sensed that knowing English was going to get him somewhere. Most of the Korean workers on the base struggled to learn some English but often became hopelessly confused. English was so strange the way the subject, not the action of the verb, came first. How "he," "she," "I," and "they" were so necessary, while in Korean you knew who was speaking or being spoken of just from the verb. Americans also habitually said "I" a lot, which seemed very conceited. Most GIs carefully kept themselves from all things Korean, as if to remain uncontaminated. They communicated through signs and silly words—"Chop-chop!"—and never bothered to learn intelligible Korean more than being able to say "How much?" They didn't bother with Korean names, and Tadpole had asked Yungman if "Hae-yi Char-Rhee" was a common Yankee name.

Another regular job for the houseboys was to relay messages to the harlots who lived in the hastily constructed shack city just outside the base. The shacks were tin-roofed and made out of wooden pallets strung together with wire, although a few flashier ones had been built from flattened C-ration cans that shined a dull gold when the sun hit them. When new GIs invariably came asking for "Sek-shi? Sek-shi?" the boys tried not to giggle, because it meant "new bride," a strange, perverted nickname for the harlots. Yungman did not understand until many years later, when his brain bent to let other meanings in, that these men were asking for "sexy."

Red enthusiastically availed himself of the harlots, but didn't beat them up like some of the GIs did. The worst ones wheedled discounts by telling the harlots they were going to bring them back to America. Many of the harlots then allowed themselves to become pregnant. As a joke, the GIs would ask their women to give the babies "American" names, like Vagina, in preparation for their trip to America. Then, when they were abandoned, the next thing you knew, the women would be showing off their Vagina to the newest crop of incomings.

Yungman couldn't help being fascinated with Americans. Everything they did was the opposite of what Koreans did—they wore their shoes inside; they sat in chairs (their Western toilets meant their ongdongis touched a dirty seat every time they shat!). They were bigger than Koreans, more clumsy, hairy, and had huge, strong teeth. Their milk wasn't wet but dry. They ate sweets all the time, even at breakfast. Also, the most beautiful colors Yungman had seen in his young life were on Buddhist texts, laboriously painted with gorgeously vivid colors, especially of the Blue Medicine Buddha. But American magazines surpassed that. No wonder they had names like *Life*. The colors—red, green, fuchsia, the blue of the skies—were unfathomable. And yet they threw these magazines out with little thought, and laughed when he begged them for them.

What if their ways *were* better? Lieutenant Jarvis, the soldiers' commander, noticed Yungman with the Bible one day and seemed astonished. "Red, is that Chinky Charlie reading the Bible?"

Yungman didn't wait. He stood up and spouted out the only verse he had memorized, imbuing it with all the conviction he had: "For God so lubbed de earth he gave his onlrlee Son, dad whosoeber believe in Him shourlrd not perlrish, but hab-u eberlrrlasting rlie-pu . . ."

"Well, I'll be darned," the lieutenant said, and he invited Yungman to attend church services on the base with the Americans. Yungman thus visited the bathhouse every Saturday night, scrubbed himself as pale as he could with pumice, abstained from kimchi, and put on his best hanbok in the morning. In church, he sang with gusto, because the music itself was beautiful.

Yungman still woke up nightly with stomach pain. He hadn't had to eat much gourd meat lately—they had even started giving their gourd leavings to the neighbor who had a chicken, and in return their mother got to make his favorite dish, custard eggs, from time to time. But Yungman felt so terrible, he hadn't eaten the last time they had custard eggs. And that night, the pain was so bad that he started to scream. His mother and Yung-sik dragged him to Hwang the acupuncturist, the closest thing the village had, besides the shaman, to a doctor. Hwang was well liked but incompetent. If his famous fertility treatments worked, women wouldn't need to buy so many Lucky Gourds.

Dr. Hwang felt his pulse and measured his fever with the back of his hand. Without warning, he pushed Yungman's hanbok blouse up and stabbed a needle right into his abdomen. Yungman screamed. There was a burning. Then a relief so instantaneous that Yungman passed out.

At home, his mother boiled the Chinese herbs Hwang had prescribed until the concoction was black and thick as sorghum syrup. Hwang also told Yungman's mother to wrap him in blankets and put him by the stove under the Chinese medicine principle of fire fighting fire. Yungman sweated under the blanket. He was awake now, and reached for the steaming cup only to pass out again. His fever still raged.

Yungman's mother knew she had to do something else. She had Yung-sik fetch Father Andrea. He helped her turn a blanket into a kind of stretcher that the three of them, gripping the corners, used to carry the groaning Yungman all the way to the entrance of the base.

The sentries immediately leaped up and pointed their guns at them.

The village had endured too many incidents of Allied troops shooting civilians "just to be safe." Yungman's mother and Father Andrea involuntarily cringed but didn't let go. If they didn't get Yungman help, they sensed, he would die for sure. Only Father Andrea had the barest amount of English from all his time with the Maryknoll Sisters.

"Sick, sick," he said, pointing to Yungman. A KATUSA was summoned. He shouted at them to go away.

"He's sick," pleaded Yungman's mother. "He needs a hospital."

"You must know they won't treat Koreans here, ma'am," the KATUSA barked while eyeing the Americans by his side, who had told him to get rid of the unwanted "Charlies"—or they would. He kept his expression fierce as he said, in a low voice, "Auntie, ma'am—please. I beg you. Go away. I could lose my job, and it isn't safe for you."

"Not . . . no . . . go away!"

Father Andrea had learned about nonviolent protests from the Sisters. He gently propped Yungman up against his mother and brother and then sat down cross-legged in the middle of the road, right in the dust, his cassock blooming as he sat.

Yungman, of course, did not remember any of this.

"There was a huge supply truck rumbling right down the road," his brother told him later, with relish. "Father Andrea refused to move unless you were let onto the base. Of course, it became a ridiculous scene with the yelling and the threats. I worried they would eventually just run him over. But the Korean cook who came out to see what was the matter knew who you were and ran and told your GIs."

Yungman always wondered: Was it Red, Ray, Hal, or Adam who got him into the base hospital? They all came to visit him, and no one took the credit—they seemed more preoccupied with how he was. He awoke from his surgery barely even feeling the post-op pain because it felt so good to be freed from the appendix pain. Apparently, it hadn't quite burst yet. "I'm not sure Koreans feel pain the same way we do," he heard a doctor say to a nurse as they fitted a mask with a foul-smelling gas inside it over his face. "They're an emotionless people; they work like machines."

"Charlie, you would have died then, from silly village superstitions that pass as medicine."

Yungman was astonished to see Lieutenant Jarvis visiting him at the base hospital, and he said so. The Lieutenant laughed.

"I'm a doctor," he said. "You didn't know? They made me a lieutenant so I would have some authority over the troops. I'm a doctor-scientist studying the effects of frostbite on the troops."

Suddenly inspired, Yungman told Jarvis in his improving English that he hoped to be a doctor someday as well. Jarvis chuckled. "Well, I never! Surprises every day here." He left the room, then returned. He showed Yungman a specimen jar with a worm in it: his appendix. Something from his body that had turned pathological was removed, safely, and would be stuck in this jar forever, where it could never hurt him again. Someone went in and took this *out of his body*—his body that was more than just a bag of skin. Things could be done if you had a great skill. Yungman gazed in awe. "I like to do dis," he said.

"Study hard, then," Jarvis said. He left behind a thick book with tiny print, the pages so thin you could see through them like onion-skin. Yungman would later learn that this book was a kind of bible, holding thousands of diseases and their Western cures.

**Bacillary dysentery**

Sulfuanidine (Rx 44) is of some value in reducing the bacterial content. Chloromycetin (Rx 36) also has shown promise in treatment. Paregoric (Rx 128) may be necessary to allay restlessness.

Streptomycin orally (Rx 33) either alone or combined with parenteral administration (Rx 32) may be superior when sulfonamides are ineffective.

The *Merck Manual*. Yungman made sure to memorize huge swaths of it, starting with A for Allergy, mumbling it to himself in the bunkhouse, reciting it like a schoolchild reciting a poem whenever Jarvis was around. *Hematocrit. Hematoma.* The GIs were amazed at him—they didn't know what he was talking about, and he was speaking English!

Back at home, Yungman's mother held up a navy schoolboy's jacket. It was splendid.

"The hat I cannot make," she said. "You will have to buy one."

"I don't understand, Mother," Yungman said.

"It's a school uniform, dummy!" Yung-sik griped.

Taking the garment in his hands, Yungman looked closely and saw that she had refashioned one of his father's jackets. Then, with a wool material she must have purchased at the Exchange Zone Market, she'd made a pair of trousers with a crisp knife-edge crease up the middle of each leg.

"You'll need a proper uniform for high school."

"There's only one uniform," Yung-sik pointed out. "Are we to share?"

"It was your father's dream that his sons should go to Seoul National University. To do that, one must attend high school first."

Because she loved Yung-sik, she refrained from pointing out that his mind was quick, yet on more days than not, he returned from school with swollen palms for his dreaminess and subpar work. That he could help her at the Exchange Zone Market by doing sums in his head and yet not do well on a test. He was as smart as Yungman, but restless and easily bored.

"If you can pass the entrance exam, I will make you a uniform as well." Her fingertips, so often pricked by the long needles she used to sew the bedcovers shut, had become so callused that she didn't need a thimble to push the head of a needle through the layers of fabric. "At least one of you needs to go," she said. "No matter which one. Someone needs to do what your father was not able to."

Both boys knew better than to ever summon their father's ghost. Almost every night they could hear their mother, the one who, in Pusan, had found a way to make a house out of scrap wood and fabric, a cooking stove out of an old American can and some bricks, who shepherded them from their home to safety and back, whom Bear Uncle had fallen a little in love with, who stayed strong during the day, weeping in the outhouse at night. She probably didn't realize how the high notes of her cries escaped. Yung-sik apologized for his impertinence. He leaped up and said he would go find some acorns; he was sure there were a few scrub oaks left. Enough that their mother could make the jellied acorn banchan she loved. He disappeared and wouldn't come back for hours, until he'd found a few and was red with sunburn.

Yungman stared at the jacket with its bright brass buttons and the trousers with a smart crease up the center. He couldn't believe how beautifully his mother had reproduced an Eagle High School uniform. It fit perfectly. The slight scent of his father—of tobacco from his pipe, pine, and clean sweat—faint but distinctive, almost overwhelmed him. He struggled not to let it show.

"Mother, you should go live in Paris," he said instead. "Become the head designer of a big fashion house."

"In another life, another history, perhaps." She smiled. Her one indulgence for herself was her obsession with the French, the wistfulness she allowed herself when staring at the Pierre Bonnard print.

"I will study hard, Mother. I will also earn enough for my cap."

"Your job is to study," she said. "I will take care of you. Don't forget that you come from the village that sold its water so its children could go to school. The water will pay for Seoul. Make your father proud."


SPRING 1953

The fighting became even more sporadic. The air force packed up and the soldiers were gone like ghosts; the houseboys left as well. On his way out, Lieutenant Jarvis gave Yungman a book, *The Five Chinese Brothers*, which was a book for little children that Yungman could easily read, but he treasured it nonetheless. Also, Lieutenant Jarvis wrote his address inside the book. A magical place: Bovey, Minnesota, USA. Jarvis had once remarked to Yungman that Bovey, Minnesota, was where the picture *Grace* was painted. In fact, the town's water tower was painted with "Home of the Picture GRACE," something you could see from miles away. And seeing that picture *Grace* all over Korea made him feel that God was telling him he had been doing the right thing, coming to Korea.

"The devil has many minions in this Gospel-deprived place, including shamans, Buddhism, Catholics. Even the language, which I believe the devil himself made so hard to learn precisely in order to keep the light of the Gospel from entering, keeping your people in darkness." He left Yungman a Bible as well.

*　　*　　*

In Water Project Village, the farmers harvested what spring barley remained, and planted their rice. Water bottling resumed. The aunties gossiped by the well about how a few more students, including one of the daughters of the House of Rhim, had moved to Seoul to attend prestigious schools. The shaman and Father Andrea tossed poisonous looks at each other when they passed, no longer united against the wartime Presbyterian missionaries who had condemned both shamanism and Catholicism as pagan religions that needed to be banned. When the coast seemed certainly clear, a few young men who'd been hidden by their mothers to keep from being snatched by the Korean People's Army emerged, pale as moths, into the light once more. One could almost forget the war was still going on.

At the market, the newspapers pasted on the poles had generals and presidents talking about "armistice." A cease-fire. That would be the end of the war, the people said. It was still easy to believe they could have a future.

Two events occurring side by side locked in that good fortune: Stalin died, and a new American president was installed. Eisenhower was a military man who, as military men do, truly understood the costs of war. By March it sounded like the fighting would indeed cease, and they could go back to being Koreans again. Perhaps the whole country could once again be like the Exchange Zone Market once the Americans left.

Only a few kilometers to the east, industrious Koreans constructed a wood-framed truce building in forty-eight hours, in the small hut village of Panmunjom, now known as the Joint Security Area.

On July 27, when the Armistice was declared—"To ensure a complete cessation of hostilities and of all acts of armed force in Korea"—a great shout of joy went up around Water Project Village. The villagers thought that meant peace.

The previous day, seventeen copies of the precious book of rules were signed into history—but instead of by South Korea's president, Syngman Rhee, it was done by the United States military. Rhee, like MacArthur, felt "In war, there is no substitute for victory." But Megadoo was an old, irrelevant soldier; worse than dying, he would just fade away. Rhee would still have all of South Korea as his fiefdom. The Americans were already focusing on Vietnam, eager to try their new expertise with napalm there. *This* time they would win through aerial firepower.

As the Korean proverb went, "When the whales fight, the shrimp get hurt." Kim Il-sung, also not at the official signing, was "given" his wreck of a country back. The global Cold War moved on, leaving behind both Korean leaders to belatedly realize their figurehead status.

At the Exchange Zone Market, a different kind of American soldier suddenly appeared. Unlike the soldiers from the Seven Arms of Mother Mountain base, who dropped in to stroll and shop, these soldiers were patrolling, their mouths set, guns ready. The Korean soldiers, North-South, South-North, stopped holding hands. Soon, no more uniforms of the NKPA were seen, even in the black marketer's tent.

The people walked more warily amid this new military show, but reminded themselves that Water Project Village sat a good hundred kilometers below the 38th Parallel. Why, the famous bay where MacArthur made his Inchon landing was within their sights. Their accents were those of good, midpeninsula people; they served their cold noodles with iced broth and not smeared with fiery pepper paste and topped with skate the way they famously did in Pyongyang. If anything, the people of this region had much more in common with the southern hicks of Cholla Nam-do (but none of their hick tolerance for Communist ideas!).

One day, the ROK and the US military pounded signs onto posts all around the Exchange Zone Market warning that the market was no longer, and this was now the site of something called

## MILITARY DEMARCATION LINE

ROK soldiers with bullhorns read from scripts:

"There will be no occupancy two kilometers to the north and two kilometers south of this line."

They were going to erect a giant fence around the periphery and seed the area with mines. It would be a no-man's-land.

As Koreans' futures disappeared like road under an M24 tank's treads, nature saw its chance. Animals from all over the world would migrate here—otters, pheasants, endangered cranes, bears, rare tigers, goral—knowing, somehow, they would be safe from the violence of man. The old rice paddies would turn into wetlands noisy with water-birds, musk deer delicately picking their way among wild blooming lotuses, looking like something out of an ancient Buddhist painting. On the northern coast, beyond the barbed wire and the machine guns trained on the rocky beaches, the sea roses would proliferate their message of love. It would once again be a place of peace, if only because there were no humans here.

In the meantime, planes with American markings were flying low again. Father Andrea returned wild-eyed from one of his rice runs. He said he had been cycling back, the bag of rice strapped to the rack of his bike, enjoying the wind blowing him along as he pedaled along the road from the Maryknoll Sisters'. Now he stood before the shocked villagers, face blackened with dirt, the whites of his eyes rolling in fear like a spooked horse. His bicycle, his pride and joy—rickety but always lovingly cared for—was but a twisted frame, with two blown tires. What had happened?

"The plane came so close that I could see the expression on the pilot's face," he said. Lee the letter writer, also in the crowd, nodded in recognition. "It just came so close, then dropped a bomb. I could hear the eerie whistling. Thank goodness for the gusty mountain wind, which blew it to the side.

"Even still, I just had time to leap off my bicycle and run into the ditch—you see what happened to my beloved bicycle!"

Rhim the village elder happened at that moment to be driving by in his car—he was the only person in the village who owned a car. He stepped out when he saw the commotion and ordered Father Andrea to repeat what had happened. "It must be a mistake," Rhim said. Rhim had come out of every war richer each time; the 6.25 war was no different. He had a genius for making himself indispensable to whoever was in power, and they, in turn, often returned the favor, grateful for someone who was so useful for steering the villagers' opinions the way Jae-hak steered Blossom, his ox.

"It was the same kind of plane that dropped the powder last week," Father Andrea said. "Remember? When people started vomiting and having seizures?" Indeed, a dozen people working out in the fields had been brought in to see Hwang the acupuncturist, who was only puzzled by their strange ailment. One child even started bleeding out of his eyes. No one had died, however, so the incident was quickly forgotten.

"Of course not, Father. What a florid imagination you have—all that silly, gory Catholic imagery with the demons and the rolling-eyed Jesus.

"The Americans are patrolling to protect us from the Reds, who could be anywhere, including among us. Who knows whether they won't try another sneak attack while the peace process is ongoing?

Maybe they mistakenly thought you were transporting munitions. They can't see from that far up. What happened to your rice?"

"The sack burst and scattered on the road."

"Well, maybe you will have planted a new rice field," Rhim said jovially. His voice, an octave lower than most men's, carried in the air as if through a megaphone. "Our village will start growing rice again. It will come back better than before." Rhim didn't seem to understand such a basic fact that hulled rice would not grow. But he was so blustery and confident that, for a while, the villagers were reassured, too. Yungman's mother, however, forbid him and Yung-sik from going anyplace far.

Of course, if the Americans started bombing again like they had before, their flimsy house wouldn't protect them. But they understood what she meant. The family needed to stay together. A few villagers, the memory of hunger not far from their minds, went to the place Father Andrea had described to gather the spilled rice, sifting it out of the dirt, while staring in awe at the lunar crater right in the middle of the road, which would bring much inconvenience.

Not long after, Jae-hak, bringing Blossom to loan to another family, was ambling along the sun-warmed road when another plane dropped a bomb. There wasn't much left of him when he was found, except for some olive drab pants and one straw shoe that had been hurled into a tree. There wasn't even a bit of the ox to salvage.

The villagers urged the elders to find the American military; perhaps the entire village should protest. How could a little boy leading his ox be bombed in broad daylight? And it was Jae-hak, whom everyone already thought was so pitiful, having no mother and half a father.

"Are you crazy?" blustered Rhim, angry now. "How could the boy be so stupid as to be wearing a military uniform?" He was talking about the cast-off olive drab pants. Yungman had received a whole GI uniform as a goodbye gift from Red. But when he saw Jae-hak peering it at stealthily, enviously, then trying to hide his envy, Yungman motioned him over to let him see the pants more closely, including the webbed belt with the magic metal buckle,. Yungman had wanted the whole uniform for himself, but again, Jae-hak's troubles, like his worn-butt farmers' pants, were so terrible as to be unspeakable, and it was often easier to just hand him gifts, just to see Jae-hak be unable to control his famous grin.

"The migun were just doing their jobs, and doing them well. The village will take care of his blind father. Case closed. Kut." And Rhim made a motion with his hand that meant the crowd should disperse, which it did, because Rhim was now about as close as they had to a village leader. He was a survivor.

Everyone waited for the good news that they all thought must inevitably come on the heels of an end to war. They didn't understand that the opposite of war is not peace; it's just more war. Wars are ongoing, like underground fires, even if you can't see them. Even a war that's officially declared done, dead, forgotten, can still be alive, every day, for those living it. The villagers looked on in shock to learn that Water Project Village was now in North Korea.

"Wait!" the villagers said. They were, and always had been, south-of-the-line people.

The soldiers putting up the notices didn't reply. They informed the villagers they had forty-eight hours to choose between being evacuated to South Korea or staying and joining the Communists of the Democratic People's Republic of Korea. However, anyone who decided to stay in the "North" would be brought in for psychological interrogation as to their reasons why. Yungman burned with curiosity when he heard that the interrogators were American civilians. What Americans would speak Korean well enough? It turned out that they weren't white Americans; they were Japanese immigrants and their children who'd been locked up as enemies during World War II. So they didn't interpret to them in Korean but *Japanese. Why would you want to become a Communist? Have you always been one?* Most villagers were so disgusted at hearing Japanese again that they decided to go south just to get out of the questioning.

Father Andrea, who had been standing quietly by during the announcement, suddenly started yelling at the soldiers. "You can't do this! You can't make us leave our home!" He kept yelling. He told people not to leave. He said the Americans had not only dropped that white powder containing sickness from the sky but they had other horrible weapons they were experimenting with putting their germs in: insects, bullets, even feathers. They didn't actually want people to stay and become North Koreans; they had plans to put germs in the town well to kill anyone who stayed behind. Father Andrea yelled so much that some military police were eventually called to bind his arms and gag him. Even still, you could see his red face, his wild eyes as he fought.

As they began to lead him away (to where, no one knew), Yungman saw an astonishing sight.

Father Andrea somehow mustered the strength the break away from the two young MPs holding him. He ran pell-mell to the well where, before anyone could stop him, he fell or jumped in. The well was so deep that they didn't even hear a splash. The soldiers drew their guns and made everyone move away, warning them not to listen to the "Communists."

"How can we help Father Andrea?" Yungman frantically pulled at his mother's sleeve. She whirled around and immediately put her hand over his mouth. "Please," she said. "He was our dear friend. But we have to concentrate on us." They heard a *MRAAAAAP!* noise behind them. Yungman started to turn back, but his mother yanked him along. Yung-sik, he noticed, was staring straight ahead, not drawn back the tiniest bit by the sound—which might have been from a gun—his eyes shiny as coal, no longer mischievous but merely cold.

As their forty-eight hours ticked down, Yungman's mother packed, but fitfully, almost distractedly. She put some things in a pile, then returned them. She paced the floor. When Yungman asked what they were going to do, she merely said, "Of course we're going to Seoul; that's where Eagle High School is."

Yungman's mother brought their few salable belongings to the Exchange Zone Market, which itself was dissolving under their feet. Shoe Aunty kissed them all and cried and handed Yungman and Yung-sik each a pair of brand-new gomushin. She held hands with her new husband, the brass seller. They were going "far away," but where, she didn't say. Yungman's mother had made her a gorgeous pojagi cloth, trimmed with silk, to wrap her belongings for the journey. Shoe Aunty had spoken once of relatives in Manchuria. Yungman hadn't considered that one could leave Korea altogether, maybe forever. Most other vendors had already vacated, gone back to their own small villages half-hidden in the mountains. It seemed unbelievable to Yungman that there were ever soldiers, of North and South, mingling here, sometimes even in the middle of the market laying their guns down to kick the feathered shuttlecock between them like boys, the winners exulting, the losers howling in defeat, laughing in the sun, eating fried silkworm larvae steaming hot from the wok as if at any market in any place in Korea at any time.

The grasses, tamped down from the tarps and other makeshift floors, were already springing back, the yellowed rectangles greening and erasing the last traces of the stalls. Yungman's mother managed to sell his father's agronomy books.

Yungman was surprised to see his mother unwrap the celadon vase. The pale green was ringed with a lovely design of clouds and white cranes, the slender-legged birds that flew with their feet gracefully extended. Halaboji would show them how, when you turned the vase in your hands, the cranes circled the skies endlessly. The special firing process made the delicate green that was a Korean potter's color and no other. This vase even had a thread of gold that followed a hairline crack that traversed its length so that you couldn't tell if the vase had been broken then repaired with a golden solder or if that lightning-shaped crack was part of the design. It was a present a magistrate had given their great-great-grandfather during the Choson Dynasty for his tenure as a civil servant.

Yungman didn't know why their mother wouldn't bring such a valuable piece to Seoul with them, the same way she had carefully packed his father's silver chopsticks and spoon or Yungman's microscope, which his father had purchased for him shortly before he'd been arrested the second time. She put all those things in the middle of the wrapping cloth. The lazy-eyed American army man his mother accosted reminded Yungman of Red, solely because he had the same Cheju tangerine hair. Yungman's mother showed him the vase, and his good eye opened wider as he recognized how valuable it was. But when his mother asked for a fair price, he shook his head. He wouldn't give her even half of what she'd asked. He handed her the coins with a laughing *what-are-you-going-to-do-about-it?* look on his face that was not Red's at all. She didn't look back, but Yungman did, seething.

She had one more errand. She slipped into a stall where she exchanged all her won for a gold ring, fat and heavy on her finger.

"We can't take much; it will be very crowded on this bus," she told Yungman.

As they walked back from the market, she pointed toward the hill and the House of Rhim. Choy had, over the war years, developed a huge bald spot on the back of his head, and it was like a beacon now, as he and the servants carried heavy, ornate chests out through the gate and onto what looked like an army truck whose insignia had been painted over. "There—that's where the girl who bought that gourd dipper to hang on her wall lived. She can take even her dipper with her if she wants, I reckon. Rich people can take what they want." They even loaded a hahm, a comically large and heavy ceremonial wedding chest, into the truck.

It had gone completely quiet in their neighborhood; all the neighbors who shared their courtyard had evacuated. They had all left their gamasots fixed into the stoves because each family was relegated to one bundle a person. They would all have to find a new way to make rice. As the minutes ticked down, Yungman was surprised to see his mother sewing.

"Mother," he said. "We need to leave."

She didn't look up. She was sewing the gold ring into the lining of Yungman's school jacket. "What is this for?" Yungman asked.

"School fees."

It occurred to Yungman that Water Project Village would no longer send its children to school. "But why don't you keep it?"

"No one will think to see if you have a gold ring," she answered. "Come," she told Yungman and Yung-sik. "We need to go to the police station."

This was the last place they had seen their father, years ago. Korea had been "liberated" from the Japanese with their surrender in 1945, but not even a month had gone by, the Koreans doing fine on their own, before the Americans came in to occupy. Yungman's father had been on the local people's committees working to redistribute the land that had been occupied by the Japanese and their collaborators. Americans didn't know anything about Korean village structure. They only knew that anything with the word "people" in it must be Communist. The American military offered bounties for neighbors to turn neighbors in. The bounties were so generous that people turned people in for the money.

The first time Yungman's father had been arrested, he was placed in the local jail, Ugimoto, now Kang's jail, for a week, then dumped in front of their house. It was Father Andrea who found him lying in the street and shouted for Yungman's mother. Their father's face was bruised and he was missing a few teeth. Every time Yungman clamored to ask him about the missing teeth—where had they gone?—his mother shook her head at him. "Just be glad he's home." At night they could hear her crying, their father whispering, "It's all right. I'll be all right. Think of all the men and women who were tortured and killed for resisting the Japanese. We have to continue their work before it's too late. Maybe now the world will finally pay attention that we Koreans want our country back. No more foreign occupation. We've been one country for ten thousand years!"

Koreans continued to resist the US unilateral occupation. There were strikes: factory workers, train workers. And when the police understood what the strikers were fighting for, some of them, too, threw off their uniforms and joined them. This insurrection by the police panicked the US and Syngman Rhee, who sent in military reinforcements and ordered them to shoot into the crowd, marking that day forever as the Autumn Uprising (and massacre). For the American military advisors, worried at how quickly and well the Koreans organized, suppressing dissent became their highest priority. Rhee was the perfect strongman. Having lived in America for forty years, he gave the elite a way to both crush leftists and distract from their collaborationist past via a shiny new nationalism based on English, the official language of the southern occupation, and Western values.

Koreans, of course, knew who had collaborated with the Japanese, and seeing many of them untouched—or even better off than before — was enraging. Water Project Village was no different. Many villagers didn't know what to think. But the friendly young thremmatologist who devoted his life to propagating better rice plants was trusted by all the villagers. He was the one who, as he went from farm to farm, whispered there was to be an anti-Rhee, anti-American rally for free elections in the Gold Sea County Seat.

That was when he disappeared.

In Seoul, Rhee's rivals were all disappearing or mysteriously dying. Generous cash bounties were offered for reporting of Communist enablers and sympathizers, children were encouraged to turn in their parents.

In the village, where people had been happy to share one battered tin cup at the well, neighbor turned on neighbor. Instead of ignoring Yungman's mother, people started pointing at her, calling her "wife of a Commie" and a "Red bitch."

"What's a Commie?" Yungman had asked. "What's a Red bitch?" He was so puzzled. His mother only wore white. She didn't answer.

His mother went to Kang's jail every day. She brought rice balls wrapped in a cloth and clean underwear.

One day, his mother came back to the house and hurriedly told Yungman to wash and put on clean clothes. She didn't explain. All of them, including Halaboji and the toddler Yung-sik, hurried to the police station. Kang the police chief roared, "I told you never to come here again!" He grabbed their mother by her chignon, dragging her into a dank hall as she screamed and as the rest of them tried to free her. But out of sight of the others, his face softened.

"Five minutes," he whispered, unlocking a cell door. "That's all I can do. I won't see you again — go through that door over there when you leave. Close it behind you."

They entered a windowless cell. It was so dark that it took a minute for their eyes to adjust. Yungman made out in one corner a rice straw mat, the kind you dry vegetables on. In the other, a large chunk of driftwood propped against the wall.

Yungman was shocked when what he'd thought was a gnarled piece of driftwood turned out to be his father. Halaboji wept, for his son looked older than he did. Kwak Gwan-su was bent like a shepherd's crook; his remaining teeth were black with decay. One eye was swollen shut. It was as if a ghoul had replaced their robust father. However, he smiled as if everything was all right. Their mother started to cry, and he shushed her.

"What would you like to do, my boy?" Yungman's father asked him.

"Whatever you want to do, Father."

"You know how I told you that you must always study hard? I know you can become a doctor—your mother tells me you have been studying Chinese characters with Halaboji."

Yungman nodded uncertainly.

"You deserve to play once in a while, then. Tell me, son: Did you bring your shuttlecock?"

Yungman, of course, had not brought any toys. He played with those with his friends. He played paduk or changgi with Father. But he didn't have the heavy stone set and wooden chess board with him.

What Yungman liked best was to go out with his father into the fields—not because he was interested in growing rice but just to spend time with him in the outdoors. When his father gave him small tasks, like holding a container in which he'd place his soil samples, it made Yungman feel proud and important. His father had taken him to the village rice field and proudly showed him the tender emerald shoots, each laboriously fixed into the mucky soil by hand. He showed Yungman the tiny land crabs that swam in the irrigation troughs. He scooped them up and emptied them into the reed strainer Yungman held. Their mother would ferment them in soy sauce to make an expensive-tasting, unutterably delicious side dish.

Occasionally, when Father returned from working with farmers in the fields, even though hot and sweaty and covered in dirt, he hoisted Yungman on his back and galloped about their small shared yard that abutted the town well. Those hazy days were some of the happiest of his life.

Yungman shyly asked for another ride on his back.

"Oh no, no," his mother said. "Father is much too tired."

Yungman's father shushed her again. "Not too tired for my first-born son," he said. He moved aside the straw mat, took Yungman on his back and jogged around as much as he could within the small confines of the small, dank cell. Yungman remembered being surprised by how thin his father had become, ribs like a washboard, the knotty nubs of his spine pressing into Yungman's young flesh. He'd also remembered the odd noises—splashing, a hum of electricity, an echo of what seemed like a scream from a faraway basement, or maybe a moan coming from the earth itself. Yet he'd been a child, with a child's outsize emotions and greed.

Even as he could sense that his father's bones had gone dry and rickety like the beams of a house about to fall, being turtled on his back, safe again, he'd wanted more, for his father to bounce him more. For this visit, for this moment, feeling his father warm and alive under his arms and legs, to never end.

That was the last time they saw their father. The guards who used to gladly take their mother's daily bundles, gobble up the jumok-bap rice balls with gusto, ordered her to stay home, threatened consequences. She showed up anyway. A single return of dirtied underclothes gave her hope that her husband was still alive. Despite their jobs, many police still secretly admired the resisters, those who stood up to power. Even though they called her a bitch, when they thrust back the under-clothes with a sneer, they added the touch of the other hand, a quick flash, a two-handed sign of respect.

How strange to be back at the station now. It was barely staffed. There was a lingering smell of dankness, like kimchi that has turned, that brought the rest of the memories flooding back. How he'd made his father carry him when surely he must have been in horrible pain. How his father's body had felt like a house with broken beams. How Yungman had shouted "Run!" and "More!"

Yungman ran outside to vomit.

When he returned, his mother and Kang were speaking in low voices. Kang had been a police chief for the Japanese during the occupation. He had grown up rough, in a poor family. However, in return for him doing whatever the Japanese asked of him, his son was sent to Tokyo for college and was now a doctor in Seoul with an entire hospital of his own. After the Japanese surrender, the Koreans set upon the hated police, driving them out with sticks and metal hoes, and clamored for official legal redress of their crimes against their own countrymen. But when the US took over, they brought the police force back. The Americans wanted, above all, the Koreans' transition from Japanese colonial subject to being wards of the US to occur as smoothly as possible. Thus, it made sense to keep the efficiently brutal Japanese police system in place.

Chief Kang had to do many unpleasant tasks to maintain his position, to stay on the correct side of the iron bars. Rhee famously took a "better be safe than sorry" approach to the elimination of political prisoners, and under this broad definition, Yungman's father would be an enemy of the state.

But Chief Kang could not forget 1938.

Rice could barely grow in Gold Sea County. The Japanese didn't care. Quotas were quotas, and the punishment for not meeting them was beating, sometimes to death. Kang's family was unused to farming; their rice seedlings turned brown immediately after transplanting. Their whole crop would be lost. Someone would die for that.

Yungman's father went to investigate and diagnosed that the patch had become infested with a root-rot blight but was still salvageable. He showed them how to use rice straw to improve their drainage. The crop survived.

Police Chief Kang therefore owed a great debt to Kwak Gwan-su's family. He leaned forward to talk to Yungman's mother quietly. Yungman could only see Kang's lips moving and his mother's face, the hardened mask descending on it; but was that a glint of tears? A statue briefly touched by morning dew.

"Red Mother," Kang said, back at his blustery volume, to Yungman's mother's impassive face. "I told you, Rhee's great purge of 1951 did not leave any Commies alive. Because of guilt by association, you are also going to have a difficult time in Seoul. Just kill yourself now and save yourself the trouble."

Their mother led them away. Time had run out. They had to go.

The staging area for the Great Move South (as the military was calling it) was down a steep path from Water Project Village. Yungman and Yung-sik lugged their bundles while their mother carried the largest one impossibly on top of her head. Yungman wore a double set of underclothes, his school jacket on top. In a smaller, silk-wrapped bundle that Yung-sik carried were Halaboji's ashes in their gray cardboard box.

The path narrowed so much that they walked in single file: the village women, spines straight, balancing great loads on their heads, some even while nursing babies, their chogoris merely pushed up to expose their breasts. The men, in contrast, were bent forward in the shape of the Korean letter ㄱ, under the weight of wooden A-frames piled high. Yungman trailed behind an old man, his A-frame stacked with a bag of rice, a bedroll, and, inexplicably, a bleating goat. Another man, moving more swiftly, overtook him; the wrapped bundle on his A-frame, Yungman saw on closer inspection, supported his wizened mother-in-law.

The Americans sprayed them with DDT while they waited to board the bus. His mother coughed delicately, the bundle on her head undisturbed. The old man was arguing about the goat, which the GI had kicked away and was now running free.

The American GI standing closest to the door of the bus yelled something, and a tide of refugees surged toward him. They had been trying to organize people by county and village, but Yungman noted how his mother subtly shifted them in line. She seemingly did not want them to be with the people they knew. Without Father Andrea, he supposed, in what was left of the villagers, there was no one who would want to help them or protect them. Yungman still didn't understand what being a "Red" was, except that you could be killed if someone decided to call you one. They would always be in danger as long as anyone knew about their father.

Yungman's mother took the bundle off her head and handed it to him. "You smaller people, wriggle in there first and make room for me," his mother said. "Yungman-ah, take care of your little brother, take care of each other."

What she said didn't make sense. Yungman looked back at her, but she was pushing him and Yung-sik forward through the crowd until they were funneled through the door along with all their bundles, two of the first people on. Yung-sik wasted no time kicking and elbowing to make space amid the crush of bodies, guarding a mother-size space on the wood floor. "Where is she?" Yung-sik asked.

"She'll be here," Yungman reassured him. The bus door shut.

"Mother!" both boys yelled.

Yung-sik wormed and shoved his way to the front, as far as he could. Yet his mother was not anywhere in sight. There was no one remaining on the sandy plain they were leaving. He shouted for the bus to stop.

The driver said, to no one in particular, that they were in what was now a highly sensitive military border zone, so the bus wouldn't stop for any reason until it got to Seoul.

There were only a few windows on this bus, like portholes on a ship. Yungman pushed and stepped heedlessly on seats and people, ignoring their shouts. He caught a scrap of sky, cloudless, incongruously beautiful. In his frantic scanning of the landscape he thought he caught a glimpse of a figure in white, a neat chignon at the base of her neck, running north, back toward the village. As the bus lumbered like a large, awakening animal, a separation of home, of friends, of family began. A collective wail arose, almost like singing, drowning out two brothers' cries for their mother.

SEOUL
1968

For the people of Seoul, the day was overpacked with so much news that it threatened to burst at the seams.

Thirty-one North Korean commandos had sneaked across the DMZ, traversed the mere fifty kilometers to Seoul, and then slipped through a busy city, heading for the presidential Blue House. Repeated, bloody demonstrations had finally gotten rid of president-for-life Syngman Rhee (flown away by the CIA under cover of night for a retirement in Hawaii). The newest occupant of the Blue House was General Park Chung-hee, who had dispatched Rhee's successor via military coup, continuing a line of military dictators flogging Korea's future. He sat unknowing how very near death was.

At the same time came the unwelcome news that North Korea had captured an American military intelligence ship in its territorial waters. The US claimed a navigational accident and demanded return of the ship. Sabers rattled.

Was the Cold War heating up again? Seoul residents wondered. Would they be hearing big guns again? Would they have to pack up and flee?

Back near the border, a farmer greeted a group of ROK soldiers on patrol. They hailed him back in Seoul accents. But the middle-aged sweet potato farmer had been a child soldier during 6.25 and recognized one of the ROK insignia patches—that it was upside down. He called the police.

Yungman, however, paid no attention to this news, both about the USS *Pueblo* and that, shockingly, a group of North Korean commandos was caught mere yards from the Blue House, the tip-off from the farmer the only thing that kept the president from assassination and a new war from breaking out. Yungman was thinking only of how he had to get to the docks. He and Young-ae had to get on the ship to America.

Young-ae was the girl who'd bought the gourd dipper as decoration all those years ago at the Exchange Zone Market—the Seoul student who found him so insignificant that she couldn't even look at him. What were the chances that, after Yungman's arrested education, they would end up in the same medical school, in the same anatomy class, on the very same team?

All of Yungman's travails, from his father's being jailed to the trek to Pusan to his years living as a refugee in Seoul, paled compared to the formidable task of getting this magnificent girl to notice him, especially since the banjang of their class was the golden-throated Lee JongDal, who never failed to get the top grades, was practically too beautiful as a man, and came from a ridiculously rich and well-placed family.

When Young-ae did pay attention to Yungman, he understood from the beginning that their love affair was one-sided. She wanted to make

JongDal the Lark jealous (when Lark seemingly only loved justice and his music). Every time Yungman tried to be sensible and feign indifference with hopes it would become real, he would fall back in love, getting wedged deeper and deeper as if into the neck of a bottle. She chased Lark; Lark flew away; Yungman chased her. It was ridiculous, really. He knew she didn't love him, and yet he fell deeper in love, and in desperation he shaved off parts of himself—including his brother, who was helping to pay his tuition by working with gangsters at a shameful hubba-hubba club—to better suit her needs. No one could say he had a disreputable family, guilt by association, anything, if he didn't have a family, if they'd all been killed in the war.

She was a sexually liberated woman, and interested in him enough that they had made love a few times (mostly after getting drunk or seeing a movie).

Yungman, however, faced the facts: Even without the competition from Lark, Young-ae was wholly uninterested in marriage. Scandalously, she only wanted to deliver babies, not have them. He had never heard such a thing. Her timing was good, as the consideration of women having a separate biology and health specialty coincided with the New Village Movement ushered in by the dictator Park, who wanted to make even the rural areas more like cities, including women going to the hospital for birth, no more of that old-fashioned squatting and clinging to a rope.

Yungman pretended to go along with her being such a new, modern woman, and he also acted much richer than he was. She didn't know—and maybe didn't care—how he paid his school fees; such was the heedlessness of the rich that they assumed everyone else also didn't have to worry about where money came from. It grew like dates on a tree for all she was concerned. She did sometimes make a slight face around their classmate Jae, who saved money by wearing the same clothes for a week, visiting the bathhouse the day his clothes were being laundered. Yungman thus made sure to take a cat-bath every night, washing his various parts using a scratchy towel, and making sure he was always shaved and sweet-smelling, sometimes by nabbing some of Lark's expensive aftershave. But the worst thing wasn't his poverty, he had to admit to himself—it was that when they made love, she shut her eyes and turned her face away. He bet she was thinking of someone else. Maybe someone braver. Someone who could be more himself even in the glare of her.

While Yungman was wooing Young-ae, Lark had begun going to protests, occasionally cutting lectures, even as he was threatened with demotion from class banjang. He kept going, and that astonished Yungman.

"Don't you hear the call of your hurting country?" Lark had asked him in rebuttal. "The movement could use someone like you, with good English to talk to the foreign journalists." Yungman had, instead, always gone to the library, even when the demonstrations were right on campus. That was his patriotism, his commitment to his family.

Lark wouldn't stop openly exhorting the students: "Why spend all our time studying when the fate of the Republic is in our hands? We need to throw out the military strongmen, institute a parliamentary system to reflect the wishes of the people!"

The closest Yungman had come to attending a demonstration was when a huge march had come down the main walk on campus, and Yungman, tiredly exiting the library at that moment, had been swept into the tide of people. Before he could extricate himself and run out into the woods in back of campus, he'd been tear-gassed by the police and narrowly missed being arrested. He could still hear the *whooom!* of the tear gas cannons, the shouts and screams, the meaty thunks of riot police batons hitting bodies, including his own, and he wondered, *Why do this?* There was no way the students would win. Why not just hit your own hand with a baton and call it a day? Did they think President Park sat in the Blue House and worried over them? No! He just had the police drag them away in what looked like kidnapping, let go after a few nights in jail with other criminals, if their fathers were prominent, or they were tortured, bused out into the country, and dumped off in the middle of nowhere.

It was because of the demonstrations that Yungman had run into Tadpole. Hurrying home from lecture to study, Yungman had passed a stout, tough-looking man smoking a cigarette, leaning against the ornate university gate, incongruously clad from head to toe in light-blue denim, the uniform of the gangsters and hired goons that university students were trained to run away from, as the professional goons were known to be even more brutal than the police.

Yungman had stopped suddenly in his tracks, recognizing the hard glint of his hair and eyes. His old friend.

"Tadpole?"

Tadpole stared, snarled—"Are you calling someone a frog?"—then squinted in dim apprehension.

"Ah, Hong Kil-dong!" he cried. Robin Hood! Yungman wondered what passersby thought of the man in the denim jumpsuit embracing the skinny student. The two of them wandered down one of the random alleys that radiated out from the SNU gate and quickly found a student place that served the flour-and-water "rags" dumpling soup, the one thing even cheaper than a bowl of curry rice at the cafeteria. Tadpole was most impressed that Yungman was a medical student. "You were just a boy of thirteen, no father, no mother, supporting your brother, and now you're here."

Yungman hung his head down modestly, but also to hide the licking flames of shame at how wrong Tadpole had it about who was supporting whom. Right now, Yung-sik was at one of his club jobs.

Tadpole recounted how at 6.25, he had also decided to take his chances in the South, and also landed friendless in Seoul. But with no schooling and almost illiterate, he joined the waifs on the street, dodging the white people hunting kids to populate their orphanages. Korea began its lurching rise from the ashes, modernizing with dizzying momentum, which left people who'd collaborated with the Japanese or who'd made connections with the Americans primed to reap all the profits. Those like Tadpole, no matter how industrious or smart, without resources would be left behind. While college students protested over the lack of democracy and justice for the poor, they still had food to eat at dinnertime. People like Tadpole did not, and out of necessity, they were recruited into the shadow economy.

He confirmed he'd become one of those denim-clad goons Rhee used to disrupt elections. Indeed, his first job had been stealing ballot boxes. In an hour or two, he whispered, he'd be cracking open the heads of students, and he advised Yungman to make sure he was far, far away. The police would be bringing tear-gas cannons that they had, recently, started sometimes firing directly into the crowds of protesters. "Those cannisters are like bullets. They're going to kill someone someday."

*Someone like Lark*, Yungman was thinking. People who had nothing to put up for resistance to autocracy but their own bodies. He thought of how lovingly his mother must have raised him, a first son. What a waste.

"I'm already getting too old for this job," Tadpole said, showing Yungman his ball-like knuckles, each one so arthritic after being broken, his arms burn-scarred from the times "the boss" was displeased. All this, and he was earning barely enough to eat. But there was little else for him to do.

Yet, it was Tadpole who paid for both their meals. Yungman protested.

"It's my pleasure to treat you," Tadpole said. "Be well, my friend. I don't think I'll see you again." He started walking back toward the arches, limping slightly. Yungman wondered whose head he would break today in the name of General Park's Third Republic.

Yungman thought about how Tadpole had named him Hong Kil-dong back at the Seven Arms of Mother Mountain base. It had pleased but puzzled him, because he didn't really feel like he was a hero, like Hong Kil-dong, the Robin Hood of the famous Korean legend. It made him feel happy that maybe Tadpole, who was so perceptive about people, had seen something in him that he himself hadn't apprehended yet. Without any education, he wouldn't even know his name was Evening Hero.

It wasn't until years later, when Yungman was filling out a form in the post office, he noticed it was prefilled "HONG [family name] KIL DONG." And he realized Tadpole hadn't seen some hero in him; in need of a nickname, he'd resorted to "John Doe." He hadn't even been worthwhile enough for Tadpole to pick out an attribute, like the Professor, or a favorite food, like Rotten Melon.

Yungman had forgotten to tell Tadpole about Lieutenant Jarvis, the one who had made the houseboys drop off condoms to the harlots, but only in the even-number shacks. And how Yungman had saved his address and written to him to see if there was any way that Jarvis could help him out of the draft, since he had in some ways "served." Jarvis had written him back to say he had a better idea. So, now, all of a sudden, he had a student visa for America. Among his peers at school, this made him a sort of celebrity. Even JongDal didn't have that. His self-worth temporarily buoyant, Yungman had swaggeringly persuaded Young-ae to make love "one last time" before he left to go to America.

Young-ae was now eight weeks pregnant. They both understood that if her father found out, it might be a death sentence—for Yungman. Rhim had enough connections that he could even pull Yungman's citizen card and have it destroyed, so if Yungman happened to, say, die in an unfortunate accident, it would be as if he hadn't existed. Yungman didn't doubt Rhim was capable of such a thing.

Young-ae was at a crossroads herself. Ironically, the harlots at the base could get an abortion anytime they wanted to, because they had US doctors (ha!) like Jarvis. Apparently, even at Yongsan Garrison now red-light district women could get abortions, but only if they were the specially licensed women who worked strictly with the US troops. For Young-ae, abortion was not an option. She couldn't even fly to another country without her father being involved. Except.

Young-ae had learned that the state where Yungman was going to redo his internship, Alabama, allowed abortions if the health of the mother was at stake. They had no way of confirming this. She would make it clear to them that she would take her life if she had to carry this baby, she said. That was a valid health claim. Yungman thought of nothing beyond having her come with him. What would happen after, they did not discuss.

Lieutenant Jarvis was a taken aback by the news that Yungman also needed a visa for his fiancée. His plan was that such a fine young chap might make productive use of two years of instruction, one foreign physician year, one seminary year. What better Trojan horse to introduce the gospel to Koreans than one of their own? Jarvis thought about it and agreed: a good Christian doctor, especially a male obstetrician, needed a wife, and so made the necessary arrangements.

Not wholly by design, Yungman had not mentioned Yung-sik to his medical-school friends. He didn't erase Yung-sik; he had always just kept his outline confined to "my younger brother." Over time, the story solidified to his "late" younger brother. A sibling dying during wartime was sadly commonplace, immediately believable. Even more, a tender empathy came into the light in Young-ae's eyes—she was probably thinking of her lost brother, Joongki—and so Yungman continued what he thought was a light charade. Seoul National University was far, far away from the club district, where Yung-sik worked, far from the barren peach orchard where they lived. This lie was also easier than explaining how they were dumped from the bus in the middle of Seoul without a father, without a mother, and without even a friend or a familiar face from their village. The Exchange Zone bus refugees were supposed to be organized by their village kun, but Yungman and Yung-sik were children and had no idea which kun Water Project Village was.

A white woman approached them and asked them where their parents were. A white man with huge horse teeth joined them and put a big paw of a hand on Yungman's shoulder. He had a cross of the Jesus, which Yungman recognized. He tensed, thinking of the houseboys' tales of the orphanages.

"You can rest at our home. You can't stay on the street," he said, leaning and stroking Yung-sik's tear-stained cheek. "It's dangerous out here. The roving gangs. You look like good, clean kids."

"I don't think they speak English—why would they, Horace?"

The man's hand moved to Yung-sik's shoulder, wrinkling the worn but clean white hanbok his mother had just starched. Yung-sik kicked the man in the shins, eliciting a "Got-tam it!" The two brothers were able to run away, but at the cost of leaving their large bundle behind.

It was Buddhist monks who finally took the wandering boys in; they took in all sorts of orphans. They did not care about them as individuals, but they also asked for nothing except work—Yung-sik in the garden, Yungman with meals. The food was basic but plentiful. Yungman let them believe they were interested in becoming monks.

There had to be a US military base in Seoul, and Yungman soon found the Yongsan Garrison. Inside its high walls were more than two hundred brick buildings; originally constructed by the invading Japanese, it was now the big headquarters for the Americans military. Yongsan had, therefore, a particularly large and splendid dump, a mountain replenished twice a day by truck, because Americans wasted that much food.

After one American Thanksgiving, Yungman came upon dozens of glass jars of tasteless pearl onions the size of marbles. Yungman recalled to Yung-sik that their shape and size reminded him of those red maraschino cherries that the Americans put in their alcoholic drinks. Yung-sik came up with the idea to inject them with cheap red dye, pack them in glucose syrup, and sell them. The black marketer found it surprisingly easy to locate American buyers with unrefined palates. "No one eats those things anyway, that's smart." Yung-sik began assisting the man at his black-market stall, which was how he procured a decent fake school ID for Yungman.

Three years later, Yungman showed up to take the college entrance exam with the boys from his class. The proctor asked him where his official family register papers were. When running away from the white people, they had saved Halaboji's ashes, their father's chopsticks and spoon, and the ring, sewn securely into Yungman's blazer. They had lost not just Yungman's microscope but all their papers. Soon, an administrator, summoned by the proctor, insisted he couldn't take the test without his family registry.

"I cannot be the only one in this situation!" Yungman had wanted to cry. There were so many rich, well-fed boys here, with two parents, smug with their papers, their Western-style clothes. He had worn his replica Eagle High School uniform, which had seemed so dashing, but now he wondered if it was obviously fake.

"I'll have you escorted out," the man said, using such low language that Yungman went faint with rage. Like Father Andrea had done for him, he sat down right on the floor of the examination hall. The administrator tugged forcefully at his arm while signaling for help.

It was the end of the Kwak family dream, wasn't it? What was the use? But he felt as if Father Andrea was with him. *Fight on until the very end*, was what he was saying.

"What in the world is going on?"

It was the English teacher, Jo. Older, still handsome, Western-suited. The side part in his hair had migrated farther to the side as his hair thinned, but he was the same man from Pusan. *How are you? I am fine.*

"This ragamuffin is trying to take the entrance exam, and he doesn't even have his family registry."

The man stared at Yungman, his eyes widening in recognition.

"This boy was the best student in my class, even in the miserable conditions in Pusan."

"But he doesn't have any papers."

Yungman ducked his eyes, waiting for whatever was going to happen next. "He's holding up the exam. He can return next year with real papers."

Next year! Once he had his papers, even if he could get them, he would be called up to do his mandatory military service—that was two whole years. Then his age would make him ineligible for the entrance exam, not to mention the danger of guilt by association finding him here. How was that fair, that the people who had suffered the most during the war continued to suffer?

He lifted his eyes to stare imploringly at Teacher Jo, who wasn't looking his way. He looked impatient and preoccupied. Indeed, he had to get back to proctor his own set of students.

"If I recall correctly, he's a distant relation to Principal Pae," he said. "Student, you're from Seoul, yes?"

"Yes," Yungman lied, making his Seoul accent as neat as possible, far away from the Gold Sea Province's drawn-out "Yeh." Whoever Principal Pae was, he was important enough that the younger subordinate was cowed. The teacher didn't look at him again, nor did Yungman ever see him again. But he was grateful. And, suddenly, he felt in his heart that it was okay to lie, if it was for a good cause.

The night before Yungman and Yung-sik were to receive their robes and have their heads shaved, they slipped away from the monastery.

Thanks to the gold ring, they were able to purchase a tiny plot of land in Kang Nam, the nebulous "south of the Han River," not far from where Rhee precipitously blew up the bridge during his shameful abandoning of Seoul on 6.25. This plain of old fruit orchards was outside the city gates, and unwanted. The one-room shack on their plot stank of pesticide and soon had blood smears on the wallpaper from all the bedbugs they killed in their sleep, but the two of them scratched their bites as they curled up together on their bedding and were thrilled to have a place of their own. There were even a few spindly peach trees remaining. They assumed those brown sticks were dead, but that summer they bore for them a few of the most delicious peaches they'd ever eaten.

While Yungman attended medical college, Yung-sik earned even more money as he had graduated from black-marketing and a new boss had installed him as a barkeep at a club near the Great East Gate that was patronized by gangsters who often tipped extravagantly to impress their molls. On the side Yung-sik continued to manufacture his "cherries." The Shirley Temple drink was all the rage, and red dye was cheap, those little onions abundant at the Yongsan dump, especially around Yankee holidays like Thanksgiving, which Yung-sik cheekily referred to as "harvest season."

Yung-sik's projects were enough to keep them afloat until Yungman received his degree from Seoul National University College of Medicine. This degree would allow Yungman to find a job anywhere, just the way anyone with a law degree from Seoul National University would end up being an important judge. "Maybe even at the famous Severance Hospital, the one set up by the Yankees!" Yung-sik mused.

Yungman had meant to do all of that. He hadn't reckoned on the girl in his anatomy class, the one with the white flash of nape under her severe haircut, the one who now strutted in Western clothes. The one who pretended she wasn't who she was, because she, too, had her family broken in two after the war, and becoming a new person in Seoul was the only way she could bear the pain of separation.

Yungman packed a cardboard suitcase, trying not to look around the hovel that he and his brother had shared for those years. He told himself that Yung-sik would eventually understand. He would get married and have a family of his own; what Yungman was doing was merely accelerating the process by a year or two. Like the proverb says, *As soon as there is affection, a separation happens*. It was because they loved each other that the separation would cause pain. But they would all be separated from each other, some day.

Yungman had made sure to leave him their father's silver chopsticks and spoon, as well as the deed to the Kang Nam house, both of which he tucked in with Yung-sik's barkeep's clothes, his name tag pin bearing his fake name: Oh Man-won, i.e., fifty thousand won.

The fatal flaw in his plan was his guilt. Just like the highly disciplined North Korean killer commandos, their perfect Seoul accents and mannerisms, their impeccable replica South Korean military uniforms, but then one man with a single upside-down insignia. Yungman had planned to leave without a note, but at the last moment he left a note on top of the clothes.

*Little Brother,*
    *By the time you read this, I will be on a ship to America . . .*

He stared at his father's chopsticks and spoon, and in an impulsive move, swiped the spoon.

It was almost like he needed to add even more to his crime, to make it irrevocable, that he *had* to leave. Pushing it deep into his suitcase, he exited the shed that had been their home.

What was also irrevocable: the departure time of the ship was two hours later than he'd written down. How could he be so stupid when he'd planned for weeks?

Yungman rushed Young-ae to the docks. She looked back at him, irritated. "Why so early?" She was wearing a stylish hat and a black bolero jacket with a pleated sky-blue skirt, beautifully made leather shoes, and nylon stockings.

"Rules for an international journey," he fibbed. He tried to keep from being too obvious about scanning the crowd. It was packed with people, and laborers were already walking up the gangways to load cargo into the hold. The pair of tickets for the *Manchurian Princess* was tucked into his jacket pocket. In his hand he had Young-ae's suitcase—she owned an actual traveling case while his would surely dissolve if it ever got wet. He could only vow to keep it dry.

He was wearing his new Western clothes, a fish scale–shiny suit that, well, he was able to afford only because Yung-sik's gangster friends had helped him procure it at a cut-rate price at the Great East Gate Market. He was also wearing Western shoes, which had heels, something he'd had to get used to after wearing gomushin for so many years. Singers and gangsters had taken to wearing Western shoes with substantial heels that made clapping noises on wooden floors, as if to declare with a snappy drumroll how done they were with the silent canoe-shaped Korean shoes of the past. Only grandpas wore gomushin now.

"Passengers, line up!"

"Come, let's be first to board," he said, as jauntily as possible.

Yungman felt a surge of hope and excitement as the crowd began to move. "Passengers, all aboard!"

"Why don't you go first?" he said to Young-ae, who, cheeks pink with close-crowd heat and excitement, nodded. As they moved forward, something caught on the collar of his Western shirt. Then that something yanked so hard that Yungman almost fell backward.

"Traitor!" Yung-sik yelled. His face was beet-red.

When Yung-sik was a boy, unlike most Korean children, who were quiet and obeyed the rules, making themselves as unobtrusive as possible, Yung-sik had fits when he was denied something he wanted. When he wasn't laid out on a mat with sickness, he tantrummed so much, despite their mother's regular spanking, that even Halaboji, in their father's absence, was called in. He half-heartedly took part, cutting the limpest branch of a willow tree to make a switch.

"On-nya," he would sigh. "The smallest pepper is always the spiciest one."

Yungman often couldn't help whispering while his dongsaeng, his little brother, was being whipped: "Tiny hot pepper. Vegetable Hero." For how could his own sibling display such idiotic intemperance when the rules were so clear?

Yungman was glad Young-ae was already several meters up the gangway. He turned and shoved his brother hard, breaking his grip. Yung-sik fell backward and hit his head. Yungman looked back in horror, felt his whole body tense in readiness to rush to him. But then his brother sat up dazedly. His familiar scowl of rage reappeared. Yungman dashed up the gangway, his heeled shoes clacking on the wooden slats. Yung-sik followed, his arms just a blessed inch or two too short. Yungman took a moment to look back and only got a momentary glimpse of the top of his brother's head, his shiny black hair. He was stuck behind in the crowd, jumping up to see over the others' heads, cut off by the ticket-taker because he didn't have a ticket.

"Traitor! Who's supposed to do the ancestor workshop now? I worked to put you through Seoul National University, and now you leave me here—with no one! Our dear mother would die twice over if she knew what you've done to me!"

Yung-sik's shriek was like the sharp report of a whistle. For a second, the movement of the crowd stopped as people looked around for the source of that unearthly noise.

"You cannot leave me!" The other passengers turned to stare at Yungman, where the ire seemed to be focused. Young-ae thankfully wouldn't know who that screaming fellow was.

Yungman reached her, standing by the prow, with a quick sigh of relief. She was staring not at the land and the people they were leaving but out at the sea beyond the bay. He leaned over, watching the crew haul in the ropes for the cargo; this reminded him, in a flash, of being with Yung-sik in Pusan, watching their fellow Koreans rush to unload the great American ships. He thought of how Bear Uncle did that work, and while every day someone slipped and fell off the ramp, they were ordered to keep working; no one checked to see if that Korean had drowned. Bear Uncle, at least, had survived. Yungman hoped he had made it back to Sokcho and his family. Something caught in his throat. "I will be back," he called to his brother, who was again lost, drowning in the boiling crowd.

Yungman took in the happy faces lined at the rail, waving to the crowd below. He looked down at the crowd, and it was just that—a crowd.

"It seems strange not to have anyone to see us off, doesn't it?" Young-ae said. She had tears in her eyes. "I'm sorry, it must be even worse having no family, but still." Yungman realized she was talking about her family. Still fearful of her father finding out, she hadn't even told her sister she was leaving. She would just explain everything when she came back. "First losing Joongki, then me; I don't know what's going to happen."

"No one knows what's going to happen," Yungman reminded her.

The deckhand of the USS *Manchurian Princess* had given them handfuls colorful confetti to throw in celebration. Yungman hurled his ferociously, but it somehow ended up blowing back in his face. He faced forward, so that Korea was behind him. It was time to go to America.

# BOOK IV

A woman named Gracie, who wore a neon-green pantsuit and high heels, showed Yungman in.

"Hi, Sir!" Einstein sat at a glass-topped desk. He wore a checkered dress shirt, no tie, and an electric-blue suit that looked like it had shrunk in the wash while he was wearing it. His hairless wrists were exposed, and there was a good inch of patterned sock between the hem of his pants and his shoes—sneakers again!

Yungman would certainly never have dressed so casually, but this was his son's private labor/delivery/surgical suite. All the medical things were hidden—there wasn't even a blood pressure cuff or an RX pad to be seen. It was just wide-open space with a wall of bookshelves, like an executive would have. Maybe an executive at an architecture firm. On the wall by his desk was a huge modern art print of a giant, unmistakably vulvar pink rose. Next to it was what would be called a "glamour shot" of Marni in a white negligee—something he'd noticed only after it was too late to avert his eyes. Who has such a picture at their place of work?

"Where is all the medical equipment?" Yungman asked.

"Behind these walls," Einstein said. "You wouldn't think it, but my desk slides away and the bookcase swivels like in the Bat Cave, and this room converts into a sterile OR. It's all controlled by my SANUSwatch."

As if on cue, Einstein's watch, the size of a prisoner's manacle, buzzed. It had a gold-link band, unlike the cheap silicone of the operator's SANUSwatch. He tapped at its oversize screen, then spoke into his pronated wrist like Dick Tracy.

"I'm on my way to lunch," he said. "I can stop by. But only for a minute.

"Midwives," Einstein said with companionable exasperation.

"The HoSPAtal uses midwives?" Yungman asked in surprise. "With all this technology?"

"It's market-driven: a subset of the Guests want a so-called natural option. If this midwife, Verna, wasn't so popular, I don't think SANUS would bother. It doesn't fit with the brand. Her office is on the way to the restaurant, if you don't mind."

"I don't mind."

The elevator, like so many other things in the Tower, was completely clear. It didn't even have buttons. Einstein had summoned it like magic with his SANUSwatch alone.

Nature's Way, said the sign that greeted them as they stepped into the crystalline hall.

"Is that onions I smell?" asked Yungman, sniffing the air. It was particularly strange because the rest of the building was neutral-smelling, that sort of staticky clean after-rain smell, fresh and wet like green tea, thanks to the ozone mist, both from generators that pumped it into the halls and from individuals' SANUSwatches.

"Unfortunately, yes," said Einstein. "Even ozone can't defeat onions."

"Hello!" said a woman whose springy hair was the gleaming white color of the inside of an oyster shell. She wore open-toed shoes, Jesus sandals, which made Yungman stare. At least her feet were immaculately clean, toenails trimmed.

"Verna, this is my father, Dr. Yungman Kwak. He's an operator at Depilation Nation."

"Honored to meet you, I'm Verna Carlson!" She extended her elbow. "To avoid unnecessary transfer of germs."

Yungman touched his rented-white-coated elbow to her naked one, feeling slightly affronted—did she think he was unclean? "I greet everyone this way," she said, as if catching his mood. "Semmelweis died hounded and insane in the poorhouse in 1865 just because he challenged his fellow doctors to wash their hands after handling corpses and before delivering babies—that's why I think your Asian bowing is much smarter. Doctors like to think they're superior to germs. But germs don't care." Einstein may have rolled his eyes a bit, for she stared right at him and said, "The most recent *Hospital Journal* showed that doctors *say* they wash one hundred percent of the time, but when they culture their hands, they find that more than fifty percent are carriers of fecal-borne infections—*uff da.*"

"What have you got cooking?" Yungman asked.

"Placenta."

Einstein now openly made a face.

"Really?" said Yungman. "May I look?"

"Be my guest."

Yungman peered into the pan. It looked like liver and onions. The placenta was an organ, after all. In Korean, the name for it was *Tae*, "life." In the village, Tae was dried and ground into a powder for a poultice to put on wounds. There were times, when food was low, that it was eaten. At the very least, it was not to be thrown away. But in the West, that hardworking organ was plopped into a plastic container, sent to the pathologist, who would give it a cursory look then incinerate it as medical waste.

Verna spread out a new placenta, rich with dark red and black endometrial veins that radiated outward, splitting off into smaller and smaller capillaries.

"The tree of life," she said.

Einstein looked impatient to get to lunch.

"In Korea, the midwives save it as well," Yungman said, despite himself.

She nodded. "We give the Guests the option to dehydrate and encapsulate it, eat it as a meal, or just put it in a smoothie. We take a remembrance picture of it regardless."

"That's great, Verna," Einstein said, "but we have a 12:15 meeting."

"All right. So, Dr. Kwak, I was thinking—"

As they talked, Yungman wandered around. While Einstein's office had been sleekly spare, this place looked like a child's gym, with brightly colored rugs and floor mats. He walked to a wicker basket that contained tennis balls and various nubbly massage tools, tubes and ovals, a squishy pillow, hot and cold packs, and a blanket that looked to be the same expansive size as the ones they used in Korea to attach babies to their mothers' backs so that the mothers could continue to go about their day in the fields or at home. Next to the basket were various exercise balls. In the other corner, a vol-cano-shaped device was spewing a cool smoke that smelled like lavender.

"And Dr. Kwak," Yungman heard Verna say, "if you feel the need to question my practice without evidence, please see my statistics first and *then* come talk to me. Oh, and on those pregnancy forums, I see what you're doing—there's a law against giving yourself good reviews under a pseudonym."

Einstein rolled his eyes and led Yungman back to the elevator.

"The downside of the Birth Boutique being for-profit is that it's harder to report people," said Einstein. "The medical board told me to report it to the Better Business Bureau and not them when I caught her letting a woman nurse a blue baby. A blue, hypoxic baby!"

"Did the baby pink up?"

"After a while—a *good while*, yes," he admitted.

"Any adverse outcomes? Sequelae?"

"Well, no. But she just got lucky."

"How are her outcomes in general?"

"They're perfect so far. Obviously using ginned-up statistics."

"What does that mean?" Yungman envisioned drunk data.

"She cherry-picks the cases, or maybe just makes them all up. She came in to SANUS having zero maternal and infant mortality."

"None?"

"None. You can imagine how appealing that would be to the rather large demographic of rich, safety-obsessed customers. In Greenwich, we had a number of successful malpractice cases seventeen years later when a hypoxic baby didn't get into Harvard; I can *totally* see that happening here. One of the medmal cases paid out *a million dollars*. That former colleague of mine is toast—although I get it; the kid ended up going to Lehigh."

Yungman considered how in the village, women got pregnant and had babies that came out blue all the time; blue was just one of the many hues newborns came in. Some of them probably died or had brain damage, but he couldn't remember any specific ones, because he'd been seven when he was no longer allowed into a laboring woman's hut. In medical school, they were taught to panic at any sight of a blue baby, to rush it to an incubator and turn up the oxygen. Only later did they find that too much supplemental oxygen could blow out the fragile newborn retina and make the babies blind.

"How can you be so sure she's using misleading numbers?"

"It's so far off the mean. If she were smarter, she would make her data more believable. Throw in at least one death or a birth injury, come on."

His son was so sure. Yungman supposed there'd been a time when he, too, was so sure about things—until age and experience had proven him wrong, time and again. He understood now why the Buddhists preferred to float along in the slipstream between the two values, good and bad.

They stepped off the elevator into a cavernous dining room on the top floor of the Quartz Tower, blue sky massively above them.

"There are six different exclusive MDiety cafés in the HoSPAtal," Einstein said excitedly. "All Michelin-starred. This one is the best, and it's Korean!"

## The M(omofuku) Diety Café

"Momofuku sounds *Japanese*," Yungman remarked. He still remembered how, as a child, he'd had to learn the Momotaro story about the infertile Japanese couple who find a boy in a peach. "'Momo' means peach," he said. "I think 'fuku' means assistant. Assistant peach?"

"I'm pretty sure the chef is Korean. He's been on that TV show, *Mind of a Chef*. David Chang. Chang is a Korean name, right?"

"It can be," said Yungman. "It depends on the underlying Chinese character."

"That makes it Chinese?"

"No. Most Korean surnames have an underlying Chinese charac-ter. Like, 'Kim' is 'gold.' " Yungman wondered if Einstein would ask what their name meant. He didn't.

"No DRones Allowed!" said the sign on the wall.

"People bring their drones in here?" said Yungman.

"No, it's a joke. Conventional doctors are called DRones. Get it?"

"I suppose."

"Our CEO/founder, Magnus Goodbetter, is a funny guy. His phi-losophy is that in the world, medical professionals are divided into service providers—the DRones—and the MDieties. It's all in good fun. Our CEO likes to think we're gangsters. I'm more formally known within the organization not just as a concierge specialist but also as a SANUS 'Doctorpreneur.' "

"Doctorpreneur," repeated Yungman.

"Yes; here we have free rein to invent and develop trademarked products."

"And yours is?"

"I'm the inventor of the Kwak Vaginal Rejuvenation, Tee Em."

"The Kwak what?" Yungman had always dreamed his son might come up with a named surgical instrument, like the Mayo scissors, the Kocher clamp, his beloved Allis, the uterine sound. Why not a Kwak obstetrical retractor? He'd even take a Kwak bladder blade.

"It's actually a suite of products. Why don't we sit down and I'll fill you in?" They followed the maître d' to a bank of seats along the outer edge of the café.

Yungman took a moment. Always so fixated on getting to where he was going, he was always forgetting to take in the view, as if he were afraid to waste the two seconds looking up or feared what might be coming down on him. The clear panels and vaulted glass ceiling of the Quartz Tower provided a panoramic perspective: you could see the nearby Minneapolis–St. Paul airport, where toylike planes were taking off and landing. If you tipped your head up, you could see the planes traversing the sky, a sight that made Yungman involuntarily tense, because he had to consciously remind himself—even so many years later—that these planes never dropped bombs.

"There's the office of Magnus Goodbetter."

"But there's nothing there," protested Yungman. "Is the CEO a ghost?"

"You see, the transparency is an illusion."

"Excuse me?"

Einstein grinned. "There are cameras outside that are projecting the view"—Yungman tracked the next plane with his eyes the entire time it moved across the sky—"in real time," Einstein continued. "So we don't see what's going on in the office."

"Ah, showing you what you expect to see. You're halfway to accepting the illusion already."

"Exactly," his son said.

"So, is your 'suite' of rejuvenation products related to aesthetics or functionality?"

"Both!" said Einstein with a gleam in his eye. "Marni helped me come up with 'suite.' She's a natural marketer. The laser can tighten and restore elasticity, but you can also use it for very precise cutting and sculpting for labiaplasties."

His son's face was the one Yungman assumed Nobel made when he'd discovered dynamite.

"I suppose that's good, Einstein—" he said now, trying to be supportive.

"Excuse me, Sir, but you're supposed to call me 'Dr. Kwak' when we're in the Tower."

"Then are you also supposed to call me 'Dr. Kwak'?" he rebutted. His son smiled weakly and pointed to his SANUS pin, the green double-snaked MDiety logo, on his collar.

All right. In the HoSPAtal hierarchy, he was just an "operator." Lower than a DRone.

"All right, Dr. Kwak, do you remember how you wanted to be a doctor so badly, even when you were little? How you visited me at the hospital? You walked over, all by yourself. The nurses were amazed."

"Oh yes. Dr. Mitzner's tonsillectomy." He smiled at the remembrance.

"Oh, well before that one." Yungman had ordered something called risotto, and a gluey lump of it went down the wrong pipe. He resented even the tiniest spark of admiration in his son's eyes for his detested colleague, his frenemy Charles Lindbergh. "You walked all the way from home to the hospital to see me. You were barely out of kindergarten. Everyone thought that was so cute. You had your little stethoscope on."

Yungman didn't mention the clucks of concern, the comments about "Who the heck is supposed to be at home watching him?" In their small town, Yungman supposed people must have noticed that it was he, the man, at the grocery store, the PTA meetings, driving Einstein to and fro. But this was not the order of things. This was a town where Mrs. Rasmussen, a newly minted PhD in chemistry, interviewed at Vermilion Mining for a job in explosives but was rejected because her husband was a doctor and "some man with a family might need this job." In fact, Vermilion Mining ended up hiring a man from Texas, moved him and his family. While longtime Horse's Breath families lined up at the First Presbyterian's food pantry, the mining company bought him the second-largest house in town as enticement. He didn't even stay a year, moving his family to the Ukraine so he could work on a new fracking venture.

Young-ae wasn't ready for Horse's Breath, it was true. And also, Horse's Breath wasn't ready for her. Housewives welcomed them to town with pies and cakes, but Young-ae didn't realize she was supposed to return the pans with *new* pies and cakes and cookies inside. She'd never had an interest in cooking; it would not have made sense to her to do anything more than give the pans a cursory rinse and return them. She did not join the park beautification committee, the neighborhood bridge club. She skipped the Ladies' Auxiliary meetings months in a row. The sharpened whispers of gossip, especially from the church ladies, made their way even to Yungman. That night when Einstein was seven triumphally cemented the "See?" they always said about Young-ae Kwak, the woman who never invited people in for coffee, even after being a guest at their house!

"Mrs. Kwak doesn't work," people remarked with their faux concern. "*What* is she doing all day?"

One night when Yungman was attending a labor, their house had caught on fire. Einstein had been trying to make doughnuts for dinner, inspired by some picture book. Not understanding that the oil wouldn't boil like water, he turned up the heat on the burner until the oil shimmered, then exploded into a fireball. The fire department, looking out its own window, saw what looked like a bomb exploding in the window of the Kwaks' kitchen, in their house perched on the lip of Pill Hill.

Yungman, as the breech presentation had devolved into an emergency C-section, received the strangest call—from the police while he was still at the hospital after midnight. He learned about the fire, which was easily put out, singed wallpaper and wasted oil the worst of the damage. But when the firemen found out Young-ae had been home (in one of her depressive sleeps, curled up in a closet) they'd called the police, who were calling him now. Both Einstein and Young-ae were at the station, and he needed to pick them up. Were they under arrest? And why?

He'd vaguely remembered yelling at his son (for he thought he was expected to do so). He didn't understand this American thing of the police meddling into family affairs. She had been home, she would have saved Einstein (he was sure) if it had come to that. Police Chief Grillo had said nothing about Einstein, only about Young-ae, shockingly using the word "neglect" and threatening all sorts of things.

It wasn't her fault. America wasn't their fault. Since the minute they'd set foot onto land at the Port of San Francisco, they'd both been laboring under misapprehensions. In 1968, abortion had turned out to be just as illegal as it was in Korea. The doctor had been shocked and disgusted when they'd inquired. By then Young-ae was into her second trimester. She accused Yungman of tricking her, but he hadn't. Her father was so wealthy that if she really wanted to get an abortion, she could have risked his wrath and disappointment. But he would have sent her to Switzerland, or one of those rich countries where it was possible, *and* gotten rid of Yungman on the way. No—she married him, and they both became undocumented and couldn't return to Korea. She probably felt terribly guilty to learn not long after they'd left that her father, who looked like a lion on the outside, had had a weak heart, which had given out. She couldn't return for the funeral. Or, she could have. She did not.

Yungman had, in fact, thought a million times about just giving up and going back. Back to what was comfortable. But he also knew that with this black mark on him, he would never be able to come to America again.

Back and forth, back and forth the terrible feelings waxed and waned. Some days less terrible, some days much worse. In this way, the last days of the nine months' gestation marched to their conclusion.

Joy had superseded everything when his fellow intern Mohan handed him the peacefully sleeping, if over-anesthetized, head dented by the forceps, form that was, then, the newest life on the planet: Einstein Albert Schweitzer Nobel Kwak, whom Yungman had named after all his heroes. He couldn't wait for Young-ae to wake up from her twilight anesthesia so they could revel in what they'd done, together.

Within a few months, however, Yungman learned he needed help. Young-ae had groggily woken, uninterested in her new son, and stayed that way, refusing to nurse, catatonic except when she was crying. Sometimes, she'd be wailing and moaning so hard, Yungman would realize the window was open, and he'd hand her a pillow "to cry into," half worried if she kept up the volume he'd panic and push it into her face, anything to make that unearthly noise stop and not make the neighbors think he was beating her or something.

Duckie Lungquist their neighbor one day came to the door with a freshly baked pie. "Oh, William," she'd said. The imperfectly latched door had swung open in the breeze, and she saw him splayed on the floor with exhaustion, mushed-up diapers and old bottles scattered everywhere, wishing he could use his male nipple to pacify his wailing son. How easily the women in the village, with their open chogoris, could nurse and then stick the kid on their backs and go about their day. He had been horribly, horribly embarrassed. There had also, however, been a kind of relief in the surrender. She knew. He knew she knew. The next day, she brought a plate of hotdish with instructions on how to heat it up. When she dropped by to say hello, she often unobtrusively tidied, once washing and sterilizing a moldy baby bottle so fungal with clotted formula even Yungman gagged at the odor when she unscrewed the vent at the top that he had missed. Someone more judgmental would be appalled. Yungman didn't even know if she'd told Clyde about the things she saw in the house: Young-ae's inconsolable crying, the stupors.

The gossip continued.

Duckie loyally never joined in. Despite what social capital it could probably bring her, she didn't leak a whit about what went on in the Kwak household: the empty fridge, the broken objects. Without even an actual discussion, she started coming over during the day, becoming both a housekeeper and surrogate mother to Einstein.

It wasn't as if Young-ae hadn't tried. She had. Valiantly so. In Birmingham, she had tried to warm up Einstein's bottle but gotten confused lighting the gas stove. Yungman had come home to find her with an astonished expression, a rabbity look in her eyes—she'd burned her eyelashes and most of her eyebrows clean off, and the neighbors were mildly curious about the explosion, her blistered face.

By the time they made it to Horse's Breath, Young-ae was done with domesticity.

Yungman paid Duckie with what was left from his salary. Duckie, who was childless, genuinely enjoyed playing with Einstein. She could pretend to answer a toy telephone over and over for hours, just to make him laugh. She instinctively knew what games—patty-cake, peekaboo, hide-and-seek, Clue—to play for every developmental age. She was never cross with him. Yungman felt every child was owed someone who was always happier, not sadder, to see them.

"I think, Bill, your wife might have the baby blues," Duckie allowed one day. "When I came in from bringing Einstein to the park, she was reading a magazine. She didn't even look up."

How terrible that their good-hearted neighbor had made such an astute diagnosis when Yungman, the doctor of women's health, did not. In Young-ae he saw a young woman who was regretful over the consequences of her decision (however, *she* had been the one to initiate their lovemaking the day Einstein was conceived). Think of it this way: they had made it to America. She was vibrantly healthy. More important, they had a healthy son—and he would grow up in a place where vaccines meant he didn't get smallpox, the measles, diptheria, or even the mumps! Of course, she couldn't forget how her brother, Joongki, had disappeared when going to Seoul to get some antibiotics for their sister, who died of TB anyway—but dying of TB in America was laughable!

*You just have the baby, I'll raise it.* It was a duty he had volunteered for; it wasn't a military draft. After the fire, he'd often ask Duckie to stay over in the evenings. But as Einstein grew older, life became easier and easier. Probably the only real upset they'd had since the night at the police station was when Einstein pulled out Yungman's father's long-handled spoon from a tangle of cutlery and started to use it to try to pry open a jar, and Yungman had what could be characterized as a disproportionate reaction.

"I remember that tonsillectomy like it was yesterday," said his son now, lost in his own reverie. "Did you know that Dr. Mitzner made the nurses tie the sleeves of my gown like a straitjacket so I wouldn't grab anything if I fainted?"

"Why would he think you'd faint?" Yungman laughed out loud. Of course, in his first medical school class, maybe about 20 percent of the students had collapsed the moment after the cadavers were unsheathed from their rubber bags. He still remembered the sounds of their bodies dropping like heavy fruit, the disgusted or amused looks of the professors. Even JongDal's ivory face had gone one shade whiter. That was maybe the first time Yungman and Young-ae had calmly locked eyes, each in exquisite control of their faculties.

To give his son a leg up, Yungman had smuggled home IV bags, suction syringes, heparin-lock catheters, and basic butterfly needles when Einstein was ten. He showed Einstein a map of the veins in the cubital fossa. He had also made a Xerox of a page from *Human Anatomy*.

Commonly cannulated for intravenous access. It variably forms as either an H or an M type pattern joining the median antebrachial, basilic, and cephalic veins.

Yungman laid both arms on the kitchen table, offering his bulging veins. He let the child practice on the easy ones, graduating to the trickier ones on the back of his hand. Einstein soon could pop the tourniquet off with one hand, as good as the phlebotomists at the hospital. Only once did he make a mistake, pushing the needle too deep.

Yungman had yanked the whole kit out of his arm, blood dripping down. "Your tears don't matter to an air embolism! Are you trying to kill your father?"

Einstein was a sensitive kid who wilted easily. Thus, it was important for him to realize, right away, that doctoring wasn't a game. Yungman let him practice until all his veins temporarily collapsed into blue lines wriggling through the map of his skin. Einstein would spray antibiotics from the little plastic container that looked like a fire extinguisher and apply Band-Aids, already taking on the confident mien of a miniature physician.

"So, what kind of doctor do you want to be?" he'd asked.

"A surgeon," Einstein said definitively. And Yungman's heart had swelled.

The next step, then, was for Einstein to observe a surgery. In their universe, availability was restricted to Mitzner, the general surgeon (Yungman had secret hopes that Einstein would pursue neurosurgery). One day when they were at the scrub sink together, Yungman casually asked Mitzner about the possibility of letting Einstein observe something simple. Ha—all he did was simple surgeries.

"Why on God's green earth would you want to do this to your kid?" Mitzner had practically yelled at him, in front of the scrub techs and nurses.

Do what? "It's my son who wants to watch," he stammered, although he couldn't remember if that was true.

"Well, *you* must have put that idea in his head."

Yungman was both outraged and abashed. Talking to Mitzner always made him feel like he was having a stressful job interview.

Mitzner wasn't finished: "I worked with an Oriental in my residency—you guys are nuts! This guy was bragging about how his kid was reading classical Chinese poetry at three years old. Let kids be kids, for God's sake!"

Yungman couldn't help noting how, years later, Mitzner complained about the dimness of four out of his five daughters, how all they cared about was makeup and TV and vapid celebrities. Yet no retroactive compliment for Yungman for what was now being admired by white Americans as "tiger parenting." Of course not—it was Mitzner! He reveled in, trafficked in, making people feel worse, not better, about themselves. In fact, even Ken had reached his limit with the "Dr. Quack" jokes and quietly parried, "Should we call you Dr. Missed-the-sponge-ner?"

Yungman took the high road, maintained decorum. "Well, Einstein wants to be a *surgeon*. He's interested in the work *you* do, Dr. *Missedner*."

Ultimately, permission to observe a single tonsillectomy was granted.

"Dr. Mitzner was such a great guy," Einstein reminisced now. "He even showed me Timmy Timmerman's tonsils up close, right before he dropped them in the jar of formalin and told me to never, ever let Timmy know I was in the OR that day. It was like our secret." Einstein gazed into the pool of his ramen, which looked more like spaghetti submerged in broth and not the poodle-curly noodles Yungman had expected. "I wrote about that surgery for both my undergraduate and medical school applications. I'm glad you arranged it."

Ah, so his restraint had paid off.

But in some ways, Yungman still felt as alienated from people like Mitzner as ever before—people he wanted to impress, and who infuriated him when they ignored him.

See, Yungman had presumed that with enough effort, anything could be achieved, including seamlessly becoming an American, with a bustling American social life.

On the ship from Korea, he'd anthropologically observed all the white people, quizzing himself on what would be the "right" thing to do in every situation, while daydreaming about the pleasantly Anglophilic ring to the name "Birmingham." Hedges. Fox hunting.

Alabama had then been a complete surprise. He hadn't been prepared for the tropical heat, how the white-white people mixed in with the Black people through certain intricate codes and verbal choreography he was at a complete loss to figure out (outside his tight-knit foreign intern clan, there were no medium-hued people like him). The syrupy smiles. And worse, he'd suddenly gone deaf to English. The odd accent of the blowsy blond nurse who'd kept asking him, at louder and louder volumes, "Is this European? European?" while poking a pen at him like an epée. *Is this your pen?*

Or, the day Yungman went to the bank to cash his first paycheck, he'd noticed that the drinking fountain offered both normal water and COLORED water. Yungman wanted to experience American ways as quickly as possible, and so he tried the COLORED water. He was disappointed when only plain water came out. He flagged down the janitor to explain that he'd used the colored water fountain but only normal water was forthcoming; could he fix it? The man stared down at Yungman for a second, bug-eyed and confused. Then a wide smile split his face. "Huh-huh-hah-ha," he laughed. Then he flagged down a fellow Black man in a suit and reiterated Yungman's "colored water" request. Both men exploded with laughter that seemed to last forever, the two even collapsing on each other in hilarity. Yungman moved on and got into line with a frown. Even the white teller looked like she was ready to laugh at him.

The only code that was easy to figure out was how all the Black patients were in one ward.

Yungman at first thought Black people were more sickly than white people, since they comprised all the patients, but then he realized it was just that all the foreign-trained physicians worked in what was called the Negro ward. "It's like an American caste system," explained Mohan the Indian intern.

On Yungman's bus commute to work, the Black people, carefully dressed, would have to shove and worm their way through a packed bus to sit in the back. Yungman often got caught up in that tide. Sometimes a bus driver would spot him and motion him forward to the "white" section, usually while beaming a benevolent, missionary-type smile. The next day, a different driver might scowl and point and make Yungman push through a packed phalanx of irritated white people to get to the back of the bus.

As non-white, foreign men, Yungman and his fellow interns didn't know where they belonged, and thus clung tightly to one another. At least they'd had one another. Yungman was grateful that he recertified in less than a year, working overnights, which paid slightly more than their indentured servitude wages. All thanks to the help of a sympathetic pharmacist who kept him supplied with Benzedrine.

At Horse's Breath General, the blond, blue-eyed patients matched more closely to Yungman's conception of "America." But here, he was all alone. With Charlie Kwak gone, the only other non-white people were a few Native Americans who lived on the reservation nearby, but they had their own separate health care system (America really *was* a caste system). Most of the doctors at Horse's Breath had been quite friendly and welcoming. It helped that he'd started the same day as Ken; they became bonded, as Yungman had with his medical-school friends.

Yungman had in fact predicted that snooty Dr. Mitzner would look down on Ken for being a mere generalist, but they were both sons of the town and were already acquainted with each other. And Ken was friends with everyone. That man was admirably incapable of making enemies. Yungman had feared Ken would melt seamlessly into this body of Horse's Breath doctors and leave him, the awkward outsider, behind. But that wasn't how Ken was. He had been a loyal friend for forty years, both to Mitzner and to Yungman.

Yungman, however, had never—not once—been invited to one of Mitzner's famous dinner parties. He and his wife, Rosemary, had them for all the big holidays (even Christmas—you wouldn't know they were Jews), as well as special themed parties where you'd dress up in costume, or figure out who a putative murderer was. Yungman longed for a single invitation, even to their all-male poker nights. But one hadn't been forthcoming. He supposed he could have had Ken intercede on his behalf, but he had pride. See, he'd done everything humanly possible to be an exemplary American, an exemplary colleague, an exemplary Horse's Breather. Maybe he was even a Super American. On the citizenship test, he told the examiner he could name all the American presidents *and* in order; did the man want to hear?

Yungman had his pride, however. He did not want to go the route of obsequious coolie—what did the kids call it? Brownie nose. Instead, he turned to study. It was in Dale Carnegie's *How to Win Friends and Influence People* that he learned that the best way to get on the good side of a man was to talk about his favorite subject: himself. Perfect for Mitzner, clearly. *Ask questions about a favorite activity.*

Yungman searched high and low for something to talk about. The weather? Too fleeting. All the doctors wore the same thing (white coat, shirt and tie). Yungman had no hobbies like Mitzner (stamp collecting, piloting a private plane—who has time for any of that? The closest thing Yungman had to a hobby was cutting the grass weekly).

Ah, but he did know that Mitzner had an almost unseemly pride in his singing voice, which he often demonstrated in the tiled acoustics of the surgical suite. So one day while he, Mitzner, and Clausen scrubbed in (even though technically the anesthesiologist didn't need to do this, since he didn't come near the surgical field), Yungman saw his chance.

"So, Dr. Mitzner—that song, you know, you're always singing: Can you tell me more about it, why you like it so much?"

"Which song?"

Which song? He'd been singing the same one for the past few weeks. In fact, because their surgical schedules had intersected three times this week, it had bored into Yungman's brain like a parasite, especially when they were at the scrub sink together; Yungman a captive audience member insipidly smiling while silently cursing the three strokes up, three strokes down needing to be done on the back and front of every finger.

"The one about the woman. The one-eyed got."

"One-eyed got? What the hell are you talking about?"

Did he have to spell it out for him? The biased woman—"one-eyed" as they said in Korean, too. And "got" must be some synonym for beautiful woman. Well, Mitzner wasn't the only one with a nice voice—the other houseboys were always complimenting Yungman on his singing voice, especially how quickly he picked up songs in English.

". . . Ain't no woman like the one-eyed got!" he belted. "To make her happy don't take a lot!"

Yungman remembered the laughter, the spasm of Clausen's foot on the water lever squirting an arc of water that pretty much rendered them unsterile and needing to rescrub. Mitzner had already finished, his hands held aloft like Moses. He said, coldly, "Good God in heaven, Kwak." And to Clausen, "Gordon, you *know* you don't need to scrub in; the anesthesiologist is dirty." And he walked away, Clausen following him, still snickering.

Out of nowhere, *Tell me, how many arteries does a uterus have?* came to mind. Yungman sat up. Mitzner hadn't been asking for an answer—he was saying, "Are you such a bad surgeon that you don't know how many arteries a uterus has?"

Yungman had puzzled over "sarcasm" over many years. Now, he finally understood how it worked.

"I'm not the quack, *you* are the quack!" Yungman had shouted after him in the physicians' lounge, making Ken, who was walking by, pause. "Are you all right, Yungman?"

Yungman now stole a glance at his physician son. His suit jacket was so closely fitting that he'd needed to unbutton it before he sat down. He was bent over his bowl, using a fork—a fork!—to eat ramen.

Had Einstein's admission to Harvard avenged these accumulated wrongs? (Einstein hadn't made it to neurosurgery, however, but that was another story.) Yungman didn't know. Einstein had been generally a quiet child, one who never gave them a moment's trouble. His report cards were always all As. His teachers praised his "beautiful behavior" and "ability to memorize." Einstein had stated that he wanted to be a doctor at such an early age—three? Four? Come to think of it, Yungman had congratulated himself about it at the time but had never really asked his son the reasoning behind his decision. Was that what he really wanted to do? Or was he making that choice out of a sense of duty, out of thinking that being who the other person wanted you to be was an act of love? At four, all boys probably wanted to emulate their daddies. But how about at ten? Twelve? Yungman didn't want to consider that Mitzner might have been correct: Einstein had only asked to watch the surgery because he thought that was what *Yungman* wanted.

He wished he'd said, both when Einstein was twelve and also when he'd announced he was going into OB-GYN (after Yungman had—earlier, regrettably—been openly scornful that he was considering plastic surgery as his surgical specialty), "Great. I'm proud of you. But please make sure this is a choice you want, and you're not doing it to make me or your mother happy. Because we're not going to be around forever, but you have a long career ahead of you. We'll be proud of you whatever you do."

However: How could his son use a *fork* to eat noodles?

Even at Golden Dragon, Yuchen Charlie Kwak would always carefully place chopsticks next to the huge wonton spoons, a silent gesture of ethnic solidarity. The Kwaks in turn would leave those chopsticks untouched and flag down the waiter (usually Charlie/ Yuchen himself) to conspicuously demand forks. In this instance they would let Einstein use the chopsticks to stir endless sugar packets into water or wear them like walrus tusks, making his parents laugh (how quickly that time had passed).

Their son studied hard and got into Harvard . . . and then was back home in three months.

Yungman almost couldn't bear how public the failure had been, people seeing Einstein around town, working at the KFC like any other kid in his class who didn't find employment in the mines.

The correct thing to do during these encounters was to murmur about how nice it must be to have Einstein home again. Even the pharmacist, when handing Yungman Einstein's lithium prescription, knew to say that.

It was Mitzner who had actually seemed concerned and suggested a few local counselors, a psychiatrist in the Cities. The concern had, at the time, felt more vampiric, triumphal maybe. Yungman had mightily wanted to tell Mitzner to mind his own beeswax.

In medical school, Einstein had announced he'd narrowed down his specialties to cardiothoracic transplant surgery and neurosurgery, two of the most difficult and prestigious specialties, something Yungman didn't mind talking at enhanced volume about at the scrub sink.

Then there was the idea of plastic surgery, which Yungman had openly derided, hoping it would push him back to transplants or neurosurgery.

Yungman was taken off guard, then, after graduation, at Einstein's sudden pivot to OB-GYN, the bomb dropped during a regular Sunday-night phone call.

"That's wonderful," Young-ae said immediately.

"Yes, I'm excited. Brigham and Women's is the best OB-GYN residency in the country."

"Of course," Young-ae said. "It's Harvard."

Yungman bit down on his tongue before he said something like, *Who goes to Harvard Medical School to just do primary care?* "Are you . . ." he had ventured, "then considering an academic career? MD-PhD? Or GYN-oncology, maternal-fetal medicine? I've been reading in the *Green Journal* that there's a lot of work being done on polyhydramnios in twins, for instance. Or advances in surgical techniques—there hasn't been a new instrument invented in quite a long time."

Einstein was quiet a moment.

"I think I just want to practice. I grew up watching you, and I've grown to like the idea of a happy specialty, focused more on life and less on pathology."

*Of course* there was the feeling of homage. Yungman was ashamed of his paternal disappointment. But weren't children supposed to do *better* than their parents? And also better than their parents' enemies?

Ugh, what would Mitzner think now, the mentally frail Harvard son returning once again as an OB-GYN "aesthetician" at the Mall of America?

The waiter wheeled over a dessert cart: cakes, puddings, pastries, petits fours, all with the logo of SANUS: a big green caduceus with double-entwined snakes making the double Ss in SANUS. The second S was a dollar sign. "What is this?" asked Yungman about a wedge of pie with a seductively glistening surface.

"Crack Pot Pie," the man said.

"Is there any crack in it?"

"No."

"Any pot?"

"No!"

"Then I will have it."

"Excellent choice. Coffee? We have the special Kopi Luwak Civet coffee. Only twenty pounds are exported from Indonesia each year. SANUS managed to get *all twenty pounds*, much to the chagrin of all those fancy coffee places."

"How'd they do that?" asked Einstein proudly. To Yungman he said, "This coffee costs three hundred dollars a pound."

"Guerilla warfare, some smuggling, a bribe to the Indonesian government," the man said.

Yungman, whose sarcasm detector was now more finely honed, was pretty certain he wasn't kidding.

Just like his need to experience the COLORED water fifty years ago, he ordered the Kopi Luwak coffee. There was always something new to the American experience.

"By the way," said Einstein. He'd ordered a regular cappuccino and took a sip. The foam left a thin white mustache on his upper lip. Yungman's Kopi Luwak coffee was smooth, but really not that different from the watery taste of Sanka, same sour note at the end. "I have something I'd like to talk to you about."

Yungman was alarmed by the change in tone. "Is Reggie okay?"

"Well, yes and no."

"Tell me." Yungman's mind raced. A young person's cancer, like Hodgkin's lymphoma? Osteosarcoma? He *had* seemed like he was limping a little bit, hadn't he? Yungman's throat seized.

"The move has been a lot harder on him than we thought."

"Oh. I'm so sorry to hear."

"Well, middle school is a pretty tender time to be moved away from your friends and everything you're used to. I mean, he was born in Greenwich and everything."

"What is happening, exactly?" Yungman was impatient for him to get the bad news out. Maybe a B-list chronic problem? Type 1 diabetes? Juvenile rheumatoid arthritis? Maybe that antisocial psychiatric syndrome everyone was talking about that Yungman had not seen spelled out but remembered it phonetically as Ass Burger syndrome.

He and Young-ae had seen Reggie for Christmas. This year, instead of buying whatever was on the list submitted by "Santa's helper" (usually expensive electronics), Yungman and Young-ae were excited about the unique present they'd found.

"Just like the ones my mother used to sell!" Yungman had laughed when Young-ae brought a gourd dipper home from church. "I used to spend so many nights scraping the guts out of them with my bro—"

"With your what?"

"With my, uh, bro, brazier. You know, the thing  I forget the Korean word—where you burn the charcoal." Actually, they'd used kerosene lamps to see by, but that was the best he could do on short notice.

The Good News Church had held a fundraiser for orphans in North Korea. They'd sold Korean party favors, and Young-ae had purchased one.

On closer inspection, Yungman saw that the gourd was plastic, a tiny gold MADE IN CHINA sticker on the handle, which he flicked off with a fingernail. But it was incredibly realistic. Both of them couldn't wait for Reggie to unwrap it.

Reggie had opened the box, pawed through it, tossed the gourd dipper aside, wailing, was that it? Really? Einstein sorrowfully explained that he was expecting a new iPhone. "I'll explain it to you later, Sir," he'd said, about Reggie's tears, but he never did. Maybe they had just gotten the Ass Burger diagnosis.

"He's been acting out. Saying he's studying when he's playing video games. Hiding his homework and saying he lost it."

"All right," said Yungman. "So what is the therapeutic plan?"

"The General Ramsey Academy is where we're thinking of sending Reggie."

"Ah," said Yungman. Maybe the most sensible thing he'd heard from his son lately. It made sense for a child who didn't even know how to make his own bed, who couldn't make it through Thanksgiving without two turkey drumsticks. "A military academy."

"No! It's a specialized private school, so he can get more individ-ualized attention. General Ramsey was the first Minnesota territorial governor, so that's why they call it that."

"I see," said Yungman, although he didn't. Since Reggie had learned to walk on his own, Yungman had been aghast at how much the two parents followed that boy around, catering to his every whim, needing to "get on his level." A grown man asking a toddler what he wants! Once, Reggie had socked Einstein in the face, and *Einstein* had apologized to the toddler for not getting his orange juice fast enough!

"Look, Sir, my son is a sensitive kid," Einstein said now. "And having to follow a dad who went to Harvard is a lot of pressure."

"Pressure," Yungman said. And then he laughed so hard that he feared his rare Indonesian coffee might spurt out of his nose. "Reg-gie? He doesn't even have to support himself or worry over making a living!"

"Sir, he's *twelve*." There was that voice of aggrieved patience for the senile old man. "Anyway, this isn't what I needed to discuss with you. We've already signed a contract to send him there."

"Okay," Yungman agreed. "You don't need to wait for my approval, or anyone's."

"Well, only: I'm a bit highly leveraged because of the new house."

Yungman tried to digest and translate in his head. "Leverage" sounded like something on Lou Dobbs's *Moneyline*. "You need money," he said.

"Yes. See, I'm in a situation where I'm cash-poor."

Yungman set his face to its professional neutral. The laughter tickled just under his diaphragm: What other kind of poor was there?

"How was your meal?" said the waiter. He placed the bill, which came in its own tiny leather briefcase, in front of Einstein.

Yungman pointed at his bowl. He felt a little bad, but he'd left it mostly untouched. It was bland, and the rice was both soupy and underdone; some of the grains almost crunched under his teeth like uncooked barley.

"This is like what we have in Korea," he said to the waiter. "Long-cooked rice is hospital food. Although I think you could have cooked it just a wee bit longer."

"'HoSPAtal food,' that's perfect," said the waiter. "Oh, my God—I *love* it."

"I just paid fifty bucks for undercooked hospital food, then," Einstein said, signing the bill. His eyes bugged out slightly when he saw the coffee charge: $110.

"Don't be sarcastic," Yungman said, addressing both of them, even though he wasn't 100 percent sure sarcasm had been committed by either. So much of his language learning had been this way, figuring out if he was right only by scrutinizing the reactions to what he'd just said. (He remembered, for instance, commenting on a 1990s stock market rally that "the stocks are really jacking off now!" and inferring quite quickly that that was not the correct thing to say.)

"SANUS really should do more with puns, even for the food," the waiter mused. "My nephew absorbed quite a nasty stick to the head during his hockey game, and I worried he'd had a concussion.

We were already close to the Mall, so we went to Dome Depot. We laughed and laughed when we saw the name. SANUS really puts fun back into health care!"

Einstein folded the bill in its little case, fastened the clasps, and handed it to the waiter. "Thank you," Einstein said coldly, and he sat rigidly until the waiter took his cue and scurried away.

"There's also something called a 'legacy,'" Einstein said. "That we really shouldn't waste."

"Legacies are important," Yungman agreed.

"I'm talking about an actual college admissions term. For the more prestigious schools, like Harvard. Harvard is proud of its legacies."

"Of course," Yungman said.

"You see if a parent went to Harvard, the child has a better chance of getting in, actually a fifty percent better chance, all other things being equal."

"What on earth does a parent's going to a school have to do with the *child*?" Yungman said in disbelief. "In Korea, we just took a test, no one knew who our parents were." Also, in that international news section of the paper, he'd seen that Korea's first woman president had hardly started her term before she'd been impeached, over helping a friend's daughter skip the test and get into Ewha. Yungman was *glad* this kind of cheating had been properly marked as scandalous and punished.

"It really has to do with money," Einstein said. "Alums are more likely to donate if there's a generational connection."

"I see," Yungman said. "Money. Of course."

"You know how many parents would kill to have a Harvard legacy? But Reggie can't use it unless he's competitive. His academics just aren't where they should be, and if he doesn't catch up somehow, the legacy won't be worth anything."

"I am sorry you have been having this trouble," Yungman said.

"It's just been one thing after another," Einstein said. "The moat froze and broke the underwater motor."

"Why did you leave it running?" Yungman said. "You should have let it freeze over. Reggie could learn to skate on it: hello, Hans Brinker!"

Einstein looked sulky. Was joking not allowed in the hallowed HoSPAtal dining room? Yungman added: "That's how I learned how to skate, you know. In the frozen runnels in the rice paddy."

"That's the first time I've ever heard you say anything about your childhood." Einstein looked slightly astonished.

"You never ask!"

"I'd like to . . . another time. Sir, let me just come out and say it: Marni and I would like to ask you and Mom for a loan."

"A loan?" said Yungman incredulously. "You live in a million-dollar house and need a loan from your father? Who's making minimum wage, I might add."

"But you have a pension," Einstein said quietly. "Things are really different for my generation. I had to empty my IRA to buy the house."

"You must have sold your house in Greenwich for a lot."

"Well, actually, I made a bad decision getting a balloon mortgage, and, to be a hundred percent transparent, SANUS is paying us in stock options."

"What does that mean?"

"It means I'm being paid in stock options."

"What does that mean, 'options'? Isn't it *good* to have options?"

"They're a kind of specific financial instrument where you have the 'option' to 'exercise' them at a later date, after a company has an IPO and goes public."

Amid the unfamiliar jargon, Yungman got the gist of it: "You're not being paid actual money right now."

"Well, yes, that's technically correct. I get tips and some fees, but that's not the bulk of my earnings. Health care is also not provided."

"Health care isn't provided at SANUS Global *Health*? What are you doing, then?"

"Well, I can get small stuff done at Employee Optimization. Luckily Minnesota has some good publicly funded plans on its exchange."

"Ah, for the not-rich. Affordable care, ACA."

"Yes. It's pretty bare-bones, but you were the one who taught me we can never go, even a day, without health insurance. Every day I pray Reggie won't need braces."

Einstein had voted for a presidential candidate who had categorically wanted to get rid of ACA, care that already absurdly didn't count the teeth in your head as part of your body, as far as health coverage went. A president who would install "strongman" health care — "to see who deserves to live or die." Yungman had found that exceedingly shocking, but apparently that kind of message was attractive to the Communist-phobic, like immigrants from Eastern Bloc countries and people at the Korean church. Conservative immigrants who fancied themselves more patriotic as Republicans, plus plain, white, bread-and-butter Americans who didn't seem to demand anything from their taxes except their minimization, found the idea of a businessman tackling America's problems with a salesman's mindset to be attractive.

"So options give you options, but you cannot eat options from your job, nor will it provide you with health care, which is what jobs are supposed to do."

"Haha, yes, you're right. But you see, that's how start-ups work. Like Facebook — a bunch of Harvard students in a dorm room. And now it's worth billions. And Zuckerberg, the founder, just like Bill Gates before him — they both dropped out of college. It's a leap of faith, if you really believe in your company's mission, like I do. Yes, it's almost like volunteer work to get it up and running. For instance, the guy they hired to paint a mural in Facebook's office, they offered him fifty thousand dollars or some stock options."

"You can't eat stock options," Yungman reiterated.

"What would you have done in that situation—say, if you had a family you were supporting?"

"Take the money, of course. How *else* are you going to eat?"

"Well, get this: The guy decided to take the *options*. He's worth millions, maybe a billion today. Just from painting that one mural."

"I still would have taken the money. Any sensible person would have." Fifty thousand!

"See, I probably would have, too," Einstein said excitedly. "But watching the movie about Facebook really helped explain how that that's an outdated way of thinking. That's also why if you work as a doctor, you get a decent income, but after you pay down your loans and then your malpractice insurance, you have almost zero opportunity for any kind of wealth advancement. Wealth, not wages, is where it's at."

Yungman thought about their 1992 diamond-mine debacle. Rasmussen had insisted it was a "sure thing" and brought all the doctors into the Future Millionaire's Club, investing in diamond mines in Rwanda. A year later, Rasmussen had bought a lake cabin and a new snowmobile, but the rest of the doctors had each lost a few thousand; Yungman actually wondered if that had been a Ponzi scheme.

"You know," he told his son, "helping people, practicing medicine for reasons *besides* wealth and wage is the reason we become doctors, right?" Yungman said. "If we want 'wealth advancement,' we should become businessmen."

"Well, under that definition, I *am* a medical businessman. You worked in a place with an extremely low cost of living, where your salary and now your Social Security goes a long way in Horse's Breath. You even had an actual defined-benefits pension, thanks to the mining company, a total artifact of the past."

"I'm not sure I understand." Wasn't that the American dream — working hard and making a living? Granted, he'd been terminated, and also that pension had been *his* money, planted like a seed.

"For my generation," said Einstein, "playing it safe means relegating yourself to a life without advancement, being stuck in a rut — as a DRone. Did you know that in college I had an opportunity to invest in a company some of my suitemates were creating called Netscape? You only needed five thousand to start."

" 'Only' five thousand?" Yungman repeated.

"Exactly. Obviously I didn't have that kind of money, but I *wanted* to invest. I suppose I could have taken out a loan or something, but you always told me never to use credit to get things with money I didn't have. But if I'd only pushed my thinking a little further, out of the old ways . . . You know, even the *intern* at Netscape became a millionaire."

"How did the *intern* get five thousand dollars?"

"No, see, he worked for the company and got paid in stock options like the graffiti-artist guy did at Facebook — and like me. But he was a young kid and could just eat a bunch of Top Ramen — and I also think he had some family help; his name literally was Rockefeller. But anyway, the situation I was in at Greenwich Medical, with my mortgage obligations, my IRA actually shrinking — the 2008 financial crisis cut it in half. And *on top* of that, my malpractice insurance premiums were going through the roof. I made a calculated decision to jump out of a dying, stagnating, conventional DRone medical field and join a start-up: SANUS."

"I thought," said Yungman, "that you wanted to move to Minnesota to be closer to us."

"Of course, of course, that was a big factor, the biggest factor. I'd wanted to move closer for a long time. I even had a headhunter working on it — Chicago was the closest I could find something. That's the pull to Minnesota, you and Mom. But as you've probably guessed, Marni isn't a huge fan of the Midwest. I also needed a *push*."

"What's wrong with the Midwest?"

"Nothing. She just doesn't particularly care for it. It's provincial. We were a quick hop away from New York City. The least I could do was get her a nice house in Minneapolis. That was part of the deal."

"The deal," said Yungman. "Your marriage is a *deal*?"

"We try to make sure everything we do as a family is equal and negotiable for both spouses. I'm trying to keep up my end of the deal—keep my son educated, her happy. Reg really needs a little something to help him be attractive to colleges. Something like, if he was good at hockey, there would be nothing to worry about." Indeed, the same year Einstein returned home for his "mental exhaustion," Yungman had been outraged to learn than the son of the baker had been accepted to Harvard despite being a mediocre student solely because he was good at skating and moving a little puck down the ice!

After a moment, Einstein glanced up now, shyly, at him. "So, what do you think?"

"How much would you need?"

"Great!" Einstein said. "It would really be more like a loan, too. Maybe a forgivable loan, but a loan. We can even come up with an installment plan."

"How much do you need?"

"Forty-five thousand."

"What?"

"You always told me not to say, 'what,' that it was rude." Einstein smiled to punctuate the gentle joke, the subtle chastisement at how obdurately strict he'd been. For some reason, hearing his child-son say, *what?!?!* seemed the height of rudeness, akin to the way some

Horse's Breath kids called their parents *by their first names*. Yungman barely knew his own parents' names, he knew most adults by their titles. But that was Korea. How was Einstein supposed to know all this? Yungman thought again about the time and attention he had not been able to give his own flesh and blood, as he had always been at work or thinking about work, always constantly worried he'd miss some ship pulling out, leaving him behind. But even if too late for his son, maybe he could make up for it with his son's son.

"I suppose it makes sense you get what you pay for," he said. "And Reggie is certainly worth it."

"What if we," Einstein said. "Considered this part of my inheritance?"

"Your what?" Yungman said. He wasn't sure he heard right.

"Like, just getting it a little bit early."

Yungman's SANUSwatch jangled, warning him that his shift would be starting in twenty minutes. "Maybe Reggie can learn to play hockey," he said to his flabbergasted son, before heading to the elevator.


At home, Young-ae had another envelope waiting for him from Sajik-Ro, Seoul-si, South Korea. She hadn't opened it, but stood there while he did.

Pictures of four young Korean women spilled out. They all had clefts in their chins, wide faces, merry eyes. Two of them wore their hair straight and pinned back with barrettes, one had a frizzy perm, and the youngest had a daring short cut that made her look like she was in a boy band.

> Bitnam, Byul, Bom, Bodul, my pride and joy.
> —Cho Bo-hae

"You going to spill the beans?" said Young-ae. "These girls . . . look a bit like you, don't they?"

"I don't know who these people are," Yungman said sincerely.

"The letter is addressed to you."

"Yes, clearly this person knows who I am."

"And you don't know her."

"That's correct." Yes, everything was going to reach a breaking point, eventually. But he was stubborn enough to wait until it happened.

"I would bother you about it more, but—" Young-ae paused. She looked so genuinely worried that Yungman began to panic.

"Everything all right? Is there bad news somewhere?"

She handed him a pile of mail. A charity letter from Doctors Without Borders. That was just a form letter. Oh, wait, also a notice that he was due for a tooth cleaning. Yes, it had been a while.

Then she handed him an envelope separately. It said "Letter of Intent." It looked very official.

He'd never seen anything like that before.

This letter is to inform you that an Affidavit of Expert Review has been requested. As per 145.68 as defined in section 145.63 subdivisions 2 and 3a, "health care provider" means a physician, surgeon, dentist, or other health care professional or hospital, including all persons or entities providing health care . . . You "health care provider" do not have to reply to this letter, it only serves as a notification that an inquiry has been opened.

He squinted. This sounded like someone was calling for a medical board complaint—or someone wanted to sue him for malpractice!

Young-ae agreed. But he had never been sued or had a board complaint, even one of those frivolous anonymous ones, in his life.

What was the protocol? Wasn't someone supposed to jump out of the bushes, trick him into touching the envelope, and say, "You've been served, Dr. Kwak"? And *who* was it? He read through all the fine print and saw only a single mention of a "C. Maki."

The first *C* name that came to mind was Christabelle Haugen, the woman who'd called him for dizziness. Of course he had secretly followed up, because he'd been worried; she'd indeed followed his advice and gone to an ER, where it turned out she had atypically presenting preeclampsia, and her baby was delivered early and safely, and before she had any terrible effects like a seizure. So it wasn't her.

*C. Maki.*

*C. Maki.*

*C. Maki.*

He racked his brain.

A full 30, maybe even 35 percent of Horse's Breathers were Makis. People laughed at him when he pronounced it "Mah-kee," like the Japanese sushi. It was "Mack-ee," reflecting how you said it in Finnish: Rantamäki, Kaunismäki, Kauramäki, Koivumäki, Myllymäki, Palomäki, Lamminmäki, Rautamäki, Peramäki, Hakomäki, Kortesmäki, Hautamäki, Niinimäki, Katajamäki; and there was Makiinen. It was hard for him to envision, but apparently the Finns were considered "undesirable" immigrants, and so they'd wanted to seem less Finnish by shortening their names until it seemed like Horse's Breath was a Maki village the same way Water Project Village was a village of almost all Parks.

He guessed it was the Maki cervical cancer case — Elmer's daughter, who'd gone untested and unvaccinated, who'd literally fallen between the cracks. A wrongful death suit — failure to diagnose cancer. He thoroughly understood the need to pin the blame, even if it belonged to the health care system itself, on someone — someone with some money that could maybe help her kids—he remembered the Tonka truck, the baby doll. It was a wacky system, but understandable on some level. While he hadn't been incompetent or had any intent to harm, per se, she was still dead.

Wait—it was a different Maki. A living one. She'd signed the Letter of Intent herself.

*Wrongful loss of fertility.*

Oh, *Cathy* Asia Suhonen Maki. Placental abruption. Aigu! The one he'd moved heaven and earth for. He'd gotten her baby, Beyoncé, into the best university-based NICU, then gotten *her* in! He'd thrown his mentor under the bus. *You saved my life*, she'd said.

"Oh, as medical officer, I've been there with a few of the other docs," said Ken, when Yungman immediately called him.

"What?" said Yungman. "How could you sue someone you're going to see in church on Sunday?" But a beat later, he also recalled how regularly high school students would drive past their house and yell "Chink!" out the window, especially if they were in the yard. They never seemed abashed when Yungman saw them in church on Sunday.

"In our health care system, unfortunately, suing is one of the few ways patients can get redress for negligence. On the other hand, there are those who use it as an opportunity to make money."

"This was a placentral abruption, arrived by ambulance already bleeding. I had to do an emergency hysterectomy, mother and the baby are healthy. I didn't make any mistakes that I know of—I even called Dr. Mitzner in for a consult."

"I'm guessing it's about the money. See, Minnesota has no cap on compensation for damages. Some people treat it like Powerball."

Yungman groaned.

"With the hospital being gone, that's probably why the patient—or her lawyer—decided to go after you."

Yungman groaned again. Hadn't Einstein often chided him for not carrying private liability insurance? He'd scoffed and said, "Who'd sue me? My patients all know I try my best. This is the benefit and the beauty of community medicine." Now, all he could imagine was himself in the poorhouse, sued into kingdom come by a disgruntled patient.

"It's not all bad news, Yungman. You can try your luck with Powerball, but Minnesota also has the highest standards for the burden of proof. She'll have to get an expert to sign an affidavit saying she has a case, plus review and approval from the state medical board. Was this just a notice of investigation, or was this a notice of a pending case, with affidavit?"

Yungman scanned the letter. "It says they're requesting an affidavit."

"Then it's just the earliest stage. Some greedy lawyer trolling the records probably got his hooks in. They work on contingency; the patient really has nothing to lose."

Yungman was feeling a peculiar stew of indignation, rage, and shame. Not unlike when he was a houseboy on the American base and some soldiers had found money missing and blamed Yungman, who had been in the room but would never touch anything of a GI's. Even as he denied it, they held him down and stripped him. The helplessness. The rage at having his privates exposed. Didn't they know the houseboys were the most trustworthy people on the base? The GIs often stole from each other, but they never would. Tadpole and the orphans depended on the job for their food and shelter. Hadn't his record of being the cleanest, the most helpful, the best-English houseboy meant anything to them? They'd let him up, satisfied, but then asked him about it a half hour later! They couldn't even tell any of the houseboys apart! It was only when Red, "his" GI, happened to come in that Yungman was spared the humiliation of being strip-searched again.

Yes, he felt the same smoldering anger now, knowing it was consuming him, but not being able to do anything to cool off.

"Yungman," said Ken. "You're a great doctor who always puts his patients first. All the doctors in the hospital would agree. That's why we fought so hard to keep you when you had your, er, immigration papers problem. If it comes to it, we'll all vouch for you." Yungman was touched that Ken didn't even ask more about the case and how he had treated it—he presumed Yungman could not, would not have committed malpractice.

"She sent me a birth announcement!" He unexpectedly felt tears starting.

"Keep that card, if you still have it, as evidence. You know, the whole time I've been doctors' liaison, I don't think a single one of these has gone to trial."

"Have there been a lot?"

"Ohyahh. I got one for saying hi to a patient in the ER. The patient was suing Rasmussen and everyone related to his care. That's all I did was say hi."

Yungman had always been under the impression that everyone understood that the "doc" did his best, even if the outcome wasn't what they wanted. They weren't God; they didn't get to control the outcome. Malpractice was a mix of incompetence and malice and dereliction of duty—he could not think of a single doctor who would fit in that category. The closest would probably be Dr. Nilsson, the GP who'd done the deliveries—Rasmussen would regale them with stories of how they'd had to cover for the man's forgetfulness, his tendency to doze off those last months before Yungman got there—but the man was ninety years old! And nothing had gone wrong. He could still do his work practically by muscle memory alone.

"Well, that's how you get health care these days—you have a fundraiser or you sue for it. The sue-ers are just copying all the people who've claimed they've injured the soft tissue in their backs from falling on the floors at Walmart. See, Walmart tends to settle quickly for modest amounts, and not require a lot of proof. And because they devastated Stuffers Drug and all the other Main Street businesses, I never felt that bad about signing those slips, to tell you the truth."

"But what should I *do*?" He heard a rustling on the other end of the line.

"How about we explore the next item on the bucket list? Madison, Minnesota, world's largest lutefisk. Got this one from a guidebook: 'A thirty-foot-long cod named Lou T. Fisk. Lutefisk, a Nordic delicacy, often served at Christmastime, combines frozen dried fish and lye and is an unforgettable taste experience.' Yep, that's the stuff I know."

Yungman had eaten it variously over the years at church suppers. It reminded him, actually, of how his family wasn't ever rich enough to eat beef, but when his mother could wheedle a hunk of knuckle cartilage from the meatmonger, boiled on the bone, it tasted of beef but with its own texture, just as lutefisk vaguely kept its fishy properties but turned to jelly in the mouth.

"Why is *this* on your bucket list?" For Ken, everything in life seemed to be a joy. Even lye-preserved fish jelly.

"No one knows who invented lutefisk—Norwegians and the Swedes are still arguing to the death about it. By celebrating it, I don't have to choose sides of my family. Myrtle's one hundred percent Swede for three generations—our mixed marriage."

"I have one question, though," said Yungman. "Do I actually have to *eat* the lutefisk if I go with you?"

Ken laughed. "According to this guidebook, they also serve wild game and frozen-from-the-summer panfish at this supper—I'd be hoping for beer batter."

"All right," said Yungman. He still had a lump in his stomach, a low-grade anxiety tethering him to his worries, as if he might open the door at any time and have someone jump out at him with a "You've been served!" and his trial would begin. At his age! And with no financial cap for damages. He and Young-ae relegated to eating dog food in their dotage—that is, if he didn't go to debtors' prison.

The bad feeling continued into the evening. Young-ae was staying late in Edina for an epic Bible-copying session. Yungman worried. Then he fumed. He racked his brain. All his cases ran together. That last week before the closure: all the unexpected admissions, the full clinic. He remembered the blood dripping onto the floor, and onto his clogs, which he'd already changed into because his shoes had been soaked by that morning's rain. He also remembered that that week he'd pretty much comped all the patients, just as he had done selectively his whole career. If someone couldn't pay, it was easier and better, in his opinion, to just let it go rather than make Rose spend her time chasing them down. The old hospital president gave it his tacit approval—all the doctors did it from time to time. But one of Tinklenberg's first "initiatives" was that the hospital hire a collection agency—the last ten years had brought in a *lot* of people who couldn't pay, adding to "debt pressures." But how could you refuse care to a person you saw at the next pew on Sundays? Theirs was a small town. Yungman wouldn't be able to imagine such a scenario, although apparently this was happening all the time now, in a newly strict and computer- and balance sheet–driven hospital world.

Indeed, in the last decade, patients were constantly bringing in coupons and rebate forms for prescription drugs. But why did people need these at all? When he prescribed drugs, he didn't know if it cost five dollars or five thousand. Wasn't that the way it was supposed to be, you just treated the condition? He wasn't a supermarket!

The envelope for Doctors Without Borders was still sitting on the pile. Now would be an excellent time for some distraction. (He *still* couldn't believe someone to whom he'd extended *so* much charity was suing him!) He'd been thinking about Doctors Without Borders a lot lately, mentally composing a letter. On a whim he typed it up:

Dear Sirs:

I am a retired doctor who still has plenty of skills left. If you ever need personnel for any kind of disaster, please keep me in mind. I have a valid Minnesota medical license and I am a board-certified OB-GYN. I speak English and Japanese and can read German.

French would probably be better, for all those Francophone African countries, but it was too late for him to learn now. Funny how he'd forgotten to include his native language.

. . . and Korean. I can be available on short notice.

Sincerely,

Yungman Kwak, MD FAACOG

He folded the letter in with his check, considering dreamily how it would be wonderful if they needed someone, say, after a tsunami somewhere. If he could just up and go like a migrating bird, from this life into a totally different one, one where any help he could provide would matter.

Yungman walked into the Depilation Nation treatment room believing routine was going to save him. Or at least get him through the day.

Like the exercise sequences they had laid out in the public park: sit-up board, then pull-ups, then balance beam. No one made you do it, but the sequence pulled you, one to two to three, and the next thing you knew, you'd done a full workout. He had made the mistake of telling his son about the suit, and Einstein exhorted him, *demanded* he immediately go "on the offensive."

"Let me call some of my Harvard buddies and find out who's the sharpest, most aggressive medmal lawyer in Minnesota."

"Ken said he saw these cases all the time at Horse's Breath General—he said they're almost all dismissed as nuisance cases."

"You don't want to be the first one that gets through, though. You have to *crush this in the bud*. Lawyers run ads that make everything seem like malpractice. They work on contingency; you just need to make up a story with a sweet plaintiff and a villain—'loss of fertility,' 'Asian butcher'—I can see the headlines already, Sir. Also, even if they settle, your name still goes into the National Medical Malpractice Practitioner Database as having been sued, and anyone in the public who searches for your name has access to that."

*Ah*, Yungman thought. No wonder his new job had asked about malpractice so many times. He would probably lose his job, that last little thread to a routine that was making his days bearable.

"Then what do *you* do, with all your rich luxury clients here?" Yungman challenged. "They must all have hungry lawyers."

"Yup—that's *exactly* an example of one of the HoSPAtal's innovations that can bring around systemic change," he said proudly. "Retailicine is governed by business laws, which are geared more to protect the business—caveat emptor and all that. Early mall retailers took advantage of that for LASIK, which can have a lot of complications because it's surgery. But when you do it at the mall, it's like getting a tattoo or your ears pierced at Earring Pagoda or stopping at the Oxygen Bar. HoSPAtal Guests sign an ironclad affidavit, and just to make sure, SANUS also puts money into lobbying the state legislature to make it almost impossible to sue medical retailers.

"Back to your situation: if someone's started a case against you, they've already gathered all these documents, done the research, hired a lawyer; they want money. So *you* have to be ready to hit them back twice as hard. This is war."

Yungman believed few things were war besides actual war. But he knew his son was trying to help him.

As he checked in with his SANUSwatch, he saw his son had sent him an intra-SANUS message.

I found a list of lawyers who are supposed to be real sharks. Plus a lead on a PI in Minneapolis to follow her around for evidence to dispute her "tragedy." Will call you later tonite. Love, E.

Joelle turned on the sign.

The Doctor is IN
YOUR OPERATOR is Youngman Kwak, MD—
\*\*\* EMPLOYEE OF THE MONTH \*\*\*

Yes, he, incompetent malpracticing Yungman, was yet employee of the month. He had received a small, shield-shaped, engraved plaque (name similarly misspelled), much like the one Einstein had gotten for reading the most books during the summer library reading program five years in a row. Every treatment bed was filled. He hurried to get ready.

As Yungman entered the treatment suite (which wasn't techni- cally a suite, but apparently that word had positive emotional asso- ciations), he could see that the customer in treatment bed 1 was a Black woman. He double-checked the safety card. Most definitely a Type IV: DANGER OF LASER BURN.

She could have gotten hurt! It was Joelle's job to do the assessment and turn people away before they went to all the trouble of disrobing.

"This customer in bed 1 is much too dark," he called admonishingly. He waited impatiently for her reply. When it didn't come, he turned around and strode into the reception area.

The front desk was abandoned.

Now what was he supposed to do?

Through the doorway, he could see the customer in bed 3, a Nordic blond, raise herself up to look at him. "Hey, the gal out front said I'd be done by three," she said warningly. "It's two thirty already."

After five awkward minutes of standing there, shifting from foot to foot, praying for Joelle to return, Yungman decided he'd have to take matters into his own hands. He went back into the treatment suite.

"Excuse me, miss," he said to the Black lady. Her eyes were closed.

"Hello," he said, louder. Waited a beat. "—Pardon me!"

There was no seepage of sound from her padded headphones. Her eyes were shut. Her eyelids twitched like she was dreaming, whisked away to her own biosphere somewhere. His customers' mental absence was something he'd gotten used to. That must be what customers meant when they cited "being comfortable" around him: they felt no self-consciousness because, due to his age or his race or both, he was invisible. The other day, two friends had come in to be depilated together. They spoke over him and had a terribly intimate discussion about "back door" sex (locational? positional?) that left him feeling like a palace eunuch.

But, for the matter at hand: How to become visible? There were all sorts of warnings in the Employee Handbook forbidding "nonprocedural touching." The Laser Defolliculator II ticked gently, as if it, too, were waiting.

He decided to touch the customer's shoulder in the zone that seemed the most neutral and professional: where the clavicle met the upper end of the long bone of the humerus. The place where you'd tap a stranger to alert them to a dropped item, right above the place where you'd administer a vaccine. A user-friendly area, in other words.

"Hunh?" the woman said, waking with a jerk. Yungman gave her a second to reorient herself.

"I'm so sorry," he said loudly, in the direction of her headphones. "We can't do the laser treatment on you."

She sat up and yanked the headphones off. Some tinny music, like a trapped yowling cat, leaked out. "What?" Yungman hated that American WHAT? "What do you mean?"

What should he say? He wasn't the one with the company-issued script that would explain in neutral terms why this laser couldn't handle her Type IV skin.

Yungman once again visited reception. Joelle's chair was— infuriatingly—still empty.

The other customers were variously doing gym-class curl-ups, eyeing him with curiosity and impatience. Yungman's SANUSwatch puffed, dousing his nervous sweat with ozone.

"I'm so sorry, Miss," he ventured. "The machine can't handle . . . your kind of skin."

"*What?*"

Yungman had, over the years, seen almost every kind of pubic hair there was, and he couldn't help noticing that this woman's hair spun itself into springy little coils—very neat. He felt an almost fatherly inclination to tell her to save her money and quit trying to adjust herself to the way whatever cultural arbiters thought she should look "down there." He was still haunted by the young redheaded customer who'd signed up for the VAL-U Pack of ten treatments with him—almost a thousand dollars! Joelle later told him there was something called the SANUS EZ Installment Credit program where they would let you have whatever depilation services you wanted ("No money down!") and would subsequently take the money (plus fees) right out of your paycheck. "You miss a payment, that's where they get you," she said. "Like that girl from the Rainforest Cafe who got fired. Wherever she works next, she'll be doing it to pay off her debt to SANUS like forever, given the interest. How can people be such dummies?"

"You don't need it," he essayed.

"What do you mean, I don't need it?"

"It's so costly—" he began. Couldn't she see he was trying to help her?

"I am here," she said, "to have a service performed. I paid just like everyone else."

"Yes, of course. What I mean to say is, you would be just fine without it."

"Are you making judgments about my *pubic hair*?"

Red lights flashed in Yungman's head. He had a sudden vision of a sexual harassment case on top of the malpractice case—could you imagine, at his age?

Yungman shut his eyes, already imagining the scandal; his stuttering explanation would make him seem guilty of *something*. His brain skipped forward to old Kimm seeing it in the local news. He could already envision Kimm after the Good News Church services, patting Young-ae's shoulder with false pity over the pathetic nohm she had married instead of the world-famous singer and peacemaker Lark.

"I misspoke," he said quickly. "I was trying to say we can't do anything for you here. Please speak to the receptionist. Maybe she can refer you to another center with a higher spectrum laser—that is, if you still want to do it." (He couldn't help adding the last part.)

She squinted at him.

"Higher spectrum? What are you saying? Can you please explain this in plain English? Are you suggesting I have autism?"

He chewed over his options. Would words like "melanocyte" or "skin pigment" be offensive to a Black person? The last time he'd had real contact with a Black person besides Bea was back in Birmingham, and before that, the very occasional Black GIs in Korea. See, America praised itself for desegregating the troops during Korea, but a lot of that had been needing to replenish the numbers of soldiers they'd unexpectedly lost to massacres like the Chosin Reservoir. In their hearts the troops remained segregated, and physically, too: the harlot camp had a separate zone for harlots who serviced Black soldiers, and apparently once you worked there, you couldn't ever go back to the "normal" harlot camp; the white soldiers would not touch a Korean woman who'd been touched by a Black man first. He recalled once selling a doughnut to a Black soldier; the man had been exceedingly polite and even said "thank you" in Korean. And, of course, GIs of all colors were always on the prowl for sek-shi and often asked the houseboys for directions to the harlot camps. It was occurring to him now that Horse's Breath had been one long all-white interregnum to now: he had never seen a single Black person in all his years in Horse's Breath, because there were none. In Apple's Gate, either. Or Crooked Fork, or Manly Rapids, or . . . So it was possible to live your whole life in Horse's Breath and never meet a single Black person outside of TV.

He instinctively felt he shouldn't make any references to Type IV skin pigmentation. How stoic but dejected the patients had looked in that Birmingham ward when corralled there by skin color. How strange it must have been—the inferior food, the crumbling walls, being attended by variously hued doctors with strange accents. The patients used to complain all the time how Mohan smelled like curry.

"I apologize for your inconvenience." He wished he could use her name, but because of the promised "discretion," customers only had numbers. She was 58387-AEJ. "It has absolutely nothing to do with you. I'm saying the laser can't handle . . . it."

She flared her nostrils. "Are you saying my bush is too *big*?"

"Oh no, no. It's for your safety," he reiterated. "Some lasers have a wider selection of frequencies they can use."

"Hello?" said Customer 58388-AEJ from bed 2. "I've been lying here with my butt hanging in the air for twenty minutes while you've just been standing there."

"Yes, I'm so sorry," said Yungman. He nudged the Defolliculator toward bed 2, nudged and pulled on the hose until it was definitively in 2's space.

VOID, said the SANUSwatch, beeping and flashing. IRREDUC-IBLE VOID.

Which "void" was it talking about? Noun? Verb? Money? Invoice? Stool? Was this a yes/no question?

"You can't just dismiss me like that," the Black lady said.

"Oh, absolutely," Yungman said, making sure not to nod. He had been trained by the Employee Handbook to say "Oh, absolutely" whenever confronted by something he was unsure of. It was reassuring, he was told, affirming—but also not legally binding.

"Absolutely—what?" said the Black lady.

"I'm going to be late," said the blond lady in bed 3. "This is bull-shit." Now what? He saw a mutiny brewing, more curl-ups all around him, like he was standing in the middle of a flower, its petals curling.

The customer always comes first, they had been told; drilled, really. But which customer? Should he stick to number order? Where *was* Joelle? Should he call the trainer?

"I'm very sorry we can't help you here," he desperately told the lady in bed 1. Since he was in bed 2's space, he had to talk to her over his shoulder, and he hoped she wouldn't take that body language as dismissive. "Sincerely. Please ask for a full refund when *the receptionist* returns."

The customer rolled her eyes. She had beautiful eyelashes that were so long and curved that they almost curled onto themselves, like an ocean wave. She gazed at him for a moment with soft brown eyes and took a deep, deliberate breath. Like with the Black doughnut-buying soldier who'd made it clear he wasn't like those hooligans who had strip-searched Yungman; similarly, this lady seemed to be communicating that she wasn't like those pushy white ladies who treated him like a servant, or worse, a robot.

"Are you saying that you don't serve my kind here?"

Yungman was relieved. He had been almost about to get out the skin-tone card to show her where he was coming from. But ah, so much better to let her paraphrase in her own words.

"Yes," he said enthusiastically.

She craned her neck. Yungman noticed that her carotid artery, pumping at a vigorous, jogging rate—approximately "Jingle Bells"—now rushed forward at a sprint, at *William Tell Overture* tempo.

"I don't need this!" she muttered, then swept her legs off the table, reattired herself (elegant business casual), kicked into her heels, hitched up her MPR tote bag (which knocked the goggles off the peg), and, with her free hand, shook a finger in his face.

"Shame on you!" she cried.

"Shame on you!" echoed bed 3, a middle-aged woman. That lady created an echo: "Shame on you!" "Shame on *you*!" on down the line.

What did he do? What could he have possible said or done that was offensive? He just said "yes"!

On her way out, the woman almost knocked over Joelle, who was just returning, sipping from a chemical-blue drink in a cup as large as a child's beach bucket.

"Whoa, how about an excuse me?" Joelle said as the woman race-walked away. She sat back down at the counter, scowling. "What's up with her?" The blue liquid in the straw went up and then down like mercury in a sphygmomanometer. She peered into the treat-ment suite, where the beds were evacuated, the remaining customers fleeing, or in the process of. "Who-whee: you sure know how to clear out a room, Dr. Kwak," she said.

However, Yungman surprised himself. Normally, he would be in a panic: he did something wrong! But the panic was overtaken by the calm realization that, no, there was something wrong with *the job*. Otherwise, why was he feeling so gleeful at having, however inadvertently, driven all those customers away?

His work had been a silly way to make things seem urgent again, when the truth was that he didn't want to face up to the fact that he was a lonely old man for whom the majority of the minutes of his life had already passed. Young-ae's sudden interest in things Korean, the occasional expressions (aigu!), had awakened something in him— including stopping to look squarely into his shadow and take an accounting of how many years had gone by without his remembering the ancestors. And not just forgetting them but trying to erase them from his mind. How could he pretend they didn't exist? How did he presume to think he got here? How could he overlook all the things he'd been through with Yung-sik, their triumph as two parentless boys dumped by war into the middle of an unfamiliar city? How could he think none of that mattered to the man he was today?

Of course it mattered. Sometimes the money Yung-sik (Oh Man-won) gave him was sticky with drink or pungent with vomit, even dotted with blood. There would be, sometimes, an odor of uhjingo—sex. Yungman would be disgusted, receiving the money with his fingertips. But *what* money did he think he paid for his medical school tuition with? Sex money that smelled like squid! Vomit money! Covering up a cancer with a Band-Aid (yes, he had a patient who had done this with a clearly metastatic bulging black melanoma) didn't change its power.

What a fool he was! So many had given up so much for him to be a doctor, to immigrate. Even Lieutenant Jarvis—had Yungman ever thanked him? No! He had only constantly, desperately asked him for favors, even after death. Did he wonder if Jarvis may have regretted ever stopping to single him out. Now, finding himself in a pool of calm, giving himself up to the machinery of days passing, was just a way to narcotize himself, here at the end of his life, into doing assembly-line work.

When he was growing up, he could barely envision a Western toilet, let alone Light Amplification by Stimulated Emission of Radiation technology, an invention of optically amplifying light once, twice, so many times that light became a *thing*, one that could precisely cut paper, do surgery, or even weld metal. Was his role in the obliteration of pubic hair a proper use of this fantastic machinery? Or of Yungman Kwak's skills?

He folded his white coat, left it in the storage room, and walked out.

"Dr. Kwak!" Joelle called after him. "It's payday; your check should be here any minute." Yungman kept walking.

When he got to the uncovered bus "shelter" (unroofed and unbenched to prevent the homeless sleeping in it) where he would catch the shuttle bus to the employee parking lot, it began to snow, heavy and wet. The kind of snow where each flake was an agglomeration of a dozen flakes. He was wearing his favorite shoes, the white ones, which would now be ruined.

Ken knew something was up the minute he opened the door and saw his friend standing there in wet, white shoes.

"Come on in, Yungman." He reached behind Yungman to hurry the door shut. Stray bits of snow came in on the wind and peppered the Hokkanens' blue Stainmaster carpet like stars. "Ohyah, it's really coming down out there." Yungman heard the *whirr—ding!* of the microwave in the kitchen. He left his soused shoes near the door, so shapeless now that they keeled over like capsized ships.

"Let's eat, Yungman," Ken said. "All I have to do is open another can. Put your shoes by the heater, but not too close or the leather will warp." He also brought out some white tube socks with thick green stripes on top. "Scotty's," he confirmed. "Circa 1976." Even though they were a child's socks, they fit Yungman. The tube was a smart invention.

They brought the stew out to living room, where Ken unfolded TV tables. It was the same living room Yungman had always remembered—the brown La-Z-Boy, the couches with the anti-macassars, the cut glass candy dish with the red-and-white peppermint candies. But even though Ken had a cleaning lady who came every week, the room had a new feeling of museum dustiness. Myrtle had always made wherever she was happy and gay. Even Ken's bear-brown La-Z-Boy would have a bright blanket folded and laid invitingly on it, both decorative and cozy. The way the cleaning lady folded the blanket was neat but somehow missing something, like the house itself missed Myrtle's touch.

Yungman wondered if there was anything Ken would have done differently had he known that his vibrant, seemingly healthy wife would one evening complain about indigestion and die right in front of him of an MI.

"I didn't realize I was going to have such a love affair with Dinty Moore," Ken said. "I should have named one of my kids that. Or how about Jiffy Pop for a son? I have so many favorite foods: Spam. Hungry-Man. Jimmy Dean. A&W. What favorite-food name would you have given Einstein if Young-ae would have let you?"

"Hmm. I would have needed to have a daughter so I could name her Steak Diane," Yungman said. There was something comforting about falling into the grooves of their conversations, like they were a two-man vaudeville act, the shortest guy in the hospital and the tallest. Yungman could be silly with Ken, but no one else. Not even Young-ae. Certainly not with Einstein.

But sometimes he wished he could talk of realer things with Ken. Maybe his marriage problems. Einstein. Or that bad decision he had made in Korea, the one so long ago that it was embedded in his life forever, like those trees that grow into metal fences, their roots bursting through the concrete of sidewalks in a way that made it difficult to trace from which tree the disorder started.

Yungman didn't even want Ken's advice, just someone to look at the wreckage with him.

Ken had always told him admiringly, "You Asians have such great family values." He noted how hard Einstein studied without having to be told. How he was so quiet and obedient while Scotty, well, ran a little wild, and even Polly had a pot-smoking phase that had made Myrtle want to tear her hair out.

Ken wasn't above winking at Yungman and letting him know he should remind his patients that having unprotected intercourse even once, even when you thought you were too old, when you thought you were *done*, was when it happened. Polly was sixteen and had gotten into Stanford early, and so Ken and Myrtle had started transitioning to being empty nesters. The pregnancy had upset this narrative. They had been shocked, but then grew into the shock with a burgeoning wonder and joy. Her pregnancy had gone on swimmingly, not even any morning sickness.

Horse's Breath General had just gotten an ultrasound machine, and Yungman had showed Ken an image of his son playing with his penis, "It's a boy!" Breaking the silly superstitions of first-time parents, they went ahead and named the fetus Ken Junior.

Yungman didn't know the baby had died in utero until it was born dead. Perfect angelic little features, fingernails long enough to be cut, a robust penis thanks to the macroorchidism of hormones. But dead.

Yungman was always amazed that Ken and Myrtle never blamed him, even a little. *He* would blame the doctor, if he were in their shoes, even though this had just been a sad, strange flash of fate, not even intrauterine growth retardation. It was only, as Dr. Rantamaki the pathologist said after the autopsy, random, inexplicable bad luck. But how could they not see Yungman's face every time they thought of their dead son? Yungman, proximate, the one who failed to deliver a live one?

Yungman knew that with each foible of Scotty's—his lassitude, his possible learning problems—Ken was, unconsciously or not, comparing him to Junior, the forever-perfect dead son. The open admiration for Einstein—"Look who's on the honor roll again!"—also came at a cost to Scotty. No wonder that, as soon as Scotty turned sixteen, he'd joined the army, then spent most of his young-adult life living on various hidden islands and withdrawing from "polite" society, which hadn't really ever done anything for him.

Yungman remembered how devastated Ken had been when Scotty was placed in a remedial reading class in fifth grade while Einstein was moved to "Great Books." But they were two different children with two different needs. Scotty had needed support, but back then children were measured by "Why can't you read?" There was one measuring funnel, and they all had to fit or be forced through it, like though a pasta extruder. The malleable ones, like Einstein, thus did the best.

Over the years, Yungman had let Ken's compliments on Yungman's superior Asian parenting go unchallenged, a tacit approval. After being thought of during his years in America as, variously, ugly, sneaky, larcenous, yellow-skinned, cowardly, diseased, dirty, meek, and robotic for so long, why not enjoy a positive stereotype?

Stan Mitzner had once said to him, quite aggressively, at a hospital Christmas party, "I heard that in Korea people just defecate on the street."

"Of course we have toilets." Yungman had given him a long, cold look to let him know he was wrong, even though, technically, if he was thinking of when Yungman and Yung-sik first got to Seoul, when it was still bombed to smithereens, he was right. They had shit in the gutters of the street, because what else could they do when Americans had bombed all the toilets?

The Americans had often bragged about how they had bombed 99 percent of all the structures in North Korea in hopes of starving out the regime (which ultimately didn't work, and also did not work when they tried it again in Vietnam). South Korea, it was never mentioned, had received almost as bad a pummeling, maybe 95 percent of its schools, hospitals, homes. There were barely any buildings left intact in Seoul or tucked away in mountain villages.

Yungman thought about when he used to scrounge at the Yongsan dump and how any copies of *Stars and Stripes* were prized—maybe even more than an intact can of Spam—for practicing English or pictures of the tantalizingly blonde "Miss Morale" (Marilyn Monroe!), but most important, if you crumpled the pages between your hands a few times, they became the most lovely, soft toilet paper.

Ha, when Reginald "the King" Kwak was little, his favorite game was hurling toilet paper into the toilet, bales of it. He'd laugh maniacally as he flushed away paper produced specially to wipe Western ongdongis, the paper washed away unthinkingly with gallons and gallons of clean, potable water.

At home Yungman had always tried to get away with leaving urine unflushed, as it was sterile water with a few salts and urea dissolved in it. But Duckie would flush it away with a clucking *tschuk*. Yungman allowed her to complain that toddler Einstein kept leaving his pee-pee in the toilet.

"You think your dad was crazy cheap," he'd once overheard Einstein say to Marni. "You should have seen my dad—he would only let me use three squares of toilet paper per dump. He monitored it." And then her complicit giggle and "Oh my God. Okay, that's way worse than being denied a Polly Pocket for Christmas."

"Well, my friend," Yungman said casually, when he got up to leave. "I'll have a lot more time for the bucket list trips. I walked off my job today."

"Whoa, whoa, whoa, Yungman," said Ken. "Way to bury the headline. Was it because of the medmal case? I told you it's nothing to worry about, nothing to put a minute's thought into."

"No, I did it voluntarily. I mean, after causing some chaos. Inadvertent chaos."

"Can't imagine what that would be, my friend. You're the steadiest person I know."

"That's the problem."

"Problem?"

"I'm not steady. I'm impulsive. I can be disloyal. I don't always do the right thing."

"You're making me laugh." Ken guffawed.

Feeling his lower lip suddenly tremble, Yungman panicked. In Korea men got together and danced and sang silly folk songs at the top of their lungs. They drank sour rice wine, and tears of nostalgia could be blamed on the alcohol, sool. Yung-sik always called those sool-pen stories, combining the words for alcohol and sad. But outside of that, men were never supposed to show these softer emotions after age seven.

"See, I fouled up my grandfather's one wish. He wanted to be buried in the mountains by our home," Yungman said. "But he died on the other end of the peninsula during the war—we'd fled from the North Koreans and the Chinese to the one place not yet overtaken by the Communists."

"I'm so sorry," Ken said.

"Ironically, cremation was a Shinto custom the Japanese forced on us during the occupation. So, in Pusan, the place where we were refugees, there was a Japanese-built crematorium that the UN forces were using for dead Allied soldiers from countries too poor to ship the bodies back. It was an awful decision for my mother—my grandfather was opposed to having his body burned—but I'm realizing we wouldn't have been able to bring him back to the village."

"Wait, where is he?" said Ken. "The ashes."

"We—my brother and I—carried them out of North Korea."

"North Korea?" said Ken. "*The* North Korea? How the heck does one get out of there?"

"We actually lived in a southern area of Korea, but after the Korean War, it was designated 'North Korea,' so to escape the Communists, we had to leave. My brother has the ashes in a box."

"This brother," Ken said, cocking his head. "This is the first time you've ever mentioned him. You've talked about your father, and about how well your mother could sew. Nothing about a brother. I always pictured you as an only child, and I've known you for forty years, Yungman." Ken seemed slightly aggrieved.

"Well, he died during the war." Yungman tasted that lie. It still tasted the same: easy to swallow. Why would anyone question it?

"You just said your brother has—present tense—your grandfather's ashes."

"You're right, I did. I tend to use the present tense. We were very close, is all. He put me through medical school."

"How the hell did he put you through medical school and die during the Korean War if you were ten when the war started?"

Ugh, Yungman kept forgetting how good Ken was with the minutest details—that's what made him such a good family practitioner. He was trained to piece together the *real* clinical story from the stew of details given to him via the patient's "history."

"Why have you never talked about him?"

"What is there to talk about?"

Ken cocked his head. Again, the family practice doc had to use all sorts of clues to figure out what was really wrong, like the mystery of the strange hematomas appearing on the Thorson baby. The Thorsons, churchgoing parents with the neatest lawn. Ken had figured out they also had the capacity to be the ones beating the kids, whose screams would be drowned out by the other parent mowing the lawn. Who could actually hit a *baby*? Well, the Thorsons did. Ken did not want to believe it, either—the Thorsons were Wednesday-night bridge friends, the kind described as "good people." But X-rays showing blunt force trauma do not lie.

"Okay. My brother didn't literally die during the war." Yungman was licked. "I just kind of left him behind in Korea. I get letters from him that I'm just too chicken to read."

"Wait, you are in touch, right?"

"I abandoned him."

"I doubt you would do a thing like that."

"I got on a ship without telling him I was leaving."

"Oh."

"Young-ae doesn't even know. She came with me. She also thinks he died during the war."

"*Oh!*"

Like those weepy Thorsons faced with the X-rays stealing a look at Ken to see if he now knew who they *really* were, Yungman wondered if Ken would still want to be friends with him. And if not, who could blame him? Who on earth betrays their brother, their literal brother, this way? Sometimes, Yungman wished he had something akin to a computer chip, a floppy disk he could just insert in his friend's head and Ken would experience and learn and know exactly what he'd gone through, from age ten to now. Maybe like those virtual reality goggles they had at Depilation Nation. It would take a lifetime of recounting stories for Ken to understand. For Pete's sake, on their march south, he and Yung-sik had seen a baby's head in a tree, a little girl trying to put pieces of her father back together. How could he leave behind the one person who had been through this with him?

"I made some terrible decisions," Yungman said. "It's too long a story, from another life. Young-ae's father didn't want me to marry her. He didn't think I was good enough."

"Ah, *that* I can understand." His friend grinned in spite of himself.

"So, coming to America was a chance to have a fresh start. Of course my brother didn't want me to leave. We'd been through a lot together. But I *had* to leave." He thought of his dear mother—that whole time, sewing the ring into his jacket, she knew she was going to leave them. Depriving them of being able to say a last goodbye. Of choosing their father, who may or may not have even been alive, *over her own children*. Wasn't she worried *they'd* die or get hurt without her? "So I did."

"I don't understand why you never went back to see him. Or why you didn't immigrate together."

"Immigration laws. Remember the problems with my papers? After my internship, I was supposed to do a year at seminary, but instead, I took the job at Horse's Breath, and my student visa ran out. That's why, for those many years, I couldn't travel."

"But I remember when Young-ae's sister visited here when the kids were small—and with her whole family."

"Yes," said Yungman. "She did, as a tourist. That was a lovely visit." Youngja had also come back to visit to celebrate her sixtieth birthday. Young-ae went to Niagara Falls with her, solo. Einstein, in the middle of his residency, had been too busy to see his aunt at all, even if he'd wanted to.

"Wait," Ken said slowly, the Enigma machine of his brain turning. "That's an amazing story. But also, you *lied* to your wife like this, for all these years? And she still doesn't know? Hoo, boy."

"I didn't really think of it as a lie," Yungman said truthfully. "It was more like those two aspects of my life didn't mix. I was pretending I was a fancy person when I was in medical school while my dear brother was working himself to a nub—for me. He had to work with all sorts of shady people and ruffians to make enough money for my medical school tuition and for us to live." Yungman had bought all those snacks and movie tickets for Young-ae with Yung-sik's sweat as well.

"Wow, Yungman."

"So, when the sudden opportunity to leave came, it was just too complicated to extricate myself from him, and I didn't want Young-ae to have the burden of feeling like after the war had split my family that she'd split it again."

"But Yungman, shouldn't Young-ae be the one to decide how she feels about your brother?"

"You're right." Yungman picked at his food. "It's like what all those old Horse's Breath ladies would say when Einstein was little: 'Oh, they grow up so *fast*.' I dismissed them as silly old ladies. And next thing I knew, my baby has a family of his own and I'm old."

"Ah, I get that. I don't want to be the Hallmark Special here, but no matter what happened between you, he'll always be your brother. Read his letters, then get on the phone, man! Believe me, I never, ever imagined I'd be in a life without Myrtle. Do it before it's too late."

Yungman thought about how the day he took his college entrance exams, amid all the parents anxiously milling, his little brother pushed his way forward so he could press a piece of rice taffy onto the building's fence, the sweetness to tempt the ancestors to come help. How he'd greeted Yungman with a cold, luxurious Seven Star cola when he'd finally emerged, drained, from the test. "I did it for all of you," he'd said to his younger brother. "Mother, Father, Grandfather, Grandmother, you, me." And Yung-sik had smiled his gap-toothed smile and . .d, "Hyung! I *know* you passed!" and gave him the cola in celebration. Even though Yung-sik called him Older Brother, it was as if Yung-sik was suddenly both parents.

"I guess my bucket wish list would include reuniting with my brother and together taking our grandfather's ashes and returning them to our village."

"But in North Korea," Ken said. "North Korea is on your bucket list." He admirably did not laugh.

"In North Korea," Yungman confirmed. "But again, we never called it that. It was always just home."

"I guess I won't be accompanying you for *that* bucket list item," Ken said. Yungman was trying to ascertain his tone—was he being funny? Sarcastic? Serious? There seemed to be only two modes for dealing with North Korea:

1. They were clowns.
2. They were such a dangerous people they needed to be annihilated.

"Honestly, though, please don't tell Young-ae any of this."

"I wouldn't dream of it—*that* task is yours, my friend," Ken said as the house's phone rang. He ignored the ringing. It stopped. But then it rang again two seconds later.

*Ring! Ring!*

"Just get it," Yungman said. "I don't mind. What if it's one of your kids?"

"Low probability," Ken said. But when the phone started to ring the fourth time, he swept up the receiver.

"Hello," he said. "Stan?"

Ah, it was Mitzner, Yungman realized, with his usual twinge of envy.

"Wait—really? How can this be? Oh no—" His voice dropped barometrically. "You're sure? He's dead?"

Yungman was surprised at how good it felt to see the Horse's Breath General doctors together again, despite the reason. He'd missed them. He would have even been happy to see Mitzner in such a gathering, but Mitzner was dead. His plane, with him in it, had crashed into the dumps behind Pill Hill. The weather had been bad, visibility poor. There was some ambiguity over whether he was instrument-rated.

The funeral was held at the Lutheran Church of the Good Shepherd, even though Mitzner was Jewish. In Horse's Breath there was no bookstore, but churches of all varieties thrived: run-of-the-mill Protestant churches, Eastern Orthodox, Christian Missionary Alliance, three separate Catholic churches, the Abundant Life Evangelical Church, an evangelical Lutheran church (which was different from "normal" Lutheran, apparently), Second Baptist but no First Baptist, and even a temple for Jehovah's Witnesses, but no temple for Jews. Supposedly Rosemary Mitzner had converted from Lutheranism, but her absence from the family church pew was whispered about with a whiff of scandal in those networks. Christianity was already so foreign to Yungman. He knew even less about Judaism. Except, from the whispers: "The Jews killed Jesus!"

Yungman was impressed by the size of the crowd: every pew was filled. And he couldn't help wondering, when the time came, who would show up. Would *he* also need one of the largest churches in town for a venue?

The minister took his place in the pulpit. "Almighty God, unto whom all hearts be open, all desires know, and from whom no secrets are hid . . ."

Yungman went through the motions: singing the hymns, shutting his eyes to pray, saying amen. He wasn't any more Christian than Mitzner! But what else could he do? He just had to playact at being a Christian for three minutes at a time. Hymn. Prayer. Hymn. The sermon took up three three-minute blocks. He wasn't Christian, he never would be. He just couldn't believe that Jesus died on the cross and came back reanimated as a zombie. He supposed these scattered denials of his true self added up over a lifetime. Like how their warm winters now meant an overabundance of woodtick nymphs; so small, but thousands and thousands of these miniscule animals could mass to suck an eight-hundred-pound moose dry—as they had with a specimen right on Highway 20, leaving behind only antlers lying in the culvert, a collapsed hide.

"This is the word of the Lord," said the reader.

"Thanks be to God," Yungman murmured with the rest of them, the woodtick congregation all nodding their tiny heads, because it was easier to just do that than to not and stick out.

The doctors got into their respective cars and headed north to Mitzner's cabin at Sand Lake for the reception, an implicitly more cheerful, Minnesota Nice affair, where it was okay to laugh.

Yungman had been to several cabins on "Sand Lake." Minnesota had so many lakes at some point someone gave up and called about 20 percent of the remaining lakes "Sand Lake." Ken's knotty-pine-board shack was on a different Sand Lake. It didn't have a proper bathroom, only an outhouse, the toilet paper stuck in a dusty coffee can to keep it dry and spider-free, a yellowed gag poster that you could only see when daylight streamed through a crescent-moon cutout in the door:

Is your bathroom breeding Bolsheviks?

Mitzner's Sand Lake place was more like a second home. Expensively appointed stainless steel appliances (much nicer than what the Kwaks had in their only home), Andersen windows, multiple bathrooms. Down the slope of the hill, a canoe, a motorboat, and a pontoon boat floated at the dock. Back inside, where there were real Kohler toilets, a double phalanx of church ladies whirled between the stove and the three-doored refrigerator. Eggs were being beaten, cream whipped, baking sheets slid into and out of the oven, the microwave dinging. Friends had also brought potluck: wild rice hotdish, stuffed manicotti, cocktail wieners. There was enough food here to feed several armies.

"Dr. Kwak: How about some potica?" asked a Mitzner daughter.
"Or some sarmas?" asked another, appearing in her place.
"Jell-O salad?"
"Lefse?"
"Bars?"
"Rumaki?"
"How about some pigs in blankets?"
"Pie?"
Connie? Bonnie? Mitzi? Gretel? Sally?
"Thank you, thank you, thank you," he said, randomly picking finger-size foods off trays, his head spinning among all the nearly identical, mousy-haired daughters. Yungman remembered ten months after Sally was born, lifting Rosemary's exhausted uterus from its pelvic cradle, having had so many placentas attached that it was worn thin in places like a dangerous tire, threatening rupture.

There was something discordant about the atmosphere, like a familiar song played in the wrong key. A more subtle electricity in the air, an intermittent buzzing noise you weren't sure you heard. The daughters were whizzing from guest to guest like automatons that had been wound a bit too tightly. The conversation was so hushed that when someone did laugh, it was like dishes crashing. Rosemary was nowhere to be found.

Rosemary finally emerged from a back room. She looked at all Mitzner's doctor colleagues. *What did they know?* her look seemed to say. Did they know about Mitzner's encroaching Parkinson's? Yes, they did. Ken had indeed happened to see him furtively take some L-dopa in the physicians' lounge, and he told the others so that they could all keep an eye on and help their colleague, but also report to Ken if he got to the point of endangering patients. But did they know some of the other things? Such as that Mitzner had wanted to try "just one more time" for a boy, and Rosemary, thoroughly depleted after a lifetime of raising all those babies despite her arthritic hands, might have been a few days pregnant (don't ask, don't tell—Yungman never tested) when she'd scheduled her hysterectomy. No, they did not know that. That was something between doctor and patient and would remain in that space, forever. They all smiled back at her with warm, professional smiles.

"Ah, Rosemary," said Ken, enveloping her in a hug.

"He was a good guy," said Rasmussen.

None of them spoke of the accident.


Young-ae and Yungman dropped Ken off and pulled into their driveway. They both noted a car, a Honda Civic, parked at the curb in front of their house. No one ever parked at "their" curb—they had a driveway. The car was rusted and dented as if someone had used it as a piñata. Yungman's breath stopped when he caught a movement, not in the front but in the back seat—it seemed someone was huddled in the back.

Yungman and Young-ae pretty much knew everyone's car in town, and now they came up blank. Also, no one owned a foreign car—people could have a house full of cheap made-in-China trinkets, but their car had to be "union made." The probably-gay tennis pro's purchase of a Volkswagen Beetle in the 1970s had produced a minor tempest. No one would dare buy an Asian car, especially now. Since the election, Yungman felt like they'd heard the c-word slur muttered at them much more often. When out, strangers seemed to glare at them with open hate, give them a "finger" while they were driving. They couldn't prove it was because they were Asian, but what else could it be? Young-ae, also having seen the movement, grabbed the CorningWare from the back seat and held it in front of her like a shield.

The car's door opened. Out came a woman stumbling heavily up the driveway, clutching her enormous belly.

It was the trainer. She was waving a piece of yellow-tinted paper at him.

"What—what—" said Yungman. "What are you doing here?"

"Your last paycheck," she gasped. It was for $36.14. "You never picked . . . it . . . up."

Yungman could tell by the way she was breathing that she was probably feeling the "ring of fire" (but when had she gotten pregnant?), the fetal crown battering the cervix, like trying to force your head through a too-small turtleneck.

"When did your water break?" he asked.

"It . . . hasn't," she gasped.

That seemed odd, given the state she was in, ready to deliver shortly. Shortly! Yungman's guts were cramping into knots.

"My wife will stay out here with you while I go in and call an ambulance."

"No!" She needed to take a gulp of air to keep panting. "Im-mi-mi-gration. They look for people like me at the ER."

Yungman's mouth was agape. None of his most beloved patients would have the temerity to do this, show up at his house in active labor. Outrageous! They'd definitely call first. And how to explain this to Young-ae?

To his surprise, Young-ae wasn't there. She had gone to the car, was peering into the back seat through the open window. There was a little girl curled in the footwell.

"Look," Yungman said, realizing he didn't even know the trainer's name. "There's no hospital around here that still has a maternity ward, or an ER that I know of. I think you need to arrange to get yourself back to the Cities as soon as possible. Duluth is a little closer, but not much. An ambulance would—"

The trainer sat down right in the driveway and began to wail. The sound, that particular pitch, made Yungman's guts clamp down. That baby inside her didn't care that there was no hospital nearby, whether Yungman knew the mother's name, or what time it was, the weather. Babies did what they did on their own schedules, and stopping that would be like trying to stop the tide. Yungman knelt down and waited for a pause in the contractions, then began to help her up. As he did so, the trainer vomited massively on herself, on the driveway, on Yungman.

"Yobo," he called to Young-ae, blurting the Korean word for *honey*. He had no doubt: "She's in transition. We need to get her into the house."

Young-ae had somehow coaxed the crying child out of the car and was leading her inside. "Don't worry—your mommy's a little sick to her stomach and just needs to rest; you all do. She's okay," she murmured into the child's hair. "Did you guys eat anything funny?"

"French fries," the little girl sobbed. "But I don't think Mommy had any, she gave them all to me."

"Ah, well, in that case, please listen: Your mommy is going to have a baby, and we need you to be a brave girl, okay?" Through the screen of his urgency, Yungman saw the ghost of the person Young-ae might have been without Einstein, without him: a skilled healer, a natural helper of women and their children.

Young-ae heaped quilts onto the bed, not to protect the mattress but to make the trainer comfortable. Yungman knew this because, squirreled away in the garage, he had a whole case of robin's-egg-blue plastic-lined chux pads that they used for messy projects. She turned on the light but dimmed it.

"We're in luck," she said. "A cephalic vertex presentation."

"I'm a multip," the trainer gasped. Young-ae cocked her head.

"From work," Yungman said. "My old boss."

"Your old boss was a doctor?"

Yungman nodded.

"Para one, gravida two." The trainer sighed between her groans. "Easy birth with Dilara. No complications." (*Dilara*, Yungman thought: Estonian? Belarusian?) She smiled. Yungman thought she was smiling at the thought of her last labor, but she was looking at his wrist. He was wearing the paper bracelet her daughter—Dilara—had made him.

"You'll be para two in just a bit," Young-ae said briskly, but her air of competence was also saturated with compassion. She seemed eager to take over, so Yungman thought: *Why not?* In medical school, while the rest of their group was still fumbling with practicing Leopold's maneuvers on the doll, she must have delivered two or three babies on her own.

"I'm going to apply fundal pressure," Young-ae said. "One . . . two . . . three . . . push."

The trainer curled her head up and strained. Young-ae paused to look between her legs to gauge how productive that had been, and she gasped.

"What?" cried the trainer.

"Your membrane is still intact."

Yungman crowded in. Most obstetricians wouldn't see this in their entire lifetime.

"I think if you do the Valsalva maneuver, the baby will be out in one more push. I have the head," Young-ae said. The trainer filled her lungs like a deep-sea diver. She would hold her breath and use that air against the diaphragm to push her baby the rest of the way out.

Yungman and Young-ae stared in fascination, both of them also unconsciously holding their breath. The baby emerged, blue as a Medicine Buddha, snuggled and surrounded in its own clear, sparkling liquid.

The umbilical cord, like a snake, pulsed strongly.

"En caul!" whispered Young-ae. Her hands were stained pink with the bloody show. She eased the baby and its jellyfish-like sac onto the trainer's chest.

Yungman had been lucky enough to have seen an en caul birth early in his career in Birmingham, but the caul had no fluid and merely draped over the baby like cobwebs. He never saw another one. They had become almost nonexistent, he supposed, because it became normal practice to manually rupture the membrane with an amnio hook. *But why?* he wondered now. At that en caul birth, they hadn't regarded it as a miracle. No, the nurses had scrubbed the membrane off right away because it looked messy.

On top of his mother's chest, this baby floated in his amnion.

"Does this baby know how to swim?" asked little Dilara.

"See," said Young-ae, "he's getting everything he needs through this cord, like a deep-sea diver. But eventually, he will also need air, because he's a human, like you and me."

The little girl's eyes sparkled in wonder.

*Thank you*, the trainer mouthed, tiredly.

As the cord slowed, Yungman and Young-ae nodded to each other. She ruptured the membrane with a finger. A single tear slid down the trainer's face. Birth was such an everyday occurrence and yet there was no way to explain in words of any language how deep this emotion went. How Yungman wished he still had one of his mother's Lucky Gourd dippers, the ones with the commemorative red chile peppers sewn lengthwise in her careful blanket stitch, to welcome this little boy into the world.

Young-ae delivered the placenta. As she had when they were students, she was able to work the baby out without tears. Yungman was clearly not needed, and so he moved to the kitchen thinking he could throw some nori—all the seaweed they had—into some Swanson's chicken broth to create a facsimile of the postpartum soup.

Yungman awoke the next morning feeling for a second like he was back in Korea; he had slept pillowless on the floor in Einstein's old room while Young-ae took the bed. Lying on the floor had been uncomfortable (his poor iliac crest, his elbows) until it wasn't, and he had fallen asleep the way he had as a child, lined up with his mother and father and Yung-sik. Halaboji, with his perfect posture, lay on the end and used a block of wood as a pillow.

He sat for a moment and watched Young-ae. In sleep the lines on her face—disappointment, anger, age—fell away, allowing an outline of a different Young-ae to assemble itself just under the surface of her visage: the fiery girl from anatomy class at Seoul National University, and the girl of twelve, so sure of herself, talking to his mother the gourd seller, and the slim figure he'd seen through the crack in the gate and then later in Water Project Village's one rice paddy in winter. She'd showed up with skates, beautiful leather boots with shining blades that she'd won in a scholastic contest at her fancy middle school in Seoul. Although the villagers gawked and gossiped over her unlady-like behavior, you could see their admiration at how undaunted she was, trying to figure out how to push herself on the blades. Even the unflappable Halaboji was shocked, he mistakenly thought he was seeing some kind of shaman spell, as the mudang often danced with bare feet atop sharp scythes to summon the spirits. Yungman couldn't help smiling—a real smile—at the remembrance. All these people made up the girl-woman whom he'd probably always loved and who had fallen into a temporary infatuation with him, a silly dalliance fired by the heat of youth and cemented by an accidental zygote. With lasting consequences. Whether they'd liked it or not, they'd made a life together.

As if she knew he was watching her, she woke.

"I thought we should check on our guests," he said. She yawned. Her breath was pungent.

They walked together to their bedroom and knocked. Yungman listened—did he hear a soft rustling? She'd asked for privacy, so they'd given it to her. If she needed any help, she could just call to them from the next room. Yungman knew some women needed help just to go to the bathroom, while some women got up and walked around as if they hadn't just given birth. He imagined the trainer, exhausted, snuggling with her new baby and her daughter beside her. Of course, the American Pediatric Association regularly sent notices to OBs that they should instruct their patients to not "co-sleep" in the same bed with their infants for danger of suffocation. Back in Korea, families, even the tiniest babies, co-slept. A separate bedroom was unthinkable in Yungman's straw-roofed dwelling—the tiny extra room they used for their father's seeds.

Yungman remembered that once, a baby was stolen from a house and eaten by a tiger. But he couldn't think of a single baby in Korea who ever died or was even injured from sleeping with its mother. And yet at Hallock's Furniture store, they'd tried to sell them a crib—a tiny barred jail for Einstein. And they had bought it! Poor Einstein had wailed in it nightly until he passed out.

Yungman knocked again, briskly, loud enough to wake her. He waited another thirty seconds, then cracked open the door and peeked in.

And found . . . nothing.

No trainer. No little girl. No baby.

A pile of quilts in the corner, neatly folded.

The blanket she'd given birth on—and bloodied—was missing. As was a box of feminine pads Young-ae kept under the sink for her post-menopausal discharge.

Yungman felt, almost inexplicably, angry and abandoned.

"That's one way to get your health care as an illegal immigrant," he grumbled. "Just look up the address of your employee that you know is an OB and show up at his house!"

"Kwak-ssi," Young-ae admonished. "She's not an illegal immigrant."

"Then what is she?"

"How can a human, immigrant or not, be illegal? That's just a way to make her seem bad, a *thing*. When she's just a desperate mother trying to do the best for her children. Haven't you been watching the news? It's not unheard of for ICE to show up at a hospital. They seem to *like* it when they can break families apart."

"Then she should have followed the rules and immigrated legally," he sniffed.

He wished Young-ae would just let him get away with the statement, given the vehement conviction he'd put into it, but she was too sharp to let that one go by. "I'm surprised you can say that with a straight face. People aren't legal or illegal; it just depends on the laws—and the laws never make white people illegal only people like us. Ever notice that? Dieter never went through half of what we did.

"You know," she went on, "I bet she left because she was afraid we'd call ICE or something."

"That's absurd," said Yungman.

"She knows she can't trust anyone. They're detaining everyone—children, the pregnant. Don't you remember that story of that poor woman from Honduras who kept telling her jailers she was feeling so bad—and she had a stillbirth a week later? Or the woman from Mexico who was shackled and fell and miscarried?"

At Young-ae's urging, he went back to Depilation Nation to try to find the trainer, follow up. It was true that if she was on her own, struggling, stressed, her normal postpartum bleeding could certainly get worse. And what about her little girl?

He couldn't find her at Depilation Nation, Joelle had no clue, and so he thought to visit Einstein.

Yungman was surprised to see his son packing. A prosaic cardboard box—CHUX PADS, 1 GROSS—held his personal effects: a *Williams Obstetrics*, a *Gray's Anatomy*, and the 1950 *Merck Manual* Yungman had given him, more talisman than useful reference (coffee enemas were still listed). On top were his framed photos: a large Reggie school picture, an outdoorsy family portrait with all of them wearing white—white polo shirts, pants, sneakers—in Cape Cod, a copy of the negligee glamour shot of Marni.

Two men in dingy coveralls passed in between Yungman and Einstein as they hauled out the luxurious treatment bed, a satin sheet trailing from it, uncaring that they stepped on it with their dirty boots. One of them took the time to unsubtly ogle the picture of Marni.

"That's a five-thousand-dollar Dux mattress," Einstein lamented. "Going right into the landfill. We aren't allowed to keep anything."

"What's going on?" asked Yungman.

"UnitedHealthcare just bought SANUS."

"The insurance company?" said Yungman. "Why would they need your retailicine hospital?"

"I think they bought it to put it out of business. Rich people were actually abandoning their insurance companies—that's how attractive our service is."

"Your CEO let this happen?"

"He's already moved on to something else—tourism hotels on the moon."

"You've got to be kidding me."

"Lots of people want to go into space."

"No, I am talking about your job, your company."

"Well, that's the risk you take with brilliant founders. They get antsy and want to move on." Einstein paused. "And I didn't realize this but some of them actively just start companies hoping they'll get bought out by bigger ones. Not sure that was the case here, but obviously he got very, very rich."

"And you're out of a job." His son nodded.

Yungman wanted to be supportive. "Well, for once you can collect unemployment—you've been paying the taxes all this while."

Einstein paused. "You didn't hear me when I said it was a start-up? That the compensation plan is a little different?"

"Okay, but some kind of unemployment insurance, even if it isn't *the* unemployment insurance. A pension? The golden parachute?"

A parachute made out of gold actually didn't seem like a good idea.

But the look on his son's face suggested free fall. "I've got nothing," he said. Yungman decided not to press, even though his inclination was to yell at him for being so precipitous. How could he not have been salting away money for this emergency, not to mention for his retirement?

Last month, Yungman had received a mystery check for $23,000 from Horse's Breath General. How could that be, when the hospital was gone? But he'd tracked down Tinklenberg, who'd moved to the Cities to work for the company that had ruined them—SANUS.

"In the carve-out, we missed a tiny piece of your pension," he explained. "What with the compounding and all that, it had turned into five figures."

"Frankly, I'm surprised and delighted you went to all the trouble to do this," Yungman said.

"It was actually Rose. I guess she's done your books for so long that she found the missing piece in some old bank statement."

Yungman thought of all that sadly. Tinklenberg had done his job as executioner, and had been rewarded for it. But Elmer's daughter had died for her consumer choice: to save money by skipping an annual checkup. She died for want of a Pap smear, for wanting *not* to be a moocher, for making the wrong decision.

"I know it's stupid to be in this position now," Einstein said. "My forties and fifties are my prime earning years—and I'm going backward."

Yungman felt a terrible urge to agree, but his son hadn't asked for counsel, so he would just keep his big fat mouth shut.

Einstein seemed to notice Yungman's restraint and continued to pack in silence. The grand office, the curtains, the expansive desk, the art—those all belonged to the company. He had very few possessions of his own. But wasn't his wealth that he had a nice family and got to have pictures of them so he could look at them whenever he wanted? Yungman would pay untold sums, a stack of whatever paper currency, for a single look back at his father, his mother, his brother, his beloved grandfather.

Yungman now noted a startlingly familiar photo that had earlier been caught in glare: Young-ae, in her twenties, standing next to him. He was awkwardly holding her purse by its lacquered bamboo handles, a hand raised against a shower of petals. In the background, trees held weightless cottony blooms that, even in black and white, looked somehow pink. He was laughing like a goon.

Their engagement photo. He hadn't seen it in almost half a century. "Where did you get this?" Yungman yelped.

"I know—funny, right?" Einstein said. "I wanted some older family photos. Mom had stored this in one of the books Duckie gave us— probably *The Apple Cider Vinegar Cure*. Perfectly preserved. Such a great candid shot. Reggie was fascinated to learn that men carry purses in Korea."

Yungman exhaled. He'd always believed that if he worked hard enough, he could make everything—all of it—right. As the photographer had set up for that photo, Yungman had taken Young-ae's purse in a silly, futile gesture to relieve her of her burdens. As if he had ever done anything in her life but make things harder. He didn't want to divulge to Einstein that *he* was in the picture, too: he was the invisible weight inside her. Her biggest burden. But somehow, through that dark Birmingham period, the photo had been transported all the way to Horse's Breath, preserved, passed on. By *her*.

Einstein carelessly plonked a trophy reading *MDiety of the Month* into the box. It was topped by a figure of a doctor riding a horse-shaped cloud, like God, and holding, instead of a thunderbolt, a scalpel. "I haven't been fired, just so you know."

"I never assumed you were," said Yungman. However, wasn't it just a few weeks ago that Einstein had been excitedly telling them about another project he was about to embark on: SANUS was getting into the internet business, creating medical "apps." The first was the Organ Trail, which would match organ donors using "machine learning" to ransack digital data and build a huge database to facilitate matching. The beauty, Einstein had explained, was that SANUS had come into ownership of the patient data from the hospitals they'd bought and then from all their customers, who signed away their (and their families') data in order to get treatment, so SANUS didn't even have to get consent for any of this (including for the results of the free blood typing tests at Depilation Nation and the other M-BROs). A journalist from CNET had come to interview him.

Back then—i.e., two weeks ago—Einstein was giddy at the "exposure" (even though at the last moment, his commentary had been edited out) and was considering taking coding classes to open up more for him at SANUS, maybe creating his own app. The only obstacle holding him back was the $30,000 he would need to do it.

"What about the Organ Trail now?" Yungman asked.

"Hopefully UnitedHealthcare will spin it off, as it could make the process of lifesaving organ donation more efficient. Theoretically, everyone with a cell phone could download it and be a potential organ donor."

"But then shouldn't this technology, along with all the data, now be turned over to the national transplant database?"

"*That* would be socialist medicine," Einstein said with umbrage. "Or maybe even Communism."

"Bringing organ donation to more people is Communism?"

"Exactly," Einstein said. "The inventor, the entrepreneur who took the chance, put in all the sunk costs, needs to be compensated, or motivation dries up."

"But *you* haven't been compensated for all the work *you* did."

"Just unfortunate timing. Also, except for the Kwak Vaginal Rejuvenation suite of services, none of this was my intellectual property."

Yungman wondered whether they taught medical history in American medical schools. In Korea they'd learned how discoveries like insulin and hormones were deemed so important that the scientists refused to patent them, feeling everyone should have access to them. Two women scientists isolated a promising bacterium they found on a dairy farm and discovered its antifungal properties. The drug they created, nystatin, was one Yungman prescribed for yeast infections. It was gentle and yet worked so well to cure antibiotic-related yeast infections that when Yungman started at Horse's Breath General Hospital, many antibiotic manufacturers thoughtfully coated their pills in nystatin—two birds, one stone. Healthier, more comfortable patients. Then antibiotics became proprietary, branded, moneymaking drugs with secret formulations, so the drug companies stopped coupling them because there was no profit in adding the patentless nystatin.

A new generation of doctors was dazzled by antibiotics, and didn't quite understand why their patients were getting thrush or genital candida. Yungman was proud that whenever he prescribed antibiotics, he wrote a secondary prescription for nystatin, and his patients always wondered what it was, exclaiming over how cheap it was—just a couple of dollars for a drug! Too cheap, actually. No one wanted to manufacture it anymore and the only way to get it was to have it (expensively) compounded, even though post-antibiotic candida infections had become so ubiquitous that pharmaceutical reps were now trying to sell doctors a special drug to treat antibiotic-related infections—another antibiotic.

"So, I'm confused, son, why you aren't benefitting from the sale at all."

"Well, some of the professional coders might get asked to join UnitedHealthcare to do claims processing."

"But what about you, the MDiety? You won't benefit from this sale at all? Of a company you helped build and put so much into?"

"No. I signed a non-compete clause. And it's not like I'm going to be a big success doing labiaplasties in a storefront medical office. How would I pay for an OR, an anesthesiologist, and at least one nurse, on my own? In business terms they're called 'barriers to entry.' SANUS or UnitedHealthcare can afford a big outlay for infrastructure. I can't."

"But what about your options?"

"I don't have a lot."

"I mean that stuff they're paying you with."

"Oh, those. You can only exercise them after a company's initial public offering, *and* if the strike price exceeds the ask. There are also some hold periods, too, so in this case, even if there was an IPO, it would have been null. In some cases the tax burden can exceed any profits, and quite significantly. So at least that didn't happen. I know a few people who bought shares of tech stuff and were paper billionaires but then later owed more in taxes."

Yungman didn't understand half the words Einstein was using, but no matter. "What does that mean for you?"

"It means I'm more financially leveraged than ever. Being 'paid' in options and bonuses, I didn't get any retirement or Social Security contributions, and I may owe for that." Einstein's eyes became red, but he manfully didn't allow a tear to fall. "I do have a severance package—I'm not *that* stupid—but I'd have to sue for it, and the court costs would make it not worth it. I'm sure they planned it that way."

"I'm sorry," Yungman said.

"I know you think I'm an idiot," Einstein said.

"I don't think that," Yungman said.

Einstein sighed. "Anyway, let's not talk about this right now. What was it you wanted?"

"Oh, it's not important. In fact, it's probably a bit irrelevant now anyway." Yungman had a vague idea that Einstein could, from his perch as a lofty executive, dig into the personnel files. Not anymore, however. And he supposed the trainer had submerged herself back into the traceless undocumented economy. As shocked as he was by her wholesale disappearance, he was also a little cheered. She'd found a way to have her baby safely; he had no doubt she'd find a way to keep her little family afloat, and away from ICE. She was scrappy in a way he recognized.

Einstein, of course, was leagues luckier. He had multitudes of safety nets, including his Harvard degrees, the Constitution, his living parents. But Yungman wished he knew what to do to comfort him.

"I guess it's good you didn't put Reggie in General Ramsey Academy."

Einstein stuck the last of his things—fancy watch case, a leather MAN-i-cure Male Grooming Kit, and a tiny mirror like the kind Yungman had kept in his desk to check his teeth—into the box.

"This is the worst day of my life," Einstein said. "I don't think you understand how much I'm suffering." Yungman couldn't tell if his son was being sarcastic.

"I'll call you," Yungman said. It was all he could think to say to his son at this very minute. "Take care."

Yungman, while lathering up in the shower, had come up with a plan for Einstein. He couldn't help it. It was too good: buy Duckie and Clyde's ranch house for a mere $45,000. That was just the listing price on the sign out front, which had been there for years. He could probably get it for even cheaper. Then together they could set up a women's clinic. His rather pleasant experience with the trainer had shown that he could deliver babies with very few resources. He would reach out to Verna, the midwife—she must be out of work, too—and look for an ambulance service, in case they needed to get a patient to a hospital. Yungman would work there, of course. And Young-ae, if she wanted to. A family business! A jangsa! A genius solution for the vast majority of the community. Much better than having to be driven—or, given the number of single women, having to drive—a hundred miles to the hospital for a glucose test.

He called his son to explain the plan:

"I'll even help you with buying the house," Yungman promised. "Cash." Hah—the $45,000 Einstein had asked for one year of Reggie's school could buy a whole house, with *a free school* within walking distance!

To his surprise, Einstein refused.

"Sir," he said, "this sounds like a great plan. Horse's Breath could sure be helped by a low-cost women's clinic. I don't want to hurt your feelings, but that sounds like something more for you."

"For me? I'm not the one who needs a job and a cheaper place to live."

"I'm talking your style of medicine. You kind of want to be seen as pure—as in purely helping people. That's fine, if maybe a little naive—I don't know if you know, but the hospital industry *hates* free clinics. It cuts into their business and they can do all sorts of things to hurt you. Me, I'm not afraid to say I wouldn't do it for a different reason: I like money. I went to Harvard and expect to be compensated for it. That's who I am. My wife and I like our creature comforts, nice vacations, our cars. I don't want to buy Duckie and Clyde's house and live in Horse's Breath and work in some cooperative. It's important for me to be fairly compensated, to see this investment I've put into myself pay off—and Marni agrees. We've decided to move back to Connecticut. All our friends are there."

"Although we'll probably have to live in Stamford—ugh!" Yungman heard Reggie say in the background.

After all the scattered and divided families, how could his own son want to move more than half a continent away again?

"You have a nice support system in Horse's Breath; it's like an old-timey village or something," Einstein went on. "But we never got to know any of our neighbors in Custom History Valley—the place is so spread out that everyone just goes to work and comes back to their specific house, and no one sees anyone. Our neighbors could care less that their giant Taj Mahal was putting our house in permanent shadow. And we hope to get Reggie back into his same school if we move by summer. We're looking for a cheap apartment to rent just inside Greenwich's borders." He covered the receiver with his hand, but Yungman could still hear. "So we technically *won't* be in Stamford, Reg!"

"You won't get *any* profit from selling your house here?"

"Probably not. But maybe I could get another balloon mortgage for my balloon mortgage. Or maybe Marni's YouTube channel will take off."

Yungman didn't know if Einstein was being sarcastic, but his son's meaning was clear. Just because Yungman didn't wholly approve of the way they lived didn't mean they couldn't live that way—it was their life, after all. Let them build an entire life supported solely by a web of IOUs and that Bitcoin thing. Yungman would always prefer the gold ring sewn inside a jacket, as well as the Buddhist resolve to never get too attached to things.

"Sometimes," Yungman said, "the hardest thing is letting go of the notion that what you think is best isn't always the best for someone else. I hope you'll come visit us often, though."

"Don't worry; we might be sending Reggie to you—for hockey lessons. If it's not too late." This time, both men laughed.

After Yungman hung up with this son, alerted by the unmuffled roar of the deliveryman's GTO, he went to the mailbox to get the newspaper. He brought it in and separated the four or five pages of actual news from the dozens of pages of ads and slippery inserts for the feed store, the general store, the hardware store, the Walmart, which was having a gun sale. He didn't realize there were so many different kinds of guns, or that they sold military-grade guns next to the fishing tackle and bows and arrows. He'd never fired a gun in his life, even though most men in Horse's Breath hunted. Men in Korea, because of the mandatory military service, would know how to shoot these automatic weapons, in readiness for whatever war might come next. Not Yungman, however. Turning back to the front page, he did a double take:

## EXPLOSION AT SECRET NUCLEAR
## FACILITY IN NORTH KOREA
## PRESIDENT SAYS PREPARE FOR WAR

A photo of a snarling Supreme Leader Kim. Yungman had remembered seeing it before. He was wearing his customary olive drab jumpsuit, standing atop an undistinguished hill. There was no context, no text. Was he shouting *Death to America*, or chewing on a particularly tough piece of dried squid? Yungman turned to the middle of the paper, looking for the story on the International News page.

The headline and the picture; that's all it was.

Yungman turned on the TV. They all had some version of the same headline:

## EXPLOSION AT SECRET NUCLEAR
## FACILITY IN NORTH KOREA
## PRESIDENT SAYS PREPARE FOR WAR!

Yungman's stomach dropped. What if the war started while Young-ae was still all the way in Edina at church? Should he go find her? Or would it be better to wait here, to not clog the roads?

Yungman called the church.

The secretary startled him by speaking in Korean. "Hello, this is the Good News Korean Church and Institute, how can I help you?"

"Um," said Yungman. Should he speak English? Korean? He would reciprocate in his rusty Korean: "I was just hoping to reach my wife, Rhim Young-ae."

"Ah, Deaconess Rhim? Yes, she's here. Just wait a small moment, please."

He heard the secretary calling boisterously in Korean: "Deaconess Rhim! Your husband is on the office phone, please."

Then, lower, an aside to someone else: "That person speaks like a missionary—he's not a Caucasian, is he?"

"Husband of our Deaconess Rhim? Oh no, that yangban is a doctor and a graduate of Seoul National University."

"Really? I've heard white people speak better Korean than that!"

Finally, Young-ae picked up the phone. "Speak," she said in Korean.

"Are you okay?" he asked in English. "Did you see there was an explosion at a North Korean nuclear facility?"

"We saw the news," she said. "Dr. Kimm called his relatives in Seoul. They aren't worried."

"How can they trust the media? Don't people remember how Rhee betrayed the Korean people, pretending nothing was happening, just so he could save his own skin?"

"Do you know about the naengmyun index?"

"Cold buckwheat noodles?" asked Yungman. Naengmyun had been one of his favorite summer treats.

"It has to do with how many dried noodles old people like us are buying, because we lived through the war. If Koreans are really worried, they'll stock up on naengmyun because buckwheat doesn't go rancid as quickly as other grains."

"So now you can predict the future—you just need naengmyun, not a shaman."

"Aigu," said Young-ae. "I need to get back to the newsletter."

"Yobo," he said, again inadvertently using the word for *honey*—again! "I'm just worried about you."

"Worry about yourself!" In Korean, she said briskly: "Hanging up!" And she did.

Yungman, thanks to Reggie, now knew how to do rudimentary Google searches. He restlessly checked CNN, ABC, the *New York Times*, the *Washington Post*.

Then he started again: CNN, ABC, the *New York Times*, the *Washington Post*. All nail-biting versions of the same tense story:

THE PRESIDENT WARNS OF APOCALYPTIC
SCENARIO ON KOREAN PENINSULA.
ASSESSING THE NUCLEAR THREAT EXPLOSION
THE EQUIVALENT OF 1,300 KILOTONS OF DYNAMITE,
EXPERT WARNS DEATH COULD BE ALL AROUND.

Yungman tried to slow himself down. The current president had oddly no government experience. He had also been caught on camera using racial epithets and assaultive language toward women. It had been an amusement when he ran for president, same thing when Jesse Ventura, the wrestler, ran for Minnesota governor decades earlier. Half the people had voted for him as a joke—but it turned out the joke was on them. And a president could do a lot more damage.

This president was caught using more racial epithets. At a news conference, the multiply married and mistressed man who also felt he was the perfect Christian got the number of children he had sired wrong.

And yet the media politely did their level best to string together his utterances into something that sounded vaguely presidential and logical. Toadying congressmen blindly took his side. "I'm pro-life because I'm also pro-climate. Climate is life. Climate is good. Climate helps us become rich as a nation."

But the world events moved on. Everyone was aware climate change was happening—many of the low-lying oil derricks in the Gulf were starting to drown in the rising seas, their oil leaking. It was also starting to affect rich people: yachts were tipped over when breaks in the jet stream caused bursts of "Turbo-wind"; a hundred-story high-rise in Manhattan had snapped like a matchstick. Scientists speculated that microbes activated by the warming permafrost unleashed a modern wave of bubonic plague in Siberia. Some days in Horse's Breath, the winter temps were the same as Bali's. Ice fishing had by now become a quaint relic of the past, as the lakes never froze solid enough anymore. Yungman realized with a start that the annual parade of hauling ice-fishing houses to the town lake (Yungman never lost his delight at seeing Duckie and Clyde—especially the taciturn Clyde!—dressed like a Viking and a Viking-ess) always the day after Thanksgiving, had at some point been replaced by the Black Friday shopping holiday. The town no longer held the Winter Frolic event, where they hid clues for the yearly treasure hunt in the snow banks around the town park. People now went to hockey games at the indoor arena to stay cool during unseasonably hot December weather. The annual smelt run still went on, but there were many fewer smelt, and last year, because of a heat wave and a long-running drought, piles of smelt became beached and literally cooked themselves on the sand. Yungman hadn't gone to that one (hospital emergency), but people talked about how the smell of piles of rotting fish was ghastly.

The president dealt with these things via his "emergency climate change directive," which was to . . . officially abolish seasons. It was now a felony to publicly reference spring, summer, winter, or fall. Even the Four Seasons had to change its name.

With the president and North Korea, it was just a matter of what odd utterance had he made today. Habitually, his only call to unity as a nation seemed to be to yell "Terrorism!" whenever he could. And, with Russia having imploded, North Korea was the only valid country from George W. Bush's hyperbolic "Axis of Evil" remaining to stir up this emotion. Yungman couldn't even remember the other two now.

Fox News:

## WHAT IS THE BIGGEST
## THREAT TO AMERICA'S FREEDOM?
## IT'S NORTH KOREA

ANNOUNCER: We need to start bombing immediately!

Yungman decided that checking outside the US media might help. He looked at the BBC: only news about the royals. Canada was barely fifty miles away from where Yungman was, but the CBC didn't mention anything about North Korea. The American news commentators speculated about where the blast happened, what it meant. The satellite photos were grainy and vague, and it was strange to see how much of the interior of North Korea was unmapped.

## WHAT ARE THE
## NORTH KOREANS HIDING?

Some news analysts thought the explosions had occurred near the DMZ. Was that a nuclear flash they'd seen in the Joint Security Area?

## PRESIDENT SAYS HE WILL ORDER
## EVACUATION OF AMERICANS IN SOUTH KOREA
## IN "OPERATION COME HOME NOW."

And, most ominously, a tweet of the president's:

Yungman thought to look at the Korean newspapers online, but he wouldn't have the slightest idea how to type hangul letters into the computer. Young-ae obviously would. He took one last look at CNN's webpage. Experts were speaking authoritatively, showing frightening pictures of missiles and mushroom clouds. AREA UNDER SUSPICION was a red circle that encompassed pretty much the whole of North Korea, part of China, (accidentally) all of Okinawa, and even a little bit of Russia.

And, not fifty miles away from the AREA OF SUSPICION, was Seoul, where almost ten million people lived. Including someone he loved.

He went to the bookshelf and extracted *Shōgun*. He had to do it now: read, not skim, the letters. He felt like he'd seen a phone number in one of them. It was time to face his past.

He started at the newest, the one already open.

*Dear Brother-in-Law,*
    *See, I don't know how to address you . . .*

Cho Bo-hae was his brother's wife.

Yungman was in such a state when Young-ae came home that she was puzzled. "I *told* you, Dr. Kimm said there's nothing to worry about."

"My brother died," Yungman managed.

"Is that what this is about? Bringing up old memories of the war? What do they call it here, triggered? Yes, I'm sad about Joongki as well. My best friend from elementary school—her whole family was lined up against a fence and shot by the Communists. Did you know *we* were almost killed?"

"No, you never told me this."

"When the Communists were retreating, chased by MacArthur that winter, a small battalion came to Water Project Village. We had food, the high wall. The soldiers chose our place to bivouac and decided to just kill us all, as capitalists.

"They let Sunja the maid and her daughter go; the rest of us they tied together in a line so as to 'waste' fewer bullets. I resigned myself to my fate."

"Then what happened?"

"One of the soldiers, a boy, really, said, 'Hyung, that's the man' to one of the other soldiers of the battalion."

"I don't understand."

"I didn't, either. But you know how my father constantly carried a bag of civilian clothes with him?"

"Yes," said Yungman. "You said it was so if someone was running away from the army, they could change their clothes."

"Yes. He had clothes and food and money, and sometime safe passage cards for both sides—I don't know how he got them; must have been on the black market. The boy was a child soldier who'd been drafted into the North Korean army, captured by the South Korean army, and then escaped by jumping out of a truck on a country road and happened to run into my father. Thanks to the civilian clothes, he managed to travel north unobtrusively until he was back with his unit. See, Pappa didn't care who was who. Everyone was a father's son. Everyone reminded him of Joongki. He hoped that by helping some of these young men, he would somehow help Joongki."

"So that action by your father saved you," Yungman said, feeling terribly grateful.

"Yes, but I suspect those were the same soldiers who killed Myung-hee's family."

"Oh."

"And it didn't bring Joongki to us. My mother and middle sister stayed behind for him, like how your mother stayed behind looking for your father. I suppose as the only son remaining, that's why she put you on that bus south and then took her chances in the North."

"She put me *and* Yung-sik on that bus," he said.

Young-ae stared at him. "You mean the bus that took the people south after the Armistice?"

"Yes. My brother came with me. You see, Yung-sik didn't die," he said. He tasted each one of those words like a stone in his mouth. "At least, not in the war."

"What are you talking about?"

"You'd better sit down," Yungman said.

He unfurled the letter, carefully smoothed its creases.

I am so sorry to tell you this now, but our Yung-sik died two years before. He said he'd been writing to you.

Perhaps you did not get the letters?

In a grand gesture, Yungman upended *Shōgun* and let the years of pale-blue aerograms fall out.

Young-ae's eyes grew large. Her hands shook. She rose. He wondered if she was rising to smite him and yell, full-lunged, about being lied to all this time—as he thought she surely would, surely must. Instead, she grew quiet. Put a hand on his shoulder.

"All that time we were students, you hid your sibling? Your last remaining relative? Why?"

"Your father already hated me so much," Yungman said miserably. "Can you imagine if he learned I was basically an orphan with a brother who worked in the red-light district? I tried to pretend I, if not *rich* rich, was from a good—non-Communist—family. You must have seen right through that. But all I could think of was that I wanted to be someone your family would approve of. You must be so angry I lied to you."

"None of that is important but are you saying you deprived yourself—and your brother—of your sibling relationship so we could get married?"

"Would you have gone to the US with me if you'd known I was abandoning him, *and* abandoning my first-son responsibilities as well?"

Young-ae took a breath, like she was going to say something. Then paused. Exhaled. "I don't know," she said at last. "I was having a lot of trouble thinking clearly then."

Yungman thought about life being like a river with a current. At first he had thought the Buddhist monks taught that you should accept where the current took you, that anything else would be suffering. But that wasn't true. Even though he had avoided the student protests, he couldn't help noticing that groups of gray-garbed monks were often at the forefront. A monk had self-immolated in protest over the government's weak response to Japan's continued lies about all the young Korean women abused as sex slaves during World War II. The monks at their temple practiced martial arts for exercise and, indeed, could get quite violent at protests; in fact, they were often the first to run headlong in only their sandals and robes into the shields and bats of the police. "We can characterize Korean Buddhism as 'defense of the nation,'" their head monk used to say. "A peaceful and stable country creates welfare of all people."

When President Park announced he was sending Koreans almost as mercenaries to help the US troops kill more Asians in Vietnam, the monks from their order went to meditate, hunger strike, clash with the police.

Nonattachment didn't mean going wherever life took you; it still meant fighting for your beliefs. And yet he, Yungman, seemed to have had few beliefs other than that he would certainly outlive his younger brother—and that as long as he was sentient, he had plenty of time to decide when and where and how to repair the rift.

When he was two years too late.

Yung-sik had done the impossible. He had managed to scrape up enough for Yungman's school fees and for them to own outright that small shack in Kangnam. How many jobs had he worked at once? Yungman couldn't remember. And this was his sickly little brother, the one he should be taking care of. He forced himself to just be still, to feel the full weight of what he had done.

"The agreement was that once I got on my feet as a doctor, I would help him pursue what he wanted to. He was a simple guy; he expressed no desires beyond cleaning up his past, starting a family. And remember how in those days we all thought *Just get rid of this dictator, maybe reunification will happen.* But then another dictator would step up in his place."

"Now I remember you practically pushing me up the ramp of the ship. He found you, didn't he?"

Yungman nodded. "I don't think he ever suspected I was thinking of leaving. Who could conceive of such a thing, after losing our mother? And I promised my parents and grandfather to take on the ancestor rites. I abandoned that, too."

Every Chusok, he and Yung-sik would prepare their ancestors' favorite foods: Mother loved wild onion pancakes, Grandmother tofu stew, Halaboji his milky sweet rice wine. For their father, a perfectly cooked bowl of Korean rice—Hanguk rice, not Japonica. After the forced migration to Seoul, the brothers had always had the idea of hiring a ferry to take them to Kanghwa Island near Inchon, which was so tantalizingly close to home, and setting Halaboji's ashes in the water there. But then, remembering Halaboji's edict about keeping bodies intact, they just positioned the box with the ashes pointing toward the village, instead.

Yungman had sent his first Chusok letter back in September of 1968, not long after he arrived in America. Not a letter so much but an envelope containing money wrapped in paper. He wrote out the address, guessing at the transliteration in English. Triple-underlining Seoul, South Korea. After that, he chose an arbitrary yearly date—August 15—so as to not even have to think about when in the lunar calendar Chusok would be that year. No matter how much or how little money he had, he sent a good sum, more than enough to equip an altar with the favorite foods of the deceased. When he had more, he sent more

He kept the envelope bare of anything except his brother's name and address. He did it all in haste, before Young-ae would see.

Yungman sent the money-laden letters to Korea all throughout the Vietnam War, the Watergate scandal, the Reagan years, the Gulf War, the Clinton years, the Clinton scandal, 9/11, and then Iraq, Afghanistan, and another Gulf War, then another—war was now endemic to America, like a chronic, low-level fever.

This was the value of being an immigrant in America: The future was what mattered, the past was immaterial. You could be what you wanted to be—a self-made man. Who cared what language Albert Einstein or, say, Horatio Alger originally spoke, what country he came from. What mattered was his immigrant success story, his American story.

He'd left Korea, left his one remaining relative. The damage was done, and nothing could change that. Why keep sending guilt money?

But then he thought of his little brother, the one he'd carried when he was too tired to walk during that exodus from their village. His brother who, upending Confucian rules of age and duty, had worked so hard to support him so he could get his medical degree. And how he had repaid this faith and loyalty.

Yungman had—once—while readying the pile of bills to mail to Korea, come close to slipping in a wallet-size school picture of Einstein in third grade (gap-toothed grin, thick amblyopia glasses). Would Yung-sik discern that his son had the squattish (indeed, gourd-shaped) torso that had long marked the males of their family? Yungman's restraint prevailed. He feared what could happen if he opened the door to his past, even just a crack.

"I don't understand why you didn't inter your grandfather's body once you returned to the village after Pusan."

"Ah," said Yungman. "One of my mother's good friends a was sort of shamaness. Not really, as in she didn't do it professionally; you know, dance on the knives and things—"

"Kwak-ssi, don't tell me your family indulged in such silly superstitions."

"That same friend came to tell my mother she was pregnant with Yung-sik and that he'd be very sick but survive—that's exactly what happened."

Young-ae shrugged. "I also predict that one day . . . you will die."

Yungman ignored her. "She said the ancestor spirits had stopped by with a message for her to pass on, that Halaboji would die far from home, and go on many voyages before he came back to rest."

"I would have buried him next to your grandmother when I had the chance. How are you going to honor his wish now?"

Yungman was stung. Of course he had thought that, maybe a million times. Their mother had spoken about it as well, wondering if they shouldn't just quietly perform an interment. However, tradition also dictated that someone of Halaboji's stature should have a long, slow funeral procession with all the village elders marching him to his final resting place, with their father at the head of the procession, dressed in dull gold mourner's clothes, a tall miter on his head, holding Halaboji's portrait, banded in black. If they did all this, perhaps they could atone for burning his body.

While they waited in hopes that things would change and their father would return, no one said it, but during this lonely time it was comforting to have Halaboji's ashes, transferred into an urn (how could the human body be that small?) on a raised altar, watching them from day to day. His mother would be grateful to be able to make the appropriate feast for the interment, if their father was home again. Why not wait a little while longer? See, that was human nature—to assume each day was one more on the way to something better, even when it had been proved time and time again to not be the case.

Yungman had edited his life to project steadiness and safety to Young-ae, and that was his advantage over Lark. Lark pushed himself to the front lines of anti-government demonstrations, singing his songs as speeches, his name and face slowly becoming known. When hordes of police converged on campus to quell an insurrection, frightening in their storm-trooper helmets and shields and tear gas guns, some heedless masked firebrand greeted them by rappelling down the side of an SNU building to unfurl a banner—DOWN WITH PARK/ WE WANT FREE ELECTIONS NOW!—*right in front of the riot police*. That turned out to be Lark, who was barely able to run away in time.

He *was* often caught and jailed, showing up with an arm in a sling, black eyes. Yet somehow he still managed to keep up with their class, optimistic that this could continue. His family had fancy lawyers who bailed him out, but how long would this last against a military dictator who snuffed out any perceived enemies like bugs, a tradition dating back to the very origins of the Republic of Korea?

Young-ae, for her part, was impatient with the grandstanding politics of left and right, while women in rural villages were dying from postpartum fistulas that were easily fixable. She was impatient with Lark for unnecessarily, flamboyantly making himself a target. For instance, Lark had publicly declared that he would resist his mandatory military service: "I will not fight and kill my Asian brothers, who have done nothing to harm me, just because Park hopes it will curry favor and bring in more American dollars." This was going to be trouble, probably even more jail—while Yungman had been quietly writing to Lieutenant Jarvis to document his service to the American military during 6.25 to plead for a release from the draft, as, worryingly, after a small medical force had been sent in, now more and more Korean combat troops were being sent to Vietnam. Yungman thought of how inept he had been in tae kwon do class in high school and could not imagine trying to take someone else's life.

On the romantic front, at least, there had been progress. Yungman could feel Young-ae's ambivalence toward Lark's passion versus his lack of common sense about how to live. Yungman pressed his advantage as the steady young man from her village, a good guy who was apolitical, studious, even a bit of a boring workhorse who would yet enjoy going to see *Hamlet* and *The Red Scarf* with her at the Changchoon Movie Theater.

And he wasn't completely unadventurous: Lieutenant Jarvis had written back to him that while he had no influence with the Korean government as far as the draft, he did have an idea how to delay it. Yungman could scarcely believe it when he had his US visa in hand; even his professors looked at him with a mixture of awe and envy.

Then, a single night with Young-ae, plied with a sool-pen story, resulting in a goodbye tryst. The meeting of an ovum and a sperm, a one-in-a-million combination of the largest cell in the body meeting the smallest and creating their son, leaving Young-ae with a life and dreams she could never go back to, and so she chose to go forward, with him.

\*     \*     \*

At the same time in his life that Yungman was sending checks to an immigration lawyer in Minneapolis, a letter had arrived, addressed to Yungman from his brother. He was so spooked when Al the mailman handed him the mail with a "Looks like you got something from over-seas, eh, Doctor?" Yungman had practically shut the door in his face.

His cheapskate tendencies had come back to haunt him. See, he received so many free address labels, especially from places where he made donations (the March of Dimes, UNICEF, the American Lung Association, and, yes, Doctors Without Borders). He tried to get rid of them wherever possible, automatically pasting them onto letters—he couldn't throw them away, and yet they kept coming! He started pasting them onto blank envelopes, and must have accidentally grabbed one of those to send Yung-sik the Chusok money.

Letters came intermittently. It was traditionally his job to bring in the mail, so Yungman easily intercepted the pale-blue aerograms and ferried them to *Shōgun* without opening them. He worried about the voluble Al mentioning something to Young-ae, but Al was actually more interested in the fact that someone on their block was receiving magazines in brown paper sleeves, and, hey, could Yungman guess which doctor had a little bit of a *Playboy* fixation?

Through this series of letters, Yungman had noted the move to Seoul-si—i.e., that Yung-sik had moved inside the gates of Seoul City instead of being in nowheresville "South of the Han River." His brother was doing all right without him, and also, depending on how this visa situation went, Yungman might be back in Korea before too long anyway. That's what he'd told himself.

Then he got his green card, but continued thinking the same thing.

Then he got his citizenship and passport. He should have gone back for a visit then. But by that time the grooves in his brain had become permanent. He'd wanted to stay married more than anything, and worried about it all coming undone.

Yungman learned that Yung-sik had sold their tiny tract of land in Kangnam and bought a small apartment in Sajik-ro, made available as part of Park's urban renewal program, which razed traditional houses and threw up apartment buildings and skyscrapers willy-nilly. Korea would continue on its modernization kick after Park's assassination, with the subsequent dictator Chun Doo-hwan using violent thugs to enact his "purification program" of ridding certain neighborhoods of distasteful poverty shacks, of the elderly and the disabled in order to gussy up the nation for the worldwide scrutiny of the '88 Olympics, a pleasing background for the snowy-white hanboks of the maidens for the opening ceremony. Certainly they couldn't have old toothless people shitting in the streets.

Yung-sik had moved to a neighborhood near the famous Kyung-bokkung Palace. He had decided to mass-produce his maraschino cherry–onions and had started a food company called Oriental Rascal. Too busy to make himself food, he often stopped by a restaurant in Sajik-ro, where he met a woman who made the best oyster sauce in all of Seoul—and married her. He packaged oyster sauce, fried chow mein noodles, and pickled mountain plums for international distribution, as these kinds of Asian foods were becoming popular in the West. So was soy sauce. Always a whiz at guessing Western tastes, Yung-sik knew that real soy sauce spoiled easily, but to Western palates, water with caramel coloring, sodium benzoate, and salt worked fine, allowing the product to sit, embalmed, on a supermarket shelf indefinitely. The fake maraschino cherries didn't do as well and were dropped.

His best product was noodles fried in a round mold, so they could fit in a paper cup and be cooked merely by having boiling water poured over them. Thanks to the Japanese forcing wheat on Koreans as a substitute for the rice they stole from them, cup noodles were gaining in popularity, and Oriental Rascal Super Hot! with dehydrated kimchi, as well as a blander Japanese style, Sweetie Honey Bee, began making the rounds.

He did not, however, foresee how inventive entrepreneurs like himself, even with superior products, would fall away one by one, crushed by the orderly march of the powerful chaebols of Hyundai, Samsung, and Lucky-Goldstar, family-run dynasties that ran over them like the T-34 tanks had run over ROK soldiers at the beginning of 6.25. Many chaebols were not unlike the Kim political dynasty in North Korea; their influence went right into the president's Blue House, which often benefitted in turn from these "family foundations." Yung-sik, in contrast, had not been educated at a prestigious university with its alumni connections, nor was he from a family that had any standing in Seoul. He didn't even speak English. He had nothing to offer but his own hard work and sweat.

In the 1970s, Chilsung Noodles, whose broth was mostly MSG, industrial salt, and caramel coloring, mixed in just enough edible oil into the industrial solvent oil it used to fry the noodles to hide the disagreeable taste and delay the deleterious health effects, easily crushed Yung-sik's noodle venture by cutting off his access to suppliers of the dried vegetables, seaweed, saccharine, and anchovy broth powder he needed; Yung-sik didn't have sufficient capital for a counter-bribe, so, with rueful shrugs and muttered apologies, his suppliers, whom he'd spent years cultivating, taking them out for extravagant nights of eating and drinking, all left him, including the paper manufacturer who'd been one of the friends he'd made scouring the Yongsan dump during the war. He made the disposable cups for the noodles, so easy and filling and delicious to eat with just hot water.

This friend at least did him one favor of introducing him to his boss, and Yung-sik applied to become a truck driver for the very company that had destroyed his business. He had four children, all girls, and for their sake (and that of their dowries), he put his head down and toiled as a common laborer, the kind given to Friday-night blackout drinking, the kind who occasionally beat his wife in frustration.

There was one letter that Yung-sik had written to Yungman two years ago but somehow never sent. Bo-hae included it; Yungman immediately recognized the blocky, impatient letters on the outside of the envelope.

Esteemed Older Brother,

I know I had harsh words for you the last time we spoke face-to-face. How long ago that was. All these years, I still never received any word of what happened to Father or Mother. I applied every time there was a family visitation program, but only one or two people would be picked each time from a million of us with missing pieces. Recently a sealed mine in Taejon was found to have more than seven thousand unidentified skeletons, men and women. The US of course was involved in some of these mass murders, so our government does not want to damage its relations with the US and covered the mine back up without investigating and sealed it. Father could just as easily be there as he could be anywhere. On the news it seems that they find a new mass grave every day. Spelunkers are finding skeletons in almost every habitable cave in the mountains. See, when the Allies wanted to get rid of a village, they were meticulous about hunting down and killing everyone. They must have somehow gotten the birth registrations. In the caves they used napalm and that either cooked the people alive or sucked all the oxygen out. Do you know about the honbul, the ghost fires? These are the eerie flames people see flickering day and night in various places, mostly out in the country, with no known cause. Investigators find mass graves at those sites. They explain it away as the phosphorus from the decomposing bones must be spontaneously combusting. Others say it's the restless souls of the violently murdered.

Ghosts or not, I like to think perhaps Father managed to escape—there are stories of people who survived mass graves; the various reconciliation commissions have revealed that the executions of political prisoners, especially in 1947, and in the first months of the war, were done in haste, as were the burials. See, what was learned was that any suspected Communists, including people like Father who just attended meetings, were made to dig their own graves and then were shot so they'd fall into the pit. Supposedly American M1 rifles and carbines were used, often with American military looking on.

But it's possible he didn't die and wriggled out of the earth from among the corpses and ran for his life. Who knows—maybe he even had a second life as an actual Communist in the North after being accused for so long. Maybe he went back to the house and found Mother there, like a fairy tale, and they lived happily ever after in the North. Maybe he even became a famous professor of agronomy, like he had always wanted to. That is the tale I wish for him.

As for me, you already know from my previous letters that my life has been difficult. I had severe back problems in my later years. The company at least gave me a menial desk job and a pension that allowed us to buy a small house.

My older brother: I am dying of cirrhosis of the liver. There will be no liver transplant for an old drunk like me. I'm not afraid. I became a Christian when I married, and I believe I have many great rewards waiting for me in heaven.

Every August, near Chusok season, I received an envelope from America. Our church strictly forbids ancestor worship, and so I put the money to good use. Please know that I am grateful. Even though I was never educated, each of my daughters has been able to graduate from college. Bitnam is a nurse, Byul a teacher, Bodul a superb housewife, Bom a travel agent. They are all wonderful, filial girls who treat their in-laws with the utmost respect, and the in-laws, in turn, let them visit their old home often, even on non-holidays. What a trick it is that life plays, that our beloved children must start families of their own and go away. Like the proverb says, "As soon as there is affection, a separation happens." I miss them every day—Bitnam even lives in Seoul! Family once is family forever.

Older brother, whatever words we had with each other are long blown away and forgotten. If we could be together, one more time, our Evening Hero, I could be so happy. I will wait for your reply.

Your Younger Brother the Evening Vegetable, Yung-sik

"Those young women," said Young-ae.

"Yes," said Yungman, tears and snot sliding down his face. "My nieces."

Bitnam ("Shining"), Byul ("Star"), Bodul ("Willow"), and Bom ("Spring")—were they in danger of being blown up by Supreme Leader Kim? Or of suffering another war started by the Americans, who always seemed to need to be at war? Perhaps it's the only way, the politicians think, such a loose collection of people can ever be united.

"You abandoned the very last of your family," Young-ae said, her voice characteristically caustic and yet blooming with wonder. "You must have really loved me."

"I still do," Yungman said, but too softly for her to hear. All his life, the thing he feared the most was her rejection, her scorn.

The phone rang, startling them both.

~ MSF ~ said the Caller ID. Minnesota State Fair?

"Allo?" said the voice. "I'm looking for Doctor Kwak."

"This is he," said Yungman, puzzled. These scams, like the one warning him his warranty for his automobile, which he obviously did *not buy from a dealer,* was running out, were getting stranger and stranger.

"This is Doctors Without Borders." *Ah, MSF,* thought Yungman. *Médecins Sans Frontières.* "*Parlez-vous Français?*" Ha, he'd become so US-centric over the years that he'd forgotten Doctors Without Borders was a French organization.

"*Non.*"

Doctors Without Borders, the woman told him in excellent French-accented English, was planning to send a medical team to North Korea. There had indeed been a destructive event—an explosion of some sort, possibly industrial, possibly a natural earthquake. Was he the Dr. Kwak who'd said he could speak Korean? Was he ready to leave at a moment's notice?

When Yungman wrote his silly bucket list all those weeks ago, he had never dreamed this could actually happen.

"Dr. Kwak," the voice on the phone said. "Are you still there?"

"Does this mean," Yungman asked, "that the regime is opening up?"

"MSF has volunteered to go in, and the North Korean premier Supreme Leader Kim has accepted."

"Was this a nuclear explosion? Weapons testing?"

"No one can ascertain that. We are not a political organization or weapons inspectors. MSF will go in—and leave again quickly if we have to. The safety of our physicians is also paramount."

"All right, then," Yungman said. "Wait—I will need to bring my nurse as well." To Young-ae, he said in a shaking voice, "Yobo—"

"What?" she said, frowning at the "yobo." Then she looked at his face.

"You need to relearn how to set an IV."

"Why?"

"Because we're going to North Korea. With Doctors Without Borders." There was a moment of stunned silence after he hung up.

"The president has threatened to prosecute anyone who defies his travel ban and goes to North Korea," Young-ae said. "Have you considered who will help us if we get stuck there, like that college kid who was sent back in a coma?"

"I'm going to go; the question is, are you going to come with me?" He googled (so proud of himself!) to show her that taking a quick class at the Red Cross could provide her with certification as a nursing assistant.

She muttered, more to herself, about whether it was possible her mother or any of her sisters were still alive. Then: "I will go with you."

Instead of calling Go Away Travel, Young-ae called Rosemary Mitzner instead. She told Rosemary she needed a discreet travel agent.

Rosemary had one. Yungman hadn't realized the Mitzners were so secretive about money.

"Would *you* want Horse's Breathers talking about your safaris in Kenya while so many of the mining families are having a hard time? They are entitled to enjoy their money, but—" said Young-ae. "I think that was smart, very good nunchi."

Rosemary gave her the name of their travel agent at North Star Travel in the Cities. Yungman wondered if they would be able to get such a quick reservation to Beijing, but the agent was able to get two tickets leaving day after tomorrow. There would be a layover in Seoul or Narita, Japan, and would get them to Beijing at the right time to meet the rest of the team, who were coming from Europe.

"We'll take it!" Young-ae said. "Seoul."

Yungman, in the meantime, returned with a few IV venipuncture kits left over from when Einstein used to practice on him. His veins were a little less robust now, but with some hydration, this would be doable. He chugged a glass of water.

"How long has it been since you set up a hep-lock catheter?" he asked his wife.

She smiled, a rare radiance. Back in the village, in her ice skates in the rice paddy, how quickly she had gone from a gangly, slipping foal to a sylph gliding along the rows of last year's rice plants. She had been a hurdler, a high jumper, a volleyball setter. It was all about training and muscle memory. "I remember everything," she said, and pushed a butterfly needle into the vein in his cubital fossa. He hardly felt it.

The last hurdle was the Good News Church.

"North Korea, tsk, tsk, tsk." It was Dr. Kimm who, despite his disapproval, insisted on throwing a send-off party for them. If he couldn't stop them, Yungman supposed, Kimm would at least make it all about himself, and he was right. "We called an emergency prayer meeting this a.m. I spent all day praying on this via conference call. It's a bit preposterous, no?"

Now in person, they were all speaking in English. Did that signal more, or less, importance? Yungman wondered. The professor, for whatever reason, suddenly had a plummy British accent—ridiculous! He'd lived his whole American life in the Midwest, and now he sounded like those people in the Harry Potter movies!

But for Young-ae's sake, Yungman would exercise restraint and decorum. He replied, evenly, "What's so preposterous about a group of doctors bringing medicine to a place that has just faced a disaster?" He had, he admitted, been hoping for a little oohing and aahing from the Good News Korean Church & Institute of Edina: *Doctors Without Borders—I've heard of it! How prestigious!*

The other half dozen of the Good News Church's "Emergency Prayer Team" eyed Kimm reverently, to see what else he would say— probably so they could ape him. After all, Kimm had a signed picture of George W. Bush thanking him personally for all his help and his large donation to the 2004 campaign sitting atop his polished black Steinway.

"It's the Axis of Evil. Communism has always been a scourge, always waiting outside the door," Kimm said. "Remember how President Rhee used to say, 'Communism is cholera, and you cannot compromise with cholera'?"

Young-ae had recently let it slip that even though they never saw her, Kimm's mother also lived in the US. Did she live in the "Kennedy Compound" with them? No! She was in a state-run nursing home for people with memory problems and received welfare.

"Honestly," Kimm said, "they're terrorists with nuclear weapons—and you're going to help them after they have a nuclear testing accident? That's only going to embolden them! Knowing these do-gooders from the outside world will rush in and fix their failures."

"Doctors Without Borders, Médecins Sans Frontières, helps people in need, irrespective of politics. They seem to think this may have been an earthquake."

"As if anyone knows what's going on there," the professor sneered.

"Actually, the French, and even the Canadians, don't have the same antagonistic relationship with North Korea as the US. They have aid workers who live there, and thus they have more information," Yungman corrected. "MSF was there most recently doing cataract surgery."

"Cataract surgery?" hooted the professor. "*I'd* like free cataract surgery."

"There, having cataracts means blindness," Yungman said, noting that besides his new accent, the professor's eyebrows looked higher, giving him a slightly surprised expression. Was it possible he'd had plastic surgery? A facelift?

"That's not the reason North Koreans are going blind," Kimm said authoritatively. "We had a defector speak at the church. Sister Kwak must have told you about him. He was talking about how during the famine, people were reduced to boiling down corncobs—Korean toilet paper!—for food. But to Supreme Leader Kim, corncobs are *too good* for his people, and he ordered them to mix the corncob gruel fifty percent with rice root. Do you know what rice root does to you? It makes you go *blind*. This man told us how one man in the village secretly refused to add the rice root to his children's corncob gruel. And so what did the 'Dearest Leader' do when his spies found out? He had the man executed! And not just a quick chop-chop beheading with a sword, but in the middle of the village, where party thugs dragged not just the man's children but all the village's children to force them to watch their father eaten by a pack of hungry dogs: an object lesson in what life is like in a dictatorship. Imagine, while Supreme Leader Kim is drinking fine French wine and eating pastries!"

"They couldn't shoot him because they had to save bullets," surmised the professor's wife.

"Wait—but how do they even have dogs there if they're so hungry?" said a parishioner from the prayer team, obviously also too trivial to trifle with and so was ignored.

"All the more reason it's important for us to at least bring in supplies," Yungman said patiently. "North Korea has a highly regulated class system, and outside of Pyongyang, they don't even have iodine or antibiotics, and patients share IV needles. Even the mountains have been stripped bare of medicinal herbs."

"But what are *you* going to do? Help create more North Korean babies?" The professor sneered.

Yungman tried not to openly sigh. He was aware that obstetricians were always in demand for mission work, because no matter the disaster, some woman was going to be having a baby.

"MSF's and the WHO's reports on women's health in Korea are particularly dire," he said. "Due to lack of basic medicine and surgical equipment, there's no infrastructure for postnatal care in the countryside. Fistulas or infections, postpartum hemorrhage. Something easily treatable becomes a death sentence."

"Whatever expensive equipment you bring in, old Supreme Leader Kim is just going to sell it all on the black market to finance his horrible weapons and fine French wine."

"That's a risk we'll have to take. Isn't that what Jesus would do? Care for the weak?" Yungman was careful not to say "your Jesus."

"No, Jesus wouldn't support terrorism," Kimm went on. "Don't you see you're just aiding a rogue state, helping it to survive?"

"Medical supplies and humanitarian aid are aiding a rogue state?"

"Absolutely! As long as the people get some semblance of things that they need, there won't be a revolution."

"So you want it to collapse."

"Of course. Why do you think we fought the Korean War?"

"I don't know," Yungman said sincerely. He thought of the GIs from bunk sixteen: Red. Adam. Hal. Ray. People who literally determined whether the person in front of them was going to live or die. People who didn't even know where Korea was on a map, and who couldn't have explained the difference between capitalism and Communism if you put a gun to their head. They were just there to, as they said, kill gooks and fight Communism. When the young army staffers Dean Rusk and Charles Bonesteel were tasked with dividing Korea in 1945, they had many other Japan-related issues to deal with and so were given a mere half an hour to deal with the whole country of Korea and weren't even given a map! Someone dug up one in an old *National Geographic* and, as if playing darts, they landed on the 38th Parallel, not the 39th or the 37th. Thirty-eight was just a rough guess, also ensured that the troublesomely northern capital of Seoul would be carefully squared away in the South. They did this so carelessly, as if they didn't see Korea as a real country, Koreans as human.

Similarly, Red was a kind individual, as were some of the others. Maybe even the higher-ups like Jarvis did actually care about Koreans. But ultimately, to a man, they just wanted, reasonably, to kill whoever they were supposed to kill and get the hell out and go home.

"The Americans were there to help *us*," said the professor, taking on some of Kimm's hectoring tone but in a posh British accent. "If not for them, we'd all be back there singing songs to the Supreme Leader and eating our corncob gruel. Tell me: You're not frightened at all for your safety—or that of your wife?"

"Yes, Brother Kwak," said Dr. Kimm. "You really need to think this through."

Yungman glanced at Young-ae, who was now sitting in a corner by herself. Usually she came alive amid her churchy brethren.

"The whole of our country above the 38th Parallel has been turned into a Stalinist dictatorship by a madman," said the professor, now in full, tedious lecture mode.

"It's not the 38th Parallel," said Yungman. "That's where the *Americans* split it in 1945. The Armistice split it again into the Military Demarcation Line—it zigzags all over the place in a ridiculous way." *Don't you even know your own country's history?* he wanted to say.

"Your going over there is sending the absolute wrong message, letting them use you for propaganda," the professor declared.

Yungman looked around. There was no food or even drink to be had. This was contrary to every Korean impulse. Even the rudest, rawest, poorest person would have at least opened a bag of shrimp chips or offered instant coffee.

"Why should we have to consider Korea as North and South when we never thought of it that way ourselves?" Yungman said. "You know, I've lived in America for most of my life now. I'm an American citizen. But I'm also Korean. In fact, in my heart, I think I'm still Korean."

The truth of these words hit him; for once he didn't measure his words as if letting out a fishing line, ready to reel it back in if it met with disapproval.

He continued: "Consider this mission my bucket list item—my opportunity to put my feet on our land again, be back under its sky and do obeisance to my parents and ancestors."

The parishoners exchanged horrified looks.

"Are you really going to bring up ancestor worship at a Christian gathering?" said Kimm, the first angry crack in his smooth facade. The missionaries told them all the time that the yearly memorial on a person's death day was tantamount to devil worship, as was astrology, feng shui, fortune-telling, blood typing, and face reading. Yungman, after all these years, still didn't see what was so wrong with acknowledging and commemorating your father and mother and those who came before them. It certainly wasn't any stranger than eating the bones and drinking the blood of the zombie Jesus, or worshipping those Catholic saints with their heads being chopped off or with all those arrows sticking out of them while they groaned. But he was hardly going to ask these people.

Instead, he said, "So, where is *your* hometown, Dr. Kimm?"

"Seoul," he said proudly, and a bit peevishly.

Yungman was undeterred. "And you, Professor?" he asked. "I believe you were saying Kaesong has the best ginseng."

"It does," he said reluctantly. Kaesong was also famous now as an industrial area in North Korea, close enough to the border that there were plans to create a North-South business consortium. "I only spent a few years there; I was a child," he added.

"I'm from Sokcho," said Mrs. Professor. "Near our sacred mountains. In South Korea."

"Ah, but Sokcho is far *above* the 38th Parallel," Yungman said. "You're more North Korean than I am!"

"Hardly," the professor retorted, but a bit weakly, as he had to know, in a reverse of what had happened to Water Project Village, that the straight line Dean Rusk and Charles Bonesteel drew put Sokcho in North Korea in 1945, and it was negotiated back, zigzag style, to put the town that was the gateway to the Gold Mountains, an important tourist hub for South Koreans, in the South. Most of the mineral reserves, however, were in North Korea, and nothing could be done about that.

"Irrespective of where we all originated in our country, at the very least," Yungman said, "as a fellow physician, I can't believe you're trying to dissuade me from a humanitarian mission. These are people — it's our countrymen and -women we're talking about."

"Brother Kwak, we aren't trying to talk you out of anything," said Kimm. "Out of love and friendship we want to express our *concern*, especially as you're exposing your precious wife, our sister in Christ, to such a dangerous place."

*My wife is a daughter of this dangerous place*, he wanted to remind them. It was their home. Imagine if Edina were suddenly made part of Canada, but at the time of partition Dante and Joyce and the grandkids were shopping at the Mall of America in Bloomington, so they were now in new, separate countries — Bloomington in North Canada, while Kimm and his wife were in South Canada, with no further communication between the two? And that North Canadians and South Canadians were now supposed to be mortal enemies and kill one another on sight?

"Ah," said the professor. "And if Supreme Leader Kim wants a photo or something, make sure not to smile; you can even give the camera a finger. They won't understand it!"

"We're not going there for photo ops."

"Do what you will, Dongbu"—Comrade—sighed the professor, leaving his seat in disgust . . . but also because Mrs. Kimm was now bringing out a platter of shrimp.

"Ah, Brother Kwak," said Kimm gently, as if speaking to a volatile, misguided child. "It is indeed Christlike to want to work with the needy. But if your thirst for action is not yet slaked, why not just come here and work with some of the poor gumdungi in south Minneapolis?"

*Gumdungi? Figures*, Yungman thought. The holiest of the holy would also use the n-word. Yungman knew if he pointed that out, Kimm would just laugh and say, "It means no such thing! 'Blackie' is a term of endearment."

Yungman excused himself. Since the way to the kitchen was blocked by the professor intently stuffing tender pink curls into his mouth as fast as they would go, his only option for temporary egress was the lavatory. He sat on the sparkling white toilet seat lid, which even had carpeting on it, and collected himself. He was going to get Young-ae and head on home. It would be preferable to live out his days in a North Korean gulag with Young-ae than spend one more minute with these pious fakers.

When he came out again, the group was gathered in a circle all looking toward Dr. Kimm, who was holding the bottle containing his ginseng root.

Not again! Enough with the show-and-tell. Yungman gestured desperately to Young-ae, pointing questioningly first at his chest and then at the door, but she came to his side and told him to shush, then whispered, "Mrs. Song dared him to decant the root so she can touch the 'penis' and prove it's not just grafted on."

"I wouldn't be surprised if it was fake," Yungman said, not bothering to whisper. How could a ginseng root be five hundred years old?

"Shhhh! That's what we're going to find out," Young-ae said. Yungman had to admit it would be funny if the ginseng man's penis fell off under prodding.

Kimm was smiling and pouring the honey into a ceramic bowl.

Yungman leaned in. "You said this came from Palgong Mountain? That's actually almost in Kyungsangdo," he noted, referring to the area where the people had particularly thick hick accents that people in Seoul made fun of. Jae, their countrified anatomy teammate in medical college, had been from that area. "When were you living there?"

"I never lived there." Kimm sniffed at the thought. "When our Seoul neighbor's house was bombed during 6.25, I managed to save it."

"What about your neighbors?"

"Unfortunately, they died. A whole family, including the grand-parents. Such a shame."

*You looted your neighbor's house?* Yungman wanted to say. But he couldn't think of a diplomatic way to say it.

Kimm inserted extra-long barbequing chopsticks and deftly pulled the root from the bottle of honey.

"Caught it on the first try!" cried the professor. "Chap-batta!"

"I'm a surgeon at heart, after all, heh, heh," Kimm said. Yungman thought he saw Kimm's wife roll her eyes.

They all leaned in. Without the surrounding glow of the honey, the root looked the color of a dead fish. The professor's wife was fixated on the thin stream of honey oozing off the ginseng man's penis. Her mouth was open; Yungman could see the tip of her pink tongue. The way the ginseng man's "legs" crossed over, it looked like he was walking casually. Strutting, even. Proud of his pepper. The professor bit into the larval body of yet another shrimp.

"This is going to be Dante and Joyce's inheritance," Kimm chuckled. "Plus tuition for my grandkids at Harvard. I hope they don't disappoint me by going to Yale or Princeton."

Yungman stood up. He'd had quite enough of this Korean P. T. Barnum. He wanted to go home right now, and as soon as possible be sitting around in his underwear with a stick of beef jerky, some marshmallows, and a tumbler of that Johnnie Walker Black Ken gave him. "Yobo—" he said.

"Just a few more minutes." She shooed him away.

Yungman walked toward the bowl of shrimp, then, like a football quarterback, feinted left, went right, and snatched the root from the tips of Kimm's chopsticks. Before anyone could react, Yungman stuffed the top half of it in his mouth and took a bite, his head tipped back, his hand and mouth dripping honey. He looked like a satyr at a Dionysian feast.

The ladies screamed. Yungman bit harder, chewed. The root was denser and more fibrous than he'd expected. It was like biting down on a stick. Underneath the cloying sweet of the honey, it was lip-curlingly bitter.

"That's a five-hundred-year-old ginseng root!" Kimm screeched.

At that moment, Yungman felt a current of ki course through his solar plexus. Pure male—yang—energy overtook him.

"Oh, it's the real thing, all right," he said, chewing faster.

"Yobo, have you gone crazy?" Young-ae's eyes were shining like he'd never seen them.

Yungman bit off the penis with his incisors as easy as a cocktail wiener, and chewed what remained of the torso with his molars. The whole thing gone in less than fifteen seconds. "Come on." He tugged his wife by the hand. She rose as if they were going to dance at a wedding, but then, as if of one mind, together they bolted toward the door.

The two jumped into the Hyundai Bongo like Bonnie and Clyde.

*Ain't no woman like the one-eyed got!*

Revving the engine, he made several circuits around the driveway like a race car driver, pulling the steering wheel sharply as he accelerated, Young-ae clinging to his elbow. All the outdoor lights of the Kimm house were winking on; silhouettes of people appeared;

there may have been shouting, but who could tell over the Hyundai's clanking "America's Best Warranty" engine?

One more revolution and the Hyundai broke free of the Kimm gravity, a satellite flying into orbit. Ginseng fire in his veins, Yungman Kwak floored it.

They were going home.

# BOOK V

# William Y. Kwak

Yungman and Young-ae had arrived at the Minneapolis–St. Paul airport as Minnesotans.

Walking by the large Snoopy statue, the Everything Minnesota store, the Prince fan club store, as they approached the gate

MSP → ICN

To Incheon Intl Airport, South Korea

they suddenly felt like they were already in Korea, being in a congregation of so many Koreans, the chatter and clatter of their language, the aura-smell of kimchi, the baggage bulging with presents. Yungman strangely felt like he was at home even though he was at the airport, a locale that's a place of transit, that's no one's home. He couldn't help feeling a strange and welcome reversal. See, here in Minneapolis, when he'd first come, nothing had ever bent to him; now they had announcements in his language, in Korean!

On the wide-bodied Korean Air jet, there was an older Korean couple across the way, about their age, the woman with a short, tight perm wearing a doubled scarf, the ends tucked through the loop in a way Yungman found very Korean. When their first meal was served, the woman looked covetously over at Yungman's and Young-ae's meals, the exact same ones.

*Ah*, thought Yungman in recognition. The scrabbling feeling he'd had during the war, always trying to get more to feed his family, alert for people or places that had more; he needed to even out the scales. That was the most Korean thing ever. He was thinking how embarrassed Einstein was when he and Young-ae came to see him work at the KFC and Yungman had walked out carrying a giant stack of napkins.

"You're not supposed to do that," Einstein said.

"They weren't chained to the register," he'd huffed to his son. They were free. This was America!

"You didn't have to take a whole dispenser's worth."

"Then why did they leave the stack out like that?"

"But you didn't even eat here."

"Were these napkins free or not?"

"Yes, but—"

"No 'yes, but'—'yes' will suffice."

He cracked his Korean Air chopsticks and rubbed them together to get rid of splinters.

"You don't have to do that," Young-ae said. "I'm sure these are sanded down right—they're Asian."

"Hah," said Yungman. "Remember the chopstick factory they built in Horse's Breath after the mines closed?" China rejected the first splintery shipments in which chopstick A and chopstick B weren't the same length, and then the company went belly-up. "I keep worrying that those chopsticks still got smuggled onto the market and I'll get a splinter in my throat."

Young-ae shrugged in agreement. "What do people in Horse's Breath know about chopsticks?" Also, the specific kind of local soft wood that worked well, the Norwegian fir, had all been sold off to the paper plant in Apple's Gate to make toilet paper—toilet paper! They'd ended up using ash, which is particularly splintery, hoping no one would notice.

"It's sad, because trees are the things that make northern Minnesota different from Minneapolis," Yungman mused. He thought of their arduous drive up from Birmingham, a catatonic Young-ae, a cranky and underfed Einstein. Once they'd crossed the Iowa border, he was excited to announce that they were finally in Minnesota. But they still had hundreds of miles to go—boring, flat prairie with only telephone poles to break up the landscape.

Yet somewhere north of Princeton (for some reason, everything in Minnesota was named after a different place: Princeton, Brooklyn, Rochester, Wyoming), a heavy but fresh scent permeated the car. It was intensely familiar to Yungman, but he couldn't quite place it. He breathed in more, like a cat, to taste this smell in the back of his throat.

"Pine!" he almost shouted. "Like Chusok rice cakes." How pretty it was up here, with so many small lakes dotting the landscape (Paul Bunyan's Babe the Blue Ox's footprints, he would be told), fringed prettily with white birches and pine and Norwegian fir.

He thought about the small sandy beach at Ken's cabin, Ken exhorting him to "Take off your shoes, Yungman! You're on the beach, geez!" as he put some brats on the grill, Blatz beer in the mini fridge. Yungman, sitting in a beach chair at the edge of the shore, had rolled up the cuffs of his pants (the same thing he did to make shorts to mow the lawn) and relaxed a little, let his feet slide into the cool, wet sand— only to extract them and see strange black globs clinging to them.

"I've never seen you run so fast, Yungman," Ken had laughed. Yungman had in his entire life never encountered leeches.

*　　*　　*

Yungman was still softly chuckling to himself as the flight attendants, having cleared away the meal debris, dimmed the lights. A bit early to go to bed, but apparently they were trying to get the passengers acclimated to Asian time. Young-ae fell fast asleep. Her head even lolled on his shoulder; he could smell the fermented sweetness from her meal on her breath.

His view of her was only of the top of her head, the tip of her nose. Dyeing her hair black was her one vanity, but he could already see a line of white growing out. When she was younger, her hair was slick and moved like ink. It was still remarkably smooth, but there were rogue hairs sprouting out of it like frazzled wires, and these hairs were entirely silver.

In the dim light, under this familiar weight, he hurtled back through the decades: 1990 . . . 1980 . . . 1970 . . .

He remembered.

Seoul National University College of Medicine. The cadaver room. He and the two young men on his team were a week into their anatomy course, terrified of their professors, terrified of life in general — although, being men, they were careful not to show it. Dissection had started far away from the head, but now they were tasked with the cadaver's face. And yes, they were eating.

Of course, no one wanted to eat in the cadaver room, with its bodies, its boxes labeled "extraneous organs," the sick-sweetness of formaldehyde, the pungent odor of the red and blue latex injected to map the veins and arteries. No one wanted to eat here — but he and his anatomy teammates JongDal and Jae did, as a dare, to pretend they weren't at all spooked about slicing open a dead person's face, especially when their cadaver, a male, had died with an unnervingly knowing smile, as if he had anticipated this very moment and relished their discomfort.

It had been the three of them ringing the table, a flap of forehead skin opened, Yungman gulping for air as he wielded the bone saw, trying to keep his hands from shaking. JongDal, following the written instructions, had tied a string around the widest part of the skull to mark the line of the calvarium in preparation to open the cranium. They had stopped to stare at a young woman who had just entered— barged in—wearing a badge that said "Rhim Young-ae." One of the few girls in their class, and by far the most striking. Unlike the others, who kept their heads down, their clothes plain, this girl took the time to brazenly accent her beauty with fuchsia lipstick, her soft-looking blouse a sweep of color below her white lab coat; her electric-blue skirt had a hundred pleats like a paper fan. She had come over, hands on hips, and stared at the three of them, one at a time. JongDal, who had just used a pen to trace the line around the string, stared open-mouthed and almost dropped both the pen and the ball of string. Jae, a country lad with shoulders like an ox, looked at the floor, his cheeks aflame.

Yungman knew he had to talk faster than his friends.

"Can I help you?" Knowing that his friends were watching him, Yungman's words probably came out more roguish, with more bravado than he actually had himself.

"You can't eat in here!"

"There's no rule against eating," he said calmly.

She ignored him to point at JongDal. "And you! I saw you bring in popcorn the other day!"

JongDal, having recovered his silky voice, grinned back at her: "Such beauty in this unlikely place!"

"One might say the same about you!" she shot back. Indeed, Jong-Dal's skin was a nacreous white that was characteristic of the rich and well-bred; the collar that poked above his white coat was simple but exquisitely cut, kind of like him. See, down to JongDal's name, he was unique: his name was a pure Korean word, not Sino-Korean. His modern and sophisticated parents had upended generational naming traditions by naming him after the jongdal sae, the lark bird.

He indeed had a beautiful voice. Yungman often joked that they should have named him Si-in, poet, because he was always under a tree dreamily reading and writing, often while sitting his ongdongi atop his medical textbooks.

> *Beautiful rivers and mountains surround me. Hello, Mr. Sun.*
> *I want to ride a rainbow to where I will feel your warm rays*

When Lark bent his head to read what he'd written, a flop of his dark hair would fall over his eyes, a look that drove girls to faint.

Desperate to win this beautiful med student's attention, Yungman speared an oblong rice cake, drowning in fermented red chili sauce, which he'd picked specifically because it looked like blood—a better choice than the grayish blood sausage that JongDal had selected as his gross-out challenge. "Want to try?" Yungman remembered not her face (for he, too, was wilting under her direct gaze) but the crooked, almost insipid smile of their cadaver.

"It's not respectful. Are you going to drop a spicy rice cake into this human's supraorbital foramen, after he's given his life to science?"

"Who are you?" said Jae the country boy, slowest on the uptake. "Where is your hometown?"

She looked at him scornfully. "I'm from Seoul, of course." She spun on her heel and walked away from them in disgust. But not without a quick glance back—at him, Yungman, despite JongDal's charismatic presence. And he was sure he had seen the sparks, like metal striking flint, in those dark eyes somewhere before.

Yungman and JongDal plied the other medical students with various treats to bribe them into telling them what they knew about this girl. The three of them were in the "A" anatomy class and she was in "B," so they never saw one another. The vague outlines that emerged: she had grown up in a family of four sisters and one brother, she was the youngest by six years, and the next-youngest daughter had died of tuberculosis around the time of 6.25.

Thus, her elder sisters doted on her unreasonably. She never learned how to cook or do dishes or care for children, in which she had no interest anyway. All she did was study. Something happened to her brother during the war, and thus, when she'd shown an interest in medicine, she had the full support of her father, who enlisted squadrons of tutors for her; he was convinced his youngest daughter was smart enough to become a famous doctor, an example for all Korean women. She had attended prestigious middle and high schools, and had sailed into Seoul National University College of Medicine. Women's health was coming up as a field, and that was what she wanted to do. Yungman, who had been searching for a novel specialty, decided that obstetrics and gynecology was what he wanted to do, too. Being first in anything was always an advantage.

"Rhim Young-ae's father is supposedly frightening," said Jong-Dal, who remained determined to court her as well. The old-timey Choson-era Changgyeong Palace was conveniently located across the street from campus, and Yungman heard they'd cut class to go skating on the frozen pond there.

Yungman racked his brain. JongDal wasn't just rich and from a good family; he was taller than Yungman, more confident, and didn't have bowlegs from rickets. No responsible parent would ever allow a match for their daughter with someone like Yungman, dirt-poor and of unquantifiable and unverifiable parentage after his and Yung-sik's documents had been lost forever on that fateful bus ride. They'd been slow to replace them because they feared being accused of being Communists.

Guilt by association was still very real.

At least, being a Seoul National University medical student went far with rich Seoulite parents seeking tutors for their dull children, and that work put food on the table. But he needed Yung-sik's work on the black market to provide his tuition. Yungman skipped lunches waiting for the days when the student cafeteria served curry rice, which came with free bean-sprout soup. He would pay the alr..dy minimal fee and fill up the tiny stainless cup ten times or more, even as the attendant yelled at him. With the few won he'd have left over, he could buy the spicy rice cakes at a pojangmacha on the street like a carefree student, not a beggar.

Yungman dreamed of her and wondered if it was possible that she, despite her fancy clothes and impeccable Seoul accent, could be of that Rhim family from his hometown. The girl who skated on rice paddies. Jae had asked her the question about her hometown because he, too, had sniffed out something of the country, as if her polished exterior had become a mirror that allowed both him and Yungman to see her and themselves more clearly; Jae came from a coal-mining area where men died standing up because that was the only way they could sleep when the black lung got them.

Yungman's village, Water Project Village, was known to all of Korea from the children's poem of the same name. Koreans loved tales of hardship and industry, and so the poem became one that all children had to memorize in kindergarten.

Modern people in the South didn't even know Water Project Village was a real place, a few miles inland from Kanghwa Island, therefore practically in Seoul. Since the Armistice had locked the village into North Korea, it had in people's minds become a village of the past, an antiquity for a folk lesson about Confucian educational mores.

This mysterious student hadn't visited their anatomy group again. Yungman waited, but he could hang around the airless, fume-filled cadaver room for only so long. She eschewed the student cafeteria and didn't join any of the study groups. Yungman skipped all lunches for a week so he could buy a single bread roll to eat out near her, when he discovered that her volleyball and track clubs practiced outside. He could stand unobtrusively among the spectators, admiring her skill and confidence (who else would devote precious time to joining a sports club in medical school?) and how shapely her legs looked in shorts. As she shouted to her teammates, Yungman swore he caught the tiniest *nng!* of their country province in her mannered Seoul speech.

Yungman and JongDal the Lark had, in the meantime, become close friends despite their disparate backgrounds. They were both near the top of their class. But the two of them glared at each other when they converged on the volleyball courts or at the track stadium. JongDal would invite Young-ae for an ice cream after these practices.

But back at the dorm, JongDal confessed that he wasn't getting too far. "She eats like a horse and then leaves me without a word!" he lamented. "She's hardly impressed that I'm to become a Seoul National University doctor because she is, too. It's hopeless!" JongDal would, at those moments, clutch his heart and fall over backward. "I'm dead! I love her so."

JongDal also reported that instead of going home to meet match-making prospects during Free Time, as the other two female students in their class did, Rhim Young-ae went to movies—alone. "Because I like movies," she simply said when asked.

JongDal was further scandalized when he confirmed that she didn't know how to cook even "rags" soup: flour-and-water dumplings, the torn dough resembling scraps of cloth. Wheat flour was dirt cheap compared to rice; this was poor people's food, filling and simple, something Yungman had made for him and Yung-sik when there was nothing in their cupboard, seasoning the broth with a single anchovy, a scrap of seaweed, sometimes just with the salt from his finger.

Yungman was determined to win. He'd learned that Rhim Young-ae had let JongDal take her out to a full pig-belly dinner, with cold noodles after. How could she accept favors from the two of them?

Indeed, she happily received the spicy rice cakes Yungman brought to her when she studied in the common area at school. After eating one, she would sometimes say, "Ah!" and Yungman would obediently but disinterestedly open his mouth to receive a dangled rice cake, quelling the growling of his stomach, restraining himself from snapping at the cake as if he were a winter-starved fish snapping at a fly.

Her "Ahs!" became more playful. Yungman, as if he didn't care either way, said he was thinking of going to a movie. Maybe she would like to come.

He had, in truth, spent a whole week running from the lecture hall to the fancy neighborhood by Kyungbok Palace to tutor an eleven-year-old blockhead. Five days with barely time to eat or sleep or take a shit, but he had scraped together enough money for two movie tickets.

Young-ae and Yungman sat in the Changchoon Movie Theater, waiting for the feature. There were mostly young couples in the theater, as this movie, *The Red Scarf*, was supposed to be romantic. A bonus, as Yungman hadn't planned it that way. What he had planned was to find out if Rhim Young-ae was from that Rhim family.

A few soldiers, who must have been on furlough, clomped in noisily and pointed at the cuddling couples and laughed through their noses. Yungman wondered if their derisive behavior was a kind of plaster over their fears of what was going to happen now that President Park Chung-hee had declared Korea would be sending soldiers to Vietnam to help the US, which, with barely a pause, was already embarking on its next war against Asians. The soldiers now sitting and cuddling with each other weren't men but silly boys, their smooth cheeks reminding Yungman that he had deferred his mandatory military service for medical school but would have to do his two years eventually. But he was good at tucking away unpleasant things in a corner of his mind, believing that if he forgot about them, they wouldn't come to pass.

He was more preoccupied with determining the right moment to deploy his test. He worried that Young-ae was disappointed he hadn't been able to buy her a drink or a snack, but she sat serenely, looking at the screen, even though the curtain was pulled over it. Occasionally she smiled inwardly at something. Before she got too deep into her daydream, he figured this time was as good as any. He leaned over and recited:

> The Water Project Village
> With the clear blue medicine water
> That they sold to send their children to school

"So?" she said, a tiny cloud of wariness coming into her eyes. "Every child in Korea has to memorize that poem."

That "so" revealed everything. Yungman spoke to her in the twangy hillbilly accent of the Gold Sea province:

> And in the mountains, the azalea bloomed
> So profusely, it looked like pink fire
> The elders collected water, speaking of tigers
> The children trudged over the mountains to school.

She laughed in spite of herself. "All right. You found me out. Water Project Village is my hometown. But that was another time." Her eyes softened. Yungman wondered if she, too, was imagining the soughing of the pines that dotted the mountain, the pink of the wild azaleas.

"The house," Yungman said. "At the top of the hill."

"Yes. That was our house. Long ago," she said. "Who are you?"

"My mother was Boon-yi the gourd seller."

"Ah, Boon-yi, the Lucky Gourd woman at the Exchange Zone Market!" Young-ae clapped her hands. "But you said 'was'—has she passed away?"

"I'm the son of a divided-and-scattered family. My mother stayed in North Korea, I think."

"What do you mean, 'think'? They made us all choose at the time."

"It's a long story," Yungman said. He felt a shuddering in his diaphragm, and for a horrible moment he worried that he might break his tough-guy exterior and cry. If she had inquired about his father, he certainly would have. He was grateful when the usher shushed them, for the movie was beginning.

Yungman actually preferred Western movies, because at least there was the opportunity to improve his English while he was watching. *The Red Scarf* was about the Korean Air Force, which was tiny. Apparently, the Americans gave the pilots red scarves to remind them of the blood of conscience and the fire of patriotism (and not Communism, the "Reds"). They were to wear the scarves every time they went out in their planes. Two pilots driving on a frozen road on a snowy night encounter a beautiful woman fleeing her village, where her family has been killed by the Communists. Both pilots fall in love with her, but the older, grizzled guy hides his heart so he can help his friend court her. The friend dies in combat, and the older guy, still in love with her, introduces her to a young daredevil pilot, as he believes she needs to be taken care of, but that he cannot impinge upon his dead best friend by following the deep love in his own heart for her.

Of course the good rural guy has to sacrifice himself for the handsome young daredevil, who is, actually, kind of an oblivious jerk. Among the action scenes of flying and bombing that made everyone ooh and aah, Yungman was quietly devastated by a small interlude in which the daredevil pilot confesses to the young woman that his heart is heavy because the tiny village they just successfully bombed was his hometown; he had seen women and children in white trying to flee just as he dropped the napalm.

On the screen, the North Korean artillery hidden in straw exploded in obliterating flames, and a slight shadow of fleeing white-clad figures, the elderly protectively curved around the young, illuminated like a flash of visible angels before the black of combustion.

"Such a small village. There could have been family—grannies and aunts and such—mixed in there," the woman said accusingly. The daredevil was sad but didn't cry. "I did what I set out to do," he said. "The same for war is the same for love."

Yungman stopped up his gulping sobs with a fist, and used that same fist to pile drive the tears back into his ducts, feigning a headache. Such a silly movie! So melodramatic! What was wrong with him?

The movie was short, and, to their delight, they learned it was part of a double feature with a Western movie, *The Great Escape*. While they were changing reels, Young-ae wanted to talk about *The Red Scarf*. Not the romance, which she thought was frivolous, and she also hated that this so-called hero beat the woman he loved, but the scene where the ROK pilots are about to bomb the village and the head pilot radios to the daredevil, confirming that this is indeed his home village—he can see the pine tree that he used to climb, his mountains, his family. It was an odd scene in which he merely said "Yes," and they went on with their bombing sortie.

"For a movie that seemed a lot like propaganda for the South Korean military, it was surprising that they would bring that up, that one of the ROK's best pilots was a North Korean," Yungman said.

"Yes!" Young-ae said. "Exactly! Sometimes I don't know why I try so hard to pretend I'm a Seoulite. We are just all Koreans!"

"How did you come here?"

"When we had to choose in 1953, my father, my older sister Youngja, and I came south. My other sisters stayed in Water Project Village because my mother wouldn't move. I had an older brother, Joongki, who disappeared during the war. My mother wanted to stay because she was worried he'd come home and not know where we'd gone."

"But," Yungman said, "how could she do that to your sisters? Knowing how harsh the regime was?"

"Don't forget that the Russians *and* the Americans did terrible things in the village—the only difference I used to hear the adults say is that the Russians would rape grannies if that's all there were, but the Americans only raped younger women and farm animals. My sisters wanted to stay with Mother and in the home they knew. At the time it was Father and Youngja and I who were thought to be taking the riskier course," Young-ae said. "No one knew how bad it would be when the Communists moved in. How could any of us? Water Project Village, after all, was one of the few places to come out of the war untouched. We didn't even get bombed!"

That was true. While 99 percent of North Korea and 95 percent of South Korea—even little mountain hamlets, because the Allies wanted to make sure the Communists had no cover and would starve—was bombed. But in Water Project Village the only victim of an Allied bombing was the train tracks, which used to go both south toward Seoul and north to Pyongyang.

"There's still a lot of prejudice against us people from the North, an immediate suspicion about Communism by people who don't even know what it is," she said. "So I tell people I'm from Seoul. However, my accent still sometimes slips out. Evidently."

"I hope it doesn't harm your marriage prospects," he teased. "To a fancy Seoul man."

"Ha," she said. "I've decided that I will not marry."

"Why not?"

"Because I want to do things. I have older cousins; I watch my sister. They do nothing but work their fingers to the bone for their husbands, their mothers-in-law, their screeching children. My father says I'm to become a famous doctor."

"But then what are you going to do?"

"What do you mean?" she said incredulously. "I said I'm to become a famous doctor. I'll travel to other places—England, France, Japan— and learn the best of their medicine and bring it here. Maybe I'll travel to the countryside and help women there. Maybe I'll become the dean of a medical school."

Yungman didn't doubt it. He had never met anyone like this. Someone so sure of herself. Someone who would step on age-old Confucian rules when they didn't suit her. She had places to go!

In the movie onscreen, Steve McQueen, playing a World War II American POW in a German prison camp, had plans of escape—but how to dispose of the rocks and dirt from the tunnel secretly being dug in their bunkhouse? He came up with the idea of making special pockets in the men's pants so they could carry out the dirt and discreetly sprinkle it around their ankles as they walked about the camp.

Thrillingly, McQueen tested his invention right in front of the Nazi guards! Yungman grasped Young-ae's hand. His palm was sweaty—he was worried she would slap him, as, reportedly, she had already done to JongDal, leaving the impression of four distinct fingers on his milky-white cheek for a week. Or, worse, take her hand back.

First, nothing.

Then she slowly, barely, squeezed back.

He was perfectly calm on the outside. On the inside, his happiness burned so bright that it seared him.

Not unlike Steve McQueen, Yungman faced a daunting obstacle: Young-ae's father, Rhim the merchant. As mentioned, he was a big man, notable for his height and girth, even coming from a province that for centuries had produced some of the best ssirum wrestlers. Rhim had also arrived in Water Project Village as a stranger, not from the Park lineage, and also penniless. The family had been famous for being wealthy for so long that it was difficult to conjure up a time when it was not. Rhim had arrived in Water Project Village with the idea of using its local water to make a kind of biscuit that was a specialty of where he came from. The biscuit, cookie-shaped, was nothing special, and most people secretly laughed at this illiterate fool. As he hired a local boy to start removing buckets of water from the Medicine Water well, which the village shared freely with anyone who cared to travel all the way there to try it, people frowned and tsched with their tongues. The biscuits weren't particularly tasty, made with wheat and the other cheap filler grains (and, it seemed, sand) the Japanese allowed, but when the local baker was mysteriously murdered—he'd had no enemies and was particularly beloved by children—Rhim took over his stall at the market in Songdo. If you wanted a baked good, you were stuck with buying what were now called "cash cookies," known not only for their disk shape but for the way Rhim pressed the dough with a stamp so they looked like a one-chon coin, perfectly fashioned for the occupation: chon was Korean but also "only redeemable for gold or Nippon Gingko," and the coin was stamped with the plum flower design of Imperial Japan.

Rhim bribed the authorities and also outsourced his violence by hiring goons. Even the granny who'd sold a popular cornbread she made from her own corn grown to feed livestock, was summarily dispatched, cursing and kicking, from the market. This kind of indifferent attitude toward his countrymen was useful for the Japanese, and Rhim was added, despite objections, despite his illiteracy, to the village council. His cash cookies became actual cash, especially when he was commissioned to run a factory that would produce hardtack for Japanese military rations. He made sure to forge good relations with the military, and Kang the police chief received regular shipments of cash cookies in bags laden with actual cash. He hired a student to read for him during Village Council meetings. He married a beautiful thirteen-year-old girl who was from one of the head Park clans in the village. It seemed, after the Liberation and beyond, that they had always lived in that house on the hill.

Rhim couldn't read, a skill he considered inessential, especially when it was so easy to hire someone to read for him. Getting ahead of the future was his specialty. Even without his firstborn son his legacy, he understood in 1953 where his next fortune would lie. After he had relocated to Seoul, Rhim left behind his biscuits and his black-market goods and, inspired by his fashionable and intelligent daughter, was moved instead to start a Western-inspired one-hundred-kinds-of-things store, a department store. This also was something novel, something you might see in Japan—like Ginza's famous Mitsukoshi—but new to Korea. Unlike the shabby Songdo open-air market where he had started selling his wheat-and-sand-filled biscuits under a repurposed military tarp, his new store would encourage people to just "shop"—to touch the merchandise without necessarily buying, to make it entertainment, like a sport. People would want to make it an outing, to see and be seen, and this outing would make buying irresistible. To help this genteel image along, prices would be fixed; no more needing to haggle with saliva-spitting merchants. The lighting would be clean and bright, the store staffed by impeccably dressed maidens.

His first, HanGaWi, failed spectacularly, perhaps because of its proximity to a smelly express bus terminal. But no matter. He immediately started another, this time selecting a neighborhood near the famous Kyungbok Palace, and made it twice as large. He asked his polyglot daughter what the French word for *snow* was and gave his new one-hundred-kinds-of-things store a pristine French name, La Neige—and by then he knew the right city officials to bribe to make the building four times as big as what he had a permit for.

When his daughter became a physician, he planned to use his considerable wealth and influence to open a hospital for her, one that would rival the famous Severance Hospital by the Great West Gate. He thus focused on this goal single-mindedly, as it kept him from thinking about his wife, son, and two other daughters, now forever inaccessible to him. He was a hard man who still loved his family deeply.

One day, in his sumptuous sixth-floor offices in a former city hall building once occupied, in fact, by Japanese administrators, bombed by Americans, and now rebuilt by himself, he received Kwak Yungman. This lad had come to his office without an appointment; strangely bold. Rhim, who had a prodigious memory for sums, for faces, for the smallest units of merchandise, recognized this young man as the son of a Communist sympathizer back in their village. Yes, the pitiable boy, already of modest means, who went door to door selling junk after his Commie father, the dirty-fingernailed seed scatterer, disappeared.

This rush sapling with no means and, even worse, from a bad family claimed he was in love with his daughter! Rhim roared when Yungman broached this impudence. Despite it, the boy straightened his spine and continued. He asked for permission to marry Young-ae— who, unbeknownst to both of them, was in the back of the office, having arrived to help with paperwork that day. She heard it all. She mistook Yungman's obsession and heedlessness for courage. Here, she thought, was a person brave enough to be her match, a man who wasn't even afraid of her father!

In cold weather, of which there was much too much in Horse's Breath, Yungman's humerus, clavicle, tibia, and ribs ached, sometimes all at once, sometimes in sequence as if Rhim had once again stalked him at the College of Medicine, pulled him into that kimchi-stinking alley, and delivered the blows from his squash-size fists.

"Your father tried to tenderize me like a piece of kalbi," he explained, laughing weakly through some loosened teeth to Young-ae, who rolled an egg on his blackening eye. She, likewise, had been told to stay away from "that young whelp from a family of Communist sympathizers," which only made him seem more exotic to her, their relationship more doomed and exciting and rebellious. To make him happy, she embarked on a single seon meeting with Lee JongDal, whom she knew her father would not see as the campus radical but as the son of a family of important government administrators, including the mayor of Seoul and a cabinet member. She felt pleasingly like a spy on a mission, a brief glimpse of a luxurious parallel life that, she had to admit, she did not find displeasing but knew that she would likely end up relaxing into its softness, becoming a pampered rich wife, a hobbyist doctor with her Seoul National University College of Medicine diploma displayed in an ornate gilded frame next to an elaborate wedding portrait, nightly meals of steak melting in her mouth. Despite Yungman's seeming like any carefree student, he was a boy from the village, the son of the gourd seller at the Exchange Zone Market. This intrigued her. He wasn't transparent but translucent, with so many layers to peel; who knew what lay at his pith?

They were both too young and inexperienced to know what those strong emotions they were feeling were, and so they just called them love.

Over their long lives together, Young-ae had told Yungman, in her usual lucid way, that if her father hadn't forbidden her to see him, she probably wouldn't have continued to date him, much less marry him. They had nothing in common. She was athletic. He wasn't. She liked to travel. He liked to stay at home. She liked trying new foods. He ate the same thing every day. Yungman was hurt by her words, but she was, after all, the same brash, honest girl she had been; just older, wiser, and, she said, sadder. The worst, she said, was watching Einstein attend medical school and approach the age they had been; all the things she should and could have done differently. To have peeled all the layers back, year after year, slogging onward, one more layer, only to find there was nothing at the pith: the last layer of the core was emptiness.

Not Yungman, she clarified. Herself. She'd been waiting in the dark all this time for her life to begin, only to learn it was already the evening of her life.

How naive they both had been!

"However, I regret *many* things, not just you." She said this to spare him.

Yungman was thinking about how, during that same leech-filled weekend at Ken's cabin, when Young-ae pulled up her feet, which she'd been dangling off the dock, she'd attracted considerably more and much larger leeches. She'd stared at the rubbery black parasites for a moment, observed them intently, then pulled them off one by one, not caring about the bright red blood running alarmingly down her leg. Yungman had blanched and run to get her a tissue, which she had waved off impatiently.

"Leeches have an anticoagulant as well as an anesthetic in their suckers," she said. "Of course it's going to bleed like crazy. It'll stop now that I've pulled them off." She actually pushed on the edge of her skin to make it bleed even more.

Yungman, just contemplating the idea of his tender skin being stealthily numbed and then bitten by a sharp-toothed leech, felt faint. Ken chuckled as he watched the whole thing, recalling Yungman's yell, his paddling his feet on the sand, then his getting up and running without destination.

"Young-ae, *you're* the one with the proper clinical detachment," Ken said. "More than us doctors."

"I *was* a doctor," Young-ae said, to his astonishment. He looked at Yungman, who said nothing. It wasn't his history to explain.

"Why didn't you ever mention that?"

"No one ever asked." She paused. "Everyone here just assumes a woman doesn't do anything. It's the same in Korea. I was in the same class as Yungman. I stopped just short of my graduation and never practiced."

"She had the highest grades," Yungman admitted. "I was number two. So I became number one."

"Well, I'll be," Ken said, surprised for the second time by this couple today.

Yungman was realizing that he had been incorrect. He'd actually been number three. Lark had been number two but dropped out just shy of graduation. Yungman the steady one had won his number-one spot solely through attrition. Solely through being steady. Solely through being decidedly not heroic and just being there.


"We will now be landing at Incheon International Airport."

Yungman wished he could look out the window at the landscape, but they were in the bank of seats in the middle, the digestive system of the plane. Other Koreans practically had their noses pressed against the panes, including the older couple.

"Ohmunah," said the woman with a sigh. "Aigu!"

When the plane touched down, everyone clapped. Korean joy.

Yungman couldn't believe he was back in Seoul, even if he was just inside its international airspace. This was Seoul's *second* airport, a result of its rapid growth, or "regrowth" from the IMF scandal of the 1990s—an ultramodern new airport with a cavernous interior, spas, restaurants, and an indoor golf course. Inchon (now spelled Incheon), where *Megadoo* had famously landed, was now part of the megalopolis that comprised metropolitan Seoul. Despite the ghosts of all the soldiers who lost their lives and limbs here, it was utterly peaceful, with fountains and piped-in traditional Korean music (a little hokey, he thought) wafting through hidden speakers. The original airport, Kimpo, was now relegated to domestic flights.

A curly-permed Korean woman without luggage emerged from the tangle of wheelie-bag-toting fliers. Her face was scarlet with exertion.

This had to be Bo-hae, Yung-sik's widow, Yungman's sister-in-law.

"Older-brother-of-husband!" she cried. At the last second she added a "nim" to show respect—a respect Yungman knew he did not deserve.

On the plane, he'd had to make an effort to listen to the Korean in the bilingual announcements. The grooves in his brain now normally fell into English. But his sister-in-law's voice triggered something in him like a radio frequency switching over to another station that at first was fuzzy, then came in loud and clear.

But even swimming in his new bandwidth, he couldn't remember the right word for a wife of a younger sibling—a term he'd never used before. He could barely remember what was proper to say to someone after a long separation. And they had been separated but hadn't even known each other; he also wasn't sure of her age. Saying *Nice to meet you for the first time* seemed too formal and cold. A wordless embrace would be scandalous, *Hello, how are you?* utterly wrong. But he must say something! Like in those dreams where you see the monster and yet cannot run, his mouth didn't move, a linguistic tetanus.

"Bo-hae!" he said instead (fleetingly wondering if he should have added the prefix for "Ms." or "dear heart"). Yungman bowed and then also shook her hand. "Nice to meet you for the first time!"

"The Chusok traffic starts earlier and earlier every year," she panted. Her Korean was thoroughly that of someone who had been born in Seoul. Yungman was happy: that standard dialect was the easiest for him to understand. "The traffic didn't move for two hours. I was so worried I would never get here!"

Yungman marveled that he had lived in a Seoul where the idea of owning a car was akin to the idea of owning your own spaceship. Everyone took a streetcar, or a bus, or a train, or walked for hours or even days to get to their destination. On holidays, the overloaded homegoing trains and buses were stuffed to the gills, but they were often merry. People always made sure to bring enough food to share, live animals they were going to slaughter at home. Now, however, even poor Seoulites were atomized into private cars, and thus for Chusok, the holiday necessitating that people travel back to their hometowns to perform the ancestor rites, the roads from the cities to the mountains became impossibly, immovably clogged.

Bo-hae bowed to Young-ae, and the two women started to chat like old friends. A song that Yungman couldn't quite place came on the speakers, and both women laughed.

"'Beautiful Rivers and Mountains'!" Young-ae said.

"Ah, such an old love song," Bo-hae said in delight. "You actually have that in America?"

Young-ae nodded. "*I have it.*"

Now Yungman remembered it. He'd heard it sometimes leaking out of the Walkman she had, from a cassette tape: the Lark, *Beautiful Rivers & Mountains*. It had been the song he'd written instead of the patriotic ballad Park Chung-hee had demanded. A love song to their country. That's when he'd been jailed up until Park's assassination in 1979. By the time he was released, his kind of music had fallen out of favor. Only covers by other singers—or this Muzak version—remained.

Bo-hae handed Yungman a doubled-up Lotte Department Store shopping bag, heavy with two cardboard boxes. Something at the bottom clanked softly—it was their father's silver chopsticks, which Bo-hae had carefully wrapped in cloth. If they made it home, Yungman could reunite it with his father's spoon.

The skin under Bo-hae's eyes sagged in soft pouches.

Yungman considered how hard things must have been with Yung-sik, whose rage, as he knew, would have been smoldering his whole life after such a betrayal by his too-quickly-modernizing country, and, even worse, by his brother. Yet here she was, not a trace of resentment or suspicion, only devotion and love as her tired but warm hands patted his. She'd thoughtfully covered up the contents of the sack with a cellophane bag of puffed, dyed rice treats. He was grateful Yung-sik had found the love of a good woman, and that she had stayed by his side.

"Korean Air Flight 3828 to Beijing . . ."

"You'd better go," she said. But Yungman took a moment to ask after his nieces. He promised Bo-hae that he and Young-ae would visit once they returned to Seoul after their work in North Korea was done.

"When will that be?" she asked worriedly. "On the news it said there had been some 'activity' near the border."

Yungman smiled at his sister-in-law and bowed, deeper than one normally would to the wife of a younger brother, but he didn't care.

"I will go and come back," he promised.

It was the same phrase he'd said to his brother every morning, including the morning he'd left to get Young-ae to sail to America.

In Beijing they met the rest of the MSF group. Jules, a Frenchman wearing a striped shirt and a scarf around his neck almost like a cartoon Frenchman, was the leader. He worked for MSF full-time and had been on dozens of missions, including several to North Korea.

After quick hellos, their flight was called. The group went outside to the tarmac.

This was Air Koryo, the North Korean airline. Yungman walked up the outdoor steps with a pleasant sense of nostalgia, like he was boarding a Northwest Orient jet at the local Iron County Airport (back when full-size airplanes still landed there) that would take him to Detroit to attend his first American College of Obstetricians and Gynecologists meeting in 1970. This plane had similar lozenge-shaped windows with individual blue curtains on curtain rods as had been on the Northwest plane in 1970. A curly-haired blond Westerner was already in the window seat of their row, his legs strangely accordioned up against a huge oxygen tank on the floor. But no matter: he hugged his large backpack, a Canadian flag patch sewn on it, and immediately fell asleep.

Yungman sat in the aisle seat, where he had a view of a 1950s-looking full-size refrigerator bolted to the floor (and spelled, oddly, in Korean as "Lefrigerator").

The propeller jet had taken off without incident, but it was now juddering like it was going to fall to pieces. Jules told them that Air Koryo was the only world airline to have received a "0" safety rating from Skytrax, but not to worry because they had, probably for the Western doctors, sent one of their newest Ilyushin Russian-made planes.

"How new?" asked an Irishman. "I thought Russia stopped supporting North Korea after the fall of the USSR."

Jules nodded. "This plane is circa 1968."

Now there was a sudden deceleration and loss of altitude. Falling and falling, beyond the point where Yungman thought, *It has to start going back up now.*

One of the flight attendants screamed, a pure, existential noise. Another put her face in her hands and started to sob, her heaving shoulders visible. Yungman had never seen such a loss of professional composure before. Nor had he seen what looked like smoke shooting from the vents by the window and filling the inside of the cabin. Yungman couldn't smell the smoke because he was holding his breath in alarm, thinking, *Okay, maybe this white stuff is some kind of condensation, like at a David Copperfield magic show—poof!* This was what he chose to believe, because why imagine the worst?

Yungman craned his head to catch Jules's eye to see how he was reacting. The stewardess who'd started crying was still sobbing. "Maybe I was foolish to do this," he said. "At the very least I should have come alone. I'm sorry to have gotten you into this."

"Shhhh," said Young-ae, pale but composed. "Don't tempt fate."

"I'm sorry if you regret—"

"Shut up," she said. "I wanted to come. I made my own decision about it." Next to them the Westerner slept, unperturbed by the chaos around him.

The plane hit what Yungman thought—*Finally!*—was the ground, but it was merely an almost-solid current of air. The plane ricocheted violently upward at a tilt; a suitcase fell out of the doorless overhead baggage compartment, crashing on top of some unlucky person's head—one of the group of foreign workers, a number of young, brown men (Filipinos? Pakistanis?) who were wearing identical blue shirts and blue pants, the kind janitors wore. The stewardesses didn't pause in their crying to glance toward the struck man. His buddies picked up the suitcase and put it back on what was essentially a shelf. Jules made his way up there, grabbing the seatbacks for support, and passed him some Neosporin and a large Band-Aid.

Yungman clung to the plastic Beijing Hilton laundry bag on his lap, his seat belt fastened over it. Normally airlines didn't let you carry things on your lap, but the North Korean airline had no such rules. It had *no* rules. No security checks, no seat belt sign, no seatbacks forward, no baggage stowed safely, no safety presentation.

Back in Beijing, Jules had eyed the Lotte bag. "Oh, lor lor, you need to get rid of that," he said.

"These are just customary Korean treats for the Lunar Harvest moon."

"Non—I am meaning the Lotte bag. You'll get immediately deported for bringing such a conspicuous sign of South Korean capitalism. Remember who you *are*."

Indeed, he was now Yuchen Kwak, MD.

Supreme Leader Kim's regime branded any Korean who lived outside North Korea a traitor to the country. Thus, it was much more likely that a white Frenchman would be able to get a visa to enter North Korea than an American. *Korean American* was double indemnity—American diasporic Koreans were despised capitalists and traitors to *both* Koreas. Yungman and Young-ae would thus have to pretend they were foreigners in the place where they were born.

In a follow-up call to arrange the visas, the MSF clerk, her English almost unintelligible through her thick French accent, had asked him if his name was Chinese. Yungman obligingly replied that the underlying Chinese character "Kwak" indeed meant "Wall Around the City." Unlike his Horse's Breath patients, MSF was a global organization; why not edify them a little bit?

*Chinese,* she checked off on the form.

The consulate in Shenyang slid into the same mistake about the Chinese-ness of "Kwak," as Yungman, when asked to sign his name, on a whim, showed off his beautiful writing, still bearing signs of Halaboji's tutelage, and signed it the formal way, with Chinese characters. This was accepted by a Chinese clerk who didn't need to care much about two Chinese Americans going to Pyongyang. Yungman's and Young-ae's passport numbers were added to the MSF group visa as

Kwak, Y
Kwak, Y, MD.

Six doctors and an obstetric nurse's assistant—i.e., the newly credentialed Young-ae. For once, a misapprehension worked to his advantage.

Jules, however, had been livid to learn of the additional distraction of having two secret Koreans on the team.

"It was MSF's mistake," Yungman said.

"This is going to be so bad if they find out," said Jules.

"But isn't it *good* we speak Korean?"

"No. They think you are Chinese—and so did we. They are providing a translator. This is going to be very bad if they find out. You can only speak English. And keep pretending you are Chinese. What should the 'Y' in your name stand for?"

Yungman grabbed the only Chinese name he knew: Yuchen. Fitting, since people mixed him up with the Golden Dragon owner even long after poor Charlie Yuchen Kwak had been run out of town.

"This is going to be very, very bad if they find out," Jules said exasperatedly.

The plane dipped, yawed, listed. Another bag fell off the shelf. The unsecured beverage cart wheeled itself up and down the aisle. Would he shout in Korean, maybe for his mother, if the plane went down? Yungman hugged the Beijing Hilton bag closer to his body. As he did so, his elbow, on the armrest, touched Young-ae's, as it had in the Changchoon Movie Theater so long ago.

"Kwak-ssi," she said, her voice unusually tender. She didn't move her arm. They flew, more steadily now, toward North Korea.

Yungman didn't know that they'd landed until he felt the thump on the ground, which turned into a worrisome thump-thump-thump—a blown tire? It was just the runway, crudely paved and pocked with potholes.

When they cut the engines, the interior of the plane immediately became sweltering. The passengers fanned themselves with paper Air Koryo fans waiting in the seatback pockets. The blond Westerner blinked and woke up. Seeing everyone else fanning themselves, he grabbed one, too.

He grinned. "North Korean air conditioning—ha-ha."

Yungman didn't reply. Did this man know where he was? A place where almost nothing was a joking matter? He didn't remember that college student who died because of his "prank"?

Doctors Without Borders had given them a long list, mostly of things not to do or say. No Bibles, but also no pornography.

No cell phones.

No telephoto lenses.

No notebooks.

No radios.

No "human biologics." Also:

Do NOT solicit conversation

Do NOT take photos without prior authorization

Do NOT go off without your guide

Do NOT make jokes or any belittling remarks about the
    Dear Leader, the Great Leader, or the Greatest Leader

Do NOT show disrespect for North Korea and the North
    Korean people AT ANY TIME

NO journalists

NO non-DPRK Koreans

He was "home."

An ancient Soviet-style bus was waiting to take them the hundred feet to the terminal. Yungman could see little more than a single wide runway and a wind sock. The land was mostly beige and tan, broken only by the turquoise roof of a windowless storage building. He sniffed the air, which also seemed tan, or beige. The bus had a wooden floor.

Three larger-than-life portraits mounted on the roof dominated their vision as the shuttle began its brief traverse to the terminal, like a ride at Disneyland. From their lofty perches, the Supreme Leaders all beamed at them with radiance.

In the immigration line marked "FOREIGNERS" in Chinese characters, Yungman handed the young, unsmiling officer his passport and visa. The man stamped the visa with a red-inked chop but left the passport itself untouched. The US State Department would have no official record of their ever having entered the country. If something happened, there was no way to ascertain that he had ever been here. For Einstein, who had tried mightily to talk him out of this trip, it would be as if he'd disappeared. This sudden realization made Yungman shiver, even in the heat.

In surprisingly fluent standard English, the young officer told Yungman to bring the shared suitcase to the table, where another uniformed man was standing at attention.

The examiner pawed through every item. He sniffed at Yungman's hair pomade, ran his fingers through Young-ae's underwear.

"What's that?" the examiner said suddenly, having pulled one of the cardboard boxes from the Beijing Hilton bag.

Yungman began to sweat even more. Bo-hae had warned him that Yung-sik's ashes could contain shards of long bones and even whole teeth. If the examiner opened it, what should he say? No human biologics. Guards had already pulled their blond seatmate out of line and pushed him in a room, closing the door. Did they suspect drugs? Contagion? Bibles? Apparently, North Koreans thought all Westerners carried swine flu and STDs and AIDS. They were also on the alert for biological weapons.

"I said to you, what is this?" the examiner barked, taking up one of the boxes—Yung-sik's—and shaking it so hard that Yungman worried it might burst.

His brother! Pieces of him flying all over the airport. He couldn't have that!

"Sir!" Young-ae said, so forcefully that the man turned, his beetle brows severe under the black brim of his military cap. "You shouldn't be handling that. The medicine mustn't be shaken—you'll denature all the antibiotics we brought all this way to help your country. Wouldn't that be a shame!"

The man paused. His olive drab uniform looked large on him, his hat dwarfing his head for an unintentionally comic effect. Yungman realized it was more because he was very thin.

"The nurse is right. You might ruin all our medicine—be careful with that," Yungman said. The man scowled, but under his hardened exterior, a flicker of fear passed. There must be many things he would be scared of at any moment. He quickly put the box back into the bag and handed it back to them.

They walked past empty food courts (Western and "Oriental"), an "Internet Room" that consisted of two computer terminals, both occupied by uniformed military airport employees staring intently at obscured screens but not typing. The Pyongyang Airport had the air of a dying mall.

Waiting at the door of the bus were their guide, Miss Moon, and a middle-aged man with a video camera. He had hair as black as a raven's wing. Remembering Kimm's acupuncture-assisted natural black hair, Yungman could easily recognize this as a bad shade of dye. He was wearing a short-sleeved white polyester shirt—the kind salarymen wore in IBM's heyday—trousers, and thin-soled blue loafers of the kind that Koreans, circa 1965, thought looked very Western, but that actual men in the West didn't wear. Miss Moon introduced him as Mr. Ryu and explained that he would be taking a "souvenir" video of their entire trip.

"Nice to meet you," Yungman said to Ryu, who was a good inch or two shorter than Yungman, a certain efficient compactness about him.

"Mr. Ryu does not speak English," Miss Moon explained.

The tour bus was surprisingly luxurious. The seats were high, with headrests; mechanical air vents blew cool air on their faces. There was even a small, clean bathroom in the back.

"Chinese," said Jules, gesturing at the interior of the bus, and then looking at Yungman. "Anything that works around here is from China."

"My country's pride," Yungman said.

They would get used to the sight of buses, streetcars, trucks, and motorbikes broken down by the side of the road, their passengers stoically sitting in the ditches as if this layover were a part of the schedule. More preoccupied with perestroika than expanding Communism,

Russia had, over the years, withdrawn most of its aid. Now when something broke, the North Koreans had to figure out a way to make it themselves.

The main road was called The Reunification Highway. It was as extravagantly wide as the airstrip and just as potholed, free of cars—as well as lanes. It was merely an expanse of gray asphalt, no dotted lines, with not even a single leaf besmirching it; the bus swerved around an old woman kneeling in the middle of it, calmly sweeping the road with a broom made of twigs, the size of the ones a waiter would use between courses to whisk breadcrumbs from a table at a fancy restaurant. Farther down, a man with his head swathed in a white towel unhurriedly coaxed an ox across the highway.

The countryside was picturesque but monotonous. There was little of visual interest except for occasional Stonehenge-like columns lining the road.

"Are those some kind of monument?" Yungman asked Miss Moon. "Or do they have shamanistic significance?"

"These mighty stone columns can create an anti-tank barrier and countervail should South Korea, as a puppet of America, restart its war of aggression."

Jules nodded wearily and took a drag on his cigarette. This bus had ashtrays built into the backs of the seats, a feature Yungman hadn't seen in a long time.

They entered Pyongyang under gigantic arches that reminded Yungman of McDonald's.

Construction cranes littered the sky, suggesting industry, but none of them moved.

Yungman felt less like they were in Korea and more like they were in an artificial city, an Oz assembled out of monuments. The statues of the different leaders were so tall that all they saw were the lower legs and feet as they drove by. In the city proper, every hundred feet or so, red banners proclaimed vigorous but opaque mottos:

LET US BAND TOGETHER AND INCREASE
PRODUCTION 50% IN THE NEXT 100 DAYS!
JOIN THE PICK-ONE-MORE-PIECE-
OF-COTTON MOVEMENT!

He thought of how little this place resonated with the Korea he had left in 1953.

South Korea was similarly alien in some respects. In the coverage of the 1988 Olympics, Seoul, with all its bright lights and traffic, even the ancient Great South Gate lit up with neon like a spectacle, could have been Buenos Aires, for all he knew. More recently, the broken-down peach orchard where he and Yung-sik had lived was supposedly Seoul's "Rodeo Drive," but he didn't believe it.

"In ancient times, there used to be eight gates representing the four directions and the intermediate directions that marked the fortress city of Seoul," he explained to Reggie. "But I lived in a nothing neighborhood that was outside the gates, far away, south of the Han River. The neighborhood was so unspecial that that's what its name is—Kangnam, south of the river."

"No, I know Kangnam," Reggie insisted. It was now spelled "Gangnam."

Yungman had been astonished. "How?"

Reggie told him about "K-pop" and played him a popular video, "Gangnam Style." He even sang along, phonetically:

*Aroom da wha—Sarang soo-ra-wha—Eyyyyy seksi lady*
*Oppan gangnam sootyle—*

In the video, the tubby singer ran around what was purportedly Kangnam/Gangnam. Yungman squinted. Not even a whisper of the gnarled peach trees that had so faithfully provided them their summer peaches. What had been built on top of the scrubland wasn't even fancy hanok houses but Western steel-and-glass high-rises, expensive stores of the same kind they had in the mall — Tiffany, Brooks Brothers, Coach. Once so far away that no one wanted to live there, now it was one of the most expensive places to live in Seoul. How could this be? Yungman gulped. Could Yung-sik have had a radically different life had he merely held on to the land longer? Who could have known?

Jules grumbled as the bus turned off into a parking lot at a ballpoint-pen-shaped tower with a red neon "flame" on top and a winding path up a mountain leading out of it. Everyone was jet-lagged, but didn't want to be impolite. They filed off the bus. The doctor from Ireland was balky, and Ryu the cameraman, sitting in the back of the bus, prodded him with the lens of his video camera as if it were the barrel of a gun. The Irishman got up with a barely disguised sigh. This was apparently the Juche — "self-reliance" — Tower, the bedrock philosophy of the Kims.

"The flame, just like Juche, never goes out," Miss Moon said. Yungman tried not to yawn.

Back on the bus, he fell asleep until Young-ae elbowed him awake. They were now at the top of some mountain.

"The birthplace of the Supreme Leader," she said. Miss Moon motioned to, of all things, a log cabin, and said, with reverence and gravitas, that this was the birthplace of the Supreme Leader, "just like Abraham Lincoln." *Ablrlaham RLrinc-orunnrnrnrn.*

The vaguely American-style picket fence surrounding it was twined with vines. Wait — could it be? Gourds, hanging like ornaments. Yungman felt dizzy, groundless, as he went up to touch one. It was smooth — and dead: plastic, like the dipper they'd given Reggie. He looked back to share this moment with Young-ae only to see the whole crowd staring at him, Ryu filming.

For a second, he forgot who he was supposed to be: Yungman Kwak? Dr. William Y. Kwak? Kwak Yungman? He was a Korean-born American doctor with a French group, pretending to be Chinese. Yuchen Kwak! He was in North Korea on an honest-to-goodness mission. What was he doing, separating himself from the group like this? This wasn't a tourist excursion, or some kind of homeland tour.

"You haven't seen a calabash gourd before?" Miss Moon asked.

Yungman froze again: in Korean one nodded yes to confirm a negative question. "You aren't cold, are you?" Yes, I am not cold. In America, "You don't mind, do you?" bedeviled him. "Yes," he'd say, to give permission—and people would flounce away with a huffily muttered, "Well, that's different."

What would be the right answer to a question in English asked by a Korean when he wished to dissemble about ever having seen the dipper gourds while pretending to be Chinese? In a non-reply, he just smiled.

Mr. Ryu filmed.

One more grand plaza—austere, spotless marble.

"This is the last stop for today, and the most important," Miss Moon said. They all perked up when she said "last."

Who would have known this would be the longest and strangest?

Divested of their cameras and even their "medicine," they were apportioned into groups of four and led into an adjacent museum, the entrance a science-fiction-type doorway reminiscent of that of the SANUS Quartz Tower, but inside, it was barely lit.

As they entered, it became apparent they had to cross what looked like an indoor river. It *was* an indoor river. In the dark, it was difficult to determine how deep the rushing water was. Miss Moon, however, confidently marched across in prim navy pumps.

*What the heck*, Yungman thought to himself. He stepped in, waited for the moisture to enter.

"I feel like Jesus," said the Irishman, a bit too cheekily for Yungman's taste. Their shoes were dry. There was a grate underneath. Next, a row of revolving brushes built into the floor buffed their shoes. Then, what Yungman guessed was a sterilizing ultraviolet light turned their shoes purple.

In the next room, an official sent Yungman, Young-ae, Jules, and the Irishman to each stand at glowing markers at four corners, representing the "four heavenly directions." A spotlight came on; they faced a raised platform atop which a glass box sat. They were supposed to bow to the taxidermied figure of Kim Il-sung!

The Irish doctor later bragged that he hadn't bowed to "the mummy." They had gotten barely a hundred feet away from the grand "Palace of the Sun" before he'd cracked up about the hidden pink light that they had trained on it to keep the corpse looking "fookin' rosy."

"Dr. O'Neill," Jules muttered. "This isn't the place to try out your stand-up comedy." Yungman wondered whether this elfin man understood that many, many people had died here during the war, right in the place they were standing. In the book Kimm had given them, *Korea's Unforgotten War*, a journalist had written that there were "no more cities in North Korea . . . My impression was that I am traveling on the moon because there was only devastation—every city was a collection of chimneys."

"Fry 'em out, burn 'em out, cook them," the cowboy movie hero John Wayne had said approvingly about the firebombs, the napalm splashed on North Korean soldiers and civilians alike, in the documentary movie *This Is Korea*, by the famous John Ford. The "fire jelly" is what the Koreans called it. It touched you and kept burning no matter what you did. People died of infection and unbearable pain days, weeks, months later. The US then declared it a success and used it in Vietnam. Yungman had splurged for a John Wayne movie extravaganza during one of Birmingham's hottest days because the pregnant Young-ae was so miserable. He and Young-ae had sat in the theater in Birmingham for an hour, aghast, not even able to enjoy the respite of coolness, unable to continue to the next movie, *The Searchers*.

No trace of napalm now. Their hotel was on an island in the middle of a river, connected to the mainland by a narrow strip of road. "On top, there is a swiveling restaurant," Miss Moon said proudly. "There is also a bowling alley, a pool room, a swimming pool, massage, herbarium, a barber shop, and a casino—anything you need, all open all the time. You also may wish for exercise," she said. "You can feel free to traverse the island, anywhere. There is a beer brewery on the beach. You can also jog at your free will. However, you must not leave the island at any time."

Yungman wondered: What if he slipped the ashes into the Taedong River? Maybe a tiny tributary of it would bring some of the remains, even the smallest bit, back to Water Project Village.

"Excuse me, Miss Moon," he said. "Which way does the Taedong River flow?"

"Our Great Taedong River flows past the Juche Tower of the Self-Reliance Ideal and the Dear Leader Kim Il-sung Square."

"That's so interesting," he said attentively.

"'Taedong' means Great East, and our Taedong is one of the deepest, mightiest rivers. Much deeper than anything in South Korea. In 1986, our Supreme Leader completed the eight-kilometer-long West Sea Barrage, which has three locks and thirty-six sluices that ingeniously provide flood control and also irrigate formerly unusable land to provide a rice field matrix to increase our food production.

"Our Supreme Leader always says, 'You must work hard to become the master of the earth, make the rice grow at your command!' As a

Chinese person, Dr. Kwak, you must empathize," she added. "You Chinese know what hard work is, through your dear Chairman Mao."

Yungman nodded while thinking about his father's other specialty besides crossbreeding: irrigation. "You must have had some master agronomists," he said, "to be able to do that, to bring arid land into cultivation."

"Of course," she said. Miss Moon was facing the other way, so she didn't see Young-ae dig her elbow into Yungman's ribs. "Supreme Leader Kim University only produces the best."

Later that night, Yungman carefully placed both cardboard boxes in Young-ae's capacious tote bag and walked with some of the MSF to the Taedonggang Beer Brewery. Miss Moon said the brewery was meant for men only. Young-ae stayed behind to browse in the gift shop.

"So there's even a Taedong Gang, eh?" remarked the Irish doctor as they walked along the paved path to the river.

Yungman was about to inform him that Taedonggang just meant "Taedong River," but he had to be mindful of who he was, Yuchen Kwak, Chinese American. He did wish the Irishman would stop joking about everything. Something about his levity reminded him about how the US regarded North Korea as a terroristic threat, but they also made fun of it, as if North Koreans were some kind of funny people who insisted on doing odd things, a country of morons. The stranger the country, whether funny or threatening, the easier to kill its inhabitants, he supposed. When the president was on one of his terrorist kicks (to cover up the fact that the Hoover Dam was deteriorating and starting to leak on his watch), he warned that he was thinking of starting a war with "the North Gookoreans."

The talk shows responded with sly amusement.

A host of a funny TV "news" show invited a bunch of six-year-olds to talk foreign policy. "What do you think *we* should do about North Korea?" he asked them.

"Let's kill all the North Gookoreans," piped a sweet little girl in pigtails.

"I'll go in and just shoot everyone! Blam! Blam!" said a cherub-faced boy. Canned laugh track. The host shrugged faux-awkwardly at the camera. "Ack, I hope we won't get cancelled," he said, to more laughs.

For Americans, lolling in a safe(ish) world created its own kind of numbness and boredom. People yearned for heroics, for something to believe in, commit to. War made things new, even when it was the same old, terrible story—but only returning soldiers knew that. The news didn't care about individual lives. They liked guns and flashes and shock and awe.

Just like how, during the first Gulf War, in Horse's Breath a big church sign was created with moveable letters:

REMEMBER OUR TROOPS

But several letters over the decades had fallen away, and now the sign said:

REMEMBER OUR     OOPS

All of the American wars since Korea had also ended in a stalemate; America could bomb every single target on its list, but it still couldn't win. It couldn't rout the North Koreans or the Vietnamese in the jungle, and now in the caves of the Middle East, it was hard to quantify what had changed at all, except that there were a lot more refugees and the Taliban had come back into power in Afghanistan. REMEMBER OUR OOPS.

＊　　＊　　＊

At the brewery, the doctors encountered a governmental delegation from Turkey, some French animators who had been in North Korea for years, and the Canadian man again, a tourist named Evan who was backpacking around the world, most recently in Nepal. He wore an armload of tasseled and beaded Buddhist bracelets, and Yungman didn't know whether they were souvenirs or signs of religious devotion.

"Why did they pull you out of line at the airport?" Yungman asked him. "Were you scared?"

"Of course I was scared! They did a temperature check and thought I had a fever; I guess they think all Westerners have swine flu. So they made me stay there for hours. It turned out that their thermometer was wonky. Big surprise: North Korean medical stuff doesn't work that great."

"That's part of why we're here," Jules said as he smoked. He'd told them earlier that whenever he traveled, he brought along a dozen packs of cigarettes. They worked as currency, and had gotten him out of jam when he'd had a Kalashnikov pointed at his head at the Afghani border. They were both peace offering and bribe, slim sticks of hope, something that always made things, in the short term, better. And they erased themselves on their own, like so many traces of American empire.

The cavernous bar could have held an additional fifty people. The beer could have been a few degrees colder, but it was surprisingly good.

In Korea, at sool houses, it was customary to serve anju, accompaniments like sweet squid jerky or savory mung bean pancakes, or maybe those tiny dried baby shrimp that crunched so satisfyingly under the teeth and were oversalted to make you thirsty. In Horse's Breath Yungman had tried to replicate this pleasurable mix of tastes with a can of smokehouse almonds, a tin of kippers, miniature marshmallows, and Spam. What would a Bavarian brewhouse in North Korea serve?

A waitress dressed like a 1960s TWA stewardess in a bright-blue vest and skirt, hair so glossily attached to her head that Yungman couldn't guarantee it wasn't painted on, approached their table. When she bent to wordlessly set down a bowl, they could all see her pins, the usual red three-headed Supreme Leaders. The open collar of her jacket exposed more bosom than he'd expected (what *did* he expect?). She bowed decorously and walked away confidently and gracefully backward, and must have turned around only once she was out of sight.

The bowl contained macaroni salad in which individual pieces of macaroni had been painted electric blue, pink, or green — hopefully with some pigment that was edible — and mixed like a bowl of candy.

A bunch of miniature forks indicated it was edible. "Whoa, this is psychedelic," observed the Canadian.

While Evan drank himself into a stupor, the MSF physicians each stopped at a single beer; the Irishman even left a quarter of his in its glass. They all wordlessly acknowledged that it was okay to experience Bavarian beer in North Korea, but they should minimize spending hard currency in tourist traps where it probably would go toward something unsavory down the line. This didn't mean the North Koreans didn't vigorously try to extort them. At half the monuments where they'd marched up and dutifully taken pictures, hands came out demanding dollars and Euros afterward. A crack had appeared in Miss Moon's carefully composed professional facade; while dropping them off at the hotel, she had pestered Young-ae to change an American hundred-dollar bill because hers had a pinhole in it. Yungman remembered that, because of trade sanctions and growing indifference from the larger Communist countries, North Korea's two biggest exports currently were counterfeit money and lab-created illicit drugs. Young-ae had politely demurred, saying that she didn't have cash on her.

While his colleagues took experimental swipes at the salad, Yung-man walked to the other side of the room, his eye caught by a topographical map of North Korea nailed to the wall. It portrayed the North as much larger than the South. The Taedong was duly illustrated running by the Tower of the Juche Idea and Kim Il-sung Square, as Miss Moon had described. He found where Namp'o was. He thought about Tadpole and his family trying to cross the Taedong in winter, the US soldiers pointing their guns at them, and their being told they were being protected and it was time to cross the icy river. Yungman could only imagine what that must have been like, being so cold and miserable, the white clothing catching and billowing in the current, the American soldiers beginning to fire at them. The screams. The water turning red. There were multiple bridges now.

Yungman ran his fingers atop the plasticine river, following the serpentine line as it flowed south, hoping, hoping it might end up in the vicinity of Water Project Village.

It emptied into the Bay of Korea hundreds of miles north. But what if this might be his only chance to lay the ashes down unobserved?

Yungman slipped out the door, not thinking about how he was leaving his compatriots stuck with an exorbitant bill, entrapped like the most naive of tourists by the food-on-the-table scam; once it was touched or eaten, the hosts could charge whatever price they wanted — here it would be twenty-five American dollars for the bowl of macaroni. But Yungman's thoughts were elsewhere as he walked, as if magnetized, down a brown gravel path that he hoped led directly to the beach, the weight of the bag heavy on his shoulder, yet incredibly light when you realized he carried the remains of two humans inside.

The path paralleled the water, and then a fork led straight down to a small patch of dark-brown sand. There was no one there — no police, no tourists, no cameras (that he could see). There were also no footprints, no signs that anyone came here — not even animals.

413

Everything was quiet. The river was wide, and from its indigo color, clearly deep. In the middle of it, there was a single man sitting in a rowboat, motionless, the silhouette of his fishing gear and net visible in the fading light. There wasn't a single ripple on the water.

Their hotel room had been set up like a slightly shabby, sterile businessman's hotel in America. No phone, of course, but where the phone would have been, on the nightstand, were the customary pad of paper reading THE YANGGAKDO HOTEL and a plastic mechanical pencil missing its lead.

Yungman had the pencil now and pushed it in the water. It floated but did not move. This river seemed to be cast in glass. It didn't give even a hint which way the current went.

The water was so still, he realized, that the ashes would probably just sit there in a turbid suspension, probably to wash back onto shore. And Halaboji and Yung-sik would be stuck in Pyongyang, in the shadow of the Tower of the Juche Idea and a Bavarian brewery, hundreds of miles away from home, forever. No, it wouldn't do.


At the hotel, a scowling Miss Moon was standing in the lobby. She handed the damp Yanggakdo pencil back to Yungman. What? How?

Surveillance cameras. The hair stood up on the back of his neck as he thought of what would have happened had he, an American, been caught placing not just this simple pencil but two boxes' worth of a strange white powder in the river. The college boy had been executed for stealing a poster.


The next morning, the doctors convened for an inedible breakfast of ersatz Western pastries and sliced cantaloupe (strangely tasty). Yungman, however, longed for a hot, spicy Korean breakfast. The list of pastries offered was suspiciously long, and didn't quite match up with what they were seeing:

> Brioche
> Bakewll Tart
> Baguette
> Blan Muffin
> Croissont
> Cronut
> German Loaf
> Souffle

The Mexican doctor put on his glasses. In the glare of the fluorescent light, they could all see the giant thumbprint—not his—in the center of the right lens. "That had to have happened while I was sleeping," he muttered, and then he tucked the glasses away and blindly picked a pastry.

The doctors loaded all their gear into the belly of the tour bus. They would be leaving the hotel, but their passports would stay behind. It wasn't their choice.

The bus ground to a halt in the middle of what seemed like a wild forest, barreled down the bumpy highway. "The road is broken," the driver muttered, in an apparently unscripted dialogue, to Miss Moon. It was impassably cratered, a giant sinkhole right in front of them.

"We will be taking a detour," she announced to the doctors in English. "Do not worry, Mr. Pak is a good driver and will get us there."

Mr. Pak piloted the bus up and then down a winding dirt road with a forty-five-degree pitch, but at a velocity that suggested he wished to maintain the speed he'd driven on the highway. The giant bus skidded around a shoulderless, guardrail-less precipice that hugged a mountain. Jules, who had a compass on his watch like a tiny crystal ball, announced they were moving generally south and west.

Yungman was becoming lost to the vertigo of motion sickness. He clung to the armrests and began to sweat. More up, more down. More swinging around. The mountainous scenery looked upside down for a moment. The Irishman threw up; Miss Moon looked back at him with pity and disgust. Oh, the weakness of the Western man.

They were back on the Reunification Highway (such as it was—it was even rougher here, like it was missing a layer of asphalt). At one point they passed what looked like a Red Cross ambulance sitting on the side of the road, but Miss Moon didn't comment. She stared straight ahead. They passed rows and rows and rows of dried cornstalks. The land that didn't have corn was neatly terraced. Maybe the corn was for livestock. But they also hadn't seen a single cow or goat or sheep. The other thing that struck Yungman as odd: there was nary a rice paddy to be seen. The road narrowed and curved. The bus actually seemed to be going around in circles. "Look at that," Young-ae said, pointing. In the distance, the mountains were growing some tiny trees. They were placed meticulously in grids, like Yungman had once seen at a Christmas tree farm.

Mr. Ryu kept filming the MSF crew, as if a bunch of nauseated doctors was all quite fascinating.

The bus veered and rumbled onto a one-lane road that curved around a steep mountain. No guardrails. So narrow in places it seemed there might not be space for all the wheels of the bus. "Someone tell us a joke or something," the Irishman whimpered. "To keep our minds off our inevitable fiery deaths."

"Do you know why cooks are mean?" offered Yungman. He didn't wait to be invited to give the punchline: "Because they whip cream and beat eggs!"

No one laughed.

Except for Mr. Ryu, whose English skills must have improved suddenly. He barked a laugh, then pretended he was coughing.

Then came Einstein.

Well, Einstein's car, the Stryker. The same model, tank-shaped body, bullet-gray. The Stryker driver had to pull over into the ditch for the bus to pass, that look of implacable patience on his face as if he was at a traffic light and not in a ditch. The driver was alone, wearing a parrot-colored polo shirt. There were golf clubs in the back, like he'd driven in from Florida.

When the bus finally came to a stop, Yungman was queasy and needed a moment to compose himself. Young-ae was already unloading supplies from the cargo hold. The Irishman staggered off the bus and threw up on a rock.

"We aren't going to work right away," said Miss Moon. "First we will get you settled in the lodgings."

"Oh, lor lor," Jules muttered. He was in a hurry to start working, but had enough field experience to understand that they would have to adapt to the vagaries of the way different countries treated time. Also, the Irishman, Phinny, had to get himself cleaned up. Young-ae made him pull down his pants so she could give him a shot of Phenergan.

"Why not take this moment to enjoy a cigarette?" Jules said to himself. Near the shoulder of the road, he squatted, looking almost indistinguishable from a North Korean waiting for his broken conveyance to be repaired. The driver, Mr. Pak, came and squatted near him. The air smelled like rain.

Yungman looked around the odd place they'd found themselves in. Ringed by mountains, they were surrounded by wild grass fields and gigantic concrete structures—apartment buildings. Some were half painted a Pepto-Bismol pink; some weren't painted at all, revealing naked gray cinder blocks the same color as the clouds that shrouded the tops of the hills right now. They looked incongruous, as if dropped from the sky.

There was no glass in the windows. Some buildings were tilted—not from the earthquake or a nuclear blast but clearly because of a lack of a proper foundation. Like early in South Korea's modernization, President Park banned foreign contractors, but then Korean construction firms became so overwhelmed, especially as the '88 Olympics approached, they were forced to cut corners doing things like diluting cement with seawater—which could shift and cause a building to collapse. The most infamous disaster was the Sampoong Department Store, whose collapse killed five hundred and injured twice that many. In one window of this listing building sat a flowerpot, one that still had a stalk of a living plant sticking out of it. Despite the deserted look, this attempt at decoration, at life, moved him.

They would be setting up the clinic and the triage area here, Miss Moon told them. The damage was beyond the ridge, she said. "But it's too unstable to go there; we will bring the patients to you."

Jules joined them now that he was done with his smoke and motioned to the buildings. "What are they for?"

"Our Supreme Leader has decided to create an industrial complex here; it will be like your American Disneyland, only a thousand times larger."

"*Disneyland*?" said Yungman.

"Maybe more like the American EPCOT center. The Exchange Zone will be a place where people from all over the world can come and see the newest innovations of the Democratic People's Republic of Korea."

"The Exchange Zone?" Yungman almost yelped. Her eyes cut over to him. But surely she was too young by twenty years to know about the first Exchange Zone. Yungman felt sweat starting to gather in his armpits. He took a few deep breaths to steady himself.

In the midst of this, Yungman noticed a fresh, wet smell, different from the rain smell. It was one that suddenly unlocked years and years of memories of the muddy ground when the snow melted. Of the mineral-rich water from the well.

"Is it possible?" he said, sniffing again. His wife, unloading boxes of surgical masks, had a strange look on her face, too.

She put down the box of masks, pointed at the ghost outline of the well.

Yungman and Young-ae then both turned to look east. There was a shaft of sun shining through a tear in the clouds.

In the foreground of the mountains, at the top of the hill, the great house was still there.

They both struggled not to audibly gasp.

"What, er, building is that?" Yungman asked Miss Moon, trying to spackle a bland boredom onto his question. "It looks different from these concrete buildings."

"That is the summer retreat center for recreation and rest times for party heroes," Miss Moon said proudly.

Young-ae was quiet. Yungman knew what she wanted him to ask. He did so as casually as he could.

"Excuse me, Miss Moon, was this once a family home? I'm an architecture buff. The terra-cotta roof is exquisite. We, er, have the same designs back in China. The Middle Kingdom!"

"Indeed, that such a huge palace was owned by one family is leftover prewar bourgeois materialism. However, the house has been preserved as a cultural example of Chosonok, traditional Korean architecture."

Chosonok, not hanok. Yungman had noted another way "North" Korea had split off and established a separate, new identity by shifting its language. The most obvious was the lack of anything that wasn't pure Korean. Most Sino-Korean language, including the use of Chinese characters, was gone. A person was a two-syllable "saram" instead of an "in," that two-legged Chinese character for "man." Most certainly they wouldn't let in any Western foreign words like bee-air. Ele-ba-tor (he'd seen at the Incheon Airport).

While Koreans had been known as "hanguk saram," people of the Han (and guk/gook meaning "country"), North Koreans now called themselves "people of the Choson," as Choson was *different* ancient name for a unified Korea, from a Korean dynasty whose name meant Land of the Morning Calm.

That familiar, proud style of architecture would always be hanok to him, their clothes hanbok. The same way that the English spelling of Pusan to him would always be "Pusan" and not the "New Revised" system's "Busan." From the beginning of the occupation, the signs had been in English as well as Korean, so accordingly all the signs were changed (the Korean "ㅂ" sound, in fact, entered the mouth as a *P* but left as a *B*). But he couldn't think of *Megadoo*'s Inchon as anything but "Inchon" and not "Incheon." (Also, he should tease Young-ae that her beloved Kimmmmmms, under the new system, would be the Gimmmmms.)

His refusal to change on these spellings made him feel slightly stuck in history, but also secured by it. Reggie—and even Einstein— floated lightly in their present, being much less interested in the past, perhaps because they'd been oversold on the future: traveling in cars to Mars, cryogenic freezing and reanimation, lab-created meat where you grew just the ham hock and not the pig itself. As if technology would advance quickly enough to solve everything, even the problem of the human heart.

Would he ever be able to properly explain to his American-born son the wisdom of taking the time to honor the deceased, of marking and looking to the past? America had "set it and forget it" birth control, and "set it and forget it" funerals as well. RIP and you were done within hours. Christianity made it so the end of your life was

Judgment Day; if you were a good person, then you'll be in heaven. Bye! But Yungman still preferred the old Korean way, where you and your dead circled back every year, and as you grew older, from each new vantage point—if you were lucky enough to get older—you could see how incidents large and small radiate out, creating new incidents, yet are still part of an age-old pattern.

Yungman would have liked to ask Miss Moon if the authoritarian North Korean government forbade ancestor worship the way the Christian missionaries had tried to extinguish it in their village. Or, how did they deal with the fact that the capital of their revered Choson, historically, was *Seoul?* He wouldn't ask, however, because there were more important things he needed to know.

"Miss Moon? Sorry, I missed what you said about the original occupants of the house. What an interesting history it must have!"

She scrunched her face in distaste. "Landowners that rich must have been capitalists, or maybe collaborators with the Japanese. They would have been punished as was seen fit."

Yungman thought about how much Young-ae's mother and sisters had sacrificed and suffered for their love of Joongki, and his mother for love of their father.

The MSF went to the bus and moved their personal things to Building 3, which looked the least tilted. Miss Moon had said they were going back to the hotel, but Jules had politely ignored her and told everyone to pick rooms to sleep in. The field hospital, a series of yurts, would be open as soon as it was up and running. The Irishman was commissioned to start digging a latrine.

The mint-green paint of the building Jules selected was peeling, but the interior was spacious and clean-looking.

Miss Moon was back on the bus, chatting with the driver. Mr. Ryu was dutifully filming the doctors hauling in boxes of Ringer's lactate, gauze, antibiotics, sutures, iodine pills to sanitize water, otoscopes, forceps, speculums, a fetal heart monitor, picnič coolers filled with vaccines, a small generator, tents, and tarps.

Yungman put down a box of Ensure and slipped back to the mint-green building. He recalled the Changchoon Movie Theater and *The Great Escape*. How Steve McQueen outsmarted the Germans, hiding the dirt from digging the tunnel by releasing it outside bit by bit through his pants.

In the crude room where they were staying, Yungman broke the seal of Yung-sik's box. He put his hand in and stirred, half hoping to bring up a piece of bone or a tooth, an identifiable shard of his brother. There were none. The ashes were the consistency of coarse-ground coffee.

Next, Halaboji's box. The ashes in there were as fine as dust.

With his house key, he poked a hole in each of his pockets, keeping them small enough that he could plug them with his fingers like the little Dutch boy sticking his finger into a hole in the dike. This also made him look casual, thoughtful.

"You did it," Young-ae said.

"Did what?"

"You know that I abhor sentimentality," she said.

"I do know that," he said.

"Then I hope you'll listen when I say my wish for you is that you could, just once, see yourself the way others see you."

"What does that mean?" He supposed she'd learned to see through him after all these years. This probably added to her contempt of him. And he would deserve it.

"You carry the weight when others can't."

"I don't understand."

"That's exactly what I'm talking about. Maybe it's your sweetest aspect. Don't think I haven't noticed the things you've given up for your family."

"Given up?" he said. "You're the one who's had to sacrifice her dreams—"

"See what I mean? Don't change, yobo."

Yobo? Dear? She said it so dangerously. So revealing of herself. And they were in North Korea pretending to be Chinese Americans: Could there be surveillance set up here, the way it clearly was in the hotel?

But he felt, oddly, that no matter what happened—no matter what—it would be all right, as long as they were together.

"Don't change, crazy boy who went up against my father, who raised our son, and who now brought me back here—Evening Hero," she said.

She helped him pour the ashes into his pockets.

Yungman walked out of the building past the doctors assembling solar panels. Holding his breath, he walked by Miss Moon. He walked one step, then two steps past her.

"Where are you going?"

Mr. Ryu started filming him.

"Er," said Yungman. He could hear the *whirr* of the camera.

He looked around. The mountains here looked so bleak, indeed were denuded of trees. The ground was parched, infertile. Any remaining Hanguk rice his father had planted, or the seedlings in their house, had long ago gone away. Gosh, if his hands were free, how he would love to scoop up a clump of dirt, as his father used to do, to smell it, to test the fertility of the soil, even place a bit of it in his mouth and work it around to taste the minerals. Yungman was no agronomist, but he could tell already that this depleted soil would just crumble to dust. There was no organic matter holding it together. He guessed North Koreans used nitrogen fertilizer to force things to grow.

He needed a distraction. "Um," he said, because he couldn't point. "What is that faded flower growing out of the rock over there? It's quite pretty." It was actually rather wilted and rotted, like a brown-limbed octopus, but he was glad when she looked.

"Ah, in Choson-mal we call that 'olleji'; 'olluk' means spot. It's a noble flower, quite vibrant in the spring. Obviously, these are dying in preparation for fall. It has been so hot that the flowers have bloomed much longer. At its apex, the flower looks like a woman's bridal chignon."

The spotted lily!

"Oh, lor lor!" cried Jules, bent over a box of surgical supplies he was rifling through. "Is the box of dissolving sutures missing? Did someone steal it?" The doctor from Mexico joined him in his rifling, muttering, "If it's true, we're fucked!" Mr. Ryu turned to the triage area to see what was going on. Miss Moon joined him. Yungman wavered, wondered whether the "right" thing to do was to stay or just risk going now.

No matter: he went.


The wild grasses grew slightly more green and dense here, nourished by the underground water that rose to the surface here, and also probably by the nitrogen-rich body of Father Andrea and his bones. Yungman walked past the ghost outline, visible only to those who knew where to look, his feet knowing exactly what to do now. He followed what would have been the lane that led to their house, their choka house. He paused for a moment at what would have been the twig fence. There was, of course, nothing left, but in his mind he could see the mud plaster, the thatched roof with the golden gourds winking atop it. How poor they were, he thought to himself. He remembered once, when a bug fell from the thatch into Yung-sik's soup; barely pausing, he ate that too. Food was food. See, when they had been together, Yungman hadn't felt poor—not for a minute. That's how dear the people who had been inside this house made him feel.

He made his way down the steep bank to where the thread of a creek widened and became a proper river. His feet remembered—the stones they overturned exposed their white sides. Yes, at the shore, there was a gentle bend, the curve of an elbow when the arm is extending to give someone a gift. This bend, Halaboji explained, created a kind of eddy where the fish could rest in the shade of the blackberry canes and willow trees, which grew right up to the water's edge. Even the Americans had a saying about how willows bend but don't break, and yes, they were still here.

In late summer, the blackberries ripened and fell into the water, where they would float languorously downstream to where he, Yungsik, their mother, and their father were waiting to scoop them up: fat, juicy, river-washed berries, in such numbers that his mother would gather her skirt like a fishing net. They'd all eat together, the juice staining their lips, laughing at one another's purple-streaked faces, saving the rest so Halaboji could later make his beloved lucky blackberry wine, bokbunja. Their father, always so strict, now allowed his eyes to twinkle on his two sons, the sun so warm, the breeze so soft in their hair. How could Yungman have known to mark that moment as one of the happiest of his life? On the other hand, perhaps that was best—his mind had been nowhere but deep within that golden moment.

Many years ago, lifetimes ago, when Yungman had ripped open the lining of his school jacket to retrieve the gold ring, he was surprised to also find a small, flexible envelope. It was made out of a piece of gold oilcloth, the kind that was piled in layers to create the warm ondol floor.

Inside was a blank police report form. Written in the white spaces was a letter in his father's beautiful handwriting, each word, the Korean letters perfectly balanced, the Chinese characters so fluidly written they almost danced off the page.

To my dearest Number One Son:

I am writing this on the most important day, the day celebrating your birth. It shatters my heart to think that we cannot celebrate this happy occasion together. It seems that it has to be this way. But no matter. We will celebrate when we are together again.

My son, as you leave your childhood season, know that you are already so quickly becoming the person I imagined when your grandfather and I chose your name. You are the pride and joy of the Family of Kwak, our Evening Hero.

If it weren't for the continued turmoil in our country, my dreams for my family would have been realized one hundred percent. Even so, they have been realized ninety-five percent. You will do our family name justice as long as you persevere and don't change the path of your heart, whatever it might be.

For your seventh year, I give you the wishes of a father. Above all, stay in good health. Survive this turmoil. Love our country. Put your family first, as I know you will do. I await the time we can enjoy each other's company as a family again.

My son: fulfill all your wishes.

From your father who loves you more than life itself

Tucked next to it was a palm-size piece of white ramie fabric, the same kind Yungman's mother made their clothes and bedding out of. A message, hastily stitched.

Beloved sons,
Be happy. Until the day
you are called to return home.
I will be there
waiting. Mother

Yungman could almost smell the blackberry sweetness, the green of the wild grasses, the spongy loam where the river lapped at the bank.

As he walked, he said little prayers for each of them. *Beloved Grandfather. Beloved Grandmother. Beloved Father. Beloved Mother. Beloved Brother. I have come back. I remember you.* As the ashes fell to the ground around him, he made sure to scuff his feet, kicking up clouds of dust, so that the good Korean earth and his family's remains could be together again.

# Author's Note

One reason this book has taken so long to complete is my attempt (destined to fall short) to render historical events with as much accuracy as possible. But what is "accuracy," and how much does it become altered by personal experience versus scholarly study? How to render what Yale historian Sam Moyn called "the most brutal war of the twentieth century, measured by the intensity of violence and per capita civilian deaths"? Many of our Korean elders, including my father, have been lost to time, and so there was a lot of urgency in gathering survivors' stories before they passed. There were frequent memories of "powders" and other substances falling from military airplanes, suggesting the use of biological weapons and/or experimentation by the Allied forces, a mystery event that has been (and continues to be) dismissed in official channels, but if you are curious, Nicholson Baker's *Baseless: My Search for Secrets in the Ruins of the Freedom of Information Act*, echoes and reifies much of what I read about or heard from these Korean elders.

Lastly, a place like the Exchange Zone did exist, where Korean soldiers momentarily set down their burdens of a war directed by foreign forces and reclaimed their time to be boys (as many of them were in their teens) and Koreans again. The city of Kaesong indeed was in "South" Korea after the post–World War II partition but then became part of "North" Korea after the Armistice in 1953. Its proximity to the border with South Korea has made it a kind of access point for both Koreas, and I've been lucky enough to look upon it from both sides of the Demilitarized Zone.

For further reading, these books, among many others, have both informed and inspired *The Evening Hero*: Monica Kim's utterly astonishing *The Interrogation Rooms of the Korean War: The Untold History*; Charles Hanley's *Ghost Flames: Life and Death in a Hidden War, Korea 1950–1953*; Su-kyoung Hwang's *Korea's Grievous War*; *The Bridge at No Gun Ri: A Hidden Nightmare from the Korean War* by Charles J. Hanley, Martha Mendoza, Sang-hun Choe; Grace M. Cho's *Haunting the Korean Diaspora*; the music of the great Shin Joong Hyun; and the poetry of the late Yearn Hong Choi, who convinced me that "Kwak" was a better transliteration of Yungman's name than "Kwok."

# Acknowledgments

My editorial team deserves the biggest shout-out for their absolute patience and engagement over the years as the book evolved and also as life intervened. So many thanks to the Simon & Schuster team, Marysue Rucci, Emily Graff, Brittany Adames, Michael Szczerban (now of Little, Brown), Claire Strickland, Shannon Hennessey, Elizabeth Breeden, Jessica Chin, Jonathan Karp, Julia Prosser, and my agenting team Kimberly Witherspoon, Jessica Mileo, William Callahan, Monika Woods (now of Triangle House), plus Nicole Dewey, friend, and also one of the most astute publishing professionals out there—I could not have done it without all of you.

For financial support, Columbia University's Humanities War and Peace Initiative, the New York Foundation for the Arts fiction fellowship, the Rhode Island Foundation/MacColl Johnson fellowship, the Rhode Island State Council on the Arts fiction fellowship, and the Barbara Deming/Money for Women fellowship.

For precious space and financial support: the Corporation of Yaddo, MacDowell, Ucross Foundation, the Virginia Center for the Creative Arts, Turkey Land Cove, Ledig House, Rowland Writers Retreat, Key West Literary Seminar (especially board member Judy Blume), the Blue Mountain Center, Cuttyhunk Island Writers'

Residency, Martha's Vineyard Writers' Residency, and the Aspen
Institute/Aspen Words. Many friends also provided space to work
(lifesaving especially during the pandemic), often without me even
asking—I wish such wonderful friends on everyone: Mary Gordon,
Mae Ngai, Susan Bernofsky, and Deborah Paredez, Frank Guridy,
and Zaya.

Thanks to my undergraduate institution and teaching home,
Brown University, especially Evelyn Hu-DeHart at the Center for
the Study of Race and Ethnicity in the Americas; my colleagues at
Columbia's Center for the Study of Ethnicity and Race, and in Narrative Medicine; the Heyman Center for the Humanities, especially
Eileen Gillooly; Brown University's Warren Alpert Medical School;
Drs. Suzy Kim and Neha Raukar—thank you for letting me follow
you into the ORs and beyond; TEDMED; my medical humanities
colleagues Drs. Randy Hutter Epstein and Anna Reisman.

Thank you to people who read drafts all or in part: Charles Yu,
R.O. Kwon, Marian Lizzi, Cathy Park Hong, Heinz Insu Fenkl, Justin
Taylor, the late Katherine Min, Dawn Tripp, Grace Talusan, John
Barnewall, Amy Remensnyder, Linda Heuman, Pamela Klinger-Horn,
Christine T. Anderson, Lauren Mechling, Jimin Han, Angie Kim,
West Moss, Dr. Kee Park, Dr. Kathy Crowley, Min Jin Lee, and Matt
Bell. My amazing writing group, Krys Lee, Leland Cheuk, Curtis
Chin, Christina Chiu.

Plus the rogues' gallery: Ed Lin's Ouija board sessions to come up
with a title; TC Charton for kitting me out in glasses my Asian face
loves and can wear forever; Choe Sang-hun for always answering my
questions about Korean proverbs; T.K. at Ask a Korean!; Mudang
Jennifer for her important work with the ancestors; my Hibbing friend
group, Patti Schmidt, Pam Tomassini, Lisa Samsa—ride or die in
borrowed jean jackets 4ever; Dr. Diane Blake; and Safa Setzer for
being so persistent and excellent working with my son, J.

## ACKNOWLEDGMENTS

And my family, the Lees: Victor, Leonard, Michelle, and my parents, Grace K. Lee and the late William Chae-sik Lee, whose migrations and sacrifices made the writing of this book possible at all. The Jacobys: Dean, Karla Vecchia, Ainara, and Lur.

And Karl and J, it begins and ends with you, always.

# About the Author

**Marie Myung-Ok Lee** is one of the few American writers granted an official visa to visit North Korea since the Korean War. She is the author of the groundbreaking young adult novel *Finding My Voice*, which was a winner of the Friends of American Writers award and has been recently reissued. Her work has appeared in the *New York Times*, the *Nation*, the *Atlantic*, and the *Paris Review*. She has been awarded a Fulbright fellowship to Korea and a New York Foundation for the Arts fellowship in fiction. She teaches fiction at Columbia University. She is a founder of the Asian American Writers' Workshop and lives in New York City with her family.